"This touching, real-world fable from Zajaczkowski draws on the insights and strategies of his nonfiction work, like *The Owner's Manual to Life* ... this story demonstrates, with a narrative more engaging than traditional self-help books, that by taking the time, exploring all possibilities offered to us, and moving at a steady pace, we can always achieve more—and become beacons of light to lead others. Readers of inspirational fiction will enjoy this story of a man, an angel, and the work it takes to build happiness and fulfillment." —**Booklife Reviews (Editor's Pick)**

"From its opening lines, the story is presented in nearly poetic language that is highly descriptive and evocative... Libraries that choose *The Color of Dreams* for its lovely descriptions, logical and compelling accounts of growth, and hope, will find it easy to recommend to readers looking for uplifting, inspirational tales of transformation that emerge from following one's dream."
—**D. Donovan, Senior Reviewer, Midwest Book Review**

"... the narrative's personal interactions and the ways in which Ben tackles his obstacles make for a diverting tale. An often-engaging entrepreneurial quest that mixes family turmoil, positive thinking, and a helpful dose of magic." —***Kirkus Reviews***

"Some novels transcend fiction. *The Color of Dreams* is such a book. Taking place in the late 1980s in the Pacific Northwest, Ben meets a tiny angel who imparts six profound lessons, guiding him to achieve his hopes and dreams. Zajaczkowski's beautiful and vivid narrative unfolds slowly to let these truths that we innately know resonate. We're with Ben as he faces obstacles and

frustration and learns to have faith in himself. His heartwarming story inspires us all to believe in the magic of dreams."
—**D. Thrush, author of *Guardian of the Light***

"Every now and then a special book comes out that changes the way you look at yourself—and your world. *The Color of Dreams* is that book. Wonderful spiritual lessons that will get you to believe in your dreams again, and that will show you how to manifest them. Read this book: it will resonate for a lifetime."
—**Julie Matheson, MA, RScP, author of *Lotus Flower Living: A Journaling Practice for Deep Discovery and Lasting Peace; Untangle your mind and heart once and for all***

"*The Color of Dreams* is a heartwarming journey through the challenges, hopes, and surprisingly delightful discoveries that come with following your dreams. This charming and enchanting tale reveals six spiritual lessons that will make your own path easier to follow. You will carry these lessons with you long after you've read it, and they will continue to encourage, uplift, and inspire you. Recommended for the dreamer in us all."
—**Katherine Woodward Thomas, *NY Times* bestselling author of *Calling in "The One"***

"In *The Color of Dreams*, Michael Zajaczkowski weaves a fable about finding and pursuing a purpose in life. Full of magic and miracles, this book is an endearing and inspiring page-turner, with something for every dreamer who dares to believe."
—**Kathleen Guthrie Woods, author of *The Mother of All Dilemmas***

"*The Color of Dreams* is a heartfelt and relatable story about resilience, family, and the courage it takes to follow your dreams. It's about second chances, quiet victories, and the small, magical moments that remind us why we keep going. Uplifting and sincere, *The Color of Dreams* is the kind of book that stays with you long after you've turned the last page." **—Lynn Dickinson, author of *The Writetress***

"Michael Zajaczkowski's *The Color of Dreams* is an inspiring story of following one's true path in the face of adversity and doubt. Through six transformative lessons, the book offers spiritual wisdom and practical advice for anyone ready to pursue their dreams. If you're ready to begin manifesting the life that has been calling you, then this book will be a trusted companion and essential guide." **—Christopher Laney, author of *Flying Colors, A Modern-Day Parable on Finding the Courage to Follow Your Dreams***

"*The Color of Dreams* weaves the yearning, struggle, and even desperation we all experience in the pursuit of our dreams. I deeply related to this story, and was moved by the way Michael reveals the ever-present magic surrounding us, along with the practical wisdom that transforms obstacles into meaningful guides. What if every setback wasn't an ending but a redirection to something 'better than we know'? This book will rekindle dreams yet to be realized by illuminating truths often overlooked along the journey." **—Pete Beebe, author of *Dream Fisher***

"Michael Zajaczkowski's *The Color of Dreams* unfolds as a poignant narrative of second chances, self-discovery, and the rekindling of lost ambitions. *The Color of Dreams* is a heartfelt exploration of resilience and the enduring power of belief in oneself, in others, and in the unseen forces that shape our lives. Zajaczkowski's writing captures both the beauty and the messiness of pursuing one's dreams, offering readers an emotional journey filled with relatable struggles and moments of quiet triumph. This book will resonate with anyone who has ever felt stuck or

doubted their ability to overcome life's challenges. It's an inspiring read for dreamers, creatives, and anyone who appreciates stories about rediscovering hope in the face of adversity."
—**Literary Titan**

"*The Color of Dreams* is an inspiring and deeply human story about fighting for your dreams, even when the world—and your own doubts—stand in the way. Michael Zajaczkowski masterfully explores the intersection of ambition, sacrifice, and self-belief, crafting a novel that feels both personal and universal. A must-read for anyone who's ever wondered if it's too late to take a leap of faith." —**Kirsten "Kiki" Ringer, Literary Manager, KLR Literary Management**

The Color of Dreams

Michael Zajaczkowski

STARLITE BOOKS

The Color of Dreams
Copyright @ 2023 by Michael Zajaczkowski
Paperback Edition: ISBN 979-8-9917691-1-2

All rights reserved. No part of this publication may be reproduced, stored in a retrieval system, or transmitted in any form or by any means, electronic, mechanical, photocopying, recording, or otherwise, without the without the prior written consent of the author, excepting brief quotes in reviews.

To receive the author's weekly quotes, samples of both previous and upcoming books, special giveaways, and more, visit:

www.MichaelZBooks.com

Cover design by Vila Design

Publisher's Cataloging-in-Publication
(Provided by Cassidy Cataloguing Services, Inc.)

Names: Zajaczkowski, Michael, author.
Title: The color of dreams / Michael Zajaczkowski.
Description: [Cary, North Carolina] : Starlite Books, [2023]
Library of Congress Control Number: 2025904681
Identifiers: ISBN: 979-8-9917691-2-9 (Hardcover) | 979-8-9917691-1-2 (Paperback) | 979-8-9917691-0-5 (eBook) | 979-8-9917691-3-6 (Audiobook) | LCCN: 2025904681
Subjects: LCSH: Inspiration--Fiction. | Spirituality--Fiction. | Angels--Fiction. | Self-realization--Fiction. | Self-help techniques--Fiction. | Magical thinking--Fiction. | Dreams--Fiction. | Self- actualization (Psychology)--Fiction. | Family problems--Fiction. | Spiritual life--Fiction. | Success--Fiction. | Fear--Fiction. | Happiness--Fiction. | Opportunity--Fiction. | Conduct of life--Fiction. | LCGFT: Magic realist fiction. | Self-help publications. | BISAC: FICTION / General.. | FICTION / Visionary & Metaphysical. | BODY, MIND & SPIRIT / Inspiration & Personal Growth. | BODY, MIND & SPIRIT / Angels & Spirit Guides. | RELIGION / Spirituality.
Classification: LCC: PS3626.A62582 C65 2023 | DDC: 813/.6--dc23

For Qi Han,
the real angel in my life.

An Unexpected Visitor

Tacoma, WA
Fall 1988

The angel told me I should write a journal of our time together, and I'm surprised I didn't think of it sooner. But maybe I shouldn't be; I mean, it's not every day that an angel comes into your life. I wasn't even sure I believed in them before, and yet one day in June, she appeared, right when I was at the bottom of my life, when I was losing everything that ever mattered to me.

If I were to read an account of what I'm about to write, I'd think the writer was mad, that *I'm* mad. I've pinched myself many times to get myself to wake up and shake off this illusion, but each time I do, I feel her presence all around me, inside of me. She was a little miracle, one I didn't know I needed, and one I didn't think I'd ever receive. But that's the thing about miracles: if you don't believe in them, you'll never experience their magic.

That's another thing: magic. Who believes in magic anymore? Maybe when I was a kid, I did, but as an adult? Magic was far away—something that had disappeared long ago. I had shed that part of my life and didn't even think to look for it again.

Kind of like my dreams: as I got older, the further away I got from them, the more they turned into hopes, wishes, somedays. And then, all at once, she appeared, and with her, a chance to recapture the magic, and another shot at making my dreams come true. The question was, could I get out of my own way and learn to believe again?

You might think that with an angel guiding you, everything would be easy, but you'd be surprised. When all the same obstacles keep coming up, and everything you try fails you, you get discouraged. After all, you can only take so much. I only wish I'd had more faith sooner, that I could have surrendered earlier. But old habits and ways of thinking can be hard, if not impossible, to overcome.

I'll always remember the shining angel, the promise of her lessons, the colors in my garden, and the light that burns inside of me. I'll remember each and every failure, all the chances I had to turn things around, and all the times I chased after the wrong things. And after all the chasing, I'll remember most what I ended up finding: something I'd always had, but that I overlooked, just as you may be overlooking it right now.

My dad always said, "You don't know what you got until you lose it." That was certainly true for me.

And I guess that's how this story really begins.

Chapter One

―――

Friday afternoon, May 27, 1988

The argument started the way it usually did, over Ryan promoting my custom mailboxes. But this time, Em said something that I never saw coming.

I got home from work before Em and the kids did, sure that she'd take my side *this* time. She had to. It was the only way I'd stand up to Ryan and finally try something on my own. Four years of working for him was way too long, and today we'd had it out.

All that time, Ryan had promised to go "all-in" to promote my mailboxes, a dream my dad and I had had ever since he taught me how to work with wood. Created as detailed replicas of customers' houses, meticulously detailed down to each tiny roof shingle, miniature window, and shutter, the mailboxes were perfect for the garden center crowd. Ryan did build an eye-catching display featuring a couple of sample mailboxes, I had to give him that, and when customers noticed the intricacy of the smallest details, from the tiny brass doorknobs to the red brick chimneys, they fell in love with them. But the bottom line was that we needed a bigger market. Three to four sales a month wasn't going to cut it anymore. The real business was in advertising to his mailing list, which extended well into Seattle and out to the islands. I knew my mailboxes would take off with that kind of exposure, but Ryan always stalled on the idea.

"Not the right time," he'd say. "Maybe next season," were some of the excuses he used.

I told him it had to be now, that I wouldn't be put off any longer, and he had finally agreed.

This should have been good news, right? Not with Ryan, though. There was always a catch. Yes, he was willing to do it, but now he wanted an exclusive on my whole mailbox business. I thought he was kidding when he said, with his smart-ass smirk, that he wanted exclusive rights for not only Tacoma and Seattle, but for all the islands as well. That meant any order that came in would go through him, and I could kiss my dream of owning my own business goodbye.

"That wasn't our deal!" I protested.

"Well, Ben, that's the deal now. Take it or leave it."

I stormed out after my shift and couldn't wait to tell Em. Now she'd believe what I'd been telling her: Ryan had never intended to promote my business, and he'd just been leading me on with every excuse. She usually told me to be patient, that he would eventually follow through. We argued over this constantly, but now I had proof of his true intentions, and I was sure she would be as angry as I was. Finally, she'd see my side of things and wouldn't have any more reservations about using our savings to start promoting my mailboxes on my own terms.

Stewing, pacing, and slamming kitchen drawers, I worked myself up as I waited for her to get home. I grabbed the sloppy joe mix for dinner from the fridge, and smelling the hamburger meat, Sadie, our old Labrador, wandered in with our cat, Oreo, on her heels. Together they sat next to their empty bowls and looked up hopefully. With a sigh, I fed them, and they wagged their tails in unison as they crunched their food, while I busied myself with dinner prep.

A little after four, the minivan pulled into the driveway, the kids chattering and slamming doors one by one. I tensed when they burst through the door, Em struggling with the backpacks, the kids racing past her into the living room. Samantha—Sammy for short, just four-and-a-half years old, yet more and more like her mother every day, complete with her curly blonde hair and stubborn confidence—took control of the radio and cranked up her favorite pop station. The brassy horns of Men at Work's "Who Can It Be Now?" blared through the house. We would joke that Sammy had gotten her love of music from her mom that night we saw David Bowie open at the Tacoma Dome in '83. Em had been pregnant, and as she sang and danced through his Serious Moonlight tour, Sammy must have soaked it all in in utero.

Em, a sixth-grade music teacher at the same school the kids went to, dumped the backpacks on the couch and quickly changed into her favorite purple University of Washington sweatpants and a cozy white T-shirt. With her blonde hair pulled back in a ponytail, she went from twenty-nine to seventeen years old in one breathtaking moment. Cheerful as always, she joined me in the kitchen, smiled, and gave me a quick kiss on the cheek. "So, what did he say?"

I frowned. "What do you think he said?"

Her smile vanished. "He didn't put you off again?"

"No, he said yes."

"What's wrong, then? You don't look happy."

I took a deep breath. "He wants total control of every order I get, including for Seattle and the islands!" I fumed.

Her expression didn't change, and with mounting frustration, I saw that she was considering his offer. I couldn't believe she was already taking his side.

"Okay, but that might not be a bad thing," she ventured. "I mean, you'll get a lot more orders from that, right?"

"Not a bad thing?! But what about me marketing them at the farmers' market and Pike Place? If I say yes to Ryan, that means my whole plan, my whole business, will be gone."

Just then, the kids rushed in and pleaded, "I'm hungry! When's dinner?"

Dylan, six years old, but as serious and sensitive as I was, immediately realized we were arguing again. "What's wrong?"

Sammy, sensing my anger, shot me a worried look and leaned against her mother's leg. Em forced a smile, bent down, and tied one of Sammy's shoes. They both stared up at me in silence.

Another tense moment.

"Nothing's wrong. It has nothing to do with you," I muttered.

"Why don't you two go and play out back before dinner?" Em said.

They attempted to argue, so Em bribed them, promising ice cream after dinner if they behaved. With that, they yelped and poured out the back door into the warm afternoon. Sadie, moving slowly these days, ambled after them.

Em started on dinner and said over her shoulder, "But you're not ready to go out on your own yet. Don't you need to expand your workshop, get new equipment and stuff? All that takes time and money, doesn't it?"

"We have money saved, and hell, I'm twenty-nine already! This is *my* business, not Ryan's. And if not now, when?"

"We can't risk all our savings on this. We've talked about that. We need a cushion for emergencies." She turned and crossed her arms. "I mean, what if the farmers' market doesn't work like you think? And how much will a stall at Pike Place cost? And what if…" Her voice trailed off, and she shook her head.

It was always about the money.

"Listen, we're fine with money. You're working, I'm working, and I'm selling four mailboxes a month at the nursery right now. With summer coming, I'll work some double shifts each week, and Ryan will be happy with the extra help. Imagine what another five or ten sales through the farmers' market would bring us—without me having to give Ryan half of the profits! That could be another seven hundred to fourteen hundred dollars a month right there. We'll be fine. Have some faith here, okay?"

"I do have faith. It's just that having access to Ryan's list is what you've always wanted, and now he's willing to do it. I know it's an exclusive, but why not try it temporarily? Get all the business you can, save even more money, and then try it on your own next spring? I'm…" She frowned at my expression and shook her head again. "I'm sick of arguing about this."

"*You're* sick of it? That doesn't even begin to describe how I feel. But I can see I'm not going to get through to you now, so let's just drop it. Besides, I don't have to agree to anything right now. This can all wait until we get back from vacation at your folks' place."

Our summer trip to her parents' house on Bainbridge Island was just what we needed. We'd spend some time as a family again and leave this stress behind us. The kids couldn't wait to see their grandparents, and they loved going to the island. It was a dream home right on the water facing Elliott Bay, with stables, a boat dock, and trails into the woods. I'd get my two weeks off and join them in the beginning, then go up every weekend over the summer.

And that's when she said it.

"I've been thinking about that." She kept her arms crossed and cast her eyes down. "I don't like the way we've been lately. You being so frustrated with Ryan, and us arguing more and more... I think that maybe we should start the vacation apart for a few weeks. It might be good for us both. The kids, too."

"What?" My stomach tightened.

"You said Ryan has been hinting that you might not even get the two weeks off because of the new Big Box store that's opening. So, if not, then why don't you save your vacation time for later in the summer? The time apart might do us all good."

So, that was it. Not only was she not taking my side with Ryan, and not letting me use our savings, but now she wanted time apart, too. Well, that wasn't going to happen.

I was about to argue, but then the kids came back and demanded dinner. Em turned her back to me and pointed to the plates.

We sat through another strained dinner, the kids eating quietly while sneaking glances at Em and me, waiting. But the heaviness didn't lift. They quickly cleared their plates and retreated to their rooms. Silently, we cleared the table, and I snuck off to my workshop. I had to cool down before bringing this up again.

Flicking on the lights, I closed my eyes and breathed in the smoky smell of sawdust and the comforting mix of burnt wood and lacquer that filled the garage. But then I opened them and frowned. I needed more room. Half-constructed mailbox frames sat drying in clamps on every available surface, spent pieces of sandpaper were strewn everywhere, and chip-carving knives and beat-up mallets were scattered over the workstations. And my ancient table saw—would it even turn on next time?—sat in the center of the garage, mocking me: *"You call this a business? Who are you kidding?"*

No, this would never do. I could make a go of it, but not in this cramped workshop. I needed to remodel, expand, double the garage space and triple the supplies. I needed more than just one sheet of three-fourths-inch plywood and a workshop full of old tools to make this work. I needed stacks of plywood and pine, and ash boards for the finish work, and I couldn't keep running to the craft stores for supplies. I'd turn every wall and each corner into useable space, with cabinets, tabletops, and shelving along three walls, and drawers for every kind of mailbox I'd make, all organized by tool use. And yes, tools! A new miter saw to start, and a better jigsaw, and not just one wood chisel, but a whole set. I was a woodworker, and any self-respecting woodworker would tell you that you could never have enough tools. I *could* do this. I *would* do this. I just needed ... money.

But besides the argument about money, now Em wanted to vacation without me? Just thinking about it turned my stomach. And why did she keep sticking up for Ryan? Old jealousy boiled inside me. I was actually glad he was being such an ass again, because I never wanted to give him a part of my business. He thought he could have anything he wanted, and for years he'd led me on, and now this.

But I had a plan. The farmers' market would be the start, and then on to Pike Place. I could get so many orders from those two places alone! Pike Place would open up the islands, and that was where the bigger mailboxes and profits were. We'd debated it for years, but we'd never pulled the trigger. It had always been about the money, but we had enough now, and it was time. I had put my dream off long enough.

Em poked her head in. "Sammy's ready for her story."

After we got the kids settled, she sat on our bed, reviewing her music lessons for the end of the semester. Oreo was sprawled on my pillow, and I nudged him over and pretended to read the latest woodworking catalogue. Then I couldn't take it any longer.

"So, I *am* going to get the two weeks off, and I *will* join you for the beginning of our vacation," I said.

She half smiled for the first time since dinner, putting her papers down. "Oh, Ben, I want you to come; I do. Just not like this. You felt the tension tonight—we all did—and I just think the kids could use a break from that for a while."

"You mean a break from me."

She groaned, and her smile disappeared. "A break from our arguing."

I tossed my catalogue to the floor and switched tactics. I'd deal with the vacation later, but right now, I wanted to rent a booth and get my business going. "Well, let's talk about it after I get the time off from work. Meanwhile, how about this: tomorrow at the farmers' market, I'll ask Bud if there's a booth available. And if so, then let's just try it out. Maybe I wouldn't need all of our savings at first, just enough to get it started, and then we can see how it goes? I've got to try something. What do you say?"

"How much would it cost?"

"I don't know yet. I don't know how much a booth is, what kind of equipment I'd need, or what I'll do about space when the orders come rolling in. I have to figure it out."

She softened a little. "Well, it doesn't hurt to ask, and I do want you to get it going. Let's see what he says, and then we can talk about how much you'd need to get started, okay?"

I reached over and kissed her, and her smile broadened as she put her hand on my cheek. Then she turned back to her papers, and I grabbed my notebook and began making a list of the things I'd need. Figuring in the remodel of my workshop, the new equipment, and supplies for an additional ten mailboxes, the total quickly chewed up most of our savings. But there weren't any shortcuts if I wanted to do this right, if I wanted a real chance at success. No, I'd need all the savings we had. But it *would* work; I was convinced of it. With both our incomes and the sales I'd make, I could earn back the money in no time. Once she realized this, she'd agree ... wouldn't she?

After we turned off the light, the familiar doubts and fears crept in. What if she was right, and the farmers' market *didn't* work out? What would happen if I spent all our savings, and my business didn't take off? How would our summer go then? I thought about how Ryan's business had taken off over the years, and I couldn't help but wonder if she thought about how different her life would have been if they had stayed together. Her father, Mitch, was successful. Ryan was successful. And then there was me. This pressure had been building for years, and we all felt it.

Like a hamster on a wheel, my thoughts chased themselves. One thing was certain: I had to get back to some sort of peace with Em over the weekend; fighting would only drive her further away. As I tossed and turned, a fitful night of sleep finally descended, with dreams I couldn't or didn't want to remember.

Chapter Two

Saturday morning, May 28, 1988

Em mumbled a sleepy good morning, her sweet mood carrying over from last night. She started breakfast, and while the smell of bacon drifted through the house, I woke Dylan and found Sammy pulling a sweater over her tangled bed head.

"Pony ride today!" she squealed.

"Yes, but just the one ride, like we agreed, okay?"

I opened the curtains in the den and noticed Sadie still sitting on her cushy brown doggy pillow next to the fireplace. Odd that she wasn't in the kitchen yet, but she had been noticeably slowing down this year. When we took her in, the vet had said she was healthy, besides her old age, and there wasn't a lot to do for her unless she stopped eating. I couldn't believe we'd had her for fourteen years already, long before the kids, and while her fur still glowed with a Labrador's golden cream, it showed a good dose of gray these days.

Oreo lifted his head and meowed and yawned at the same time. He had sauntered in one day while Dylan sat in his high chair, munching an Oreo cookie. Dylan had pointed at the cat and called him Oreo, and the name stuck. He had never left us since.

I helped Sadie up, and the three of us moseyed into the kitchen, where Em was separating egg yolks for hollandaise sauce. Humming to a song playing in the living room, she began beating the eggs to the rhythm. Her singing usually put me at ease, but it unsettled me this morning. We would *not* be spending the summer apart. She called the kids to breakfast, and while Dylan came in, Sammy stayed in the living room and turned up the music on a new song.

I found her singing to "Girls Just Wanna Have Fun" by Cyndi Lauper, holding a hairbrush as a microphone, dancing and swinging her head from side to side. I didn't know why it upset me so, but it did. I grabbed at the hairbrush, but she jerked it away.

"Put that down and come to breakfast!" I shouted above the music.

Sammy ignored me and kept on singing and dancing.

"Stop messing around!" I yelled and cut the volume on the boom box.

"But I'm going to be a famous singer!" she yelled back.

"Not everyone can be a famous singer!" With the music turned down, my voice boomed through the house.

Sammy froze and started whimpering.

I softened. "But if you study hard in school, you can be a teacher, like your mommy."

"I don't want to be a teacher! I wanna be a singer!"

"It's good to dream, but dreams aren't gonna pay the rent. Now, c'mon, it's time to eat."

Dylan raced in. "I'm gonna be a fireman! They save lives!"

"Yes, and they get a steady paycheck," I added.

Em appeared in the doorway. "Breakfast is getting cold!"

The kids, oblivious to the edge in her voice, filed in and took their seats, and she hushed me by putting a finger to her mouth. Her sweet mood gone, she glared at me and said, "I've told you to leave her alone! It's good for her to dream. Just because you..." Her words trailed off, her cheeks burning red, and she quickly turned her back on me.

Within minutes, I sat stewing at the kitchen table again, worrying about how the day was starting out. Definitely not in the right direction, and I had to calm down and find a way to turn it around.

After getting ready, we piled into Em's Voyager and pulled out of the driveway. Already, I could smell the odor of rotten eggs—the so-called "Aroma of Tacoma." The Tacoma Pulp & Paper Mill's rendering plant had been here even longer than me, and I pretty much ignored it now. But when the wind kicked up and the plant was in full operation, the smell smothered the city. It had driven Bruce Springsteen out of town after he played at the Tacoma Dome a few years ago. Rumor had it that the stench was so bad, he became ill and left town early, forgoing his post-concert TV appearances.

I hit the air recycle button while the kids fidgeted and argued about who was going to ride the ponies first. Em and I relaxed a bit and kept our conversation light. Twenty minutes to the farmers' market felt like a long time this morning, and I caught myself several times wanting to talk about the booth, but I bit my tongue. Instead, we talked about booking a dinner reservation at The Lonely Pines, where we'd spent many a summer evening on the deck, watching the trout nip at the insects in the icy stream that ran along the back. Dylan always liked to see the three lone pine trees on the east side of the huge, wooded property, where Em and I had carved a heart with our initials years ago.

We pulled in, and I got excited seeing all the other cars already here—they all seemed like dollar signs to me now—and watching all the vendors setting up their stalls and booths made me envious and anxious to join them.

The parking lot of The Lonely Pines was large enough for over two hundred cars, and the sellers were packed in tight this morning. Most anything one could imagine was sold here, and the foot traffic was heavy throughout the day. Eighty stalls packed the market, selling locally grown vegetables and fruits, like Wenatchee apples and the new honeydews. My favorite were the delicious-smelling gourmet coffee stands, including a new addition, Starbucks, which had become quite the talk of Seattle these days. I couldn't wait to get a cup.

Craft booths were scattered throughout the market, selling everything from homemade soap and candles to cleaning solutions. I was most interested in the woodworking booths. Some sold smaller items, like oak cutting boards, but there were also larger booths selling furniture, like pine rocking chairs and tables. There was even a high-end stall offering maple and red oak kitchen cabinets. I needed to be here! With all the shoppers, I'd get plenty of orders to make a profit and make Em happy.

The carnival-like atmosphere buzzed with people talking and laughing and live bluegrass music. Kids ran, shouted, and begged their parents for one more pony ride, or a bigger bag of fresh caramel popcorn. Em and the kids joined the long line for the pony rides.

"Let me see if I can find Bud," I said. "I'll be back in a minute."

I waded into the market and spotted him near a booth selling assorted sprouts, and I rushed to catch up with him. A typical ex-hippie, Bud had long hair pulled back in a ponytail, a salt-and-pepper beard, and a faded Hawaiian shirt that screamed the sixties. He might have looked behind the times, but he was a business shark who had started this market with just a few local growers and built it into the thriving business he had today—"the pride of Tacoma," a local paper had called it.

"Hey, Bud!" I called as I approached him.

"Oh, hey, Ben, how goes it?"

"Do you have a minute?"

He was already moving on to the next booth. "Well, I'm kind of busy right now..."

"It's about renting a booth."

That stopped him. "Oh?"

"Yeah, ah, I wanted to see if you have any booths available right now?"

He stepped closer. "How big are you looking for?"

"Oh, I don't know... What sizes are available?"

He squinted, even though the sun was in back of him, and asked, "What are you selling?"

"I make custom mailboxes modeled after people's homes, so, I don't know..." I pointed to a medium-sized booth. "Maybe like that one. What does something like that run?"

Barely glancing at it, he said, "That's a ten-by-twelve booth, and those run four hundred dollars a month. Right now, I've got one coming up for rent the first of July. I've got other people asking me about it, so if you're serious, I'd need a deposit no later than Monday morning. Deposit is two hundred, and then I'd need the first and last months' rent a week before you open up. Still interested?"

I quickly added everything up and tried to calculate the additional costs. "Do you supply the actual booth itself?"

"Nope. That's on you."

Building a booth frame would be easy enough, but what about the other costs? Mailbox samples, lumber, supplies, the workshop remodel... But all the shoppers! Hundreds of people crowded around the booths and lumbered their way down the aisles, their bags and carts overflowing with items. Dollar signs danced as I added up all the sales I could make. Then I flashed to Ryan's face, and the knot in my stomach returned. I blurted out, "I'll take it!"

Bud's eyes got big, and he grinned and grabbed my hand hard. "Great! It's yours!" He pulled a business card from his pocket. "My address is on there. Can you swing by Monday morning with the deposit check?"

I cleared my throat. "You bet!"

"Great! Then welcome to the market, and I'll see you Monday!" He tapped his clipboard, spun around, and hurried off toward the next booth.

So, just like that, I had a booth. Jostling against the crowd, I felt like a salmon swimming upstream as now I was going against the flow of shoppers pouring into the market.

I reached my family just as Dylan and Sammy were getting on their ponies.

Em raised her eyebrows. "Did you find him?"

"Yeah, and we've got a booth starting July first!" I held my breath.

"Whoa! We didn't agree you'd *take* the booth, just see if one was available," she said, a little peeved. "How much will it cost?"

Might as well go for it all. "Well, here's the thing... It's around two thousand dollars to get the booth started, but I figured out last night that if I'm gonna really make this work, I need more space and tools and supplies to fill all the orders I'll get. I can build out the workshop and get everything I need for about ten thousand, and I can do all the work myself, and—"

"I thought you said we wouldn't need all our savings for this?" She crossed her arms.

"Yeah, but my workshop is bursting at the seams, and if I'm going to do this right, and be successful at it, then we need to go for it."

"No way, Ben! I can't believe you'd commit to this without talking to me first! We're not using all our savings on this. No way." She backed away and glared at me.

"But just hear me out..." I stammered.

"Listen, I'm not making a decision like this right now." The ponies had stopped, and the kids ran over, begging for another ride. "We'll talk about it later."

She pushed the cart toward me, grabbed Sammy's and Dylan's hands, and led them into the market. Burning up inside, I moved through the aisles, picking out items on my list. Em fell behind me as we snaked through the crowded booths, and I kept glancing back, but she kept her head down and went on shopping.

My mood lightened when I smelled the incense wafting from Sirena's stall. Sirena was our favorite of all the vendors in the market, and she often surprised Sammy and Dylan with little gifts of colorful polished stones or small glittering crystals. She had set up one of the liveliest stalls in the market and created a little world in her booth. Brown, green, and red paisley scarves fluttered from the clotheslines connecting the top corners of the booth, and hens and a rooster ran free on the ground around her, scratching and pecking and crowing. She had long golden-brown hair and kind green eyes, and she dressed more like a gypsy than a farmer, always in flowing, colorful long skirts and blouses, with a silk scarf on her head, her wrists and arms covered with the silver and turquoise bracelets she made. Sirena had been one of my first customers in town. Her mailbox had been a challenge for me at the time: a miniature version of a two-story farmhouse, with a small covered porch and an A-frame barn door on the right side that opened for the mail.

"Well, good morning, Ben!" she called to me. "Where's the family?"

"Oh, they're shopping away."

"Hey, I hear you're joining the market!"

How in the world did she know about that already?

She saw my look. "Bud just came by, and I felt that something special was happening today. How wonderful—finally bringing your dream to life! Hey, I have something I need help with, and it may end up helping you, too."

Sirena turned and disappeared behind the canvas curtain at the back of her booth. I looked down at the hens, who now sat quietly on some hay. They both turned their little heads toward the opening Sirena had just gone through. A moment later, she emerged with something I hadn't expected: her mailbox.

"What's this?"

"It needs some attention. One of the hinges is stuck; I think some rain leaked in and made it rusty. Do you think you can fix it for me?" She placed it on the counter.

"Sure, ah, sorry about that."

"Oh, that's fine. I've enjoyed it for years, and it just needs some special care now." She paused and smiled again, her eyes sparkling in the sunlight. "And take your time. I'll be away for a couple of months, so I won't need it 'til the end of summer."

I collected my eggs and put them in the basket, then lifted the mailbox and placed it on top of my shopping cart, its roofline nestled against the sides. Sirena bowed her head slightly, all the while holding my gaze, her eyes clear and confident. The hens now studied my cart, and I followed their stare, pausing for several moments, looking down at the mailbox.

"Everything will work out, Ben. You'll see."

I thanked her as a group of shoppers approached her stall. As I turned to leave, the hens stood up and slowly stretched their bony legs, bobbing their heads and scratching at the ground.

All at once, the outside world rushed back in, and I became aware of the hustle of the marketplace again: the music from the band at one end, the steady hum of shoppers' voices, the calls of the vendors, the screams and laughter of children as they darted in and out of the crowd, their tethered balloons bouncing behind them.

I joined Em, and we sauntered around the other booths for an hour, then stopped for coffee and bags of steaming-hot kettle corn. All the while, I checked out how the booths were constructed and mentally made a list of the supplies I'd need. We stopped by a booth that sold all kinds of seeds for planting, and Sammy and Dylan combed the rows and picked out what they wanted to plant on Sunday. On the way out, we got some freshly made ice cream, the first apricot flavor of the season. The guy who'd scored the ice cream booth at the exit had a great marketing ploy; location really was everything. Where the heck would my booth be located? It hadn't even occurred to me to ask Bud, but I made a note to do so later.

On the drive home, Sammy fell asleep, and Dylan's head dropped to his shoulder. Em stared out her window, ignoring me, until I finally broke the silence.

"Well?"

"Well, what?"

"Can I use the savings to get the business going?"

She paused for a moment. "I know how important this is—for both of us. The sooner you can get the business going, the closer we'll be to the home we want in Seattle. I get it. And you know that I support you in doing that."

"But?"

"Well, how about this... How 'bout we make a plan to save up for another year? That way, we'll have more savings, and this will be more thought out and planned for. Maybe you try his list for a year, and—"

"Ryan? He isn't going to give me a year to try his list out. Besides, Bud has a booth open right now, and with my income from the nursery and the business I'll get here, I can probably replace our savings within the year."

"You *hope* you can replace them. And if Bud has a booth now, he'll have a booth open next spring, too," she pointed out.

"Dammit, Em!" My raised voice almost woke the kids.

She went silent for a moment, then said, "I'm just not ready to risk all our savings at this moment."

She reached over and touched my elbow. I jerked it away.

"Don't be like that," she said.

We drove in silence the rest of the way home.

Later that evening, I passed by my workshop and found the door ajar. I looked in and saw both Sadie and Oreo sitting side by side, looking up at Sirena's mailbox, which I had put on a counter. *Strange*, I thought. I entered the room, and they both glanced over at me, then looked straight back up at the mailbox. Lifting the roof, I peeked inside and saw the edges of a bird's nest. Not wanting to disturb it, I gently closed the lid, shooed both Sadie and Oreo out, and closed the door. I'd deal with the nest later.

Chapter Three

Sunday, May 29, 1988

I woke from a fitful night of dreaming. My dreams were the same old unrelated nonsense, but it was like they were filmed in Technicolor—vivid, in a vintage Hollywood kind of way. Shaking them off, I stepped out back and into a cool spring morning, the pale blue sky painted with billowing, vibrant white clouds, the maple and dogwood trees bursting with new green leaves. Insects swarmed everywhere, with bees, dragonflies, butterflies, and gnats buzzing and zooming around the yard. The aroma from the mill had drifted past, replaced by the sweet scent of our neighbors' white jasmine. It was a perfect day for our annual planting in the back garden.

Em helped Sammy struggle into her little red rain boots on the porch, while Dylan stepped into his black rubber boots with the yellow trim on top, just like real firemen wore. Em slipped into a tight-fitting, one-piece black bathing suit, with a floppy wide-brim hat and big, round black sunglasses, and took up her post on a lounge chair in the sun. She looked like a movie star.

"I want to grow pumpkins as big as the house this year!" Sammy said.

"We aren't planting pumpkin seeds," I said. "You only get what you plant, so because you're planting carrots and tomatoes and beets, you're going to get yummy orange carrots, big juicy tomatoes, and bright red beets! That's how it works. As they say, 'You reap what you sow.'"

"But we aren't sewing, daddy. We're *planting*," she corrected me.

"I meant sowing with an *O*, not an *E*. It means planting."

Em, hearing everything, glanced over and smiled. She shook her head and sipped her iced tea. Adjusting the volume on the boom box, she bobbed her head to The Go-Go's "Vacation." I marveled at how sexy she could be just sitting on a lounge chair as I smiled and resumed digging, happy to see that the kids were behaving themselves. I had learned long ago that the secret to having a peaceful day with kids was to make sure they had something to do.

We finished a couple of hours later, and I joined Em on the lounge chair while the kids hauled their gear back to the shed.

She took my hand. "This has been a nice afternoon. I miss that." She leaned over and kissed me.

A flurry of butterflies flew through me. She still had that effect on me. "I've missed it, too."

"Yeah, we ought to have more of these days." She lingered for a moment, then released my hand as the kids charged up to us. She ushered them inside to shower, reminding them to straighten up their rooms before we left for dinner. I adjusted the drip system and put things away. When I got back inside, they were arguing.

"Told you I'd finish before you!" Dylan taunted from Sammy's bedroom doorway.

Sammy yelled back, "That's not fair! I have more toys than you!"

"That's because you still have little baby toys!" Dylan laughed.

Sammy started crying and stomped past him into the hallway, right into Em's arms. Their mother had heard them fighting and gently put her hands on Sammy's shoulders. "What's wrong, sweetheart?"

"I hate Dylan!" she whimpered.

"Was he being mean to you?"

"Yes!"

She bent down and met Sammy's teary eyes. "It doesn't feel very good when people make fun of you, does it?"

"No! He's mean." Sammy shook her head so hard that a little tear flew off her cheek.

"Sometimes we can say things that hurt other people's feelings, so that just means we have to be extra careful before we say them. Do you think if Dylan apologized to you, you'd feel better?"

Sammy glanced over at Dylan, who pretended to ignore what his mom was saying, but all eyes were on him.

"He'd better mean it." Sammy sniffled.

"Dylan? Would you come over here, please?"

Dylan reluctantly looked at his mom, and if he'd had a tail, it would have been between his legs the way he shuffled over to her.

"Now, Dylan, I'm sure you didn't mean to hurt your sister's feelings, did you?"

Dylan stared at his feet and mumbled, "No."

"Can you look at your sister and tell her you're sorry?"

Sammy sniffled and turned to Dylan, and he said, "I'm sorry."

"Sammy, do you accept his apology?" Em asked.

"Yeah, I guess so."

"Okay, now I want you two to give each other a hug, and then you can get back to your chores."

Dylan hesitated.

"Go on."

It might have been the quickest hug on record, but it made Sammy smile, and that was good enough for me. Sammy then darted past us and into the living room, where she turned up the radio for one of her favorite songs, "Walk Like an Egyptian." Dylan and Em, both smiling now, raced after her, and I quickly followed them to take part in a family ritual: singing together, while making flat hand movements and jutting our heads in and out, like we imagined the ancient Egyptians did. Sammy and Dylan sang along with the chorus.

We pranced around the living room, singing and swaying, looking very Egyptian. We laughed and smiled, and I was thankful that we could forget the tension and be a happy family again. Em tilted her head and tossed her silky blonde hair back from her forehead and over her left ear. I fell in love with her all over again, just like that day in high school. I wouldn't let her down. I'd keep my promise and get us that home on Queen Anne Hill, with her own music studio.

"My mailbox business will make it all come true for us, you'll see," I had sworn to her on our wedding night. But the years had passed quickly, and I was no closer to making my business work than I had ever been. I shook this off and strengthened my resolve to get my dad's help that night.

We headed over to my parents' house that evening, passing neighbors who were busy with their gardens, planting purple and yellow daises and adjusting sprinkler heads for the warmer weather ahead. I wasn't telling Em about my plan; my dad had drilled into me that it was easier to get forgiveness than permission. Once I had the money in hand, I would let her know how I'd pay it back.

We pulled into my old neighborhood near the mill, where my dad still worked. It looked older each time I saw it, and there always seemed to be one more heating and air conditioning truck or painting van parked in people's driveways. The kids jumped out and ran to my mom, who was wearing her sunflower-yellow apron, standing on the porch with her arms outstretched. They crashed into her, and she waved to us and then wrapped them in a big hug. She nodded at Em—no doubt something going on at Garfield Elementary, where they both taught. Em's privileged background had always intimidated me, and I'd worried how she'd fit in with my family, but she and my mom had hit it off from the start over their love for teaching and kids. The rich smell of butter and barbequed chicken—the smell of home—welcomed us inside.

On the patio, my dad was smoking a cigarette. He flicked it away, stepped into the house, and picked up Dylan, who was wearing his number 80 Seahawks jersey, and gave him a big, smoky kiss on the cheek.

"How's Steve Largent today, eh?" he asked.

Dylan playfully pushed him away. "I'm ready to start this week!"

"That's what I like to hear," Dad said.

He lowered Dylan, and I caught a glimpse of his bulging biceps. Fifty-seven, and he could still bench two hundred. Not to mention, his wavy black hair with a bit of gray still turned women's heads. I worried about how much he smoked, especially when he was nervous, and how much beer he packed away, especially on Sunday game days, but he was as fit as a horse from years of working at the paper mill. Standing near him, I caught the faint scent of wet carboard mixed with cigarette smoke, a smell I'd associated with him for sixteen years.

He made a drinking motion and grabbed two beers. We sat at the dining room table and started our ritual.

"So, how's work?" he asked.

"Well, Ryan won't market to his mailing list without totally taking over. He wants an exclusive on the whole thing," I fumed.

My dad knew all about my struggles with Ryan, had shared my frustration over the years, and he stood firmly on my side.

"He's a jerk. Always has been, always will be," he muttered.

"Yeah, well, I've got an idea I want to run by you. In fact—"

At that moment, my mom and Em burst out of the kitchen with plates of steaming, delicious-smelling food. We loved my mom's cooking. It was pure comfort: mashed potatoes with sour cream and chives, fried chicken in her secret barbeque breading, steaming creamed spinach, and a basket of hot dinner rolls with a slab of soft, salted butter on the side—my personal favorite.

"So, how's work?" Emily asked my dad.

"Oh, same ol', same ol'," he said vaguely.

My mom snuck a quick look at my dad. "Well, there's actually some talk around the plant on account of that Big Box store that's set to open soon."

"How's that?" I asked.

My dad, with a mouth full of mashed potatoes, said, "It's always something, you know? The Big Box store has got a lot of the smaller hardware stores and lumber outlets worried, and the competition is gonna get rough out there. No one can buy in bulk like they can. They have to get their lumber from somewhere, though, and our mill is the logical place. But like I always say, if something can go wrong, it will. We'll have to wait and see."

My mom frowned and quickly looked down. She picked up her napkin and wiped her hands forcefully, put the napkin down, and kept on wringing them as if she were drying them.

"But, so, what if they don't, right? I mean, one store? That can't make *that* much of a difference," I said, glancing at my mom again.

She opened her mouth, but my dad shook his head and took over. "Well, it's one store for now. Heck, they've really caught on, taken over the whole southeast over the last five years, and if they do well in Tacoma, there's talk that they could open additional stores up and down the west coast. That's a lot of business for the mill, and a lot of competition for the smaller suppliers."

"But still, the mill's been in business forever. They sell lumber all over the country, don't they?"

"Oh, the mill will be fine; it's not going anywhere. There've been some rumors about possible layoffs of some of the new hires, but I've been there for over sixteen years. Four more, and my pension is fully vested, so I'll be fine."

My mom couldn't remain silent any longer. "We'll *probably* be fine," she said. "If worse comes to worst, we have our savings, and as my mother used to say, 'Whatever happens, we'll just cut our cloth accordingly.'"

After dinner, my mom and Em cleared the table, and I joined my dad on the back patio while he had a smoke. It was a little after eight by then, and the sky had turned a burnt orange, dotted with dark gray clouds. He went through the familiar routine of patting his breast pocket, then his pants for his cigarettes and lighter. He lit one and took a deep drag, then a pull from his beer. Exhaling the blue smoke, he said, "So, what's on your mind?"

"Well, I got a little bit of good news today. You know Bud, down at the farmers' market?"

"That old hippie? Yeah, I know Bud. Watch out for him, though. He looks mellow, but that mind of his is always moving and scheming."

"I know, but he runs a good business there, built it up from just a few vegetable stalls to almost a hundred booths now. You know I've always wanted a booth there, to put out some nice samples, some photos of other mailboxes I've made, and heck, there are hundreds of people shopping there every Saturday."

I paused and waited for him to bite. He just kept smoking and staring at the sky.

"Anyway, I spoke to Bud today about renting a booth, and there's one coming available in July. It's four hundred dollars a month, and I know I could sell enough mailboxes to easily cover that and make a profit."

"Sounds good." He nodded.

So far, so good.

"Yeah, it's a great opportunity, and it means I don't have to rely on Ryan, which makes it even better. Anyway, the thing is, I'm not interested in just this booth. I want to go all-out: remodel and expand my workshop, outfit it with new tools and supplies, and after the booth is up and running, add a stall in Pike Place, too. All in, I'd need about ten thousand dollars to start the business the right way." I stopped and held my breath.

"Ten thousand, huh? That's a good chunk of change. What's Em say?"

"She's… Well, she's on board with the idea, but she wants to wait another year, save up more. But I'm through with waiting! It's time for me to do this."

He faced me. "And?"

I took a deep breath. "Well, Dad, here's the thing… I've thought all this through, and I figure if you could loan me the money, then I could pay you back in twelve months—sixteen, at most. I'll pull some double shifts at the nursery, and with the booth, I'll be keeping all the profit from each mailbox. Ryan is selling three to four a month from the nursery alone, and the foot traffic at the farmers' market is twenty times what he gets." I paused. "What do you think?"

My dad considered it. Then he raised his eyebrows and said, "I think you ought to do it. Hell, you should have done it a while ago. And I'd love you to show Ryan up, too. I know you're good for the money, and if it takes a little longer, that's okay. Just pay me something each month—like five hundred or so, and that'll make your mother feel better. Could you handle that?"

"Absolutely! The money I would have saved for this, like Em wants, I'll just route to you each month. And I'll pay even more once the orders come in."

"By the way," my dad added, "does Em know you're asking to borrow this money from me?"

He always could see through me. "Well, no… I thought I'd run it by her if you said yes. No need getting into anything if you wouldn't do it."

"Ah, wise man," he said. "When do you need the money?"

"I need to give Bud a check on Monday for the deposit, and

get some lumber for the build-out, order some tools, and get to work preparing. Is there any way—"

"How about I write you a check for seven thousand tonight to get you started, then give you the rest in two weeks? Just don't cash it 'til Tuesday; I've got to move some money around. Will that work?"

"That would be great! Thank you." I glanced back at the house. "And do me a favor... Don't tell Em tonight, okay?"

My dad chuckled, stooped down, and crushed the cigarette out in an ashtray. "I'll let you handle that one."

Back in the house, my mom clapped her hands. "Who wants rocky road ice cream?"

"I do, I do!" the kids cried in unison.

She asked me to go out to the garage freezer to fetch it, and Dylan volunteered to help carry it. The garage smelled musty and cool, packed with boxes, bags, and backpacks and littered with dull woodworking equipment. An old table saw still sat in the middle with cobwebs on the base, and we stepped around rusty bicycles, old kayaks, and camping gear from a life that had long passed by. Dusty old pink insulation hung from the open rafters in the ceiling. Against two of the walls, a dented and stained workstation sagged, scattered with forgotten tools, and above it hung worn-out sandpaper and frozen-together clamps.

"How does Grandpa get anything made in here?" Dylan asked.

"He doesn't have time for woodworking anymore."

Dylan furrowed his little brows. "Was he as good as you?"

"Grandpa was actually a lot better than me. He taught me how to work with wood. In fact, we were going to make mailboxes together—make them right here and sell them all over the state."

"And why didn't you?"

I suppressed a sigh. "Because things change."

I turned away from him, and a dullness filled my chest as that memory boiled up again—the day I came home from my first day of junior high school, and my world changed. Ever since I was a kid about Dylan's age, my dad and I had spent all our free time in this garage, working on wood together. He showed me how to measure and cut wood, how to shape and sand and stain it, and those afternoons and weekends of ripping, smoothing, gluing, and painting were the happiest memories I had.

Until they weren't.

Coming home from school that hot September day, I couldn't wait to join my dad in the garage for an afternoon of woodworking. Only, the garage was closed. Something was wrong.

I had found my dad on the patio, pacing and smoking. He cleared his throat and looked away from me when I approached him.

"What's wrong?" I asked. "Why's the garage closed?"

"Son, sit down. I've got something to tell you."

"I don't want to sit down. What's wrong?" I jammed my hands under my armpits and stared at him.

"I got a job down at the mill. It's a good job, with a future and a pension, unlike the contracting work I've been doing. It's where I'll be working from now on." He took a deep drag on his cigarette and studied the smoke as it drifted away.

"But, but ... what about our business? Are we going to do that at night?" I asked.

He flinched, then snapped back around. "That was just a dream, Ben." His voice was raspy. "Dreams don't pay the bills, son. Jobs do. And that's what I've got now. Evenings won't be enough time to work on the mailboxes. You'll have to take that up in your woodworking class."

He patted his pocket for his smokes, then realized he already had one going. Clearing his throat again, he turned away from me.

And just like that, our dream was over.

Dylan drifted over to the table and looked up at an old silver-and-blue Seahawks sign: SEAHAWKS FAN PARKING ONLY. A small, dusty hand planer with a mahogany handle lay on the table. Dylan picked it up. "Does this still work?"

I hadn't seen that planer in years; I'd forgotten all about it. It was a birthday gift my dad had given me when he told me about his dream for us to do woodworking together. After he told me about his new job at the mill, I'd sworn I would never use it again. I didn't know why, but I slipped it into my jacket pocket.

"Let's get the ice cream and get out of here," I said.

The evening ended the way it began: my mom in her yellow apron on the front doorstep, this time hugging the kids goodbye. My dad and I shook hands, and he pulled me aside and slipped me a check for seven thousand dollars. He whispered, "Take it slow, and let her talk her feelings out."

He patted me on the shoulder, and I followed Em and the kids, who were full and sleepy, to the minivan. We drove off down the dark street.

She didn't wait long. "What was that about?"

"What was what about?"

"It looked like your dad gave you something."

I had hoped to have this conversation tomorrow, once I'd decided how to approach it. But Em, too sharp for me, was on it. It was time to get to the forgiveness part.

"Well, I was thinking. You know how you said we could save up the money and start the business later?"

"Yeah."

"Well, I figured I could ask my dad for a loan, so we can get started now. You know, take advantage of the summer and fall months, without waiting and losing out. So, instead of saving money each month, I'll just pay him back a little at a time."

She shifted in her seat and faced me. "Why didn't you ask me first?"

"Well, I ... I wasn't sure he'd even loan me the money."

"How much?"

"The whole amount."

She shot a look into the back seat and saw that the kids were both dozing.

"Ten thousand dollars?! Ben, that's a *huge* loan for them! And it's a big debt for us to take on! What if you don't sell enough mailboxes to pay that off?"

She started twirling her wedding ring and shifted in her seat. The forgiveness part felt far away.

"I've thought about that, and here's the thing. With my income from the nursery, and the sales from the market, he'll have his money back within a year. This is finally my chance, and I have to take it. It's a loan that I can and will pay back."

She remained silent.

"Without touching our savings," I added.

The back of my spine tingled as she shook her head back and forth. I almost said something, but remembered what my dad told me: just let her talk her feelings out. I bit my tongue.

Finally, she softened and said, "Well, it does make some kind of sense, I guess. You know I want this for you. As you said, we both have incomes, and we won't have to risk our savings, and if you can get orders right away, it could all work out, right?"

I squeezed her hand. "Absolutely! And I *will* get orders—plenty of them. I'll make this work, I'm telling you."

"You've got a lot to do to get ready to open the booth and build out your workshop." She hesitated. "I mean, that's only a month away. I've been thinking about it, and the kids do want you to join us on vacation, but I can't see how you can take two weeks off now, right?"

"Oh, yes, I can! I've almost got three samples done right now, and I can make a frame for the booth in a week. I'll get the two weeks off, and we'll start the vacation together, just like we always do. We'll have a relaxing time as a family, right before the booth opens. It's just what we need. You know it is."

"Let's see how things go, but I'm open to it, if you think there's enough time."

"There's plenty of time, don't worry."

She squeezed my hand back, and I relaxed.

"It'll work out," I assured her.

We both fell silent and stared straight ahead as a soft snore came from the back seat.

Once we got home, we carried the kids in, and while Em got ready for bed, I opened a new can of dog food and waited for Sadie to come into the kitchen. Normally, both Oreo and Sadie instantly reacted to that sound, but they were nowhere in sight. I looked around and found them back in my workshop, leaning against each other and staring up at the mailbox again. How had they gotten in here? I was sure I had closed my workshop door. This time, they didn't even glance at me; instead, they remained fixated on the mailbox. I picked Oreo up and carried him into the kitchen, then had to go back and nudge Sadie out as well. I closed the door and pushed on it to make sure it was secure.

In the bedroom, once Em's slow, steady breathing began, I tried to turn my mind off, but that wasn't happening. My dad's warning resurfaced: *"If something can go wrong, it will."*

I'd get enough orders from the booth, wouldn't I? Of course I would. But why had Em brought up Ryan's list again yesterday? They had broken up so long ago, right after his parents died in that car accident. Surely, she couldn't still have feelings for him?

Or was it because he'd been so successful with the nursery his parents left him? He'd bottled up his grief and poured it into dominating the business, and boy, had he succeeded. He borrowed, he expanded, and over the years, he put smaller nurseries out of business. He was cutthroat and unrelenting in the way he ran the nursery, and damn, he was smart. He'd jumped on the new mail-out coupon idea and drove business through a barrage of seasonal advertising: spring specials, summer discounts, fall closeouts. Why didn't I think of doing that? Now his mailing list reached people all the way into Seattle and even the islands, and I could have gotten so much business there!

But Friday, he had put an end to that hope. Well, he wasn't getting any exclusive from me; I'd start my own business on my own terms. Now I had the booth and the money, and after the vacation with Em and the kids, it'd be smooth sailing. Finally, I'd show him.

Chapter Four

Monday, May 30, 1988

I dropped off the booth deposit at Bud's house before my shift. Paying it relaxed me a bit, but the closer I got to the nursery, the more I worried about Ryan. I pulled into the broad parking area and saw him in the side yard, supervising a large delivery of steaming brown mulch. He barked orders at his laborers as they scurried around with their wheelbarrows and snowplow-sized shovels. I took short breaths as the stench of the moist mulch filled the air.

Ryan's Nursery—just like him to rename it after himself—was an attractive, well-stocked, and well-run business. I'd helped build the landscaped island that sat in the middle of the huge circular driveway, and it had been my idea to feature a waterfall with lush green ferns, and to showcase in-season plants and flowers around it. The mulch and soil delivery were on the south side, housed in an original big barn, and the entrance to the nursery on the north side was fronted with aisles of saplings, shrubs, flowers, and anything else needed for spring planting.

I punched in, put my lunch box in my locker, and grabbed my gloves and work belt, which had my order pad in it. Outside, the sun glared down on the rows of newly potted trees, and I wiped the sweat off my forehead and squinted into the yard. Early shoppers swarmed the outside lot, and three yard workers jostled around the crowded aisles, answering questions and loading customers' carts with potted plants and flowers.

I glanced back to the mulch area and saw Ryan marching toward me. As he passed, he hissed, "I want to see you in my office, right now!"

Now what?

I followed him into his corner office, which had walls of glass so he could survey the shoppers—and keep an eye on his employees. He stood in front of his big, messy desk, his arms folded, his mouth tightened into a scowl. He nodded at the door and boomed, "So, how long have you known?"

"Excuse me?" His hostile tone startled me.

"You heard me. How. Long. Have. You. Known?"

"I'm sorry, known what?"

He unfolded his arms and stepped toward me. Ryan was only about five-foot-seven, but he was wiry, and at thirty years old, still fearless, and not beyond a barroom brawl. But I was six-foot-one and in good shape, and I wasn't backing down. He stared up at me and growled, "Big Man Mitch, putting up the Big Box store. How long have you known he was planning to do that?"

"What are you talking about? Mitch's Big Box store? What do you mean?"

"Yeah, it's on *his* property!" He took another step toward me. Just twelve inches away now, the vein on his forehead bulged blue, and his jaw popped as he chomped his gum. He glared and snapped, "Don't pretend you don't know anything about it. Does he have a piece of it? Do you?"

I flinched as he spun around, cut back around his desk, and began pacing.

My stomach collapsed. "I don't know anything about that." There were many implications here, and none of them were good.

He stopped and turned on me. "That store is going to have a *major* impact on my business. You know they undercut every local business within a hundred miles. I don't believe for a second that you and Em didn't know about this. I mean, Mitch is her *father*, isn't he?"

"Yeah, but—"

"'Yeah but' nothing. This isn't going to be good for my business—and that means it's not going to be good for you."

I grasped for something to say, and it slipped out. "What about promoting my mailboxes to the list?"

He sneered at me. "Yeah, well, you can forget about that. I need higher-profit items to resell now that the Big Box store is coming. The only way I'd even consider it is if we changed the percentage split. Instead of fifty/fifty, it's got to be sixty percent to me and forty percent to you. And the exclusive. Take it or leave it."

Sixty percent to Ryan? Ridiculous! The exclusive was bad enough. I grinned and said, "I'll leave it. Besides, I don't need that now, because I'm starting my business at the farmers' market in July."

"With Bud?" He snickered. "Yeah, good luck with that."

"What's that supposed to mean?"

"How many mailbox buyers do you think you'll get at the farmers' market? They're a bunch of cheapos looking for discount vegetables and handmade soap. Without me, you don't have a business." He gave me a quick, disgusted snort and added, "In fact, you don't understand the first thing about business. Never did, never will. If you want something, you have to go out and take it. And you don't have that in you."

"Well, we'll see about that."

With that, he stopped pacing and plopped behind his desk. He reached into a drawer and pulled out the big nursery checkbook.

My ears burned, and I was about to walk out—but the two weeks' vacation! Bad timing, but I was too charged up to care. "I'll think about the sixty percent, and then I'll let you know after my vacation with Em." I hoped bringing up her name would sting. "I've scheduled a week off starting Friday the tenth, and like last year, I'm going to extend it an extra week. I've already cleared it with the day shift manager." I let that settle in.

Ryan didn't react. Instead, he calmly opened the checkbook. "How many hours have you worked since your last paycheck?"

I calculated briefly. "Twenty-eight. Why?"

He started writing a check. "I'm done with you, and Mitch, and your mailboxes. You can take two months or two years off, as far as I'm concerned."

He finished writing the check, ripped it out slowly, and held it out, smiling up at me. Confused, I grabbed it, and he said, "That pays you for the hours you've done. From this moment on, you no longer work here. You're fired. Leave your order pad and work belt, grab your mailbox samples, and clear out."

He dismissed me by lowering his head and shuffling through a stack of papers on his desk.

"What the hell?!"

He looked back up with steely eyes and spoke evenly. "Do

you need me to get Jim and a few of the boys in here to help you find your locker?"

Moments later, I peeled out of the nursery, burning some rubber on his pristine driveway. How could Em have betrayed me like that? She must have known about Mitch! I blasted through a yellow light and changed lanes to avoid rear-ending a slower driver. Man! I had to slow down and think about this.

My thoughts raged like a tornado, twisting out of control. What about the booth now?

Em was only okay with it because we'd both had income. Should I go back to Bud's and get my deposit back? No... The booth still had to happen, especially now. And what about Em knowing about Mitch? She spoke to her folks several times a week, and this deal must have been in the works for months. Why had she kept it from me? I couldn't wait to talk to her, but I had to calm down and make some sense of it first.

A little after three-thirty, the minivan rumbled into the driveway, and three doors opened and slammed shut. The pitter-patter of feet mixed with the soft pitter-patter of the rain, and then they all tumbled through the front door, Em's hands full of the usual backpacks. They all stopped short when they saw me, surprised that I was home so early on a Monday.

"Daddy!" Sammy called out, running over and hugging me. "What are you doing home?"

Em and Dylan stood by the front door, looking me over.

"It's a long story, honey, and I'll tell you all about it later. Why don't you and Dylan go change clothes?"

"Okay." And off they went.

"Yeah, what *are* you doing home so early?" Em frowned, dropping the backpacks on the couch.

I got in her face. "When were you going to tell me?"

Em stepped back. "Tell you what? What's going on?"

"What's going *on*?" I grabbed her damp wrist and led her into the kitchen, but she jerked away.

"Stop this! What the hell is going on? Tell you what?"

"That Mitch, *your* father, is behind the Big Box store coming to town! When were you going to give me that bit of information?"

"What are you talking about?" She stared at me and didn't back down.

"Ryan told me—hell, he *ambushed* me—and said we must have known all about your dad's plan to bring the Big Box store here. It's being built on land that Mitch sold them! Don't tell me you didn't know anything about it!"

"Of course I didn't! Why would I know anything about that? I don't know what he does in his business! What has that got to do with anything? And why aren't you at work?"

"Oh, yeah, I forgot to tell you: Ryan fired me today. That's why I'm not at work."

She covered her mouth, and her eyebrows shot up. "Oh my God! He *fired* you?!"

"Yeah, he fired me. Said I was hiding Mitch's involvement in the Big Box store, probably even making money off the deal. He told me you knew all about it. Well, did you?"

She stared at me, too angry to answer. Then she said steadily, "I can't believe you. How *dare* you think I'd keep something like that from you?! See?" She shivered. "This is just what I'm talking about! Something is wrong with you—with us. This..." Her voice trailed off, and she bumped past me and stormed out of the kitchen.

I moved to go after her, but the kids rushed in.

"I'm hungry," Dylan said.

"When are we gonna eat?" Sammy asked.

I grabbed a couple of apples and almost threw them at them, then ushered them into the living room before stalking off to find Em. I needed to cool down, plan my next steps carefully, but I was steaming. I should have gone into my workshop and waited until later, but I didn't.

She was in the bedroom, changing, and I dived back in. "So, you didn't know about it, huh? Is that what you're telling me?"

She kept her back to me. "I'm not even going to answer that."

"Well, what the hell is Mitch doing with the Big Box store? How long has he known about it?"

She whipped around and exploded. "Who knows?! Who cares? He's in real estate! That's what he does, Ben! The real question, is what are you going to do for work now?"

"I'll get a job, I guess. What else am I going to do?"

"What about the farmers' market? Did you give Bud the deposit check yet?"

"I told you I was dropping it off this morning, so of course I did. What about it?" There was no way I was giving up the booth.

"You should go get that back. Unless you get a job in a week or so, we can't afford to take that risk now." She stood tall and still, her slender arms folded in front of her chest, daring me to disagree.

"My dad gave me the loan, and he doesn't care when I pay it back. Besides, that's a source of income right there. And meanwhile, I'll find a job!"

"Yeah, well, you'd better hustle if you want that to work out."

She turned her back on me again and said over her shoulder, "I know you don't like to hear this, but you should have taken the deal when he offered it last week. That nursery is a little gold mine, and the list could have really paid off for us."

The thought had crossed my mind at the nursery, but her bringing it up now ticked me off. "I can't believe you're going back to that! Why are you always taking his side?"

She flipped around, her cheeks burning red. "Christ, Ben! I'm *not* taking his side. I'm on *our* side. That was a great opportunity. It's why you went to work for him to begin with, and even taking it temporarily could have given us a nice cushion to launch your business."

"I'll make it work at the farmers' market, you'll see," I said. "Now I've got plenty of time to make it just right. Right after I get back from vacation, I'll—"

Her eyes grew large. "Vacation? You gotta be kidding me! You don't have time for a vacation!"

"Actually, it's just the opposite," I said, perhaps a little too smugly. "I've got nothing but time now."

She moved to the bathroom doorway, turned, and said, "You're staying home and getting a job. I'm not bringing this attitude on vacation with me and the kids. That's not gonna happen. I knew we needed time apart, and this just confirms it."

She whirled into the bathroom and slammed the door.

Things only got tenser between us over the next ten days. As the kids finished school and Em prepared to leave on vacation without me, she'd often pick up the classifieds, scan the jobs, and say,

"This is a perfect job for you. It uses all your skills and pays well. Why don't you apply for it?" Then she'd stand there, hands on her hips, ready to get into it with me.

"Because it requires every other Saturday. I can't work the farmers' market and take this job at the same time. Just read the ad all the way to the end, and you'll see that."

That week and a half had been hard on the kids, too. They stopped checking on the vegetable garden, and Sammy didn't even attempt to sing along with the radio anymore. The distance between us all had grown into a chasm I couldn't seem to cross. The kids couldn't wait to go on vacation, and I couldn't blame them.

They left on a Thursday morning, a bright June day that should have been happy and full of joy for the upcoming summer. A couple of our retired neighbors were already out mowing and planting colorful annuals in their yards. We loaded the minivan with all the backpacks, suitcases, and snacks for the drive.

My eyes burned as I knelt down and kissed Dylan and Sammy goodbye, then watched as they raced down the driveway to fight over the front seat. I followed them to the minivan and hugged Sammy tightly once again, trying to hold on, but she pushed me away after the second kiss and said, "Okay, Daddy, I want to go!" She broke free and tried to pull Dylan off the front seat.

Em put an end to the fight. "You'll both be sitting in the back, and you'll behave yourselves."

We buckled them in. Dylan leaned over and whispered for me to make sure his broccoli was okay, and Sammy asked me to take special care of Sadie while she was gone. I nodded and stood in the driveway, wiping away a stray tear. Em's eyes welled up as well, and we didn't know what to say to each other as we stood side by side, staring at the kids.

"I'll call you when we get there," she said, looking straight ahead.

"Yeah, ah, that'll be good. Drive carefully," was all I could manage.

She took my arm and said tenderly, "Hey, I just need some space right now. We both do. We'll speak on the phone, and you'll come up soon enough." She kissed me on the cheek. "We'd better get going if we want to catch the ten-thirty ferry."

With that, she got in the minivan and backed out of the driveway, and my little family drove away. I watched them until the very end. When they reached the corner, I hoped they would turn and wave, but instead they simply turned and disappeared.

I shuffled back into the empty and quiet house, in need of caffeine. Maybe it would give me courage to keep searching for a job, but just thinking about the classifieds turned my stomach. I looked around for Sadie, but she wasn't in the den. On the way to the backyard, I passed by the workshop and found its door pushed open wide, and I slumped next to Sadie and Oreo and stared up at Sirena's mailbox absently. Gradually, my thoughts cleared. The familiar and soothing smells of wood and lacquer comforted me, and for the first time in days, I relaxed.

That evening, I ate in the glow of twilight in the backyard. The clear night still held the cool of spring. Damn, the house was quiet. Sharp pangs of longing for Em and the kids stabbed at me. I stared into the woods as a chorus of crickets roared. My head swirled as I tried to figure a way out of and back into my life at the same time.

It all came crashing down on me. How had it come to this? What if Ryan was right—that I didn't understand business or have it in me? I hadn't had the silver spoon, the head start, like

Ryan or Mitch did. What would become of Em and me? Was this the beginning of the end? I shook those thoughts away and took a long pull on my beer, tipped my head back, and gazed at the twinkling stars overhead.

Our house was far from the bustle and lights of downtown. I loved coming out, looking up at the stars, and wondering how many other people or beings, on all the other planets, were doing the same thing at the same time, looking back at me. There had to be more than just us.

A shooting star with a long white tail pierced the night, then faded over the horizon. It snapped me back to the moment. I was supposed to make a wish. Caught in a tangle of thoughts, I went through all the things I could wish for: better feelings between Em and me, my family being back together, my mailboxes working out.

Finally, I cleared my mind. I let out a deep breath and imagined all my worries and fears leaving me with that breath.

I surrendered.

And I wished.

Chapter Five

Friday morning, June 10, 1988

I found Sadie and Oreo in the workshop that morning, seemingly unmoved since yesterday; their bowls of food in the kitchen hadn't been touched. Had they slept here all night?

As I entered, I saw it: a faint blue glow flickering from inside the mailbox. I stared at it, unbelieving at first, but the glow increased and sparkled behind the little windows, like fireflies after a summer rain. Sadie and Oreo looked up at me and then back toward the light.

Instinctively, I moved to the table, removed the roof of the mailbox, and held my breath. A wonderland of pastel colors and light unfolded before me. Lining the bottom of the mailbox was one of Sirena's paisley scarves, its folds forming a bed, with the ends bunching up a few inches on each side. Cradled in the scarf sat a perfectly shaped nest made of the finest straw, each strand glistening with light. The center of the nest pulsed with a swirling galaxy of color, a surging energy that shimmered and gently vibrated. Fascinated, I held my hands over it, and like a magnet, warmth from the light radiated up my arms and across my shoulders, filling me with peace and connecting me to the presence of life that glowed before me. What in the world was happening?

I stood entranced, then heard a soft humming coming from deep within the nest. I had an overpowering urge to protect it, so I replaced the roof and carefully carried the mailbox into the den, where I placed it beside the couch, facing the fireplace. Sadie and Oreo were right behind me, and keeping the mailbox in view, they took their places on either side of the fire, like two sentinels.

I slid onto the couch and sat staring down at the mailbox, dumbfounded. I fell into what I could only describe as a kind of trance, where all my thoughts cleared and time seemed to stand still. When I came out of it, shafts of blue light now blazed through every opening of the mailbox: around and through each window, around the front door frame, along the roofline, and even up through the little chimney. Like rays of sunshine, the light reflected off every surface in the room, casting striped shadows on the walls and ceiling of the den. I sat absorbed in this radiating glow, and it took a few moments before I became aware of the sound.

The hum from earlier now sounded like a chorus of a thousand soft voices, all chanting the same tone or vowel. This sound was barely perceptible at first, but once I became aware of it, it expanded and filled the room, as softly and yet as fully as did the light. I staggered to my feet and leaned against the couch, enchanted by the mystery unfolding around me.

I had no desire to lift off the roof again, nor to disturb the mailbox in any way. Instead, I went over and petted Sadie and Oreo, who led me into the kitchen and sat next to their bowls. I fed them, but was too dazed to think about eating anything myself, so I went back into the den and lit a crackling fire. Settling on the sofa, I stared at the shining, humming little house for the next couple of hours, alternating between gazing and meditating, dozing and dreaming.

Then something snapped me out of my trance, and I refocused on the mailbox. All at once, the shimmering light that had been streaming through it faded and withdrew back into the house. At the same time, the song that filled the den also faded, like music being turned down on a stereo. As the room dimmed and quieted, I slid over on the sofa and examined the windows of the mailbox, but the opaque plastic was too cloudy for me to make out what was happening inside. I sat still for several minutes, watching the last of the light disappear inside, and listened as the sound softened to a whisper, then faded out. I froze in the sudden stillness of the room, barely breathing, trying not to make a sound, waiting eagerly for what would happen next.

And then I heard it.

First, a gentle rustling, then another, and then a soft movement came in an uneven rhythm that lasted about three minutes. Something was moving within the nest.

I waited and listened for a few more minutes, but the sounds soon settled, and the room fell silent once more. I looked over at Sadie and Oreo, who had wandered back in and were sitting on either side of the mailbox, alert now and looking up at me. I wasn't sure what to do, but instinct took over, so I gripped the roof and slowly removed it.

Nestled on top of the scarf, with the tattered pieces of the nest pushed aside, lay a glistening, softly glowing figure. Her shape was like a miniature person, about the size of my forefinger. Her body, however, was covered with delicate feathers, like the finest down, snowy white, yet tinged with soft grays, oranges, and yellows. The only parts of her body not covered with these feathers were her tiny face, hands, and feet.

She had the face of a little girl, no larger than a button on one of Sammy's sweaters, yet with exquisite features: almond-shaped eyes with miniscule lashes, a tiny nose, and a delicate little mouth, all surrounded by long, golden curls of blonde hair. Her hands and feet were perfectly formed, with the precise detail of the finest porcelain doll. She lay sleeping on her side, her body curled with her knees tucked into her chest. Her skin glowed the color of a ripe peach, slightly translucent, and it shone with the brilliance of a light from deep within.

Then she moved, and it startled all of us. Sadie and Oreo were standing closer to me now, attentive and tracking the little being below. As we stared at her together, she shifted again and rolled onto her stomach, and I spied two small bumps along each side of her back. These bumps had thicker feathers than the rest of her body, and they were both sky blue, edged with gray at the bottom. It didn't occur to me at the time what they might be. Her little body rose and fell with her soft, rhythmic breathing, and the three of us sat still, mesmerized by the small, gleaming figure before us. After a while, I replaced the roof and set it at an angle to allow air to flow in.

Suddenly, I was starving; when was the last time I had eaten? I mechanically made a pot of coffee and a bowl of cereal and wolfed it down while trying to make sense of all this. What the heck was happening? Had I lost my mind?

Too energized to sit still, I spent the early afternoon straightening up the house and organizing my workshop, making frequent trips into the den to check on my little guest. She was changing rapidly, and each time I lifted the roof and peeked in, she had developed a bit more—not necessarily growing bigger, but rather filling out and becoming more defined. Her coat of feathers had changed as she dried off, becoming thicker and more spread out. The colors marking their edges had faded, and she was now a more uniform color, a soft pearl white, except for a hint of yellow around her neck, which gave the appearance of a faint golden necklace.

Her radiance had changed as well. Her glow had turned to a kind of gloss that was still evident when looking at her from certain angles. It seemed like the light was retreating deeper inside her, and as it did, her skin lost much of its translucence, but this made it easier to see her features. Her miniature fingernails and toenails and her little eyes and nose became more distinct, and occasionally, her lips moved. I bent closer; was she whispering something? The lumps on her back were expanding and taking on a vaguely familiar shape. They stretched from her shoulder blades all the way to the top of her waist now, and they protruded out nearly a quarter of an inch.

Sadie, Oreo, and I were all watching her sleep, and as she turned from one side to the next, her eyelids fluttered, and she blinked a few times—then she opened her eyes! I couldn't imagine what she made of the three of us looking down at her—a golden Lab, a black-and-white cat, and me with my thick black hair and two-day-old beard. She gazed up at us, blinked several more times, and then scrunched her tiny brow and broke out into a warm smile. I grinned, Oreo purred, and Sadie thumped her tail on the hardwood floor. She gently rubbed her eyes with tiny fists, blinked, and peered into me, her eyes beaming with the innocence of a child, yet filled with the love and wisdom of a grandmother. She was captivating.

She held my eyes, and a deep sense of warmth, of peace, surged through me. My mind cleared. I suddenly felt immersed in a deep meditative state, and yet I was aware of where I was and what was happening. We locked onto each other, and she sensed my many questions, my curiosity, my wonder.

Her eyes closed for a long moment, and in my head came a soft voice: in time, she would tell me everything I wanted to know. She then opened her sparkling little eyes and added, *"And many things you could never even think of asking."*

I didn't understand how I could hear her, but I did. Questions swam in my mind: What *was* she? Was she real? Was I hallucinating? She sensed these questions, the biggest being, *Who are you, and what is happening?*

A voice whispered inside me, *"I am here, Ben, because your dream called to me. What is happening is something powerful that can change your life and others' lives—if you're able to embrace a great truth. But now, you've already taken in much more than you can process, and I need to grow stronger. Let me rest, and let's continue tomorrow, when the day is fresh and the light is young."*

With that, she curled up in her nest, and I placed the roof back on the mailbox, the blue light from before barely visible behind the windows. Sadie and Oreo drifted back to their places beside the fire, and I went onto the back patio and tried to make sense of the avalanche of questions overwhelming me.

First of all, was I hallucinating? Had I lost my grip on reality? But if I had, then Sadie and Oreo must have as well, because they definitely seemed to see her, too. And what *was* she, exactly? She "came because my dream called to her"? Really? How did she know about my dream? And why me? What great truth? My mind hurt just thinking about it all; it was too much, and I had no answers to any of these questions. What would happen next? Would tomorrow make any more sense, or just bring more questions?

The sharp report of a gunshot snapped me back to reality. I flinched and whipped to attention. In a quick movement, I bounded back into the house, glanced into the den, and was out the front door. Wound up and shaking, I heard the raucous caws of crows circling the telephone wires above the houses. And then I saw Toby. He stood ramrod straight in his driveway, pointing a pellet gun up at the gray sky, aiming at the crows on the wire.

I rushed over to him just as he was about to fire again. Six large black crows hopped on and off the telephone wire, and several others circled in alarm. The crows screeched, their cries echoing down the street, while the ones on the wire pecked aggressively at their neighbors. The day had turned overcast, with heavy dark clouds carried in by the wind from the harbor.

He saw me at the last moment and hesitated. I grabbed the gun barrel and pushed it to the ground. With one quick, firm movement, I yanked it from his grasp. "What the heck are you doing, Toby?!"

"Nothing."

Toby was big on one-word answers, a favorite being "whatever." He was wearing his black sweatshirt with the big red *A* in a circle on the back—the symbol for anarchy—with safety pins littered across the chest. The latest punk rock rebellion wear. I doubted he even knew what anarchy really meant. He pulled the hoodie down, and a tangle of red hair spilled out onto the top of his chest. He moved to the curb and sat, head down, rubbing his right thumb and index finger together, a nervous habit I had seen him do many times before.

I caught my breath and calmed down a little. "Geez, Toby! You shouldn't shoot a gun in front of your house! Where'd you get it from?"

"I don't know, a friend from school loaned it to me," he muttered and looked away. He sat down on the curb, and when I joined him, he scooted away nervously.

I needed to settle him down. "Looks like a twenty-two-caliber pellet air rifle. I used to have one of those when I was a kid."

He looked up at me. "Really?"

"Really. My dad used to take me into the woods, and we'd set up targets, and I learned how to aim and shoot. I got pretty good at it."

Toby fidgeted, but didn't say anything.

"Would you like me to teach you how to aim and shoot too?"

He studied me, gauging whether I was serious or not. "I don't know."

"I can teach you how to use this—that is, if your grandparents are okay with it."

At the mention of his grandparents, he flashed a look of fear and then immediate resignation. He knew it was over; he wasn't getting the gun back any time soon.

"Let's go ask them, huh?"

Toby squirmed. "Ah, I don't think they'll let me. They, ah, they don't know I have it."

"Well, they should know, and if they also know that I'll teach you how to use it safely, then maybe they'll let you keep it. What do you say?"

"I don't know…"

"Well, let's go and ask." I rose and waited for him to stand. Reluctantly, he got up and followed me to his grandparents' front door, his head down like he was going to the principal's office.

I knocked on the door and waited. I liked Tom and Laura, his grandparents. They had stepped up when Patty disappeared after having Toby. Patty and I had dated in high school for a while, until she got deep into drugs and other boys. She got pregnant at sixteen, and she'd had Toby when she turned seventeen. No one knew who Toby's dad was. After he was born, it was obvious that Patty wasn't getting clean, and she took off for the city. When she left, Tom and Laura didn't hesitate; they took Toby in and raised him like he was their own kid. I hadn't seen Patty in over a year, and I didn't think he had either.

Toby had always had a wild streak, and he'd had his share of trouble: breaking some school windows during the summer, and a couple of suspected home break-ins, never proven, as well as a serious runaway attempt a couple of years ago, when he was just eleven. I'd had to fetch him after he snuck onto a bus to downtown Seattle, and when the police caught up with him, he said he was trying to find his mom. He was a good kid, and I'd always had a soft spot for him, but his grandparents were clearly overwhelmed at this point.

We both heard footsteps, and as Tom opened the door, I saw Laura standing behind his left shoulder. Tom, a retired engineer, was in good shape for a sixty-six-year-old, and when he saw us, his mouth fell open as he stared at the gun in my hands. He put his hands on his hips. "What's this?"

"I found Toby with it in the driveway. Thought I should let you know, and—"

Before I could finish my sentence, Laura rushed forward, grabbed Toby by the elbow, and dragged him into the house. "Toby, what were you thinking?!"

Toby mumbled, "I didn't hurt anybody."

Tom frowned. "Didn't hurt anybody *yet*, you mean. Toby, all guns are dangerous. You know better than that. Who gave it to you?" he demanded.

"Just someone."

"Well, 'someone's' parents are going to hear about this!"

That was all he needed to hear. He shook loose from Laura and darted down the hallway and into the kitchen at the back of the house.

Tom and Laura stared at me, and Tom finally said, "I just don't know sometimes. Glad you found him before he shot something—or someone, or even himself."

"I'm glad, too, but you know how kids like guns. They're gonna do all kinds of things if you're not constantly on them. I'll keep this safe at my house until you find out who it belongs to. Let me know when you do, okay?"

"Yes, we will," Tom said.

Laura added, "How are the kids? And Emily?"

"They're fine. Left for the island yesterday." It was odd, but I realized I hadn't thought about them today until that moment.

Tom told me he'd be in touch.

When I got home, I peeked into the den and found the mailbox still dim. Sadie looked up and gently swished her tail on the floor. This calmed me a bit. In my workshop, I unlocked one of the bottom drawers filled with cans of paint and cleansers, slid the gun in, and locked it away.

I spent the rest of the evening hovering around the den, adjusting the logs on the fire, wrestling with the events of the day. I thought of checking in with Em, but she had left a message earlier saying they had arrived safely and that the kids were busy settling in. So, I turned in, my head still swimming with questions. When I finally fell asleep, the colors began again, washing through my dreams like waves lapping on the shore.

Chapter Six

―

Saturday, June 11, 1988

I awoke alert yet uncertain, the turbulent dreams I'd had spilling into the morning. Soft light streamed into the bedroom, and everything descended on me at once—the nest, the birth, the little being in the mailbox.

I rushed into the den, and the mailbox was still there, softly glowing, with Sadie and Oreo sitting on either side of it.

So, this *was* real. But what was "this"?

I held my breath and removed the roof. There, in the middle of the scarf, next to the sparkling pieces of the nest, sat our little guest. Her face flushed a light pink when she looked up at me, and I blushed, wondering if she wanted some privacy. She sensed this and immediately shook her head and shifted to the side, showing me her back.

The bumps from before had transformed into a stunningly beautiful pair of wings! They were shaped like butterfly wings, nearly three inches long, but translucent like those of a dragonfly, and their vibrant colors glinted as she lazily opened and closed them. All at once, they snapped and buzzed, moving so fast that they merged into a brilliant blur of color, undulating and vibrating at a terrific speed. Just as suddenly, they stopped, resuming their soft, easy fluttering. I stared at her, my mouth agape. She looked back up at me, quickly flapped her wings once more, and laughed at my reaction.

In that moment, I knew. She was a little angel.

As she read my thoughts, her expression changed, and she stopped giggling. But she kept smiling, her eyes half closed, like tiny half-moons. She crinkled her little brow, tilting her head, and as we sat gazing at each other, a warm flush of peace and a quiet feeling of knowing flowed into me.

Slowly, she stood up, spread her wings, and shot out of the mailbox, soaring around the den! She flew as silent as a shadow, leaving a glittering trail of vanishing colorful light. It startled me at first, but I relaxed when she returned and floated down to the table, standing and fluttering her wings in an easy rhythm. She put her left hand on her tiny waist and smiled playfully. She seemed quite proud of her new wings, and they seemed to complete her in a way, adding to a confidence that emanated from her look, her posture, and her mesmerizing eyes.

By this time, Sadie and Oreo were sitting attentively next to me, and she looked at the three of us, her golden necklace shining. Oreo meowed, and he and Sadie turned toward the kitchen. My stomach growled, and I followed them in for a much-needed breakfast. I fed them, then poured myself some cereal, and as I ate, the questions stabbed at me again. Who? What? Why?

As if she'd heard me, the angel soared into the kitchen and landed on the dining room table. She looked up at me, and my mind calmed.

"I know you have many questions, and you should." She

spoke directly into me. "But everything will become clear as we work through the lessons together."

"Lessons? But who are you, and what are you doing here?"

"The music of your dream sang to me, Ben. I have come to help you answer its call by revealing to you the truth of being and the laws of creation."

"Laws of creation?" The question clouded my mind, and the angel gently pushed it aside.

"There is much I have to teach you, and much for you to accept, and it will take time. Above all things, Ben, be patient with yourself, and I will walk each step of this journey with you."

She led me back into the den and floated onto the couch, and her tiny hand patted the cushion. I settled in next to her, and she directed me to close my eyes and deepen my breathing.

"We are going to do all our work in the depths of your consciousness, in the secret reaches where all thought originates and the forces of manifestation begin..."

Blue. A soft, watercolor sky blue enveloped me. I immediately thought of the colors in my dreams, the undulating waves, like the silent movement of the sea. I was lulled into a deep relaxation, but I was aware and open to receive.

She said, "Today, we will start with the first lesson, the foundational truth upon which everything in the universe is based, from which all else springs. And it is this:

"We are all individualized points of consciousness of the one Source, and our purpose is to express its vision for us in this world. And that vision is the dream you hold most dear in your heart."

She waited.

The light blue in my mind shifted to a darker blue, and she continued, "The Source is yearning for expression, always trying to manifest itself at the point of being, which is ourselves. The way we know its particular vision for us is by acknowledging and accepting our deepest dream."

Images of my mailboxes flooded my mind. Miniature carved doors with tiny doorknobs, windows with matching shutters, covered porches with little swings... In my mind, I caressed the surface of smooth ash wood and cut and shaped it to resemble individual bricks of a chimney, while my dad finished them off with paint and sweet-smelling lacquer. I saw my workshop filled with completed mailboxes of all shapes and designs and colors, lined up neatly along one wall, like a new housing development springing up in my shop. I filled with the joy and pride of accomplishment. Yes, the dream of making mailboxes with my dad was still alive, vivid, and clear to me.

"Yes, Ben, that dream. That is why I have come: to help you manifest this vision that burns within you, and to help you release the energy of the Source that has given you such clear direction. And once you follow it and learn how to make your dream come true, then you will transform not only your life, but the lives of countless others as well."

Suddenly, threatening gray clouds darkened my mind, smothering out the blue. The angel frowned. She sensed my doubt, my lingering questions, my disbelief and even fear, and she felt my frustration from years of wanting and trying to make my dream work. The onrushing storm of my thoughts swirled and crashed like lightning. Then the angel rose up in my mind, and her light dispersed the clouds. The blue sky returned.

"All in time, Ben. I will teach you the universal laws of creation, and you will come to see that as part of the great Source, you share its essential qualities, the most important one being the ability to create. As a conscious being, you hold that power, and I'm here to show you how to use and direct it to create the things, the life, that you are here to manifest."

My mind kept coming back to that word: the Source. "But what is the Source?"

The angel raised her eyebrows. "Why, the Source is everything, of course. It is the ocean and origin of all life, the field of consciousness and intent from which all living things flow. You are like a drop of that ocean, an individualized expression of its great whole. And inside, you have the same qualities and abilities as the Source itself—you, me, and everyone you see." She paused to let me take that in.

"All from the same Source? What does that mean?" The colors in my mind shifted toward blue again, and lavender appeared at the edges.

"All beings are just different expressions of the one Source. All the life on this planet, and on all the other planets, is an individualized expression of the one Source."

Overload now. The colors in my head swirled and shifted to darker shades—grays to charcoal, lavenders to purple, blues to navy.

The angel saw this. "This is a lot to take in, and you are at the start of your journey. When you are ready, more will be revealed, and you will learn how you are constantly interacting with and directing the Source. Once you make that connection, things will begin to change for you."

"Directing the Source?"

"Not today, Ben. Your colors are too heavy, and I am not yet at full strength. Take some time and consider all I've shared today, and just be open to the Source and try to feel its presence.

We will pause here now, so you can begin to take in this lesson, and I need time to rest and continue my development."

Slowly, our connection faded, like a television picture disappearing from the screen. The colors in my mind retreated, and the awareness of the den returned. Daylight filtered in through the windows, and the sounds of a car outside and kids playing in the street crowded back in. Sadie and Oreo were back on their pillows, and both gazed over at me dreamily.

I instinctively put my hand out, and the angel climbed onto my palm, light as a sparrow. I set her down in the middle of the scarf. She looked up at me with shining little eyes and said, "It's all going to be all right. Everything will become clearer as we move along together." Then she sat and folded her wings, and I replaced the roof. The light inside the mailbox faded, turning a soft, warm amber.

A familiar whistling outside the front door brought me back to the world, and I realized that Alan was here to deliver the mail. Alan was always whistling that same tune—I knew it, but could never remember what it was—and sometimes you could hear him coming from halfway down the block. I swung the front door open and caught him rummaging through his bag for our mail.

Startled, he recovered quickly. "Well, hiya, Ben! How's your side of the world?"

Talk about a loaded question. "Ah ... it's good. How are you doing?"

"Livin' the dream, man, livin' the dream," he said as always.

I hoped I'd look as good as Alan when I was in my forties; he was as fit and lean as I was. Nothing seemed to faze this guy. He wore his standard-issue shorts, blue wool with a navy stripe down the sides, even in the rain and cold. He was the most positive person I'd ever met, always in a good mood. I wished I knew his secret.

"How's your Saturday going?" he asked me with a grin.

I peered across the street. "A little drama with Toby. Caught him shooting a pellet gun in his driveway yesterday."

"No kidding! Heck, what did you do?"

"I took it away from him and told Tom to keep an eye on him."

"Geez. I'll have a word with him if I see him. He's a sweet kid, but he needs the right kind of attention, if you know what I mean."

"Do I ever."

Alan handed me the mail, resumed whistling, and crossed my driveway to the sidewalk.

I spent the rest of the late afternoon in the backyard, enjoying the warm spring air, listening to the buzz of insects mix with the whistling of the wind rustling the leaves in the forest. What the heck was the Source? I couldn't keep my attention on it, and soon my thoughts drifted back to the farmers' market and the progress I was supposed to be making on the samples and the booth. I still had time, but I needed to regain my focus.

As if to snap me back to reality, Em called after dinner.

"Just calling to check in," she began. "How's the job search going?"

Job search? That was the last thing on my mind. Still preoccupied by the angel's lesson, I answered vaguely, which didn't make her too happy. Then she put Dylan on, and he prattled on about his day. Next Sammy came on and asked about Sadie.

"She's doing about the same," I told her.

"Tell her I love her, and that I miss her!"

Em got back on the phone, and sensing that I had no news for her, she said a quick good night.

When the sky darkened and the first stars appeared, I was reminded of the angel's nest again, and thoughts of the Source returned. Where did the Source come from? How many other lives was it weaving through? The distant stars twinkled, and I wondered what its vision for the universe might be. Did it really include my dream, too?

Chapter Seven

―

Sunday morning, June 12, 1988

A small polished stone was on my pillow when I awoke the next morning. Light salmon in color, its depths held a marbled mix of earth-toned rose and faint orange, engraved with the words *Your Dreams Are Inspired by the Source* glowing a golden shade of amber and pulsing with light. The entire stone shimmered as if river water poured over it, but to my touch, it was warm and comforting. What in the world? Where did…?

The angel. Our first lesson, of course. And today, there would be even more.

Sadie and Oreo weren't in the den when I got there, and the roof of the mailbox was askew, tilted at an awkward angle. I rushed over to it, and the angel was gone!

Frantically, I scanned the den, but she was nowhere in sight. As I leapt up, a sparkle of light shot into the room, and in an instant, the angel was perched on my shoulder. She touched my earlobe. "Oh, Ben, I didn't mean for you to be afraid! You don't ever have to worry about me; always know that. I felt my energy return this morning, so I got up to stretch my wings."

"But the roof…?"

"The roof isn't heavy. Besides, I can do a lot more than you can imagine." She was delicate, but confident at the same time, and I relaxed.

Sadie ambled into the den and struggled onto her pillow. The angel studied her movements, and I held Sadie's legs steady, reaching under her rib cage to gently help her down. I looked back at the angel, who furrowed her brow and pursed her lips. Then Oreo appeared at my feet and bumped up against me, purring. He wanted breakfast. I glanced back at the angel; what in the world might she eat? She flew onto my shoulder, and I carried her into the kitchen. She sat on the counter, her wings slowly beating, while I heated milk and made oatmeal. Then she buzzed onto the dining table as I searched the pantry for some pistachios from the farmers' market, broke one open, and poured a couple of drops of milk into it. She carefully cupped it in her little hands and gingerly sipped the warm milk. Her glow increased, and she wiggled her nose in satisfaction. I brought my oatmeal over, and we sat like that for a while, eating breakfast together, just me and an angel.

Afterwards, she directed me into the living room, and I sat facing the TV while she landed on the back of the couch just above my right shoulder. Our reflection glinted off the TV screen, her wings sparkling in the morning sunlight shining through the windows. My mind clouded over with a soft lilac, and she appeared in the center of my thoughts, as if she were a part of my consciousness. We were together now in a sort of garden in my mind—a garden surrounded by color, in which we sat side by side. My questioning and disbelief were gone, replaced by the peace of her presence. Next to her was the stone I had found on my pillow.

She said, "After each lesson, I will give you a stone to remind you of the essence of the teaching. In the beginning, your mind will drift back to the illusion of separation from the Source, so keep these stones close by and concentrate on the truth they hold."

"I was wondering what that stone was for. How many lessons are there?"

"Six, but you won't be able to take them all in at once. You will need time to work with them, to accept and apply their wisdom. The first lesson is the foundation for all that comes after it, and it is a lesson that you will reflect back upon throughout our time together. From that great foundation will come the revelations showing you how to work with the Source, how to direct its power to manifest your dreams. Today, if you feel ready, I can reveal the second lesson."

She paused and observed the colors in my consciousness. They were a mixture of soft lilac and blue hues. I felt ready, relaxed, and quiet, hungry for more.

She then took a deep breath, and the colors above moved toward us. As she exhaled, they expanded, and I heard, "The second lesson is this:

"*As part of the one Source, we share its essential quality: the power to create. And the way we create is through directing our thoughts. Thoughts are things. As within, so without.*"

She let this sit in the colors of my garden, and she sensed my questions bubbling up, so she explained, "The Source constantly flows into our lives, needing to express itself, and we direct it through the power and focus of our thoughts, through the constant things we consistently dwell on over and over again. Thoughts are things; this is the universal truth. The manifestations of our lives start with the seeds we plant in the garden of our mind, which we then consistently water and nourish with our feelings and beliefs. These beliefs are the springboard for the actions we take that shape our destiny. Once you understand and accept this, you will see this universal truth in action: you cannot think one thing and produce another."

She paused and monitored the color of my thoughts. Gray appeared now.

The angel peered into my eyes. "What did you tell Sammy about getting pumpkins?"

I thought of our vegetable garden and imagined the green sprouts popping through the cracked soil. How did she know about that?

"I know a lot more than you think. When Sammy asked about getting big pumpkins, what did you tell her?"

I thought back to that Sunday afternoon, planting seeds in our garden. "Oh, yeah! She wanted to get big pumpkins, but I told her we weren't planting pumpkin seeds, and she would only get the kinds of vegetables she was planting: carrots, tomatoes, and beets."

The angel fluttered her glistening wings, and color tumbled from them like pixie dust, shimmering and evaporating in the light of my garden. "The thoughts you plant in the garden of your mind are watered and nourished by your feelings and beliefs. They will always bring you the fruit of those seeds, whether they are what you want or not. Whichever you have the most belief in."

I said the first thing that came to me. "But what about Em and the kids going on vacation without me? I didn't want that to happen."

"No, you didn't. But how many of your thoughts were colored with the dread that it *might* happen? How much energy and belief did you give to that possibility?"

She saw my colors darkening, billowing and blowing in like a storm.

"Ben, once you fully examine all the things you constantly dwell on, you'll see that they match all the situations in your life. The illusion is that people think they dwell on the things that bother them *because* they are in their lives, but what if it were the other way around? What if those circumstances appear and persist in their lives because they dwell on them and give them so much energy?"

That seemed way too simple, and my mind argued with it. "But what about car crashes? Cancer? All the bad things that people *aren't* thinking about, aren't expecting? Does that mean I'm to blame for all the bad things in my life as well?"

She frowned and thought deeply before answering. "It isn't a matter of blame, Ben. It's a matter of understanding the truth and living in alignment with it. Yes, things happen that are outside our control. What you *do* have control of, however, are the thoughts you choose to dwell on after each unplanned event. What you choose to do next, and what you choose to believe is possible afterwards always determines the actions you then take. And your consistent actions, as we'll see, always determine the course your life eventually takes.

"Ultimately, Ben, all things, all circumstances are temporary, always changing, and they have the potential to become what you choose to make them. Once you embrace this, you'll realize you have the power to change any situation, as long as you carefully choose what you focus on, and then act in accordance with what you dream for your life to be."

I considered all she said, and for a moment, the burden of blame I had assigned myself lightened. As it did, the color in my mind changed towards golden yellows and blues.

She monitored my swirling colors and continued, "Everyone is creating all the time. Look around you. The airplanes that fly overhead, each piece of their engines, the fabric and design of their seats, and all the houses and buildings you see, down to the very nails holding them all together—everything you see first started as a thought in someone's mind. Were there setbacks? Accidental occurrences? Deaths and tragedies, even? Yes. Yet through persistence in believing in what was still possible, and the action that followed, that belief, that dream was manifested into the world."

My head was spinning now, but as I took in what she said, its truth resonated within me. I thought about all the things around me, and then about all the inventors and minds that had conjured up the world we lived in.

"Each mailbox you make begins as a thought and an intention in your mind, doesn't it?" she asked.

"I guess. I mean, each mailbox starts with the pictures I take and the plans I make."

But it all started as a thought, it was true. The angel watched my mind shift to a deeper blue, and as I envisioned each item in my workshop, I glimpsed that the angel was with me, looking over my shoulder. Each tool, all the planed wood, and all the pieces that made up each mailbox held a story—a story of their origin and the thoughts and actions that created them. Suddenly, I glimpsed that the world was alive with energy and specific intent. Everything started with the kernel of intention and belief, with a thought, and then it became a reality once someone acted on that belief.

She breathed in my colors once more. "That's it. You're now looking at the world as the field of energy it truly is."

We spent another hour lost in the sights, smells, and surfaces of my workshop. After a while, the vision faded, and the angel disappeared from my mind. I was back in the living room, staring at the beaming white being next to me. Her wings drooped a bit; she was tired. I carried her back into the den and set her down in the soft folds of the paisley scarf. She gazed up at me, smothered a tiny yawn, and curled up for a nap.

I spent the rest of the afternoon looking at the world with new eyes. As I fetched the Sunday paper, I took in the details of each house on the block and imagined the ideas and thoughts that had given birth to the various designs, the textures and materials used, and the hundreds of items inside each one. A truck droned by, and the whirling combustion engine filled me with new wonderment. Somewhere in the distance, a leaf blower buzzed along a driveway, and I thought about the gasoline that powered it, the wells that drilled for the oil, and the refinery that transformed it into useable form. I thought of all the problems, setbacks, and naysayers who'd said it couldn't be done, yet I marveled at all the minds that believed and dreamed of what was possible. The sun appeared from behind a cloud, and the light glinted off the millions of leaves on the trees. I wondered about the Source and its unlimited power and ability to manifest.

"Thoughts are things," the angel had said. What about the thoughts I dwelled on all day long? I flashed on the years of frustration I had suffered through. It occurred to me that I had never really believed Ryan would promote my mailboxes, and sure enough, he didn't. And Em and the kids going on vacation without me? I had known I'd lose that fight, and I did. What about

the farmers' market, though? Would that work? I shivered. It could be just another struggle, couldn't it? A money pit that would drain our savings, just as Em predicted.

But what if I changed my thoughts about it? Could it possibly work then? No, that was way too simple... But the angel, the colors, the wisdom in those sparkling eyes—could they be wrong? How *did* it all work? How could I make it work in my life? I was itching to ask these and other questions and couldn't wait to spend time with her again.

The angel awoke a little before four o'clock. Warm afternoon light lit the den, and when I lifted the roof from the mailbox, I found her sitting serenely. As she flapped her wings, I noticed they had filled out and the translucence was gone; they were now a deep yellow blending into shimmering blue, accented with black borders and veins like a butterfly's wings, with amber spots along the edges. Her face shone with a light from within, and her peach color had warmed to a light honey. She flew onto my shoulder, and I inhaled the faint fragrance of spring peonies, delicate and slightly sweet. She gave my left earlobe a little tug, and I carried her out the kitchen door and onto the back patio.

Sadie and Oreo were already enjoying the day, with Oreo walking along the top of the side fence, and Sadie sauntering unsteadily into the woods at the back of the yard, barking in the distance. I squinted as the angled sunlight sliced through the trees. Overhead, birds soared and sang, and dogs in other yards joined Sadie in barking, their chorus charging the air. The sudden amount of energy and action in our surroundings made me feel protective of the angel, and sensing this, she gave my ear a tight squeeze.

"I'll be fine, really. Don't worry about a thing."

Whizz! came the high whine of her wings, like a mosquito close to your ear, and she surprised me when she shot away and raced into the forest. I tried to trace her colorful trail of light, but it dissolved quickly in the sunlight. Then I caught her dazzling reflection at the very top of one of the lodge pole pines. Seeing her perched up there made me think of a Christmas tree topped with a little angel.

"Can you see me?"

I nodded and waved at her. "You're so fast!"

"Actually, I'm slowing down for you. Keep your eyes on me."

Snap! She landed back on my shoulder, and I jerked my head in surprise. "I can't keep up with you!"

"You'll get used to it. Relax a bit while I try my new wings." She burst into a blur of color and shot off once again.

I followed her the best I could, searching for faint trails of glitter in hopes of seeing her direction, but she was just a blur. I saw two hummingbirds twisting and dancing around my neighbor's apple trees, and all at once, the angel darted over and buzzed around them. The speed of the angel made it seem like the hummingbirds were moving in slow motion. As they became aware of her, they immediately came to rest on a branch near the top of the tree, and the angel settled in between them. Both hummingbirds turned their needlelike beaks toward her, and then all three of them leapt off the branch and raced into the sky, banking left and right in a tight, perfect formation. They flew like this for several minutes, and I smiled at the show. Then the angel broke off, and the hummingbirds soared away over my roof.

Suddenly, the angel returned. "They want to know why you don't put red nectar in the feeder anymore."

I looked over at the empty hummingbird feeder we'd bought last year. "I haven't gotten around to it, I guess," I answered. "Do you mean to tell me you can—"

"Hummingbirds have thoughts, too, you know." She winked, and then she was gone.

She spent the next hour zooming around the yard and through the forest, playing and "talking" with all the insects, birds, and animals she met. I found the red syrup, mixed it, and filled the hummingbird feeder, then sat and watched for her. Occasionally, she returned and reported things like, "Have you seen the new family of red foxes? Three baby girl kits and one boy, nested just a hundred yards into the forest."

Overhead, a sudden raucous cawing and flapping pierced the air, and a swarm of shiny black crows bounced on the branches of the trees behind my neighbor's yard. Squawking, fluttering, and jumping restlessly from limb to limb, they were as agitated as I had seen them in front of Toby's house the other day. The angel raced over to them and sat in the middle of their group, and they instantly grew silent. For fifteen minutes, they sat looking at her and then at one another. Her white glow contrasted sharply against their deep black feathers, and her radiance seemed to infect them with the serenity I'd felt, because soon they were not only silent, but still as well. A breeze ruffled the broad leaves, and then she left them and was back on my shoulder.

Casting her little eyebrows down, she said, "The flock of crows that arrived a week ago—the ones you saw jumping on the telephone wires and cawing all afternoon—are still here because they're in mourning. Toby shot one of their elders. Did you know that?"

I blushed. "You know about Toby, too?"

She frowned. "Of course, I do—and so do they. They're terrified of him and can't understand why he would do something like that."

"He's just bored, I guess, looking for trouble. He hasn't had an easy life," I tried to explain.

"You're closer to the truth than you know," she said. "Toby is just as much a point of expression of the Source as you are. But without direction, the energy of the Source is scattered, feeding fear, giving expression to consequences we don't want. Toby's fear and unhappiness lead to thoughts of anger, rejection, and frustration. These must and will always be expressed without."

She paused and looked up at me. "Just like I'm helping you, you must do all you can to help Toby find his way."

"But how?"

"By applying these lessons and pursuing your dream."

Blue in my mind's eye again. I thought about the lesson, and something deep within me resonated with the idea of my mind being like a garden. I could imagine my thoughts digging deep, taking root, and then sprouting into my life.

She read these thoughts and said, "That's the beginning, Ben. It's happening."

"What *is* happening?" I asked.

"Something wonderful."

It was after seven, the early evening still warm, and the angel had been flying for several hours. Now she slumped on my shoulder, the tips of her wings droopy and the glow of her necklace faded. She touched my earlobe, and she seemed warmer than before. From the corner of my eye, I could see that her light had dimmed.

"Are you okay?" I asked.

She wiggled my ear tenderly. "I may have overdone it a bit, but there's so much to do and see! I'll be fine after a good night's rest."

I carried the sleepy angel into the den and lowered her into the mailbox. She looked up dreamily and whispered, "You're taking a lot in, but you're doing well. Just be patient." Once again, she had read the questions, the doubts, and even the hope swimming in my mind. I gently set the roof at an angle, allowing space for her to get out if she needed to. Sadie and Oreo settled in on either side of the fireplace, and I lit a small fire and went into the kitchen.

The red light on the answering machine blinked twice: two messages. I hit the button, and Em's messaged played first. Just checking in, she said, wondering where I was and how my day had gone. She didn't ask me to call back. The second message was from my mom.

"Oh, hi, honey, are you around? If you hear this, can you please pick up?" An anxious pause. "Well, something's come up, and... Um, we need to talk. Later tonight won't be good, but could you call me in the morning? I need to talk to you about something. Okay, dear, ah... Yes, please call me tomorrow." *Click.*

That was odd. She sounded worried—scared, even. I called her right back, but it went straight to their answering machine.

Chapter Eight

Monday, June 13, 1988

I woke to the pitter-patter of rain on the window and thick gray clouds hiding the sun. A second polished stone, a light brownish-yellow with tints of pink and white, lay on the pillow next to me. Words in script, *Thoughts Are Things*, glowed in soft amber. This must be the second stone! Thoughts of the previous two days filled me with warmth and colors. How strange to be thinking in colors!

In the den, the angel sat on the floor next to Sadie. Her head was nestled between her paws, her eyes closed, and she didn't move when I came in. The angel held Sadie's left ear in both her tiny hands, her glow pulsing softly. She creased her little forehead and motioned for me to sit on the couch. Oreo, sitting on his pillow like a sphinx, gazed over at them, as if in a trance.

After a while, the angel let go, her glow fading, and Sadie opened her eyes. Seeing me, she thumped her tail on the floor, and with difficulty, she pushed herself up and struggled over to me. The angel remained on the floor and said, "I've been up with her for several hours now. She's weak, but she's no longer afraid. She really loves you, but she's confused, and she asked me where her family has gone. It's best that you give her some extra attention for a while. She needs to feel your love now more than ever," she said.

"Is she going to die?" I asked.

"She's going to transition soon and become free."

"Transition? Free? I don't—"

"She won't die. Nobody will, in the sense that you understand it. Right now, she's struggling to hold onto the life she's known and loved for many years—a life that has centered around you and your family."

I instantly thought of Em and the kids. I wished more than anything that they were here to be with Sadie, and I almost called them. But that would ruin their summer, and maybe she would hang on until they returned? I'd monitor her and decide in the coming weeks, if it came to that. As I thought this, Sadie rested her paw on my foot, placed her head on it, and looked up at me. I teared up and looked over to the angel.

"She knows she's loved, and I will comfort her and work with her to help her make sense of what's happening."

I bent down and stroked her head, and she soon closed her eyes as her belly rose and fell. I leaned back on the couch and exhaled. *Oh, Sadie!* Colors rushed in that I didn't have words for, and shades of charcoal returned.

"We have much to cover in the rest of the lessons, and so much will become clearer to you. You'll see," she said. "But first, I need some time today. I didn't get the rest I needed, and between the garden—which I enjoyed so much—and last night with Sadie, I need to gather and restore my energy. Would it be all right if I ate a little something and then rested this morning?"

A few drops of oatmeal in a pistachio shell, and her color returned. I carried her back to the mailbox. She snuggled down in the scarf and closed her eyes. The rain outside had softened to a drizzle, turning the early morning misty and cooler. I lit another fire and decided I'd take this time to work on samples and the booth for the farmers' market.

I had the table saw running, and only after its whining blade died down did I hear the banging on my front door. I hurried out of my shop and shot a glance into the den on my way to answer it. The fire had died down a bit, and the small lamp cast a soft glow over the still-quiet mailbox.

I jerked open the door and was surprised to see my dad, moist from the drizzle, looking impatient and worried. Then I remembered my mom's call. What was wrong? I stood inadvertently blocking the door, and he tapped impatiently on the doorframe, so I stepped aside, and he plunged past me. Thinking fast, I guided him into the kitchen and raised my eyebrows.

"What are you doing here? Aren't you supposed to be at work?"

"So, your mother didn't tell you yet, huh?" he said as he took a seat at the dining table. He glanced at the kitchen counter and added, "You got any coffee going?"

"Tell me what?" I asked.

He just glared at the kitchen counter, so I boiled water for some instant coffee.

"Yeah, well, it happened. Friday, the mill announced that they didn't get the Big Box contract like they thought they would, so they cut twenty-five workers. They called me in, and Chuck gave me an envelope with a check for two weeks' pay, then told me to clear out my locker and go home," he said, shaking slightly.

Fear stabbed at me. "They can't do that!"

"Not only can they do it, but they did. And that's not the worst of it. Because I'm not fully vested yet, with them cutting me now, my pension will be a lot less than I can live on." He was shaking even more now, his forehead red and his eyes wide. He absently patted his shirt pocket for his smokes, brought them halfway out, then pushed them back down again.

The pot whistled, and I brought the coffee over. "They can't do that to you," I said, though I lacked conviction. "I mean, can't you talk to a lawyer or something?"

"They know exactly what they're doing. Almost all the people they let go today are in the same boat I'm in—close to being fully vested, but not quite there yet. They screwed over a lot of people today. You can never win with these guys, I'm telling you. I knew something would go wrong." He exhaled deeply, and all the energy, all the life seemed to drain out of him. He slumped slightly, clutching his coffee cup.

"So, what ... what are you going to do now?"

"What am I gonna do? What *is* there to do? I've got a check for a couple of weeks, enough savings for a few months, and then I need to get a job. *That's* what I gotta do: find another job, pronto. And twenty-four other people are going to be looking for a job, too," he said.

Twenty-five, I thought grimly, adding myself to that list. I glanced over to the classifieds on the corner of the counter. Suddenly, I was afraid.

"Mom called last night, left me a message. She sounded worried... Now I know why. How's she doing?"

"Not good. She's in shock, I think. We both are. We've been counting on my pension for years, for everything. We don't have the savings to make up what they just took away. Hell, I'm fifty-seven years old! All I know is working at the mill. I might find some part-time construction work, but the money isn't gonna be like what I was making at the mill, and I'm not gonna get the kind of benefits or pension I had before. I don't know what I'll do." He slurped his coffee and looked down at the table, then back up at me.

I was dumbfounded. I couldn't believe my dad was sitting at my kitchen table in the middle of the week, telling me he was unemployed. I just couldn't wrap my head around it.

He raised his eyebrows and cocked his head. "Listen, things are about to get very tight for us. Every penny counts. I hate to do this to you, but I need the seven thousand back that I loaned you. I just can't spare it right now." He dropped his head and gulped his coffee.

My forehead tingled. "But ... I've already ordered, I mean, I've already spent most of it." Where was I going to get *that* money from?

"You told me you have savings, so you can use that. I'm real sorry to do this to you, Ben, but it's like I always say: if anything can go wrong, it will. And it did. So, if you can give me a check now, I'd really appreciate it." He paused, looked up at me expectantly, and added, "It'll make your mother feel a lot better."

"But what about the booth and the remodel?" I said, panicking. "I've spent a ton of money already on lumber and new tools. I mean, this is how I'm going to make money now; I'm not working either." Fear shaded into me as I saw my one chance disappearing.

He shifted uncomfortably and looked around the kitchen. "I know, Ben, and again, I'm sorry. But what choice do I have? Your mother is sick with worry, and we need all the money we have right now."

Then he turned back to me and said, "You can get the money elsewhere. I mean, what about Mitch? He's loaded. Hell, ten or fifteen grand is nothing to him. Have you thought about asking him for a loan?"

"Mitch?" My voice faltered. Em would kill me if I asked him! He had the money, sure, but I couldn't ask him without getting permission from her first. Besides, borrowing from Mitch was a long shot at best.

He continued, "Yeah, of course. Why wouldn't he want to help you and Em out? Again, he has the dough. I'd think about it if I were you. It's either that, or use your own savings. You have enough, don't you?"

"There's no way Em would let me use our savings. I already asked. That's why I came to you."

"Well, it's something you should think about. But I'd ask Mitch, if I were you—or get Em to ask him," he added.

This was going from bad to worse. I cringed, and he softened. "Anyway, what you do is up to you. But right now, I've got to get to my bank and deposit this two weeks' pay and the seven grand. That will give me some breathing room, and then I've got to start looking for work. Would you mind writing me that check, so I can get going?"

And that was it. In a daze, I wrote a check for seven thousand dollars out of our savings. What the hell would Em say? Given that I wasn't working right now, well, that wasn't going to be pretty. Signing the check reminded me of signing for the down payment for the booth, and I vaguely wondered if that was refundable.

My dad took the check and drained his coffee. He shook his head as he walked to the front door, then shook my hand—an odd gesture that was awkward for us both—and headed off into the dull, gray drizzle. He lit a cigarette, smoke curling over his shoulder.

I flashed on that day after school, when he'd turned his back on me, and our dream had ended. Shades of frustration returned, and old resentment colored my thoughts. I clenched my hands. Damn him! But I wasn't a little boy anymore, and this wasn't going to stop me. I'd find a way, with the angel's help.

I sneaked a look in the den, but her little house was quiet and dim. I slumped back at the kitchen table and brooded. My palms sweated, and my heart thumped. What was I going to do now? I glanced over at the pile of newspapers and filled with dread, remembering Em asking me how the job search was going. I had wanted to tell her that the farmers' market *was* my new job—hell, much more than that: it was my business now.

My mind was scrambling. What about the booth deposit, and the first and last months' rent? Was I on the hook for that? I dreaded the conversation with Bud and chided myself for not getting clear on it in advance. And what about all the equipment, lumber, and supplies for the samples I'd already spent money on? I couldn't take those back. I could just hear Em telling me to forget that now and get a real paying job.

No, I couldn't give up on the booth, my only shot at finally making my dream come true. And wasn't that what the Source wanted me to do? I was in a time crunch, though. Bud needed the first and last months' rent in just fourteen days, and then a week later, my booth would open. I now had less than two weeks to find the money somewhere, complete the samples, make the booth, make progress on the remodel, *and* find a job.

Me getting a job—or even a decent lead on a job—would calm Em down, and maybe if I did get work, she'd let me use our savings. And my dad was right: asking Mitch for the money did make some sense. He definitely had it, and why wouldn't he want to help out Em and me?

I collected the stack of newspapers and went through them with renewed vigor. One thing stood out: the Big Box store's ads dominated each paper. They were hiring for all departments and accepting applications. I hated the idea of working there, just another guy in an orange apron shuffling up and down the massive aisles like a zombie, but I figured I needed to at least apply. Nothing would probably come of it, but at least I could tell Em I was trying. I hauled out our typewriter and addressed all the questions in the Big Box ad. I'd mail it the next time Alan came by.

The angel awoke around noon, and I couldn't wait to talk to her. I was in the backyard, and the day had turned glorious, the sun peeking through the woods, and bright yellow goldfinches chased each other around the yard. Save for the acrid smell spiking the air, it was a nearly perfect day—a stark contrast to the thoughts of worry I was nursing. I didn't realize it, but I had slipped into the garden of my consciousness again, and there I found the angel. She peered up at me, and colors seeped into my mind: blues and yellows, all enclosed by grays and blacks.

She said, "You're worried, I know. Today was an example of outside things coming into your life that you hadn't thought about. The question now becomes how you respond and what you choose to focus on next. The answer to that is contained in lesson three. Do you feel up to it?"

By way of an answer, I retreated from the outer colors and settled in the central blue that surrounded the angel. She reflected a warm white light against the cocoon of blue, her necklace pulsating with a golden glow. Together we were bathed in a wondrous garden of warmth and color, and I relaxed for the first time that day.

"You always have access to this peace, and it will welcome you in the most empowering way once you learn to dwell here rather than in the darkness of worry and fear." She looked up, and I followed her gaze to the dark clouds circling high above.

"Ben, the third lesson speaks to what blocks the flow of the Source, resulting in failure and frustration across all worlds. It is this fundamental law:

"The thought that blocks creative expression and keeps you from your dreams is fear. And fear is always the belief in the illusion of separateness from the Source."

She looked up at me and into my colors of awareness. The grays and blacks darted above and tried to penetrate the layer of yellow holding them at bay.

"You are not separate from the Source, Ben; you are its channel. But this channel gets blocked when you hold onto fear instead of acknowledging this fundamental truth."

I teetered on the edge of my colors as the gray tried to punch through the yellow to the blue. My fear grew. How could I stop it?

"Fear is caused by thinking we are separate from the Source, from one another, and from all life around us, and especially by the mistaken belief that we are separate from our thoughts and the results they create in our lives. Remember, Ben, thoughts are things."

I longed to believe her, knew intuitively that she spoke a deep truth, but I couldn't make the connection. I felt lost in wanting, needing to believe, but being unable—or maybe unwilling—to accept it.

She touched my hand. "There comes a point in everyone's life when a choice has to be made: the choice between living in the darkness of illusion, or in the light of truth. Those who choose illusion retreat and live in that darkness, and they pour out energy covering up their truth. This is a great cause of emotional sorrow and suffering."

A mix of conflicting feelings bubbled up inside me: confusion, resentment, desperation.

She saw my reaction and said, "But this illusion can be cast off at any time, and once it is, the temporary circumstances it has built up instantly begin to crumble. Always remember, Ben, your troubles have power because of the attention you give them, by choosing to believe in them. All the emotional energy you give to situations you do not want—your doubt, worry, fear, and anger, your sadness and resentment—they build up and maintain unwanted conditions in your life. Cease giving them power, and they begin to dissolve."

She paused again and examined my eyes and the colors hovering above. "Redirect the flow of the Source's energy by focusing solely on your dream, and concentrate on the joy that dream will bring you and others—and you will, sooner or later, bring this into being. As within, so without. It cannot be any other way."

She shook, and magically, the colorful, shimmering dust from her wings changed direction. Instead of falling down around us, it gently floated *up*, mixing with the blues and golds in my mind's garden. The colors became lighter, and my mind cleared.

She said, "Once you have more faith in your destiny and your dreams than you have in your fears and obstacles, that is when you own your power as the co-creator of your own life."

I wanted to believe, and the angel read the urgency in my eyes.

"But what about my dad needing the money back, or the lucky breaks Mitch has had, or the nursery business that Ryan got handed to him? There's just so much I have to overcome."

She gazed at me and furrowed her little brow. "Ben, this is the secret: what you believe in most—your potential, or your limitations—is what ultimately determines your results. Every time you look outside of yourself for the answer, you stray further from the only real cause and the only real solution: your power to direct the Source using your thoughts. Both of these things reside within you. What you feed with your beliefs and thoughts grows. Always ask yourself in any given moment: what are you feeding? Your vision and possibilities, or your fear and limitations?"

We sat in the garden of my mind for a while longer, and the angel remained quiet, her body emanating a soft light that illuminated her down feathers and made their colorful tips glisten. Her wings, quietly opening and closing, cast off bits of glitter as she sat amid her color and light. Slowly, as if awakening from a deep dream, I shook out of the color of our cocoon and looked down at her sitting on the patio table.

She smiled reassuringly and put her little hand on mine again, and her warmth coursed through me. Her whole figure blurred into a cascade of color and motion, and she shot off in a shimmering burst toward the trees. All at once, the sounds of life rushed back in: the barking of distant dogs, the buzzing of a nearby bumblebee, and a familiar whistling growing louder out front. It was Alan coming to deliver the mail.

Suddenly, the day's events returned, and I thought of the Big Box store application. I still didn't think I was a good fit for it, but ... what if? I rushed inside to get it.

Chapter Nine

Monday afternoon, June 13, 1988

When I opened the door, Alan had my mail wrapped in the latest woodworking magazine. "Oh, hey, Ben," he said as he handed it to me.

"Hiya, Alan. Thanks." I gave him the Big Box application. "By the way, did you ever catch up with Toby?"

"Oh, man, geez," he said, shaking his head. "He wasn't around when I looked for him. Come to think about it, I haven't seen him for several days now."

"That's odd. Usually he's out and about."

I glanced over his shoulder—and then I saw it. In front of Toby's house sat a beat-up, faded brown Toyota, missing a front hubcap. White streaks down the driver's side door suggested it had scraped the side of a pretty big concrete post. My heartbeat quickened. She was back.

At that moment, the front door opened, and Tom, Laura, Toby, and Patty spilled out onto their front steps, then stood awkwardly facing one another. Toby fidgeted nervously, then moved behind his grandmother, keeping as far away from his mom as he could. Tom noticed me first and nodded my way, and

Patty's eyes followed his gaze. Spotting me, she stood up taller, ran both hands through her long, light strawberry-blonde hair, and then nervously caressed the outsides of both thighs.

Alan took all this in and said, "His mom is back. Maybe that explains it." He adjusted his bag and whistled his way down my driveway to the next house.

I strolled across the street, and when I reached their bottom step, Patty came down, leering up at me with her bloodshot hazel eyes. She grinned and said, "Hey, Ben, I didn't know you were home today. How ya doing?" She inched next to me and stood so close that our elbows were touching. She wore an off-the-shoulder light pink sweater, her black bra straps a sharp contrast. I stared at them just a beat too long, then finally looked up at her face and gazed at the familiar freckles on her nose and high cheekbones. She arched her eyebrows, and her mischievous eyes bored into mine.

I turned and blushed. Sexy Patty... She was daring and edgy, and I couldn't get enough of her back in high school. Adventurous and progressive, she wanted to experience everything—including, eventually, heroin. She had become more and more wild, and I had to let her go—my first love, and the breakup of that relationship still hurt. A year later, she had gotten pregnant with Toby. She dropped out of school, lived with her parents for a while, and then left to pursue her life and her drugs, without Toby. She came around less and less, and by the looks of her car, things hadn't been easy on her.

"What's going on?" I focused on Tom, and Toby moved in between and slightly behind both Tom and Laura.

"Well, Patty showed up out of the blue, and we were all just visiting and talking," he said.

Toby, visibly agitated, blurted out, "I'm not going with her!"

We all turned, and he searched our faces and yelled, "I'm not! And you can't make me!" He spun around and stomped back into the house.

Patty looked nervously at her dad, then reached into her pocket and pulled out a crushed pack of Salems. She flicked a red Bic lighter, then took a big drag, and while blowing out a cloud of smoke, she looked at her parents and said, "Well, if you can't get him under control, what are you going to do with him? I mean, I can't take him yet, but when I find a job, I will." She hesitated and added, "Of course, if you could help pay for me to support him now, I could take him for the rest of the summer. I mean, I have my own apartment now, and I could—"

"We'll get him sorted out, and you'll get no money from us, as long as..." Tom shot a quick glance at me and continued, "... as long as you're still using!"

Patty flicked her cigarette down and ground it out with her sandal. Her toenails were coated with faded pink nail polish that had half chipped off. Fiercely, she said, "You don't know the first thing about me! I've been clean for almost a month now, and I can take care of him better than you can!"

She cast her eyes down, then peered back up at me, softening a little, as if pleading for some support. I looked back up at Tom and Laura and said, "Toby's a good kid; he just needs something to do over the summer. It's tough being out of school. Not enough structure right now."

Laura nodded and looked at Tom, but he just cast his eyes down and shook his head. Clearly, they didn't want Toby to go with Patty, and obviously, he didn't want to go with her either.

"You know, I've got a lot of work to do in my workshop. I'm opening a booth at the farmers' market in a couple of weeks. I could sure use some help, and if Toby is up for it, I'd be happy to keep him busy. Maybe even give him some woodshop lessons he can use when he's back at school in the fall. You know, if it's all right with you guys."

Tom exhaled sharply and smiled, and Laura looked relieved and grateful. Tom said, "I'd have to ask Toby, but that would be good for him, I think." Laura nodded.

Patty flashed me a challenging look. "What'll Emily think about that?"

"Em is up at her folks' for the summer, so it won't be a problem. I've got a lot to do to get ready, so the help would do me good. Again, if it's okay with Toby," I added.

"That's nice of you to offer, Ben. We'll talk to him about it," Tom said.

"It would actually be a great help to me. I think I can keep him busy all summer, and then school will start before you know it." I turned to Patty and said without thinking, "What about you? What are you doing this summer?"

Patty shot me a sly smile. "What, you want me to come over and help, too?" She half closed her eyes and bumped me with her hip.

I turned red and stepped away. "No! That's not what I meant. I mean, what are your plans for the summer?"

Still smiling, she said, "Oh, you know, same old. I need a job, so I'll be looking for one. I got a few leads, though."

A door slammed inside the house, and Laura went back in. Tom said, "Well, we'll let you know, Ben. Again, mighty nice of you to offer." He scrutinized Patty with concern and exasperation. "I hope you do get a job soon, and stay off that stuff. We're here for you when you want help."

Patty glared at him, turned, and shuffled back down to her car. I looked up at Tom, and he shrugged his shoulders and blew out a big breath.

I followed Patty to her car and stood facing her as she unlocked the door. She turned and took a step toward me, and I froze. She looked up at me, cocked her head to one side, and whispered, "It could have worked for us, you know. I still have a sweet spot in here for you." She took my hand and placed it on her warm chest.

I left my hand there for just a moment, then pulled it away, feeling ashamed for the attraction still simmering inside me.

She smirked and said, "Maybe I'll see you around this summer, since you'll be all alone and in need of help." Her hands fell to her thighs again, and she stroked her torn jeans. Then she touched my cheek and climbed into her car. Fast food trash littered the inside, and the back seats were stuffed with large black plastic bags. Was she homeless?

She lit another cigarette and cranked the car, which choked to life. Another long, smooth drag of the Salem. She grinned again. "Good seeing you, Ben. You look as good as always. I'll check in with you once in a while, see how you're doing, huh?"

Before I could say anything, she put the car in gear and roared off. I stared after her, feeling a familiar craving. I glanced up at Tom's house, and the curtains fell closed, Toby's head disappearing from the window.

I found the third polished stone in my workshop. It was dark charcoal gray, almost black, with faint veins and specks of lighter gray sparkling through it. It reminded me of the flat stones the kids and I would skip across the sea while hiking along the shore. The words *Fear or Faith?* glowed vibrantly against its smooth, dark surface, and as I picked it up, Toby's face appeared before me again. He was terrified of being taken by his mother. Fear had creased both Tom and Laura's faces, and I felt Patty's fear and desperation as well. And what about my own fears? Fear over money, fear of the farmers' market not working out, fear of Em's reaction, and so much more.

All the situations in my life *were* exactly as I had worried about them. Had I worried them into being? Could fear be dictating the results in my life? In all our lives? The angel's teachings on this were clear, and now I connected to their truth. She said I needed to change my thinking, and while that sounded simple enough, it was hard to shift away from the fear I constantly felt. How was I to do that?

Fear or Faith? The stone beckoned me to choose.

The flash of the angel's wings appeared in the mirror over the workshop counter, and in an instant, she appeared next to one of the half-completed mailboxes. I gazed at the dazzling being sitting in front of me, and in that moment, it *was* all real. An angel had come to teach me a truth that was awakening within me.

She sensed these thoughts. "Ben, when you overcome fear, you overcome failure."

The power of these words resonated deeply, and my mind wasn't processing any longer. Instead, a new awareness was emerging, an inner knowing connected to the lessons the angel had given me. As I gave in to this new feeling, fear faded away, replaced with a faith that went beyond my thoughts.

She held my gaze. "When you choose to live in faith rather

than in fear, the Source flows more freely to complete its vision through you. Look around you, Ben. This is your dream, your destiny to bring into the world. This is what the Source will help you accomplish, if you can live in faith while the Source finds the best path for it."

I looked in the mirror and saw both myself and the angel reflected back. We were bathed in an aura of sparkling light, like sunlight reflecting off a rippling river, and behind me, my workshop glowed. It called to me to embrace it, and in that instant, I saw that it held everything I needed to make my dream come true, and it had always been waiting for me. I surveyed the intricate pieces of each mailbox, the small window frames, the miniature doors, the siding and frames lined up awaiting completion. The only thing that had been lacking was sustained faith—the kind of faith that would lead to continuous action, no matter the obstacles.

In a rush of feeling, accompanied by an ocean of blue in my mind's eye, I decided then and there to cultivate faith, to learn from the angel how to harness my thoughts and consciously direct the flow of the Source. I surrendered to the miracle of the angel's presence and asked her to show me the way.

I spent the rest of the evening in a serene state, my thoughts calm and unattached. I tucked the angel into her cozy little house, and Sadie and Oreo, sleepy now, climbed onto their pillows and took their places next to the gently crackling fireplace. I lay on the couch and watched my thoughts float by. Patty and Toby. My dad and the other mill workers now looking for a job. Bud and the booth. Em and our savings. Getting a job. All these thoughts drifted through my mind, but I didn't attach myself to them. Instead, I looked at them as pieces of a giant jigsaw puzzle and wondered how they would all fit together.

And then I saw a new piece appear: Mitch. My dad had said he could afford to loan us the money, no problem, and he could—but would he? Was Mitch the channel the Source had chosen to help me make all this happen? I thought back to when Em took me to meet Mitch for the first time. What a roller coaster that day was! I had known there was no way I'd measure up to what he expected for his only daughter, and his custom-built home on Bainbridge, with its breathtaking view of the bay and its lush, manicured grounds, didn't boost my confidence. Mitch had opened their massive stained-glass front door, and I got my first peek into his world of wealth and privilege. He looked the part in his green polo shirt with the little red alligator logo, his words fast and focused. His wife, Dianna, self-assured and attractive, appraised me with a fixed smile. I shrank into myself and wanted to go home.

Thankfully, I'd had my secret weapon: my Polaroid camera. I took pictures of their new mansion and did what I always did. I made them a detailed, exact replica mailbox of their home. I didn't tell Em. A couple of months later, we attended a catered summer party on that magnificent lawn, the kind with rented tables decked out with white linens, servers mingling to offer hors d'oeuvres to the guests. When the string quartet took a break, I snuck the mailbox over to their table and surprised them both. The memory of Mitch's reaction triggered a cascade of blue light through my secret garden; what a triumph it had been! For once, Mitch was speechless. The entire gathering had applauded. I could still see Em beaming at me, her eyes moist. Mitch still talked about his mailbox. He'd loan me the money, wouldn't he?

Fear or Faith?

Determined, I reached for the phone to tell Em about what

had happened with my dad and that I needed to ask Mitch for a loan to keep my dream going.

The phone rang for a long time before someone finally picked up: Mitch.

"Hello?"

"Oh, hi, Mitch, it's Ben."

"Yes, I know. How are you doing?"

"Okay, I guess. Ah, is Em available?"

"Nope. She and the kids went out for dinner, but I expect they'll be back within an hour. You want to call back?"

I didn't think; I just acted. "Yeah, maybe... Ah, Mitch, I also wanted to ask you something."

"Shoot."

"Well, I've got an idea I want to run by you, but it's something you need to see. Just wondering if you're going to be in Tacoma next week. Maybe you could drop by for a few minutes?" I held my breath.

Silence as he considered this. "Let me see... I have some paperwork I need to run into town, um... I'm going to be there a week from this Thursday. I suppose I could swing by around lunchtime. Would that work?"

My stomach fluttered. "Yeah, that'd be great!"

"Okay, then, I'll count on it. You want to give me a preview?"

"Not yet. As I said, it's better if you see everything first. By the way, do me a favor and don't tell Em you're coming over. I want to surprise her later, okay?"

"Works for me," he said.

We hung up, and I stared at the phone. Had that really just happened? Exciting, sure, but I felt some guilt, too. I had called with the intention of asking Em first, but ... it seemed the Source had given me Mitch instead. Maybe this was how the Source worked? I was supposed to ask *him*; that was why the thought had occurred to me so quickly, and it just came out. Yes, that had to be it!

I had a lot of work to do to prepare for Mitch's visit: samples to complete, the booth to finish, new flyers to write and take to the printer, and I had to be ready to sell him on my idea that very day—because the next day, Bud would need another check for the first and last months' rent. It was cutting it close, and I'd need some help, but tomorrow I'd ask my dad if he could spare some time in the evenings to help get the work done. And Toby might be open to helping as well.

After a quick dinner, I went into the front yard to adjust the sprinklers, and there was Toby, sitting on the curb with his hoodie up. I approached him, and he looked up hopefully.

"How are you doing?" I asked.

He just shrugged and mumbled something. He kept his eyes on mine, though, and I ventured forward.

"Did your grandparents mention anything about maybe working with me on my mailboxes?"

"Yeah…" While it was only one word, he shook off the hoodie and looked up at me expectantly.

"I don't think you've ever been in my workshop, have you?"

"No." Again, one word, but there was hope in it.

"C'mon." I led him into the house and straight into my workshop.

He looked around curiously, shy at first, but he warmed up quickly as I took him around to the various stations and explained the stages of making the mailboxes.

"These are the pictures I take of the houses, and these are the frames I use to build the structure."

"You use quarter-inch plywood. That should make them pretty solid," he said as he ran his hand down the sheets of plywood leaning against the wall.

"Wow! You know your wood. Where'd you learn that?"

"In Mr. Campbell's woodshop class."

"Have you ever used a table saw before?"

"Yeah, but we have to have supervision to do that. But I know how to use dowels to fit things together," he said proudly.

We spent an hour going through the various tools, processes, and pieces I used for the mailboxes, and after we were done, I was more than impressed by his knowledge. He, too, seemed engaged and more alive than I'd seen him before.

"Well, how about it? Would you like to help me this summer?"

"Sure!"

"Great. Then let's start tomorrow. I have Em's dad coming over next week, and I need to be ready to pitch to him and get him on board."

Toby promised to be there first thing the next day, and after he left, I thought about how things seemed to be coming together. Maybe the angel was right: all I needed to do was have faith and act on it.

Chapter Ten

Thursday, June 23, 1988

It had been a good week and a half, and I needed it. Despite being nervous about meeting with Mitch, I mostly stayed positive and focused on the angel's three lessons. Surrounded by the early sun pouring through the pines and dogwoods in the backyard, I started each day in my secret garden with her, cultivating faith and focusing on the clear color and intensity of the Source. It was strange, but color had become my guide. It was hard at times to maintain the baby-blue aura around us, as high above floated the ever-present darker colors of the "what ifs" and worries and uncertainties that still surrounded me. But little by little, I grew better at identifying these thoughts, and at redirecting my energy and intention away from my doubts and more toward faith. I got in a groove of concentrating only on the feelings of things working out, and each time I did, I summoned the blues and attracted the amber-yellows and whites that mimicked the angel's colors.

The stones helped, too—especially the third stone, which held the simple reminder, *Fear or Faith?* I moved all three stones, including the first one, *Your Dreams Are Inspired by the Source,* and the second stone, *Thoughts Are Things,* into my workshop, placed on a shelf at eye level, so I could watch them flicker while I worked. At the end of each evening, I'd carry a stone with me into the backyard, its warmth comforting in my pocket. The angel flew and played in the forest on these warmer nights, while I retreated into my inner garden alone. I passed through the familiar worries and into my center, visualizing it all working out: the farmers' market, Em and the kids being back, building my business on my own terms. This became the vision I focused on cultivating throughout the week.

And my workshop came alive! Toby had been more helpful than I could have imagined, and his experience from his woodshop classes was deeper than I expected. He was genuinely interested in the designs of my mailboxes and intuitively grasped the assembly process, and best of all, he was eager to help.

At one point, while showing him pictures of various houses and how I'd made the plans for each one, he spotted the planer I had taken from my dad's garage. I had cleaned it up and polished the mahogany handle to a smooth red glow, just as shiny as it was all those years ago.

"What's this for?" Toby asked as he picked it up and weighed it in his hand.

"After I rip the large pieces of plywood or pine, I need to smooth them out before I can sand them. I have a power planer for that, but sometimes it's nice having a hand planer for smaller or more delicate work," I explained.

"Is this what I'm gonna use?"

"At some point, sure. I'll start you on the small sander first, but definitely, it's something you can use. Be careful with it now, though; the blade underneath is very sharp."

Toby showed up every day, and it was heartening to see how

positive he'd become now that he had something to work on. Not only had his attitude improved, but the black sweatshirt was gone, replaced by T-shirts and even the occasional button-down shirt. I hadn't even known he owned one. He also had a new attitude toward his mom.

"It's not good for me to be with my mom right now," he said as he handed me a piece of wood he was working on.

Surprised, I asked, "What do you mean?"

"Well, until she gets better. I mean, it might be okay later, but right now, she has to take care of herself first."

I could just imagine the discussions Tom and Laura had had with him.

"One day, hopefully, she will. And then you two can try it. Would you like that?"

There was a long pause as Toby's eyes darted around the room. "I think so, but I have to wait."

I felt good that he'd opened up to me, and I looked forward to talking with him more about it, when he was ready.

My dad showed up most nights and helped as well. He seemed tired, though, listless at times.

"Are you okay?" I asked him one night.

He stopped what he was doing, patted his pocket, and led me into the backyard for a smoke. The tip of the cigarette glowed a fiery red as he hit it hard.

"There's not much work out there, and the little I've found is mostly one-off day jobs at construction sites."

"What about the paper? Anything in there?"

"Not much that suits me... A lot of ads for that Big Box store, but I don't know what the hell I'd do there. I'll keep at it, though."

"You'll find something, you'll see," I assured him, with more conviction than I felt.

"I'm glad you decided to ask Mitch for the money. What did Em say about it?"

"Ah, I haven't told her."

He raised his eyebrows.

"I was going to, but Mitch answered instead, and... Well, it just seemed like it was meant to be. After he said he'd come over, I didn't want to jinx it."

"Well, if he'll loan you the money, that must mean he thinks it's a good investment in both you and Em. She should be okay with it."

"Yeah, well, we'll see." I felt bad that I hadn't asked her, but I kept focusing on faith and my dream, and I hoped it would all work out.

Meanwhile, my dad had great suggestions, like creating a facing for the booth itself, including a roofline that would give the whole booth the look of a little house. Now anyone walking by would be drawn to my booth in its own right, and the booth itself would act as a kind of mailbox sample. Just brilliant! Dad had been ripping plywood, and Toby sanded it smooth to create the facing, while I spent the week finishing the mailbox samples to show Mitch. Dad also helped me build the framing for the workshop remodel—work that would have taken me much longer on my own. Having my dad and Toby over each day filled the house with energy, purpose, and most of all, hope—all of which helped me stay in faith. And it all came down to today.

At eleven o'clock, the throaty roar of Mitch's red convertible Porsche 911 echoed down the street, and he pulled up to the curb. The morning had started out sunny, but had faded to a dull gray. I peeked out the den window and made a quick calculation: it probably wasn't going to rain in the next hour, so if Mitch put the top up, then he planned to stay a bit; if he left it down, then this would be a quick meeting. He sat in the rumbling car for a while, shuffling things about, then he killed the engine and headed my way.

He left the top down.

Mitch was dressed for battle in the real estate world: white button-down work shirt with the sleeves rolled up, revealing a huge gold Rolex, and dark blue wool slacks with cuffs draped over shiny black leather loafers. He was the epitome of business casual meets college prep. Still in his fifties, with jet-black hair parted on the side and combed in a wave across a broad forehead, he reminded me of Cary Grant in the Hitchcock film *North by Northwest*. He sauntered up the walkway and gave the house a steady stare, appraising it from end to end. I could only imagine what he was thinking, given this had been his home for almost fifteen years while he fought his way to the top of the real estate market. Coming closer, he sniffed the air and made a face. *Welcome back to the Aroma of Tacoma,* I thought wryly; it had to be thick and heavy today.

The doorbell chimed, and when I opened the door, he filled the doorway. He thrust his hand out and gripped mine, giving it a viselike squeeze, then passed me and charged into the house.

"How ya doing, Ben?" he asked with a smile I couldn't read.

"Good, good! Thanks for coming." I directed him into the kitchen. "Would you like some iced tea?"

"Sounds great. Ah, no sugar for me, thanks."

He sipped his tea while unconsciously shaking his left hand down, trying to get his Rolex to straighten and fall over the top of his wrist.

"So, what's going on?" He quickly raised his eyebrows twice, as if to compel me to answer. I always found that gesture annoying.

"Well, I have a business opportunity I wanted to talk to you about..." My voice broke.

Mitch just raised his eyebrows and waited.

"I've got everything set up in the living room, if you'd like to have a look."

"Okay, lead the way." He held his hand out, and I led him into the living room, which Toby and I had set up earlier.

I turned and tried to gauge his reaction as he took it all in. He raised both eyebrows, tightened his lips, and scanned the room. We had leaned the façade of the booth next to the TV, and it made quite an impression in the small room. Lined up on the coffee table were four mailbox samples we had finished during the week, and they were striking. There were two one-story ranch designs that mimicked many of the houses in neighborhoods around Tacoma. I had painted the first one bluish-gray with white trim, like our house, and it had a white garage door that opened for the mail. The other was also a stand-alone ranch, but without a garage. I had stained this one clear with yellow trim, and you simply grabbed the red chimney and tilted it back, and the whole roofline opened on hinges for the mail. But the other two samples were my favorites: classic two-story Craftsman homes, with overhanging roofs covering end-to-end miniature front porches. The paneling had been tricky to make, but I ended up using layered popsicle sticks, a half inch each. They gave the impression of a custom wood front and were painstakingly stained, one a bluish-gray, the other a deep beige-yellow. The angel had beamed at me when she saw them; they could have been mistaken for intricately made dollhouses. Toby had watched in fascination as I did the finish work, and once we carried them from the shop and set them up on the coffee table, he stepped back and whistled.

Lastly, there were the new flyers my dad had helped me create, fanned out in front of the mailboxes. We had three designs—a yellow, blue, and purple one—each showcasing a different house layout: one for the ranch houses, one for the Craftsman designs, and another for the newer homes sprouting up in the expanding housing developments around Tacoma. I was sure Mitch owned some of the properties on which these housing developments were being built, and this had to pique his interest.

"Very impressive," he said, nodding. "Em told me you were opening a booth at the farmers' market. I'm assuming this is it?" He raised his eyebrows again.

"Yeah, this is the start of it. I'm going to build more samples and put together a photo book of the mailboxes I've made through the years—you know, kind of give people an idea of what their own mailbox could look like. I'm also well along on expanding my workshop to handle all the orders I'll get."

I waited.

"Well, Ben, 'nothing to it but to do it,' I always say. Good for you!"

Hope fluttered through me, and I sped on, "Yeah, I'm pretty stoked about it all. The booth rental starts on Saturday, July second, and I'll have another sample done by then, and a lot of the photo book completed, too." I paused.

He looked expectantly at me and raised his eyebrows in quick succession.

"Yeah, well, I've run into a little snag, and I need to ask you something."

He stood still and waited for me to continue. At least he had stopped raising his eyebrows.

"Ah, I had secured some funding for this—about ten thousand dollars—but my backer had to, ah... It was my dad, and he needed the money back for an emergency. Anyway, I now need a loan to help see me through this, and I was wondering—hoping—that I could maybe borrow the money from you. As the orders come in, I'll make monthly payments to pay you back. Plus, soon I'll have a job, and I'll be able to pay you even more each month."

Mitch glanced back down at the mailboxes and then moved to the couch, motioning for me to pull up a chair opposite him. Setting his iced tea down on a purple coaster featuring a big W, he picked up two of the flyers. He creased his forehead and asked, "So, this booth at the farmers' market... I'm assuming there are other booths there selling woodworking items as well?"

I shifted uneasily. Where was *this* going? I simply nodded.

"And what is the volume of sales—you know, week to week—of the other booths featuring woodworking products?" he asked.

I squirmed, and my forehead tingled. "Ah, I don't know."

He raised his eyebrows and nodded knowingly. "How about the amount of foot traffic to those booths? How many people visit the woodworking booths compared to, say, the food booths?"

Dammit! I didn't have any of these answers; I hadn't even thought of them. I shrugged and shook my head. The tingling on my forehead turned into a small bead of sweat, and suddenly the living room seemed crowded and warm. Why hadn't I opened the window before he got here?

"Then I guess you also can't tell me about the demographics of the shoppers themselves? I mean, I'd assume these are local residents from the Tacoma area, probably within a, what, five-to-ten-mile radius, I'd guess?" He stopped and looked like he expected an answer.

I shrugged and nodded again, searching his face and hoping my agreement would in some way show I had at least considered this. My stomach dropped, though, as I watched the farmers' market begin to slip away.

He grunted and put the flyers back down. Then he touched the roofline of the blue-gray Craftsman house and forced a smile. Staring at the samples, he said, "Ben, you don't have to sell me on your mailboxes. They're beautifully made, and I love mine, as you know. Still get compliments on it all the time." He hesitated, then raised his eyes to mine, his expression softening a little. Lowering his voice, he slowed his pace, as one might do when speaking to a child. "Here's the thing, Ben. The farmers' market is a good venue for selling certain things, mainly locally grown food at a discount on what people would pay in a store. That's always been the draw to any farmers' market, and it's what makes them successful, right?" He waited for me to answer.

"Yeah, I guess. I mean, sure. But there's a lot of other stuff sold there, too. Handmade crafts, wooden patio furniture, cooked food, candles and soaps..."

Candles and soaps?! Geez. Ryan's smirking, laughing face flashed through my mind, and I knew I had just lost. A bead of sweat dripped down and stung the right side of my cheek.

"Well, for any business to be successful, there not only has to be a market for it, but the business has to be able to scale if it's going to last and grow. Now, I don't doubt you could get a few orders initially, but what I worry about is the long-term viability of this—for you and for Em. What's the monthly rent on the booth, for example?"

"Four hundred a month."

"And how much do you charge for each mailbox?"

"Between two hundred to three hundred and fifty dollars, or even four hundred plus for the elaborate ones," I said, shifting in my seat.

"And what's your average profit per mailbox?"

"Well, it depends on the design, but anywhere from a hundred dollars on the lower end, up to one seventy-five or even two fifty on the more expensive ones."

"Okay, that's what I thought. So, you'd need four orders of the lower design, or one of those and a couple of midrange houses..." He pointed to the Craftsman house in the middle. "...to make your rent on the space—and that doesn't cover your expenses yet. I mean, you still have to buy supplies, right?"

My head whirled. Why hadn't I drilled down to this level? I had just assumed I'd get lots of orders from all the foot traffic, but as Mitch broke it down, it seemed almost like wishful thinking. Still, I tried to think about what the angel had told me, and I shifted my thoughts and tried to recapture my faith in this. When I glimpsed my colors, however, the blue was gone, and the dark gray from before billowed in like smoke.

Mitch studied me and said slowly, "I'm sorry, Ben. I just don't see it."

Suddenly, my eyes stung. I quickly turned away, but caught him shaking his left hand down and glancing at the time.

Abruptly, he stood, waiting for me to join him. I stumbled to my feet. He scanned the booth façade, then the samples, then slowly shook his head once and raised his eyebrows again. Then he made his way back into the kitchen. I followed.

He put his glass of half-finished iced tea on the counter and went to the front door. Over his shoulder, he said, "So, when are you coming up to the island?"

Not any time soon, once Em finds out about this, I thought bitterly.

"Not sure yet."

An awkward pause.

"Well, I'd better be going, got a meeting downtown with some builders." He paused on the front porch, and I hovered in the doorway.

"Listen, I hope I'm wrong about this," he said earnestly. "I've been wrong before. Good luck with it, regardless. If it doesn't work out, you'll find something else, I'm sure." He stuck out his stiff hand and crushed mine, then whirled and marched down to his gleaming car. I shut the door, the Porsche roared to life, and then he was gone.

Chapter Eleven

Thursday afternoon, June 23, 1988

What had just happened? Dazed, I drifted back into the crowded living room and stared at the booth façade. A money hole was all I saw. The samples and flyers? All a big waste of time and more money. The beads of sweat returned, and my stomach flip-flopped as my business crumbled and disappeared before I had even made a go of it.

Business? Who was I kidding? Ryan was right: I didn't have a head for business. Mitch had a head for business, clearly, and Ryan had the ruthlessness, the relentlessness to drive his business. But me? I was just a dreamer, and as my dad said, if something could go wrong, it would.

And it had—again.

Dark shades of color flooded my mind, but a flash of light streaked in, and the angel landed on top of the Craftsman mailbox. She perched on the roof, her body glistening with iridescence from the partial rays of the sun now filtering in through the living room window.

"Are you in faith or fear right now, Ben?"

I was instantly ashamed, but I couldn't control my disappointment. "It's all over."

"What's over?" she asked with a steady gaze, her wings opening and closing hypnotically.

I plopped down on the couch and let out a deep sigh. "All of it. Mitch won't loan me the money. He thinks it's a bad idea and won't work, so now it's over. It's just all over."

The angel zoomed into my consciousness, raised her little hands, and scattered the choking darkness. Murky colors retreated to the edges of the bubble that now surrounded us, and the angel's glow warmed it to a sapphire blue. She sat beside me, and I calmed, basking in the blue and watching the dark disappointment retreat above us.

She asked, "How did you think Mitch would react to this?"

"I thought he could loan me the money." Even as I said these words, the feelings surrounding them were flat and detached.

"What did you *believe*, though?"

This stopped me cold. I had just told her what I thought, and now I considered what I'd said. I thought he *could* loan me the money. But did I believe he would? I shook my head. Not really. Sure, I'd hoped he would, and I'd tried to convince myself that he might. But deep down, I hadn't truly believed he would do it.

I caught sight of the angel nodding her head, patiently looking up at me with her mesmerizing clear blue eyes. She remained silent for a while, letting this realization settle in.

Then she said, "Thinking and thoughts by themselves are powerless if those thoughts are not anchored in belief. What you truly believe about any situation—this is what directs the Source. You can hope and wish all you want, but without the conviction of unshakable belief, and the sustained action that follows, those thoughts will not manifest. The Source will only flow along the lines of your deepest truth, your belief, and it will always bring into being either what you fear with deep feeling, or believe with great faith. You never really believed Mitch would loan you the money, and your true belief was borne out in the circumstances that unfolded. This is the law exactly as I have been teaching it to you. Everything is as it should be, Ben."

The angel scanned my colors and said, "Each feeling you have paints your consciousness with a color, and each color determines how easy or difficult it is for the Source to flow through you. The clearer and lighter the color of your consciousness, the easier the Source moves through you, and this determines the speed and ease of manifestation. The fastest way to manifest your dream is by focusing on what you want, rather than what you don't want, thereby keeping the colors as light and clear as possible. This is the essence of lesson four."

Once again, she inhaled deeply, and the membrane of blue bent toward us. Then she exhaled, and our space expanded. She said:

"The key to manifesting our dreams is to stay focused, with feeling, on what we want, rather than what we don't want."

She paused, and I weighed the gravity of her meaning. Her tiny eyebrows scrunched, and the effect infinitely endeared her to me. My heart warmed and brimmed over with inexpressible love. How could I not believe, not cherish everything this incredible little being was teaching me?

"It's crucial not to let worry or doubt dilute your ability to channel the Source. You must strive to allow the Source to flow unobstructed through your life. Worry, doubt, or fear of any kind interrupts the flow, diverts its course. Only by rising in consciousness, by casting off worry and focusing on your dream, will you be able to create an unimpeded path for the Source to flow.

"Your goal, Ben, is to focus with complete feeling and faith on the joyful accomplishment of your dream, to believe in its reality beyond doubt. Once you do, the Source will bring that vision into your life. The image you hold in your secret garden will always become a reality in your life—just as it's doing right now. The secret is staying focused on what you want to create, rather than what you don't want."

The colors surrounding us were energized now; almost every color, in every shade, raced around us. I gazed down at the angel, who radiated a vibrant white, and I understood: that color meant pure and immediate manifestation. Her golden necklace pulsed brightly, and she nodded at my realization.

She said, "Once you are able to create and sustain absolute belief in your dream, and hold that vision *as if it has already come true*, then you will be ready. And at that moment, you will find that the whole world is ready, too. Everything you need to bring forth your dream, in the most efficient way possible, will automatically appear to help you. In fact, everything you need is already here, all around you. You just can't see it yet, but you will."

The grays of my doubts collected and darkened. "But how?"

"By working on this lesson. Whenever you find yourself focused on any situation, fear, or feeling that goes against your dream, withdraw your attention from those thoughts and redirect them to the Source and its vision for you. Hold this positive vision in your thoughts, wait for the colors to clear, and stay focused only on what it *feels* like to have your dream come true.

"This is the key to this lesson. You will experience many moments of doubt and worry and even setbacks on your journey, but remember, these are simply temporary states. When you find that you are dwelling on these, immediately shift your thoughts to what you want to happen instead. Return to your garden and cultivate the vision of having already succeeded, and *feel* the joyful emotions you'll have once you manifest your dream. And with this vision firmly in your consciousness, take a positive action that is in alignment with your dream. Act as if it were so, and it will become so."

The blue surrounding us darkened for a moment. Why hadn't she told me it would turn out this way? All that time I'd spent in my secret garden trying to cultivate faith, hoping Mitch would say yes—was all that just a waste of time?

She read this and watched the gray above us deepen to charcoal, and as she glanced at it, it retreated. She locked onto my worried eyes and asked, "Now that you know the difference between hoping and believing, what do you believe about the farmers' market itself? Is that the way?"

Utter confusion now. I wasn't sure what I thought, or rather, felt about it—really felt on the level of belief. I hoped the booth would work. I thought it could work, if everything fell into place. But did I truly believe, with unshakeable conviction, that it would? No. I didn't have that level of faith in it.

And then it hit me. What about my dream itself? What were my true feelings about that? Was my dream just a hope? A wish? I suspected Em didn't think I could do this on my own, but what did *I* think, truly believe? As these thoughts swam in my head, the charcoal gray above us swirled menacingly and coalesced into ominous black clouds. I shivered, scared—even threatened, as if my life were about to end.

The angel put her hand, as light as a feather, on top of my thumb, and her energy raced through me, filling me with not only warmth, but with knowing as well. She peered into my eyes and asked if I remembered the truth of the first lesson. What were the words again? I couldn't tell her, but the light, the purpose, and the urgency of the truth they held still resonated within me.

And then they returned: "I am a point of consciousness of the one Source, and my purpose is to express its vision for me. And this vision is the dream that burns in my soul."

The angel fluttered her wings, and jewels of light cascaded from them and bounced around us. Her necklace vibrated and glowed, and her soft hum grew. Then, in a charge of energy, my whole consciousness erupted with radiant light, the color of an ivory-white rose, which transmuted into baby blue. Instantly, we were bathed in the center of this light and color, and I knew.

She gazed up at me and asked, "Do you believe in your dream, Ben?"

My feelings went beyond words, and my vision filled me: the comfortable feeling of smooth ash wood in my hands; the intoxicating smell of freshly cut and planed wood; the consuming satisfaction of working on the intimate details of assembling a roof, of cutting the delicate lines of bricks for a chimney; and most of all, the serenity of purpose and the indescribable gratification of a completed mailbox delivered to a happy homeowner. I caressed these feelings, and all thought stopped. Unfettered belief coursed through me. I was one with the angel and with the Source. I was still. And I knew.

We sat in silence, and time sat beside us. Reluctantly, I returned first to the awareness of the angel sitting next to me in my garden, and then to the living room, where she perched on the back of the couch next to my head. Her soft touch brushed my earlobe, and the same sense of warmth and certainty flowed through me. I opened my eyes and looked down at the mailbox samples, and there it was: the fourth stone, a gleaming violet, shot through with pale hues of red and blue. The words *Focus on What You Want* danced with golden light.

I studied the perfect mailbox samples on the coffee table and fell in love with them all over again. Then I glanced at the big surround of the booth, and it seemed distant and awkward and rough—a sharp contrast to the delicacy of the mailboxes. Dropping my head, I sighed and faced what I'd been too afraid to admit: the farmers' market had never been the way.

The angel let go of my ear and scooted down the back of the couch. I faced her and said, "How, then?"

"That will be a lesson for another day. Today, you accepted the most important thing: you claimed your dream and made it yours. Today, you went from understanding the first lesson to becoming one with it by going beyond thinking and wishing to knowing and believing. Now the other lessons will become tools for you to use, rather than abstract concepts to think about. And once you integrate and practice them with the belief and certainty you have now, you will hold the secret to all manifestation."

The evening came gently, fading light spilling into the den as cool air seeped through the open window. The aroma had long since drifted away, replaced by the sweet smell of moisture. The shock of my meeting with Mitch had drifted by as well, and I was centered now, empowered, and certain about my dream. I tucked the angel into her little house and glanced at Sadie, who lay peacefully on her pillow, her ribs filling and falling in short but steady bursts. I stood in the doorway, my eyes fixed on the fire, my mind finally still—until the phone rang.

I caught it on the third ring. Then I heard Em say in a slow and deliberate voice that started softly, but rose quickly in tone, "Ben, what the hell?!"

Silence for a moment, and then it came.

"My dad just got home and told me he'd been over to see you today—that you asked to borrow money from him for the farmers' market? What's going on?" At this point, she seemed more curious than mad, but that would change quickly.

"Yeah, ah, turns out my dad needed the seven thousand dollars back. He, um, lost his job, and... Anyway, he needs the money and won't be able to loan it to me now. So, I thought maybe Mitch wouldn't mind, you know..." I paused. "I'd pay it back, of course, like I planned to with my dad."

"Your dad lost his *job*? Why didn't you tell me? When did that happen?"

"About a week ago, I guess."

"And you gave him the seven thousand dollars back?" Her voice grew serious. "Where'd you get that money from?"

"I borrowed it from our savings—you know, temporarily, until I get something else lined up." Hearing myself say it aloud, I squirmed, feeling guilty and suddenly shocked by how much I hadn't told her. What had I been thinking?

"Are you kidding me, Ben? You took money out of *our* savings and didn't even tell me? Then you went behind my back and asked *my* dad for the money? What were you thinking?! Why didn't you talk to me?"

Her voice trembled now, and the heat of our tension stung through the phone. Worse than the tension was the fact that I didn't have an answer for her.

"I thought it would all work out. You know, me getting a part-time job, the opening of the booth, the orders... I just figured, well, I figured I'd make it all work out, and you'd be happy in the end."

Hearing myself say it, I realized I had taken a big risk, and my justification didn't excuse what I had done. I should have talked to her first. It would have been much easier to ask for permission rather than hope for forgiveness that didn't seem to be coming.

There was a long silence—an uncomfortable silence.

"Em? Are you still there?"

Quietly controlled anger came back at me. "I'm pretty shocked right now. I don't even know what to say. I just, ah, I can't quite believe it." She stopped abruptly, then continued, "How much of the seven thousand have you spent so far?"

"About fifty-three hundred."

"When is the first and last months' rent due on the booth, and can you still get your deposit back?"

"It's due tomorrow."

"Well, you can't pay it, obviously. In fact, tomorrow you need to go see Bud and see if you can get the deposit back. Just tell him something came up," she said.

"Yeah, I know. I'll call him tomorrow."

She paused, and I held my breath. "Are you even looking for work?"

Another wave of guilt passed through me. "Yeah... I don't have any interviews yet, but I've submitted some applications, and yeah, I'm looking. But part-time work is kind of unpredictable," I said.

"Well, you can get a full-time job now that you aren't doing the farmers' market, can't you?" It was more of a command than a question.

"But what about…" I stalled for a moment, then continued. "What about the mailboxes? What about my business?"

"Business? You *have* no business, no job, and no money! What part of this aren't you getting? The mailbox business will have to wait!"

"But…" My voice faded.

Em's tone softened, but she remained firm. "Listen, Ben, you don't have a choice on this. Now is not the time. We need income, and we need to replace our savings, and you need to start acting … more responsibly. If you want your business to get going, maybe you should go see Ryan again. Now that you're not doing the farmers' market, he can have the exclusive, and you could get some business right there."

I didn't think I could feel any lower, but that did it. "You don't think I can do this, do you?"

She hesitated. "Well, I'm not hearing any better ideas from you. I mean, why don't you offer him an exclusive or something, for, like, a year? Tell him you want to see how it goes. After that, you can renegotiate. At least this way, you can get the business going in some way while you get a job and income coming in. At least it's an option… I mean, unless you've got a better idea?"

"Not right now, but I'm working on it. I'll think about asking Ryan."

"You should. In the meantime, you've got to promise me you won't do anything like this again without talking to me, okay?"

"I'm sorry, I just thought…" But I didn't know what I'd thought.

I heard the kids in the background, and Em put them on. They gushed about all the things they were doing: horseback riding, kayaking, fishing. Their innocence and excitement warmed my heart, and my eyes burned. I missed them. When would I get to see them? Em came back on, and I wanted to ask her, but it didn't seem like the right time.

"And what else is going on over there? How's Sadie doing?"

A new wave of guilt washed over me. A lot was going on with Sadie, but how to tell her without revealing the work the angel was doing with her...?

"She's struggling more, it seems, but I'm keeping my eye on her."

"Is she still eating?"

"Yeah, a little."

"If she stops, take her to the vet and call me. I could come back home, even bring the kids."

I was torn now. What would I do with the angel? And was it even a good idea for the kids to see Sadie so weak?

"I will, I will."

That calmed her down a bit, and although the rest of the conversation was still strained, it was short, at least. We hung up, and I staggered around the kitchen, feeling like a boxer who had just lost a tough round. It was clear she didn't think I could do this without Ryan. I burned as that sunk in, and I would have argued more, but she had settled down, and that was victory enough for one night. Her tone had stung, and I was ashamed. Why hadn't I told her about Mitch? I was disappointed in myself, and I was worried.

The best thing I could do to start repairing the damage was to see Bud tomorrow, get the deposit back, and get out of the first and last months' rent. After all, I didn't remember discussing any specific terms, and I hadn't signed anything. Still, facing Bud and giving him this news wasn't something I was looking forward to. And begging Ryan for a one-year deal? It turned my stomach just thinking about it.

Overwhelmed by these thoughts and the dark colors they brought, I tossed and turned in bed and eventually fell into an uneasy sleep, dreaming of outcomes I didn't want.

Chapter Twelve

Friday, June 24, 1988

I arrived at Bud's a little after nine o'clock that warm and sunny morning. When he answered the door, he stifled a yawn, his long hair loose now, matted and shaped to his pillow. Had I woken him up? He wore a faded yellow Hawaiian shirt and stonewashed, frayed blue jean shorts. He grunted at me, led me into his cramped kitchen, and offered me a cup of Folgers.

"No thanks," I said.

He poured himself a cup, studied my worried expression, and went into pitch mode.

"I'm putting you in the back area with the other high-end wood sellers. You'll do well there, I'm telling you. I've cleared out the space next to the other vendors and let them know not to spread into yours, something you'll always be dickering about, but any trouble, and you come and talk to me. But we're all excited to have you, and I'm sure you'll sell a lot of dollhouses."

"Mailboxes," I corrected him.

"Oh, yeah. But they look like dollhouses, right? I mean, there's a lot of kids at the market. Have you ever thought of making dollhouses, too? I bet they'd be a big seller for you."

I hadn't thought about that, and a new revenue stream briefly passed before my eyes. Suddenly, I was sorry I wasn't getting the booth and wondered how I could still swing it.

Then he got down to business. "So, you owe the first and last today, eight hundred, and after that, rent is due the last Friday of each month, so that'll be..." He paused and flipped the calendar on the wall—one of Ryan's promotional nursery calendars, I noted—and said, "July twenty-ninth." He put his hands on his hips and stared at me.

I glanced down to his Hawaiian shirt and said, "Yeah, about that... Ah, unfortunately, I can't take the booth after all." I braced myself.

Instantly alert, he narrowed his eyes. "What do you mean? The booth's already yours!" He took a small step towards me, and I stiffened.

"My financing didn't come through, so I can't afford it. In fact, I need the deposit back, and I was sort of hoping you could give the space to one of those other people who were interested."

No hesitation, no consideration. "Not possible. Your deposit is nonrefundable. I've been turning down other new vendors all month, holding this space for you! And if no one else can take this, then you'll also owe me the first and last months' rent: eight hundred dollars." He stood as rigid as a marble pillar, put his coffee cup down, and crossed his arms.

I shifted uncomfortably, surprised not just by what he said, but by how much force he said it with. "But I ... I don't have the first and last. And I need the two-hundred-dollar deposit back, because I'm not taking the booth."

As I said this, I realized how feeble my argument sounded. And he was right: I had reserved the booth, and I hadn't given him any indication I wasn't going to take it. But another eight hundred dollars out of our savings? I shuddered.

Bud studied me intensely, uncrossed his arms, and demanded, "Why didn't you tell me this sooner? You can't just stick this on me. What am I supposed to do?"

"Well, can't you call one of the other people? Won't they be happy that a booth space is available?"

He shook his head and shot me a disappointed look. "I can try, but if I can't get anyone to take your space... I mean, the opening is only a week away. Then you'll owe what we agreed on. And regardless, you won't be getting your deposit back." He huffed, snatched his coffee cup off the counter, and turned to the sink. He said over his shoulder, "You can let yourself out. Let me make some calls and see what I can do. I'll be in touch with you as soon as I know."

I was even more motivated to see Ryan now.

When I got to the nursery, things had changed a lot. It seemed that rather than scale business back with the Big Box store opening soon, Ryan had gone on a buying spree. The outside garden area had expanded into part of the parking lot, and now the plants of early summer spilled into the first row of spaces. Neatly arranged tables of colorful annuals, new perennials, and bright red, yellow, and peach rose bushes were on display. Under a green awning, vibrant houseplants—including pink orchids, and Em's favorite, white peace lilies—were lined up by color. Ryan had been busy, and I begrudgingly admired his passion for and belief in his business.

Cars crowded the parking lot, and shoppers in wide-brimmed summer hats and baseball caps roamed around the aisles, loading up their carts with the new harvest. Business was good, and that should be good for me and my pitch today. I gathered up the flyers, scooped up a new mailbox sample, and marched into the store.

I hovered outside Ryan's office, and when he looked up through the glass door, his beady eyes locked onto mine. His messy office overflowed with damaged potted plants scattered around the floor. Rickety metal bookcases sagged under the weight of returned landscaping tools and assorted pots, and a deep layer of soil lay swept up in the corner. Invoices, unopened mail, and coupon flyers littered his desk. That annoying smirk returned when he eyed the mailbox under my arm, and he slowly shook his head.

"Mailboxes at the farmers' market fail already?" he asked and grinned.

Asshole. What had I been thinking? It was Ryan—the same old piece of work. But steady, now... There was a higher purpose here, and today I was going to get what I wanted.

"And good morning to you, too." I set the sample Craftsman mailbox on the corner of the desk, then fanned out the new flyers. "Nursery looks good out there. How's business?" I asked, trying to divert him.

"Business is humming. Best time of year, as you know. Oh, and have you heard the news? We're expanding—and no, I won't tell you where yet, so don't ask. How's Em?"

Such a prick. *"None of your business,"* I wanted to say. "Good, good."

Ryan, ignoring the mailbox and the flyers, leaned back in his chair, smirk firmly in place. "I'm kinda busy. What do you want?"

I picked up one of the flyers, cleared my throat, and started in on my well-rehearsed pitch. "Well, as you know, the Big Box store opens in September, and it's going to affect a lot of smaller hardware stores and nurseries." I paused.

His eyes bored into mine, unblinking.

"And I figure you'd benefit from having something they don't—you know, an edge they can't compete with." I handed him the flyer.

He took it, scanned it, and flung it onto his desk.

"Anyway, I've got some new designs and new flyers, and I thought I could help you compete by us partnering up on a full mailbox display, at both this location and the new one you're planning, wherever that is. The Big Box store will have bulk—"

He waved his hand, dismissing me. "What happened to the farmers' market?" he asked, grinning.

"Well, it didn't work out. I mean, I've decided to delay it for a year or so."

"Didn't work out? Of course it didn't. I told you it was a foolish idea." He smirked as I shifted uncomfortably. The hair on the back of my neck tingled, and I wanted to argue, but I waited.

He had me right where he wanted me. He glanced at the colorful flyers and looked back up at me. "I agree with you: having something they don't is a good idea. But I've also been thinking that I don't need you. If I want to, I can sell custom mailboxes without you at all."

Fear surged through me. "What do you mean?"

"Yeah, well, anyone can make a mailbox. Hell, it's just a few pieces of wood glued together, right? Scott is a pretty good carpenter, and he told me he could make a couple a day, no problem. All he needs, he said, is a picture of a house, and then he can make a decent copy." He rocked in his chair, laced his hands behind his head, and glared at me.

I tightened my hands into fists. "You can't do that!"

Exasperated, he dropped his hands hard onto his desk. "Ben, you're not the only one trying to make a living here, and you don't own the idea of making custom mailboxes. It's not like you have a patent or anything. Anyone can make those, and besides, what's important is being able to market them—and that's something I can do that you obviously can't." He leaned back in his chair and put his hands behind his head again, taunting me to disagree with him.

I paced the office, my fists opening and closing. I had never suspected he would steal my idea, but that was exactly what he was doing. So, I did the only thing I could think of: I bargained.

"But listen, I'll give you an exclusive. Em and I thought it'd be fair to give you a yearlong exclusive to see how it goes. If you sell a lot and business is good, then we can extend the..." I stopped and scowled at his broadening grin.

"There's no deal, simple as that. I don't need you or your mailboxes. My business is going strong, and I'm expanding, and it's going to get even stronger, trust me. If I decide to make and sell mailboxes in my nurseries, I have every right to. I'll simply have Scott make the displays, and I'll advertise them to my list and keep all the money myself. It's the better business decision for me. So, if there's nothing else...?"

I looked down at the broken pots on the office floor, barely controlling my anger. In a flash, I watched my mailbox business, my summer with Em, and my future get flushed down the toilet. I fumbled and pleaded one more time, "Well, what about a two-year exclusive? You'd at least get to—"

His grin turned into a chuckle, and he shook his head. "You're hopeless. You don't understand anything about business, and you never will. So, you want me to spend, what, two whole years marketing and building up your business, so after *I* make it into a success, you can then come in and undercut my share and profits? That's the 'deal' you're offering me?" He closed his eyes and shook his head again, like he was talking to a nine-year-old.

"Tell you what..." He picked up the flyers and tossed them back at me. "Take your little mailbox and your little fantasy of a business and get out of my office."

He jumped up and hurried around the desk, passing so close that I prepared for impact. Instead, he brushed by me and went out into the store. I stood frozen, stunned, seeing black and shaking. I wanted to punch something and scream at the same time. I snatched up my flyers and the sample and stormed out to my truck. I didn't see him anywhere in the yard, but I did see Scott at the far end of the building. He caught my eye, winked at me, and then disappeared around a corner.

I jammed the truck into reverse and almost hit someone, slamming on the brakes just in time. Seething with resentment and fear, I sensed the swirl of dark clouds descending. Dammit! Ryan could have more mailboxes made in a week than I could make in a month, and I imagined his flyers and mailers blanketing the city and the islands. How the hell could I compete with that?

Without my dream, who would I be? Who would I become without my mailboxes? Just getting a dead-end job and working for a paycheck would be like a slow death, a misery that would infect my relationship with Em and the kids. No, I wouldn't let that happen! He wasn't taking this from me; I wouldn't let him. I'd find a way, no matter what.

When I pulled into my driveway, Toby was sitting on his curb.

"How'd it go with Mitch?" he asked when I approached.

Mitch? Oh, yeah... I hadn't told him about that yet.

"Not too good. He won't loan me the money."

He frowned and studied the curb. "What are you gonna do?" he mumbled.

"I'm going to find a different way."

"But what way?"

"I don't know exactly yet, but there are a lot of ways I can market this. Flyers, for one, around local shops and businesses. Even the library and supermarkets and stuff." I paused and added, "And there are ways I may not even know about yet, but they're out there, and I'll find them. It just takes faith."

I said all these things without thinking, without doubting; they spilled out of me as easily and as naturally as my breath. I *would* find other ways, better ways. I sat on the curb next to him and asked if he'd continue to help me until I found the right direction, and he smiled for the first time and nodded hopefully.

"There are two more samples I could use some help with. Wanna come over and learn how to do some of the delicate work with ash?"

He shot up. "Yeah!"

We worked through lunch, and I taught him how to use the router to do the detail work with the chimneys and rooflines. He did well, his smaller fingers clearing the wood shavings from the grooves of the roofline. He was serious and easily became absorbed in the work.

"I've been riding over to some of the new housing developments nearby. Have you seen the new houses yet?" he asked.

"No, I haven't. What do they look like?" I was surprised he had taken the initiative.

"The paneling is pretty nice, and there are even some second-story balconies."

"Maybe we should check it out some time," I said.

With his safety glasses on, his head bent over the clamped wood, his tongue out slightly as he concentrated, he reminded me of myself at his age. Who knew he had so much potential?

We finished working in the late afternoon, and after he left, I went into the den first, then peeked out back, looking for the angel. I didn't see her, but I did see Sadie lying against the house; she hadn't moved since this morning. I went over and sat with her a while, stroking her head and scratching under her chin the way she always liked it. She gazed up at me and drooled a little. I looked up at the trees and searched for the familiar sparkle, but there was no sign of the angel.

I went back into the workshop to clean up a bit, then collected and set out the four stones on the worktable. They were striking as they glowed a golden amber, their light flickering and bouncing off the tools and pieces of wood. The color of the stones merged with the colors in my mind, and I closed my eyes and embraced the lessons. I shifted my attention to the Source, and as I did, the familiar warmth of the angel surged through me. I grew quiet. Colors swirled through my garden, and as I pushed away the darkness lingering in the distance, I found and settled into a soft blue.

And in this center of calm and warmth, I became determined—and then empowered.

I deepened my breathing, and soon the baby blue faded to a translucent white. I remembered the angel beckoning me to bask in these colors and dwell on what I wanted, not what I didn't want. In this garden of peace, it was clear: Ryan didn't deserve my dream, and he would never have it, no matter what he did. The Source directed me now, and I believed, deep within, that I would find a way to make my dream come true. I just didn't know how yet...

Two phone calls came in quick succession. Bud called first with both good and bad news: he had found someone to take the booth, and that let me off the hook for the first and last months' rent, but he wasn't willing to refund the deposit.

"You gave me a deposit to hold the space for you, and I did. It's not my fault you reneged on the deal. Hey, you're lucky I found a replacement for you," he said.

And I *was* grateful. This would make Em feel better, and I was about to call her when the phone rang again.

"Hi, Ben," she began. "Just calling to check in. Any news from Bud?"

"Believe it or not, I literally just hung up with him. He told me he got someone to take the booth, so we don't owe the first and last months' rent."

"What about the deposit?"

"I asked for it back, but he said I paid him to hold the space, and he's done that, so it's nonrefundable. I guess he's right there, but at least we don't owe eight hundred more."

"No, I guess not. I'd have liked to get two hundred back, though; I hate wasting money like that. So, how did it go with Ryan today? Did he go for the idea of a one-year exclusive?"

"Oh, yeah ... Ryan." My scalp burned. "I know you're always thinking he's the answer, but guess what? Not only does he have no interest in promoting my mailboxes, he told me today he's going to go ahead and make them without me! Yeah, he said he doesn't need me at all. He'll have Scott make them, and he'll market them to his list with his mailers," I seethed.

"What?! *Ryan* make them? He can't do that! They're your mailboxes!"

"Well, he may not be able to make *my* mailboxes, but he's going to make some kind of custom mailboxes and promote them through his nurseries. Did you know he's expanding and opening another location?" I asked, barely keeping my anger down.

"How would I know what he's doing? Another nursery? That's ambitious. Where's it going to be?"

"How the hell should I know? He wouldn't tell me. Just kept that smug look on his face and then told me there'd be no deal."

"So, what are you going to do?" she asked.

"I'm going to find another way to market my mailboxes, whether you believe I can or not."

"That's not fair, Ben." She hesitated, then said, "Look, I know you'll find a way, but we need income. I mean, if you're not going to be marketing your mailboxes right now, this clears the way for you to get something full-time. How's that going?"

I spoke without thinking. "It's not going! I haven't had time to look. I've been too busy trying to get the mailboxes to work."

"Well, you're going to have a lot more time now. Maybe after the Fourth, there'll be more jobs in the paper."

I had been thinking about the upcoming Fourth of July. I really missed the kids, and Em and I hadn't spent a Fourth apart since our wedding night—still the happiest day of my life. During that warm evening on her parents' sweeping lawn on Bainbridge, with the wedding party in full swing, we'd wandered down to the waterside and sipped champagne, watching the fireworks over Seattle burst their reflections over Elliott Bay. It seemed like a lifetime ago that she had leaned her head on my shoulder, and I asked her what her dream was. She told me she wanted a home on Queen Anne Hill in Seattle, with a private music studio. She dreamed of having her own music tutoring business, of giving lessons from our home. I vowed to get her that home one day...

"We've never missed a Fourth together. How about I come up next weekend, and then hit the job search hard when I come home?"

A carefully controlled tone brought me back to reality. "We're not in the right space for you to come up yet."

"But it's not just about what *you* want. What about me? What about the kids?" I said, my voice rising.

"I'm thinking about the kids! They're happy for once! How do you think they'll feel when you and I start fighting? No. Now isn't a good time. Get yourself settled, find some work, and let's put the mailbox business behind us for a while."

That tone meant the conversation was over, and no amount of pleading or yelling was going to change it. I hung up, and frustration filled me. She was right, sure, but I had to see the kids, and I had to find some way to restore her faith in me—and in us. Her refusal to see me unsettled me even more than my fight with Ryan had.

I drifted to the doorway of the den, and my mood lightened when I saw the golden glow seeping through the windows of the little house. I felt the warmth of the angel's light even from here, our connection stronger than ever. I closed my eyes and sensed the power of the Source, embraced the wisdom in the lessons, and I knew: I wasn't going to take Em's advice of putting my mailboxes on hold, especially with Ryan conniving to steal the idea from me. I wanted to make my mailboxes a success now more than ever. I *had* to make them a success.

And I would.

Chapter Thirteen

Saturday, June 25, 1988

When I woke up, I went into the den, looking for the angel, when out the window, I saw Patty's Toyota parked in front of Toby's house again. Now what? Should I go over? No, I needed to find the angel; I was worried about her. And as I thought this, a whirl of light raced up and hovered in front of me.

"Where have you been?" I asked.

"Gathering energy. We have much work yet to do, and there are still challenges ahead. I have to be ready, and so do you."

I fixed us both breakfast, and we went into the backyard, the cool morning air crisp, the patio chair glistening with dew, the cushion slightly sticky. I nudged it out from under the shade of the umbrella and basked in the weak sunlight. The yard buzzed as insects swarmed and zoomed through the bushes, birds flittered and flirted and chased one another around the trees, and the vegetable garden glinted with a sea of hopeful green leaves.

The angel sat on a pot holder patterned with bright spring flowers. She blinked, and we tumbled into the turbulent river of colors in my thoughts, the blues and whites pushing against the grays from the day before. I frowned down at her, but she remained calm, the soft tips of her feathers glittering like a hummingbird's, her gleaming wings flapping lazily. She stared back up at me and gently raised her tiny eyebrows.

"Ryan is trying to steal my mailbox business, but I won't let him! It's *my* dream, and I must find a way to make it happen. I just don't know how yet."

The angel remained silent, and in my garden, she watched the familiar struggle as the blues and golds of my vision fought for dominance against the grays and blacks of my worry.

"I believe in my dream, I believe in you and the Source, but I just can't see my way through it. I don't know what to do—don't know *how* to make it happen." I longed for an answer, for a solution. I was ready, and the angel knew it. She glanced at the darkening colors, and they retreated. The colors around us lightened and pulsated with the rhythm of her breathing.

She faced me. "I can feel your belief, and so can the Source. You have reached the stage where your faith has become stronger than your fear, and from this place, your dream *will* find expression. The final secret to allowing your faith to lead you to your dream is contained in lesson five. Let's be quiet together, and I will reveal this truth to you."

We closed our eyes and took a deep breath together, and when we exhaled, it came:

"Take continuous action, and stay focused only on the why, not the how. Your role is to take action with faith, and let the Source find the most effective channel for its expression."

She paused and monitored my colors. My thoughts danced with questions, and a multitude of colors crowded into my garden. *But...*

The angel answered, "You don't need to know the *how* or the right channel; you just need to develop a strong enough *why* and continue taking action. This is the final work for you to do in your secret garden. You'll see it when you believe it."

"You mean I'll believe it when I see it? That's how the expression goes," I corrected her.

"No, it's the opposite, Ben. You have to believe in something first, before it can become reality."

My colors darkened, shaded by my confusion. "But I don't understand. Yes, I believe in my dream, but besides taking action, I need to know the right path, find out *how* I'm going to make it happen ... don't I?"

I watched the radiance of the white light sparkle and shine, expand and contract, as if the light itself were breathing.

"Ben, the laws of thought, of manifestation, move in silent grandeur, ever present and guided not only by your thoughts, but also by your beliefs. Your part has always been to envision the final outcome, to feel and believe each part of its expression —as if your dream has already come true. Once the Source has this clear direction, it will present you with different paths. As you go down each one, you'll develop distinctions that will help you bring your dream into greater clarity."

"But how can I know what to focus on if I don't know which way to go?"

"The Source has infinite resources, so it acts and moves beyond the limitations of what you know, and beyond the limitations you unconsciously impose upon it. A reminder to help you go beyond your limits is to *imagine better than the best you know*. Always keep reaching, with faith, beyond your boundaries. Remember, once you are ready, everything else will be ready, too."

We sat in the garden of my thoughts, and I merged with the

angel and perceived through her eyes. The Source blazed within and around us, and I fell into its all-consuming light, surrendered to its burning vision, and became one with its urgent need to express through me. My mailboxes were my destiny, and this truth resonated within and washed over me like waves caressing the shore. I completely let go and let in its divine power and purpose.

But which path did the Source want me to take? At first, I had hoped it would be Ryan and his list, but that had collapsed in the disaster of me getting fired. Next, I was sure that the booth at the farmers' market would be the way, but without the funds, that path had also evaporated. Today, I had sheepishly knocked on Ryan's door again, but without real belief, and not only was that still the wrong path, it got darker as I went down it.

Now I saw these experiences in a new way: not as failures, but rather as simply efforts, attempts, miscues. They weren't an end; instead, each represented a fork in the road of my ultimate manifestation. These were paths I had to try, learning along the way, and there would be others as I continued to do my part: acting with growing faith. It also occurred to me that as part of taking action, I had to refine my plans and prepare for all possibilities. I didn't want a repeat of my pitch to Mitch, where I hadn't taken the relative costs and size limitations of the market into account.

We sat still together and took in the endlessly changing colors. Navy blues, purples, deep pinks, pineapple yellows, and more floated in front of the familiar grays and blacks. These darker colors still hovered ominously, but for the first time, they appeared farther away. As I stared at them, I saw them for what they were: old ideas and limitations I had long believed in, coupled with my anxiety over not knowing how to manifest my dream. I withdrew any attention or belief in their ability to limit me, and like letting go of a balloon, they retreated and sailed far away.

In their place, waves of joyful emotions rose up, and my vision engulfed me: I was in my workshop with my dad and Toby, busily constructing several mailboxes at once. I envisioned an assembly line, with each of us focused on a particular stage of design: ripping, sanding, and assembling; detailing the tiny doors, windows, and chimneys; priming, painting, and varnishing; and finally rolling out new and varied beautiful mailboxes, one by one. It reminded me of Santa's workshop, all of us merrily working together. The air was heavily scented with the burnt smell of freshly ripped and sanded wood, mixed with glue and varnish. It was intoxicating, vivid and real, and I easily lost myself in this vision.

Next, I saw beyond the door of my workshop, and my vision wandered into the house, where Em sat playing our old upright piano, humming softly, her head tilted back the way I loved, her delicate features capturing the light from the window. Sammy sat beside her, singing along deliberately, her little forehead furrowed in serious concentration while following the piano keys. Dylan opened the door of the workshop, and the delicious aroma of a casserole floated in and mixed with the heady scent of the shop.

Dylan, helping in the workshop now, picked out some light grit sandpaper and began carefully sanding the roofline of a sample. Anxious to do more, he asked if he could paint the chimney today, and I told him we'd do it together. I scanned the workshop and became mesmerized by the five glowing stones blazing in front of five finished mailboxes: *Your Dreams Are Inspired by* the Source; Thoughts Are Things; Fear or Faith?; Focus on What You Want; and the fifth stone, a light taupe with soft shades of pale green and fawn, inscribed with the words *Vision the Why; the How Will Come.* The stones radiated a soft rainbow of earthy-colored light that danced over the mailboxes. I caressed this smooth fifth stone, its delicate colors luminous, and basked in my vision and the emotions attached to each part of it. The more I concentrated on my feelings, the more the color of my garden shifted to a transparent baby blue, the edges tinged with the softest whites.

I looked down at the angel. Her eyes were closed, and she rocked gently back and forth as her wings, almost at a standstill, shimmered with color. Slowly, she opened her eyes and mouthed the words, *"Imagine better than the best you know,"* and her golden necklace pulsed.

I closed my eyes and dived further into the emotions of my dream. Soon, I floated above the workshop, out over my house and neighborhood, and the angel flew by my side. Looking down, I spotted houses dotted with brand-new custom mailboxes—*my* mailboxes—each glistening in the dawn of a new day, sparkling like lights on an early morning Christmas tree. As we rose higher, I followed the highway stretching into Seattle, and I soared along with it as it snaked into the city. The sun twinkled off the skyscrapers downtown, and I watched the ferries ply through the deep blue sea to the wooded islands in the distance. I soared over the surrounding neighborhoods of Seattle and followed the hills up as they spilled out into First Hill, then Capitol Hill, and finally the Queen Anne Hill neighborhood.

We zoomed lower and swept past colorful Queen Anne Hill homes with their large porches and pitched roofs, and soon I spied Dylan and Sammy playing down the street with other kids in our new neighborhood. I imagined Em in her large front room studio, giving piano lessons, but this time on a white baby grand piano—the one she'd always wanted. I beamed with delight as she smiled and hummed the tune she was teaching. The house was light and spacious and all ours. I moved over to the garage at the end of the long driveway, and inside I found my new workshop, neatly organized with the finest hand tools and saws and sanders, along with newly built cabinets lined up like toy soldiers standing at attention.

From here, we climbed up over Elliott Bay, then out over Puget Sound, and as we crisscrossed the islands, there, too, my mailboxes lit up the forest like fireflies dancing through the trees. I swelled with pride and tingled with emotion, bursting with a bliss beyond color, beyond words. I felt the Source pouring through me, flowing, undulating like the shimmering sea below.

In a dizzying mix of emotions, I almost exploded with joy, but instead I landed back in my secret garden, with the angel beside me. We sat together, exhilarated, and the baby blue of faith and vision enveloped and cuddled us. The angel smiled up at me—and in a flash, we returned to the patio table with the angel sitting on the pot holder, her shining radiance pulsating, her warmth reverberating through me.

"This is the vision of your *why*. From now on, your goal is to meditate on it several times a day, to embrace and enhance it, and to maintain the blue color by bringing this vision into even more focus. Build it, color it with emotion, and make it burn with the fuel of your desire. Once you believe it with all your being, it will come true. The Source will find the *how*, the *way*, and it will be better than you could ever have imagined."

As the vision faded, a vague sense of doubt encroached. "But what if—"

"There are no buts, and no ifs. There is only the Source. This is the ultimate and unchanging cause and effect. Do not be distracted or worried by temporary circumstances; do not let unsatisfactory results take root in your garden. Whenever these false thoughts come, immediately shift your attention to the light of the Source. You may have to do this multiple times a day, but each time you do, you reinforce the truth of being, and this will strengthen and grow your vision. Retreat, always, to the vision of your truth within."

As the angel spoke these words, the light of the Source surged through me, and my dream returned and resonated once again. It all came together. Everything the angel had taught me coalesced into a beautiful order, an ultimate reality that went beyond the illusion of doubt, beyond wishing and hoping. It was up to me to maintain this vision and keep taking action, and if I did, the Source would find the best way to manifest it.

June 26 – July 4, 1988

I immediately developed this visioning process into a daily practice, and throughout the week, I retreated into my secret garden and spent time living in the emotions and feelings of my dream coming true. Each time I returned to the real world, it changed a little; the colors of the leaves, the airy blue sky, the complex whites of the clouds all appeared sharper, more radiant, pulsing with a hidden heartbeat. The world was becoming more alive, changing from a stagnant thing into something interactive and responsive to the color and emotion of my thoughts. I was becoming a co-creator with the infinite possibilities of life itself.

But I had work to do. The angel taught me to "act as if," to take continuous action toward the manifestation of my dream. So, Toby and I kept working in the shop. I sent him off with my Polaroid to take pictures of houses he liked, and together we started in on a couple of new designs. Doing so allowed me to expand my vision, and I incorporated new feelings and emotions into my dream. I tried to get him to open up about his mom, even asking him a couple times about seeing her car parked in front of his house again, but he just shrugged it off and kept working.

My dad came over a few evenings that week and helped with the expansion of the workshop. I often looked at both Toby and my dad working away, surrounded by the sights, sounds, and smells of the workshop, and I'd spontaneously slip into my garden, where my reality mixed with my dream. Each day, I solidified my vision, increased the vibrancy of my feelings, and grew more assured, calmer—even though the *how* hadn't shown up yet. After working together, we'd gather in the backyard, barbecuing and joking and taking in the early summer evenings.

I also continued looking through the classifieds for jobs, making it a daily practice, and my dad and I compared notes on opportunities we found. I sent off several more applications, mostly for carpentry work. My calls with Em and the kids changed in tone during the week as well. While I was bummed that we weren't spending the Fourth of July weekend together, I was grateful that the animosity between us had lifted. Em was relieved that I was actively looking for work, but most of all, she was encouraged by my new attitude.

"I don't know what's gotten into you," she said, "but it's been so good talking to you this week! You sound so ... well, happy. You sound like the old Ben I haven't had around for a while."

Finally, Em had calmed down and was coming back to my side. By painting the picture of my dream coming true, feeling the immense joy and relief of my vision being manifested, I was becoming more and more the person I had always wanted to be. I couldn't remember being this excited, this positive before.

The angel was always there. She flew around the house and darted around the back garden and between the brown bark and the heavy boughs of the trees. At times, she joined me in my secret garden, where day by day, I became more relaxed, more confident—even though I still didn't have clear direction on the *how*. But by the end of the week, that somehow didn't matter. To me, my dream had already come true in the most important place of all: in the garden of my thoughts.

Now, I was just waiting for the outside world to catch up.

Chapter Fourteen

Tuesday, July 5, 1988

The phone call came a little after nine o'clock that morning.

"Is this Ben Davidson?" a woman asked.

"Yeah?" Now what?

"This is Betty Ickler, down at the Big Box store HR department in Tacoma. I'm calling about an application you submitted several weeks ago. Are you still looking for employment?"

The Big Box store? Oh, dang, the application I'd sent! Relief and dread surged through me at the same time. The Big Box store was still the last place I wanted to work, but I tried to remain open.

"Ah, yeah," I said noncommittally.

"Well, we're conducting interviews for several positions, including one in the lumber department. After reviewing your application, we think you might be a good fit. Are you available for an interview later today?"

Scribbling down the information, I confirmed an appointment for two-thirty. She told me to bring contact info for any references I had. References...? I told her I didn't have any, only the experience I had listed, and she said she could always get those later if the interview process went to the next step.

I spent an unsettled morning in my regular routine, visualizing alone. The angel was off zooming around the forest, mingling with the insects and charging through the already bright and hot morning. Toby and I had already put in several hours on some samples, so after lunch, I sent him home and got ready for my interview. My thoughts wouldn't leave me alone. How in the world could the Big Box store help me with my dream? It couldn't. Frustrated and annoyed by the intrusion, I half hoped it wouldn't lead to anything.

The Big Box store had replaced a large corner of dilapidated strip malls and turned it into a sprawling complex: a huge, single-story warehouse-like building, bigger than any store I'd ever seen. A large open area lay to one side with a giant NURSERY sign over it. The store itself had large double glass doors on one end marked ENTRANCE, and on the other end, separated by rows of gleaming orange shopping carts and endless checkout aisles, was another large set of glass doors marked EXIT. The parking lot reminded me of the one at the the Seahawks Kingdome stadium: hundreds of parking spaces, each freshly painted with gleaming white lines. Dotted here and there were shopping cart corrals for people's returned carts. Impressive, but intimidating at the same time. They were going to put a serious dent in local business.

The stench of the newly poured asphalt hit me hard. Baking in the midday sun, it steamed a little and mixed with the Aroma of Tacoma, and the combined smell overwhelmed me. Taking short breaths, I scurried through the entrance and joined the back of a line of fifteen other applicants. What was that saying? *"Even if you win the rat race, you're still a rat"*? A rat baking on steaming asphalt. Thankfully, the line moved quickly, and the guy at the door, wearing an orange vest printed with THE BIG BOX—YOUR

NEIGHBORHOOD STORE in blue, checked off my name and handed me a clipboard with an additional questionnaire, then directed me to a row of seats inside next to the other rats.

After a forty-five-minute wait, during which I thought about leaving several times, another orange vest came over to the seating area and called my name. He led me down the towering, empty aisles of shelving that formed the interior of the cavernous warehouse, through a set of black rubber swinging doors, and into a long hallway with offices lining either side. He peeked through a slightly open door, found another applicant already waiting inside, and double-checked his list.

I was about done with all this. If he took me back to the waiting area, I was going to leave—but no, he ushered me into another room instead. Unfinished, stark white, and empty, except for a large beige folding table and two metal chairs across from each other, the small space looked like a police interrogation room. The only adornments were a loudly ticking clock and an orange Big Box store calendar, complete with tear-off coupons at the bottom, very much like Ryan's nursery calendars. Bored, I watched the long, slow arms of the clock inch by.

Fifteen minutes later, a burly guy strode in with lots of energy and thrust out his hand. "Hi, my name is Mike Donavon, VP of sales. Pleased to meet you." He glanced down at my paperwork and added, "... Ben."

Mike didn't have an orange vest on. Instead, he wore a short-sleeve, pin-striped light blue business shirt, khaki work pants, and shiny brown shoes. His eyes darted with a restless energy, bright and intense. His black hair, glistening with hair gel, was cut short and parted on the side. He looked like a linebacker stuffed into a business suit.

He moved to the chair opposite me and rifled through my application, then looked up and asked expectantly, "So, what do you have for me?"

What? He'd said "sales," but I definitely hadn't applied for a sales position. I had no idea what he was asking me. "What do you mean?"

His broad smile contracted as he glanced back down at my application, then his eyes shot back up at me as he asked, "What line of products do you represent?"

Products? I frowned and looked down at the table.

He reacted to my confusion and said, "I'm in charge of new product development and acquisitions. Aren't you here to discuss a new product for the store, or am I in the wrong interview room?" He quickly glanced down at his watch, then up at the big clock, and then at me.

Clicking, clicking, clicking, my mind rolled like the tumblers of a combination safe, and it suddenly sprung open. "Ah, well, yes! I do have something that would be a perfect fit for the Big Box store!"

My heart sped up as I saw Mike ease back in his chair. Thinking fast now, I said, "I manufacture a product I've been selling in the local market here for several years now, and with the exposure it could get through this kind of store, it could be a really big seller for you." I paused, waiting for a sign of interest.

"Go on," Mike said.

"Well, I have a workshop, and I take orders from local homeowners for a customized mailbox that is an exact replica of their home. They're individually handmade, and people love them. Once I make a sale in a particular neighborhood, their neighbors often want one as well. It's word-of-mouth sales right now."

Mike's face drooped a bit.

"But a display in a store like this could really help this take off." Mike didn't look convinced, so I quickly added, "Plus, it would give you a way to connect with the local homeowners market. You should see them; then you'd get an idea of how they could work here."

Mike's face shifted to neutral. "All right, let's see one."

My eyes got bigger than I wanted. "I ... I didn't know I'd be meeting with the VP of sales this first time, so, ah, I didn't bring any samples." Disappointment colored Mike's face, so I pushed on, "But now that I've seen the store, I'll create a custom display and sample mailboxes and show you both at the same time. Believe me, once you see the whole display and the samples, you'll want to carry them."

Mike checked his watch, made a quick decision, and gave me his card. "Call this number and talk to Shirley; she'll set something up. I'll have a look at what you've got, and we'll go from there, okay?" He stood up to go.

I jumped out of my seat, and his powerful grip reminded me of shaking Mitch's hand, but I gripped it right back and pumped it up and down. I glanced at the clock; only ten minutes had gone by. It seemed a lot longer.

Back in my truck, in a flash of inspiration, I searched for the Polaroid camera. A sample mailbox of the Big Box store itself would blow him away. The roof of the store was flat and made of heavy aluminum. I could spray-paint a thin piece of plywood silver, and it would imitate it perfectly. I took pictures of the orange carts in front, the glass doors on either side, and the open nursery area on the side. It would be perfect as a placeholder for newspapers, flyers, and magazines.

As I drove home, my mind wouldn't stay in one place. Like fireworks, it burst with color. This was better than anything I could have imagined! A booth at the Big Box store would certainly solve the problem of limited foot traffic. Unlike the farmers' market, the store was open seven days a week, and hundreds, maybe thousands of people would go in there every week! I thought back to what the angel had said about refining my vision, and that had certainly happened here: the business I could get would make all my dreams come true!

Back home, I dialed the number on Mike's card, and Shirley put me on hold while she checked his calendar. Coming back on the line, she said he had an opening on July 18, a Monday. Did I want it? Absolutely.

The angel zoomed onto my shoulder and placed both hands down to steady herself.

Shaking with excitement, I cried out, "I can't believe it! I met the VP of sales by mistake, and then I pitched him my mailbox idea, and he wants to see my samples!"

The angel studied me thoughtfully. "Mistake? There are no mistakes with the Source; this was synchronicity."

"What's synchronicity?"

"It's when the Source uses chance encounters, or even so-called mistakes, to further its grand design."

"Well, this is it! I feel it! This is exactly what you've been telling me about, exactly what I've been visioning and feeling in my secret garden! It's all coming true! He's in charge of sales, and this is going to lead to a huge display, bigger than what Ryan ever could have given me at his nursery. This is even better than I thought—just like you said!"

The angel furrowed her tiny eyebrows. "Ben, try not to outline the end result. The way is still up to the Source. You must remain open to what the Source has in store for you."

"What do you mean, 'outline'?" I asked.

"When you start dictating what the *how* will look like, you are once again imposing your limited will on the manifestation. Instead, you must remain focused on the feelings, on the *why*, and leave the actual ways and means to the Source, no matter how hard that might be."

"But he's in charge of new products, and this is a new product! He's got to see how this is perfect for the store," I said, though I didn't like what she was hinting at.

"And that may well be it, but always remember, your job is to stay in faith, keep affirming your vision, take action, and leave the results up to the Source. Your next action is to make new samples and meet with Mike again, right?"

"Right, but—"

"Right, and that's all. Take the next indicated action with complete faith, but leave the results of that action up to the Source, just like you've been doing," she said.

But I didn't want to give up on the results. The perfect opportunity had opened up before me, and I was ready to step through to the other side. I could already imagine the display, the mailboxes, the flyers, and I could envision the orders pouring in. Maybe I could even work the display and help sell them, too! My mind rushed ahead.

The angel followed my thoughts and peered into me. I could feel her concern, her love and support. She said, "Stay focused, take the actions, and let the path unfold."

It was hard not to "outline" as I charged ahead. I imagined many different scenarios, all of them good: Mike might want to start with a big display in this store first, then expand to other stores in the Northwest, or Mike might like the idea so much that he'd want to start in several stores at once—even across the nation! Another scenario had him hiring me as the marketing manager for the entire West Coast. It was all so amazing!

I rushed over and told Toby the good news, and he jumped and grinned and asked when we would start working on the samples. Next, I called my dad, and he said he couldn't come for the next couple of days, but he'd be there on Friday and throughout the weekend. When I mentioned the Big Box store, though, he grew irritated, still sore about losing his job on account of the mill not getting the contract, but he soon got caught up in my enthusiasm. We hung up, and I spent several hours in my workshop, reviewing the supplies I'd need for the store sample.

My next call was to Em. I couldn't wait to tell her the good news! When I called her, though, she sounded down.

"Hi, Ben," she answered listlessly.

"Are you okay?"

"Just a lot going on, I don't know..."

"Well, I've got some news that might make you feel better: I went on an interview today, and it turned out better than I could have ever hoped for!"

"Really?" She perked up a bit. "What happened?"

I told her the whole story, and about the upcoming second interview, and she said, "Wow, that's... I don't know what to say."

"Em, this is it! This is why the thing with Ryan didn't work out. It's why the booth at the farmers' market didn't work out. This is what I've been waiting for and working for these last few weeks. It's gonna be huge. It's just what we've always wanted!"

Em said cautiously, "Well, it sounds good, but he hasn't seen the mailboxes yet and hasn't actually said he wants to feature them, right?"

"Not yet, but don't you see? This is exactly how I envisioned it. This is my dream coming true. I can feel it!"

"Well, I'll keep my fingers crossed, but just don't get too ahead of yourself, okay? Let's see what he says after you show him your mailboxes."

Em's attitude deflated me a bit, but my enthusiasm remained steady. And besides, she didn't know about the angel, about synchronicity, about all the work in my secret garden. But I'd show her.

I pushed on, "I know this is it, and you just wait. Monday the eighteenth, it's all going to work out for us."

I was too excited to listen to anything else she might say, so we chatted briefly about what she and the kids had been up to, and then we promised to talk soon.

After we spoke, I tried to hold onto the good feelings I had, but some fear and doubt crept in. Both the angel and Em seemed supportive, but they were also cautious and warned me not to get too far ahead of myself. I searched my garden for colors and found a steady shade of blue, with a hint of lilac at the edges. Gray clouds lingered in the distance, and I wondered, just for a moment, what would happen if Mike didn't like the idea.

Naw, that wouldn't happen.

By early evening, I checked on the angel and found her sitting on the floor in the den, her inner light dim, her wings hanging limply down her back. She leaned against Sadie, holding the dog's ear, which glowed a deep amber yellow. Oreo lay on his pillow, gazing over at them. The angel studied me, her delicate lips shut tight, and nodded for me to sit next to her. Sadie's eyes were closed, and she lay still, barely breathing.

"She doesn't have much time left."

Shivers ran down my spine, and my heart sped up.

"Her transition is almost complete," she said, gently pressing Sadie's ear. I wondered why she was doing that, and she sensed this. "I'm accessing Sadie's memories of her life with you and your family. It's one of the ways I'm able to learn more about all of you and about Sadie. By replaying each memory, Sadie gets to relive her life again, and she feels each moment of joy she's spent with you and the kids. Even though her energy wanes, she looks forward to this precious time we spend together."

"How is she feeling right now?" I asked.

"She misses the kids and Em so much, but by living in those memories one last time, she's comforted to no end."

But I didn't *want* Sadie to go. My colors shifted to dark gray with my sadness, and the angel interrupted my thoughts once again.

"Don't be sad, Ben. Transitioning is a miraculous process—a rebirth, really—and Sadie is in a deep state of peace and acceptance now."

I touched Sadie's ear and glimpsed a portion of her memories, and the unconditional joy in them washed through me.

"Wow, the feelings, the memories are so real! How can you access memories like that? Can you do it with anyone?"

"With any living creature."

We sat like that for a while, and I experienced some of the joy of Sadie's life with us. There was the time in the backyard when Dylan had chased Sadie around with the garden hose, and the time she'd brought back a stick so big that Sammy couldn't even throw it for her. We had laughed so hard when Sammy tried. In doing so, I got to relive that joy myself, and soon I was overcome with longing for my family, and with sadness that we wouldn't be creating any new memories with Sadie after this summer.

Later in the evening, the angel flew into her little house and nuzzled down for the night, and soon afterwards, the light from inside dimmed. I helped Sadie onto her sleeping pillow and spent time with her, stroking her head gently and talking to her softly. She moved her head from side to side so I could scratch behind each ear. Her eyes were moist, and so were mine, and my heart ached when I thought about how the kids would react. After a while, she became still, and her breathing evened out.

As I brushed my teeth, I reviewed the day. It had been a really good day with Mike and the Big Box store, but it had been a sad day with Sadie as well. It seemed unfair that the same day could hold both major promises and major challenges. I gazed into the mirror and wondered how everything would turn out, how far I'd come, and what the Source had in store for me and my family. I had a lot of work to do to prepare for my meeting with Mike, and I kept my mind and colors focused there, making list after list of things I had to do to for the opportunity ahead. This time, I'd be prepared.

Chapter Fifteen

Sunday, July 17, 1988

The last week and a half had been a whirlwind of activity, and we had much to do to be ready for my presentation with Mike. I hadn't realized I needed so much help until I had it, and I couldn't have accomplished even half of it without both Toby and my dad. Having them working beside me, bantering about ideas, strengthened the action part of the vision I'd been painting in my secret garden.

On the third day of working together, my dad asked, "So, how are you going to display the samples for Mike?"

I hadn't given this much thought. "I guess I was thinking of just putting them on a table, you know, with the flyers in front of them." My shoulders fell as I said this, though; the small table in the interview room probably wouldn't hold all the samples and flyers.

"I have a better idea. Why don't you use the booth structure we made for the farmers' market? You told him you wanted to make a display, and you've still got the façade that looks like a house, so why not make a small frame for it, and you can then put folding tables inside the booth and set the samples up on the tables?" He paused and put his finger to his lips. "What you can do is simply set up the whole stand by attaching it to the end of one of the aisles you told me about, and that way, it'll give him a good idea of what the actual display would look like for customers entering the store." He paused again and then added, "Toby and I can come with you, set up the booth and tables, and help you carry in the samples and set those up, too. It'll make a real impression."

"That's an awesome idea! In fact, I'll paint the booth so it matches the orange-and-blue color scheme of the store, and with a few adjustments to the frame, you're right, I could attach it to one of the aisles and make it blend in perfectly!"

Toby showed up every day right after breakfast, and he no longer asked for direction from me. He simply came in, grabbed his work apron, fastened it securely, and then resumed the part of the project he had left off with the day before. He listened carefully to each suggestion my dad had, and after hearing about the façade, he reached for something in a stack of papers he had brought in.

"Why don't you redo the flyers so they have the Big Box logo at the top, so it looks like they're from the store, too?" he suggested.

"But where would I get a copy of the Big Box logo?" I asked him.

"You can use this," he said and handed me a flyer about the grand opening of the store.

"Holy smokes, where'd you get this?"

"It was in the paper the other day. They're sending out flyers now, announcing the opening."

A tinge of guilt washed through me; I hadn't even thought about looking through the classifieds. Once again, though, Toby's growth shone through, and I was proud of him. Together, their ideas were spot on, and each time they came up with something, another piece of the puzzle, of my dream, fell into place.

The Big Box mailbox turned out the best. It was a perfect replica of the store, with the exact colors, sliding front doors, and aluminum roof, and we'd even found little shopping carts at the craft store, which we painted orange and arranged in a row between the front doors. This alone was surely impressive enough to get Mike on board!

During the week, with Toby and my dad working alongside me, the vibrancy and color of my thoughts improved as they fed off the energy and atmosphere in the shop: saws and power tools buzzing, the sticky aroma of glue and stain and paint, the friendly joking between us, all accompanied by a music mix of Neil Young and Bob Dylan. My dad even brought over a Roy Orbison tape and crooned along to the song "Only the Lonely," which turned Toby's cheeks red as he giggled. I made ham-and-cheese sandwiches for lunch, and we took breaks on the back patio, painting bigger and bigger scenarios of how this could all go. After Toby went home, my dad would stick around in the evenings, and we'd share some beers and talk like we used to all those years ago: close, open sharing, the kind that had ended when he went to work at the mill.

"I never thought they'd let me go," he said one night. "How they could cut a man off like that, so close to being vested... I just don't get it. I won't forget it, and I'll never forgive them for it."

I remained silent and let him talk.

"There's no work out there—not for someone like me. Hell, I'm too old to haul lumber around a construction site, and too old to work for starter wages elsewhere."

My heart sank, hearing my dad sound so defeated, and I said, "When Mike says yes to my business, I'm going to ask him if you can work with me on it, too. Even Toby."

My dad raised his eyebrows. "Oh, yeah? You think? Well, wouldn't that be something?"

"It will be, you'll see."

"Yeah, well, I'll believe it when I see it."

"No, you'll see it when you believe it. Like I do."

My dad took a pull from his beer, patted his pocket for smokes, and chuckled. "You keep saying that, but I still don't get it. Whatever you say, though."

One evening, we had been talking in the kitchen, and I had my back to him while finishing up the dishes. When he didn't answer my question, I turned—and he was headed for the den! I hurried after him, and when I caught up, he was standing over and peering at the angel's little house. My heart froze. I rushed up beside him, and my heart only began beating again when I saw that she wasn't there. He stared at the little house, which thankfully had the roof attached, and asked if we were going to finish this sample as well. I shook my head, and he then looked over at Sadie.

Sadie had had a particularly bad week, and for the last few days, she had hardly touched her food. Each day when my dad arrived, he'd gently pick her up and carry her out back to rest beside the house, and then he'd bring her back in each evening. He went over to her, and she didn't even have the strength to lift her head, so he just sat next to her. I sat opposite him, watching as Sadie took short, shallow breaths. My heart broke seeing her like that.

"I remember when you got her." My dad slowly stroked her

head, and her tail limply brushed the floor. "She's been a good dog to you all."

"She's been a good dog, for sure, and the kids love her. They grew up with her. I'm sad they aren't here to say goodbye to her. Do you think I should go get them and bring them home to see her one last time?"

"Naw. Won't do any good for them; they're too young to see death up close like this. Let them have their nice summer, and when she goes, you can tell them she's in doggy heaven, waiting to see them another day," he said.

He continued petting her, and our presence seemed to ease her breathing. We sat quietly across from each other under the light of the small lamp next to the couch, and I thought about the work the angel had done with Sadie. God, I wanted to tell him about her. But where would I even begin? She had been a shock for me in the beginning, and I could only imagine what my dad would think of it. After a while, he went out for his last cigarette of the day, and then I walked him out to his truck.

It was a perfect July evening, full of the warmth of the day and still light outside, even though the sun had long since slipped down. My dad glanced back at the garage, took a final drag on his cigarette, and reached into his truck to stub it out in the ashtray. He stood staring off into the distance, and it seemed like he didn't want to go. Finally, he reached out his hand and stiffly shook mine in what felt like an odd gesture.

"Son, I'm proud of you. You didn't give up on your dream, and now it's all coming true. I know how much you want it, and God knows you deserve it."

I looked up at my dad's slightly defeated yet sincere face. With the way things were going for him, I could only imagine how he felt. I vowed to myself that I'd find room for my dad in my dream as well.

"We both deserve a break, and I believe the Big Box is it," I said.

He stood awkwardly for a moment, opening his mouth, but then just nodded. Then he got in his truck and pulled into the street, and I watched as the taillights disappeared around the corner.

During the evenings, the angel joined me in my workshop while I cleaned up, and she flittered around as I checked the clamps and lined up the small pieces of window molding and trim for the next day's finish work. Together, we'd arrange the five stones, lining them up against the completed mailbox samples, and she'd sit on the counter as the lights from the shining stones rose, flickered, and fell in unison with the rhythm of her breathing. The stones' dim glow glinted against the fringed plume of her ivory-white body, each tiny feather tinted with subtle yellows, greens, and light pinks. Her beauty was sublime in these quiet moments, and I breathed in the magical scene before me and concentrated on the lessons inscribed on each of the five polished stones:

> The light salmon-colored first stone, with its mix of earth-toned rose and orange:
> *Your Dreams Are Inspired by the Source*
>
> The second stone, light brownish-yellow with playful tints of pink and white:
> *Thoughts Are Things*
>
> The serious, dark charcoal gray, almost black third stone:
> *Fear or Faith?*

The gleaming violet fourth stone, with its pale hues of red and blue:
Focus on What You Want

And the fifth stone, one of my favorites, a light taupe with soft shades of pale green and fawn:
Vision the Why; the How Will Come

I meditated on each of these lessons, measuring in both feeling and color how far I'd come, how much the angel had changed my consciousness, and how these truths had become my truths. I also spoke with Em, and often with Sammy and Dylan, several nights that week. I ached and wished I could be with them. We arranged for me to come up Friday, July 22, after my meeting with Mike.

The only thing that colored these calls darker was Sadie.

One night Em asked, "How's Sadie doing?"

"Oh, Em, not well. She's not eating much."

"Should you take her to the vet?"

"I don't think that'll help. Besides, she's so weak. She doesn't seem to be in any pain, and I don't want to put her down; I want to be with her."

"I wanna be there, too! I'll bring the kids down, and we'll—"

"I've thought about that, but it wouldn't be good for the kids to see her like this. She's barely opening her eyes now, and it would just upset them. I don't want that to be the last memory they have of her; I want them to remember the better days. I say let them keep those memories."

"Oh, Ben. I don't want her to die alone. I'll come down myself. I can come tomorrow—"

"Tomorrow I've got my pitch with Mike. How about Tuesday?"

"Good. I'll catch the early ferry, and I'll be there by noon."

I briefly thought about the angel, but I knew she'd stay away ... or would she?

"That'd be great."

Em remained quiet, and I thought she was still thinking about Sadie. But then she said, "Ben, I know you're hopeful about the meeting with the Big Box store, but I ... I—"

"Now, don't worry, Em, it's all going to happen. In fact, it's all happening right now. This will be the best thing for us," I assured her.

"I know, and it all sounds so good, but..." She hesitated. "I just don't want you to be let down if for some reason it doesn't turn out the way you want. I'm afraid, well... I don't want it to go back to the way it was between us, you know?"

I paused for a moment, and yes, I did know. "I have faith that this is the way. I believe this will work. This opportunity is what I've been waiting for, what I've been envisioning every day, and it's better than anything I could have thought of. Trust me, it'll all work out."

"It just seems too good to be true. I mean, I guess it *is* true; that's why he wants to meet with you. I don't know, I hope it happens is all," she said.

"Have faith. This is what I'm meant to do."

Sunday night finally arrived. Tomorrow, my dad and Toby would come over to help load the booth and the samples into my truck, and together we'd go and set up the display, and I'd pitch to Mike.

Everything was ready, and I felt sure that the world was now ready, too.

Chapter Sixteen

Monday, July 18, 1988

"Wow!" Toby said as we pulled up to the Big Box store. My dad whistled as we passed the outdoor nursery, which was now packed with potted flowers, an endless variety of shrubs, and assorted small trees in large containers. Stacks of fertilizer piled onto shelving reached over twenty feet high, and three orange-vested employees scurried back and forth, hauling out more. Two counters were set up inside the gates, and new orange shopping carts gleamed in rows. Flat metal pallets for heavier items were lined up, waiting for the many orders to come. I smiled smugly; this would put a serious dent in Ryan's business, and in his ego.

"I think before we bring everything in, we first go inside and figure out where to set things up," I suggested. My dad and Toby both nodded and followed me into the store.

The inside of the store had filled out as well. The waiting area had been replaced by rows of shelving that held all the supplies needed to garden around your home. Insecticides, lawn treatments, hand tools, buckets, and gleaming green garden hoses crowded the aisles. The rest of the store had now burst into life as well, each aisle organized with signs like PAINT, CARPET, HARDWARE, KITCHEN, their shelves bulging with every item imaginable.

I told the employee about my appointment at one o'clock with Mike Donavan. She brightened considerably and told me she would let him know I was here, but I asked her to wait a few minutes while we set up the display.

We hauled the parts for the booth into the store and assembled them in front of the first row. The orange of the façade matched the orange of the sign above it perfectly, and the booth blended right in as if it were designed for the space. Next, we carried the mailboxes in and set the sample of the Big Box store in front on the right side of the display, and the two-story blue Craftsman on the other side. They sat on large outer shelves attached to the front of the booth and made an impressive pair. We then lined up the other samples along the sides of the booth on the inner tables. Finally, I brought the flyers in and laid them out, and they also looked like they were made for the store, thanks to Toby's suggestion of putting the Big Box logo at the top. Once finished, all three of us stood back and admired our work. It looked fantastic!

The employee came back and asked if we were ready. I glanced at my dad and Toby, who both smiled, and I asked if Mike could come out to see the booth. She left, and Toby and my dad wandered over to the gardening aisles, making sure they faced the booth, so they could judge his reaction from a distance.

Within minutes, Mike came marching over from the far end of the warehouse, looking exactly like he did a couple of weeks ago: short-sleeve pin-striped business shirt, the same khaki slacks, hair parted the same way. His stride had a purposeful, forceful gait, and he wasn't smiling. This put me on guard for a moment; maybe I should have followed the woman into the back offices, as I had done before. Reaching the end of the aisle, though, he stuck out his hand. "Good morning again."

Then he glanced to his right and noticed the display for the first time. He did a double take and moved to take a closer look. Scanning the booth, his eyes flittered from the Big Box store replica to the Craftsman, and then over to the other mailboxes. He walked around the sides of the booth, examining them all, then stood in front, grinning and gazing down at the Big Box sample. He turned and said, "Did you make all these yourself?"

I quickly moved over to the Craftsman house and pulled open the front. "Yep! And this is where the postman puts the mail."

Mike peered into it, and then I went over to the Big Box store sample and opened the front of it.

"Ah..." He nodded.

I pointed out the open nursery area on the side of it and said, "This is where the magazines and larger envelopes go."

Mike stepped over to the other samples, opening and closing their fronts, and saw that each mailbox had a red metal flag on the side. He lifted one up and said, "I see. Very clever!"

Warmth pulsed through me, and I relaxed and slowly let out a long breath. I stepped back to let him take in the whole booth and quickly stole a look over at my dad and Toby. They flipped me a quick thumbs-up, and I turned back to Mike. He walked into the booth and carefully examined the details of the mailboxes and shot questions at me: How did I make the roofs? What about the chimneys? Where did I get the parts for the little doors and windows? I explained each process in detail, and he nodded thoughtfully. I handed him a flyer and showed him how they could be used to collect people's information, as each had a tear-away section for filling out contact information. The flyers were made for the homeowner to take the other part with the pictures and description of the mailboxes home with them.

Mike examined the flyer and nodded. "Very impressive."

I smiled and began breathing normally.

"So, how long have you been marketing these in the community?" he asked.

I hadn't expected this question and tried to think of the right answer. What was he really asking me, and what did he want to hear?

"I've had a small display at a local nursery for a couple of years, and I've been marketing them there. I've also thought about opening a booth at the farmers' market, and maybe even a stall at Pike Place Market, but so far, I haven't decided on which way to go yet."

"How long have you been making these, and how many have you sold to date?"

Dang! Another hard question I didn't know how to answer correctly. I went with the truth, dressed up as positively as I could make it. "I've been making these since high school, and on and off, I've probably sold about two hundred or so."

"Over how long a time period?" he persisted. He wasn't smiling anymore.

I frowned. "About ten years, I guess."

He looked away from me and back down to the flyers on the table. Once more, he went over to the intricately designed blue Craftsman, opened and shut the front of it, and then stepped back. "These sure are beautifully built... But let's talk in my office." He turned and headed down the aisle, and I followed without casting a glance back toward my dad and Toby.

In the white interview room, the interrogation continued. He sat down opposite me, put the flyer down on the table, and leaned back, interlacing his hands behind his head. He began with "So, how do you see yourself marketing these across the chain of Big Box stores nationwide?"

I gasped at the prospect of national exposure, and the thought intimidated me. I stared at him, and he must have seen the deer-in-the-headlights look on my face.

"How do you go about making these, for example?" he asked.

I explained how I planned each mailbox, starting with taking photos and getting an idea of how intricate the homeowner wanted their mailbox to be. Next, I explained the process of making and assembling them in my workshop. He then asked how long it took to make a mailbox, and when I told him two to three days, he frowned. I could see where this was going, and I didn't like it. The small room grew warm, and the plain white walls reminded me again of a police interrogation room.

Mike finally said, "I won't tell you I don't like them. They're really unique. Heck, when I get a home here, I'll be the first to order one from you. What I'm trying to wrap my head around, though, is how to scale this to accommodate the number of orders we could get nationwide. That's if it actually took off, and we got enough orders to start with here." He leaned forward and folded his arms across his chest.

The second hand on the clock sounded like it had been hooked up to an amplifier.

Mike continued, "Now, the second part about getting orders, that's a concern. You see, the majority of our in-store purchases are made by residential do-it-yourselfers who want a low-cost solution to common household jobs. They're weekend warriors looking to save a buck. That's our core bread and butter. I'm not at all sure they'd buy a..." He scanned the flyer and noted the price. "... a two-hundred-to-four-hundred-dollar custom mailbox, when they already have one that works just fine."

He paused when he saw the disappointment on my face, then quickly continued, "I'm sure we'd make a few sales. I mean, again, they're beautifully constructed, and for the right buyer, some would sell, no doubt. But how many is the question." He paused again and considered his next words. "You see, we buy in bulk. We price low, package big, and make our margins on volume. I just don't see a lot of volume here. I don't see the scalability."

He stared at me, searching for an answer, or even a rebuttal, but I had none. He went on, "And as for the first part, the production of these, if it takes you two or three days to make one, and say we get an initial order of... Well, if we did a limited release across our ten West Coast stores, an order of, say, a hundred —how would you handle those? You mentioned that you take several pictures of each house first, so, what about the logistics of getting, what, four or five hundred pictures sent to you? All these would be custom mailboxes with different-size windows and doors and garages. I mean, are you set up to handle that kind of volume and diversity? How long before you're backed up for months with so many orders?"

I gulped and wiped the sweat from my forehead, and my lower back prickled, but I resisted reaching back to scratch it. I sat staring at Mike, much as I'd stared at Mitch, and at first I didn't know what to say.

Finally, I asked, "Well, what if we started small, like with just this store, to see how they sell?" He creased his brow, and I kept going. "I could get some help in making these, from my dad and Toby, and if they do sell well, I could enlarge my workshop. Heck, I could hire some workers and scale up as the orders came in, even expand as we brought more stores on—"

I stopped as he shook his head and pushed the flyer back to me. "That's not how the store operates. We're looking for scalability of concept, looking for ways to sell in volume across our national footprint, and with the time and labor involved with these, I just don't see it. Besides, this is now outside of my purview anyway. I've been promoted to the pro market section of our stores and won't be dealing with residential any longer. The pro market is made up of professional local builders who need material in bulk for new housing projects and other building construction. It also serves local contractors who need lumber and supplies in bulk. The pro market is where we make our money: higher margins, larger orders, and that's where the real growth of our nationwide expansion is."

He could see what I was thinking and added, "Brandon, the new VP of the residential market, will have the same thoughts on this that I have, so there's no use pitching to him. I'll run it by him, but I wouldn't get my hopes up."

Mike glanced up at the clock, pushed his chair out, and stood. "I'm sorry to disappoint you, but that's the way it is."

He extended his hand, and when I took it, a bolt of charcoal colors coursed through me. Numb on the inside, my knees weak, I followed him to the office door. As I stumbled through, he offered, "There's always a way to get a good idea done, and this is a good idea. It's just not a fit for us. But don't give up on it." Then he turned down the corridor and disappeared into an office at the end.

My scowl told Toby and my dad that it hadn't gone well. "What happened?" they said at the same time.

"He said no, that's what happened," I said flatly.

Before they could launch into their questions, I said, "Let's pack this up, and I'll fill you in on the ride home."

We broke the booth down in silence and lugged it, piece by piece, back to the truck. Then we collected the samples, loaded them, and secured everything. Slowly, I pulled out of the massive parking lot and headed home. The atmosphere in the little cabin of the truck was tense, and my dad kept glancing over at me. He lit a cigarette, blowing the smoke out his window, and finally asked, "So, what did he say?"

"He said I couldn't scale the production of these to meet the hundreds of orders we might get."

"*Hundreds* of orders?" my dad said, his eyebrows arching up.

"Yeah, and that's just with the West Coast stores!" I growled. My frustration got the better of me. Why hadn't I thought of that? I thought the problem of not having enough foot traffic and orders had been solved; why hadn't I considered the fulfillment of all the new orders I would get?

My dad, ignoring my mood and trying to be helpful, said, "Well, what about hiring a whole crew to make these, like ten or twenty people? There's a bunch of guys from the mill still looking for work—"

"Woodworkers?" I snapped at him. "Do they know how to make mailboxes? And how are we going to pay them?"

Heat jetted across my face, and I instantly felt ashamed for jumping on him like that. He stirred awkwardly, glanced back out his window, lit another cigarette, and fell quiet. Toby shrank into his seat and stared straight ahead, nervously rubbing his fingers together, and I was left alone with my dark thoughts.

I stewed and fumed and fought for a way out. Suddenly, the angel appeared in my garden, and I calmed myself. I exhaled deeply several times, and with each breath, my frustration drained out of me. As my mind cleared, the white light of the Source surged in, and with it, determination. My anger gave way to courage, and soon a burning blue resolve flooded through me. This should have worked! I'd felt so certain about this—in fact, I still did. I had a strong urge to turn around, haul the Big Box sample back in, and pitch to Mike again, but I needed the answers to his hard questions. And I'd find them. I would.

Toby peered up hopefully, and my dad, now smoking a second cigarette, turned back from the window and searched my face. I stiffened and said, "This isn't over. It may not have worked out this time, but I'm not giving up. There has to be a way—I know there's a way! And I'm going to find it. I promise you, I'll find it."

Back at the house, Toby and my dad carried the booth into the workshop, and with renewed determination, I carried the samples in and lined them up on the counter. After unloading, I walked them to the front door, where my dad put his hand on my shoulder and said, "I'm sorry, son. I know how excited you were about this." Toby quickly mumbled sorry as well. My mind raced, searching for another solution. I told them that today just meant this wasn't the way, but it wasn't the end of my dream. I reaffirmed that I wasn't giving up and vowed to them both that I would find a way, and I meant it.

After an awkward moment, my dad and Toby left, and I retreated to the workshop. I paced like a caged tiger and searched my garden. I found that my colors were deep blue, but they churned like the sea. Above them, the dark clouds of fear were collecting, and I fought to keep them away. Questions bombarded me: How could this not have worked? I had done everything I had been taught to do. The image I held in my mind's eye was so clear, so real. I'd felt sure this would work, and still felt it should have. But it didn't; something had changed. And now what? All paths seemed closed to me. The farmers' market, Ryan, and now the Big Box store, all gone. What was left? How would Em react to this? The thought of telling her, of letting her down yet again, was unbearable. My mind chased itself in circles as I desperately fought for another way, but nothing came to me.

As my thoughts continued to spiral, I wavered, and the dark clouds swirling above my garden picked up speed. Once again, I hadn't had the answers to basic questions about my business. How *was* I going to scale this? I obviously hadn't thought this through—or if I had, I had still been thinking too small. *"Imagine better than the best you know,"* the angel had told me.

When Mike talked about the West Coast stores—*just* the West Coast—and about a hundred orders or more, that was so much better than I'd been imagining. I did have to think bigger ... but where to start?

Fear or Faith? In an instant, I made a decision and a commitment to myself: this wouldn't happen again. The next time I pitched my business to someone, I would have these answers, and I would let the Source direct me to them. As I thought this, the gray clouds dispersed, and the navy blue settled down and lightened in both density and hue.

Instinctively, I reached into a drawer, pulled out the five

stones, and put them in front of the sample mailboxes. I put the fifth stone, *Vision the Why; the How Will Come*, in front of the Big Box store mailbox. It glowed brightly before the miniature orange carts and reflected off the perfect glass doors we had found. I stared at the flickering golden light of the words, and all I could think of was that I still believed the Big Box store was the answer.

I really believed it.

Chapter Seventeen

Monday afternoon, July 18, 1988

The sun blazed high over the backyard, and in the distance, the rumbling start and stop of the weekly garbage truck lunged up and down the street, triggering the dogs in the neighborhood to yelp and cry. I needed to talk to the angel, to get her guidance and see her light.

I went outside to find her, but instead I found Sadie. There she was, lying motionless against the back of the house. My heart fell. I rushed over and laid my hand on her, but she didn't raise her head nor open her eyes. God, she was so thin and frail, her breathing shallow and sharp. I sat beside her, resting my hand on her rib cage, and gently stroked her fur, which was matted with sweat. My tears fell freely.

"Oh, Sadie, oh, girl, no..."

She nudged her head just slightly, trying to respond to me, an intimate, familiar gesture that let me know she heard me. I knew she wanted to nuzzle my hand as she always did, lick me one last time, but she just didn't have the strength. I cried even more at this, deeper this time, with the grief of a loss I couldn't begin to understand or accept. She was so much a part of me, of our family. I just couldn't bear to lose her.

"Sadie, I love you so much. Oh, I love you, girl. And Sammy and Dylan love you, and Em... We all love you. Oh, girl..." My voice choked off, and my eyes blurred. My heart was completely broken.

The angel floated down beside us and landed on the other side of Sadie's head. She placed her tiny hands on Sadie's ear for a moment, then withdrew them and furrowed her brow. "It will be soon."

I collapsed against the back of the house, weeping uncontrollably now, wiping my nose on my sleeve and gazing into the forest and down the trail Sadie loved so much. A new wave of sadness overcame me as I thought of walking down that trail without her. How could I ever do that again without breaking down at the memory of her?

The angel buzzed to the other side of me, and we sat on the cool patio, the three of us in the shade of the house, quiet and still. The angel put her hand on the coolness of my thumbnail, and we shifted seamlessly into my inner garden. It had shaded to dark blue, like the color of Puget Sound in the late afternoon, and it undulated around us, the slow, rhythmic waves of energy floating above and between us.

My sorrow burst into questions. "But why does she have to go? Why couldn't we have all been with her at the end? Why now? Oh, I'm going to miss her so much..."

The angel, her warm hand still on mine, her eyes soft and sincere, said, "Everything is transitory, Ben, and when our current form is finished, we all move on. Sadie is sad to be leaving you, too, but she knows she'll live through you, through the love you have for her, through the memories and joy she was a part of. She loves you all, and while she doesn't want to go, she knows how important she was and is to you. That love has given her peace."

With these words, a release of sorts loosened in my heart, though it was still heavy with loss. I knew Sadie would never leave me, not the essential part of her—her love for me and our family. I would always carry her with me.

I studied the colors above me and watched as the deep blue tilted into charcoal—a color that reminded me of Mike. Soon, my restless thoughts turned to the events of the morning, and a new loss loomed.

"Why didn't it work? All that time I spent in my garden—the colors, the vision, the feelings I had... I believed it with all my heart."

The angel gazed at me and said, "It didn't work *this* time, in *this way*. The Source, though, has power beyond your understanding, unlimited channels for manifestation. And if this wasn't the way today, then your faith will lead you to a better way. Do you still believe this, Ben?"

I relaxed as she said this, and despite my disappointment, I did. I truly believed everything the angel had taught me, everything I had seen and felt. And now I wanted it even more than before. After each setback over the years, I had been resigned to putting my dream on hold, to getting a job, to waiting and hoping. But not now. The Source, the miracle of the angel, the vibrancy of my vision, and the urgent desire to bring my dream to life overpowered any doubt and drove away thoughts of giving up or giving in to fear. I had crossed a threshold into true faith, and because I burned with the *why*, I knew there was a *how*.

But I was also frustrated and disappointed in myself. Scalability! The same issue Mitch had brought up, and I still didn't have an answer for it. Why hadn't I thought more about the volume of orders, about this being even better than I could have imagined?

All at once, the awareness came to me: perhaps I had been limiting the power of the Source by outlining, as the angel had warned me about. I was so locked in on my vision of a new workshop in Seattle that I hadn't been open to other possibilities. Maybe my workshop was only a part of the answer. Maybe my dad's suggestion of hiring some of guys from the mill could work out after all. We could definitely scale up the business with more help, but I hadn't seen it, hadn't even considered it, because I was so invested in the *how* as I envisioned it.

Merely thinking this turned the dark blue of my garden to the clear blue of a summer sky, and the soft white of the Source warmed the edges of the vastness around us. The angel glimmered at my side, her necklace shimmering with the Source's light, and said, "Keep building your vision of the *why*. Continue refining the parts of that vision, and keep taking action. Trust the Source to provide the right opportunity, and you will be ready."

We sat like this for over an hour, and in the glowing, colorful radiance of my garden, I surrendered again and again. Over and over, I fell into the mystery of the Source. I painted a picture of Em and the kids, happy in our home on Queen Anne Hill in Seattle, and of my mailbox business humming along and generating all the income we needed, and I filled up with the feelings of this vision alone. The various pieces of how I could scale this tumbled through my head: working out of my workshop with others, renting a warehouse space and hiring workers, hiring woodworkers to work out of their own garages, and more. But I resisted fitting them together. These were just a small portion of the available channels, the various *hows* I was aware of. Many more possibilities existed, and when the time came, I had faith that the Source would show me the way.

I emerged from my secret garden and back into the warmth of the July evening. The sounds and smells of summer drifted through the yard: the sweet scent of nearby gardenias crowding out the fading aroma, kids yelling and laughing as they chased and played and hid from one another, the chorus of birdsong from the finches and the screeches of the jays. The angel whirled her wings and darted off. She shot up to the top of the trees, rounded them, and zoomed back down, crisscrossing and flying so fast that she painted the sky, her colors dripping and sparkling down like fading fireworks.

I caught a glimpse of Sadie watching the show. She had raised her head, and her glassy eyes reflected the dazzling light. I turned to her and gently caressed her ear. "I'm here, girl." I cupped my other hand under her head, so light and barely warm now, and her tail feebly swished over the patio. Her head nuzzled my hand, and she drooled a bit as I held her. Tears clouded my eyes.

"Oh, Sadie, I know you can hear me, I know you can understand. I love you, girl. I love you so much." My nose tingled with tears, and my voice faltered again. I couldn't speak anymore; I could only hold her, love her, miss her.

Finally, I whispered, "It's okay to move on now. We know you have to leave us, and we'll love you still. You'll always be with us."

She closed her eyes, and her tail came to rest on the patio. Tears stung my cheeks as I flashed on our life together. The day at the animal shelter when we got her as a rescue, just a couple of years old, as frisky as a puppy, her whole body shaking with excitement at the feel of Em's touch. The early mornings, when she'd pounce onto our bed and wake us up with her wet nose. The long walks through the forest, and the joy she showed in fetching any stick I threw. And of course, her tenderness with both Dylan and Sammy, instantly accepting, loving, and protective of them. They loved her, and she adored them in her unconditional way.

Sadie's head settled into my hand, and I laid it gently between her paws and wiped away my tears. The angel, sitting next to her now, suggested that I bring Sadie inside and lay her on her pillow in the den. I carefully lifted her, and she was light as a puppy again, just fur and bones now. Oreo hurried over and circled my feet, then sat with his tail wrapped around his front paws, watching me intensely. He sprung up and followed me as I carried Sadie into the den, and he sat opposite her, alert and quiet, with a sleepy yet steady stare.

I lit a small fire, thinking it would comfort Sadie, even though it wasn't chilly in the den. Together, the three of us sat close to her, and over the next hour, the room dimmed, lit only by the flickering light of the fire. The crackling logs, the dancing flames... I must have dozed off, because when I awoke, Sadie had stopped breathing.

She was gone.

I sat in the stillness for a while, then gently moved her, along with her bed underneath, into the workshop, where I covered her with a thick wool blanket. The next day, I'd take her into the forest and bury her next to her favorite trail. I'd dig a deep hole, wrap her firmly in the blanket, bury her, and cover her with fallen leaves and the sticks she loved to chase.

Back in the kitchen, I fed Oreo, and he ate alone next to Sadie's empty bowl. The angel settled on the dining table, and I pulled up a chair. Together, we sat in silence. The quiet house seemed even lonelier than before, and I longed to see Em and the kids and wanted more than anything to talk to them, to hear the life and promise they held.

As if thinking about it made it so, the phone rang, and Em's bright voice asked, "So, how did your meeting with Mike go?"

My meeting with Mike! That suddenly seemed long ago. I wanted to be strong, wanted to hold onto the determination I'd felt earlier, but the weight of the day drained me.

I said simply, "It didn't go like I wanted it to. He turned it down."

Flustered, she asked, "What? Why?"

"He said it isn't scalable. He liked the samples—even wants one himself—but he said he couldn't see a big future in the residential market."

Em paused a moment, then started to say, "But—"

"And," I continued, "he asked me how I'd handle hundreds of orders—or more—if this took off across his stores. I didn't have an answer for him." The stab of defeat was sharp.

"Oh, Ben," she said. "I'm so sorry, babe."

She hadn't called me "babe" in a long, long time. It opened a chamber in my heart I had closed off a long while ago, and it made me determined to win back her confidence and trust in me.

"Don't be sorry. It just means this wasn't the way this time. But there is a way, I just know there is."

Her voice went quiet and soft. "We can talk about it tomorrow when I come down. How's Sadie doing?"

My heart broke open, and I teared up. "Oh, Em..." My voice faltered, and I mumbled, "Sadie died this afternoon." I choked up and covered the mouthpiece.

"Oh, no!" she breathed into the phone. I could hear her crying, softly at first. Then her words faltered, and between hiccupped sobs, she whispered, "Oh, Ben, no. Oh, no! I wanted to be there with her, wanted to see her, tell her..." Quiet sobbing through the phone mixed with the sadness of my own tears. My head clogged, and my nose stuffed up. I felt helpless and missed Sadie with a shared longing, and I wished Em had been here with us.

Silence, and then I heard her blow her nose. "Oh, Ben, I'm so, so sorry. Did she suffer?"

"No. No pain. We were with her here in the den."

"'We'? Was your dad there?" She sniffled some more and blew her nose again.

I caught myself. "No, just Oreo and me, and ... you know. We were there for her. I told her that you and the kids love her. She knew she was loved." My trembling voice died away.

"Oh, I wish I had come up today! I'll miss her so much, the kids will miss her... Oh, Ben." She paused, then asked softly, "Where is she? What are you going to do?"

"I wrapped her in her bed and covered her with a blanket. She's in my workshop now, but tomorrow, I'll take her to that trail she loved and bury her alongside it, so when we take our walks, we'll pass by her. Maybe she'll know we're near."

This triggered a new wave of tears from her, and I heard the thump of the phone as she put it down and blew her nose again.

"Oh, Ben, I just can't take it. I can't bear the thought that I'll never see her again. I just, I can't..."

"I know, I know." I tried to be strong for her. "I'm worried about Sammy and Dylan. This will devastate them. Should we tell them tonight?"

Em thought about this and said, "No, not tonight. I think you should wait until you come up on Friday. Tell them in person, and be here for them. That would be best. Oh, Ben... What a tough day for you! I wish we were all there together. It'll be good to see you this weekend."

"I could come up tomorrow and spend the week with you," I offered.

She hesitated, and the distance between us almost returned, but only for a moment. "Well, the kids have the whole week planned out. Sammy is going with my mom to a horse show tomorrow, and dad is taking Dylan fishing. They're both looking forward to seeing you on Friday, and so am I. You coming up early would be a bit of a disruption, and I'm afraid the news of Sadie would ruin a week they've been counting on... I hope you understand."

I did understand, and while I wanted to go up sooner, I could wait until Friday. "That's okay. I just want to see you and see them. I'll wait."

We hung up shortly after that, and I drifted into the den, fell onto the couch, and stared at the empty space where Sadie's bed used to be. My heart was dull, my eyes sore from crying. How would the kids take—

Plop! Oreo landed on the couch next to me, meowed sweetly, and crawled onto my lap and collapsed against me. I stroked him, and he purred deeply as we both focused on where Sadie used to sit. Not long after, the angel landed on the arm of the couch, her glow flickering and her wings moving slowly. For a long while, we all sat in silence, mesmerized by the fading embers.

Later in the evening, I laid my head on my pillow and sorted through the events of the day. Prominent among them were my feelings for Sadie and the loss of something I could never replace. It was too soon to process that, and each time I went there, my world crumbled, and a sadness beyond words—beyond color, even—threatened to engulf me. Switching to the matter of the Big Box store, I found that the anticipation and hope I'd had over the last two weeks had completely drained out of me, as did the belief and surety of feeling I had built up for it. Oddly, I didn't feel deflated, though. Instead, the feelings of defeat I'd known for so long were replaced with a strange stirring—a wonderment, even, an openness to what might come next.

Chapter Eighteen

Wednesday, July 20, 1988

The blaring phone woke me out of a colorful sleep a little before 6:00 a.m. I sprang out of bed and caught it on the fourth ring.

A soft, slurry voice said, "Hi, Ben. Whatcha doin'?"

Patty? Why was Patty calling my house at 6:00 a.m.? How had she even gotten my number?

"I'm sleeping, Patty. Are you all right?"

In a dreamy way, she sighed. "Yeah, I'm fine, all good here." Then a pause. "I miss you, Ben." Another pause. "Ah, I need to see you ... about Toby."

The robot from the TV show *Lost in Space* flashed in my mind, its arms flailing, its metallic voice spewing out, *"Danger, danger!"* I knew I should run as fast as I could, but Toby... I had just lost Sadie; I wasn't going to lose Toby as well.

"Where are you?"

"Downtown."

"Where downtown? Tacoma?"

Heavy exhalation. "No, silly, Seattle. Can you come over?"

My mind raced. Had Toby gotten into some kind of trouble? Why had her car been in front of his house lately? Had she threatened to take him? I knew I had to go to the large craft store, Kit Kraft, to get some supplies, so I needed to do some shopping in Seattle at some point anyway. Maybe I could pick those up and head off anything bad that was coming.

"I might be in town later today. Want to meet for lunch?"

"No! I need to see you now. Can't you come for breakfast?" she moaned.

My heart beat a little faster. What time did the store open on Saturday? Nine o'clock? I made a split-second decision. "Yeah, um, it'll take me an hour or so. Can you get to Briggs Diner on Spring?"

Silence.

"Patty, are you still there?"

"Yeah, um, where?" she mumbled, as if in a haze.

"Briggs Diner. We've been there before. You know the place —on Spring, near Pike Place."

"Yeah, yeah, yeah. When? How soon?" she asked.

I glanced at the clock by the bed. "A little before seven. Can you make it by then?"

"Sure. Hurry." *Click.*

The morning sun sparkled on the water as I approached downtown Seattle. The air smelled like the ocean, and seagulls made small circles over the docks. I alternated between worrying for Toby and about this being a bad idea. What was I doing meeting Patty downtown? Those thoughts mixed with the excitement and danger I'd always felt around Patty, but I stuffed them in the back of my mind and shifted to Toby and what might be going on. Flushed with emotions I'd buried long ago, I plunged ahead.

I parked around the block from the diner and checked the

time. We'd have plenty of time for some waffles or pancakes and coffee. Yes, coffee—Patty sounded like she could definitely use a strong pot of that.

I'd always loved going to Briggs Diner, and it seemed like it had been there forever. As a kid, I'd gawk at the black-and-white photographs showing off its history over the years, and what I loved most were the cars. While the building looked the same in each photo, what changed through the years were each era's cars: Pontiacs and Plymouths with big chrome fenders from the forties; sleeker, finned Cadillacs and Chevys from the fifties and sixties; and muscle cars, GTOs, and Mustangs from the sixties and seventies. In fact, I still dreamed about owning one of those GTOs.

Walking into Briggs was like walking right into a black-and-white movie from the forties. I imagined Humphrey Bogart sipping a cup of joe at the half-horseshoe wraparound counter with red-leather-topped stools anchored to the faded tile floor, and I couldn't help but drool, breathing in the greasy grill sizzling with bacon and eggs. I was hungry as soon as I opened the door. An ancient Bunn coffee machine was dripping a new pot on the counter, and next to it were two round glass displays filled with chocolate, glazed, and colorful sprinkled donuts. Dark wood booths lined the side wall from the front of the diner all the way to the back, and the first booth had just been cleared, so I took a seat facing the street. I slurped coffee and watched for Patty's Toyota.

After twenty minutes, two cups of coffee, and two donuts, I almost gave up and left. But then a white-and-yellow city bus pulled up to the curb across the street, and a pack of people poured out. As the bus took off, I scanned the knot of people, and there, dressed in torn jeans, sandals, and a light linen strap top was Patty. She cut across the corner and crossed when the light turned yellow, and even from this distance, her long strawberry-blonde hair appeared knotted and tangled. She looked like she hadn't showered in a few days.

She didn't see me at first, even though I was in the front booth, so I waved her over. She slid into the booth across from me and glanced around, flashing bloodshot eyes. Suddenly perky, she said, "So good to see you! How are you, Ben?"

A grumpy waitress arrived, wearing a pink apron with *Briggs* in red script on the top right pocket. She looked suspiciously at Patty and held up a coffee pot.

"Yes! Coffee is good," Patty said.

The waitress poured a steaming cup and set it in front of her. She left a menu, but Patty pushed it aside. I shoved my half-eaten chocolate donut over to her. She attacked it, chocolate smearing her upper lip, and she wiped it with the top of her freckled hand. Her fingernails were broken and dirty. I suddenly felt bad for her—worried, even.

"Are you okay? Where's your car?" I asked.

She wolfed down the rest of the donut, then picked up the sugar bottle and upended it, pouring a quarter of its contents into the coffee cup. She put a spoon in, and it stood straight up. She slowly worked it around, and when she had it the consistency she wanted, she took a big gulp and said, "Car got towed somewhere. I don't have the fifty bucks to get it out."

I thought of my savings and hoped she wasn't going to ask me to loan it to her. I wouldn't, that was for sure. Changing the subject, I asked, "Where are you living? I mean, you don't look too good. Are you okay?"

She shot me a look of anger, maybe even hurt pride. Then her face changed in an instant, melting, registering my concern. She smiled up at me and said, "No, I'm fine. Just going through a transition, I guess. How are you, Ben? How's Emily? Still with her folks?"

That was a loaded question. Geez, what was I doing here?

"Fine. Ah, you mentioned Toby... What's going on with him?"

Patty examined her empty coffee cup, then glanced over at the sprinkled donuts on the counter. "Can I get some more of those?"

I waved the waitress over. "Ah, could we get some more of those sprinkled donuts, please?"

"Sure can. What about breakfast?" She pointed to the menu in front of Patty.

"Naw, I don't need any," Patty said, shaking her head.

The waitress snatched the menu away, then promptly returned with the three donuts and slid them across to Patty, who devoured the first one. I waited for her to stop chewing and then tried again.

"So, Toby...?"

Patty seemed to be stabilizing after ingesting all the sugar. Her eyes cleared a bit, and still chewing, she said, "Yeah, well, I've been thinking. I think Toby should come live with me here in Seattle. I could get us an apartment—"

"Patty, what would you do with a teenage boy? You just said you don't even have fifty dollars. You're in no condition to look after him..." I hesitated while she ate her donuts and chugged her coffee. "Listen, you don't look so good. Are you still using? Are you high right now?"

Her face flashed with defiance: an addict's indignation. "You don't know anything about me. Sure, I like to have fun once in a while, and I'm allowed to. It's my life, and this is still a free country!" she snarled, and people turned and glanced over at us.

"Patty, I'm just worried for you is all—and your parents are worried, too. You need to get clean before you can even think about taking care of Toby. You know that." I reiterated, "I'm worried about you."

At this, Patty's eyes softened, and her frown turned naughty. She leaned across the table, and her loose top pinched open, revealing the tops of her breasts—no bra. I quickly returned my eyes to hers, but she had caught me looking. She took my hands and said, "I wanna get clean, I really do! I just, I mean... I'm lonely sometimes, and I just need a little relief. I won't be using forever. I won't. I just, you know, need a little help."

She rubbed my hands, and I slowly pulled them away. She looked up at me, hurt almost, before smiling a warm, soft smile and tilting her head. "I just need a little company sometimes, you know, Ben? We all get lonely, right?"

In one quick movement, she slid out of the booth, slinked over to my side, and scooted onto the seat, bumping me aside with her bony hip. I scooted over, too, trying to keep a safe distance between us. I didn't have much space in the small booth, so I put my hand on her bare leg, more to keep her away than as an advance.

That was a mistake. She grinned up at me and leaned in to whisper something just as the door of the diner opened, and in walked the last person I expected—and the last person I wanted to see.

Ryan.

He locked eyes with me, then lustily scanned Patty up and down, then trained his sharp eyes back on me. He smirked, winked at me, and made his way to the counter. I jumped in my seat and pushed Patty toward the edge of the cushion. "Listen, you need to go back to your side." I physically helped her out, but she wouldn't sit back down.

"What are you doing? I don't wanna sit there!" she yelped, causing the people at nearby tables to stop chewing and gawk over at us. Ryan and the young blonde waitress he was chatting up both turned, too, and they leaned on the counter, smiling, enjoying the show. My face burned. I pulled out a ten-dollar bill, slammed it on the table, grabbed Patty by the elbow, and dragged her out the front door with me.

She shuffled along, arguing and resisting, and we finally moved past the glass front of the restaurant. She yanked her arm away from me, stomped to a stop, and viciously spit out, "What the hell, Ben?!"

"This was a bad idea! I can't do anything to help you if you're not willing to help yourself. And as far as Toby is concerned, you're out of your mind if you think you can take care of him.

It's not even about him, is it? It's about you getting money, so you can keep using!" I shook with anger and glared at her.

Patty wasn't taking anything from me. In an instant, her street persona burst out, and she yelled, "I'll party any time I want to! I don't need anything from you! You go on back to your pretty house and perfect Emily! And I'll get Toby any damn time I want!" She balled her fists, stormed off down the sidewalk, and turned the corner, heading down toward Pike Place Market.

I glanced over my shoulder, but didn't see Ryan. Embarrassed and guilty, I took the long way back to my truck, hoping I wouldn't run into him. That was the last thing I needed. What the hell was he doing in Seattle? Was this where his new store was opening? It had to be—and that meant he'd not only tie up the Seattle market, he'd have easy access to the islands as well.

As I reached my truck, I stared out at the water and saw the ferries. I started the engine, a slight panic seeping into me. The islands. It made some kind of sense. People there had money; they wouldn't be shopping at the Big Box store. If he was making his own mailboxes now, he already had a list that included all the islands. I shook it off. Naw, that would be just too much of a coincidence. He had to be opening a store in Seattle; that made much more sense.

I skidded away, thinking back to Patty and her threat of taking Toby any time she wanted. That wasn't going to happen. I wouldn't let it.

I made it to the craft store when they opened, got my supplies, and headed back to Tacoma, trying to shake off the uneasy feeling from breakfast.

Toby was waiting for me on my doorstep. He jumped up as I pulled in.

"Where ya been?" he asked.

"Seattle," I answered quickly. Then I added, "Craft store, for supplies."

"Did you find anything for the railing for that top-story balcony?"

"Yeah, come in and let me show you." I led him into the workshop and showed him the thin railing the store had for a dollhouse balcony. Toby had found some new homes that had a second-story balcony, and we had begun working on a sample. He was more than just a helper now—a partner, really—and his eagerness for new ideas and his enthusiasm for the new railing lifted the weight from the morning. It also made me even more determined to protect him.

Right before lunch, Oreo came in and meowed. Toby led him into the kitchen to feed him, and when he came back, he said, "Sadie's bowl is missing."

A frozen feeling crawled up my back.

"Ah, yeah... Sadie passed a few days ago." I turned away quickly as my eyes began to burn.

"Passed?"

I turned to him, and he shifted uncomfortably when he saw my tears.

"Sadie died on Monday. I buried her along the forest trail, so we can say hello to her when we go for our walks."

Toby went rigid, and his eyes scanned the floor. Slowly, with a faltering voice, he mumbled, "Do Sammy and Dylan know?"

I wasn't expecting that question. "Not yet. I'm going up soon to tell them."

He looked up at the worktable and absently brushed some wood shavings away. "They're gonna be sad she's gone." He hesitated, then added, "They're gonna be mad they didn't get to say goodbye."

He turned before I could see his eyes, but from behind, I saw that his hand went to his face.

For the first time, I fully felt the pain and betrayal Toby had endured. I wanted to hug him and let him know he'd be okay, but I still felt weird about just having seen his mom, and mad, too. I doubled my commitment to help him in any way I could.

I tried to explain, "Sometimes things don't go the way we want. Sometimes we have to move on, and this was her time. She had a good life with us, and she knew she was loved." My eyes cleared. "It's just something we gotta accept. We don't have to like it, but it's a part of life. What matters is what we do in the meantime, what we do next. Like making this dream come true, like we're doing together."

Toby turned and scrunched his eyebrows. "Do you really think it'll come true now?"

I grasped his arm. "It will if we both believe it will. I'm not gonna quit. Are you?"

"Heck, no!"

"Then let's get to it."

We spent the rest of the afternoon working on the new two-story sample. After Toby left, I organized the workshop and thought more about the new homes that were springing up in the area. It seemed like new opportunities were coming up every day.

Em didn't call, and for some reason, that worried me. Thoughts of Ryan's glare and glee at seeing Patty and me stormed back into my head—as did my guilt. Thinking about Toby's reaction to Sadie dying and his comments about Sammy and Dylan made me miss them, and I longed to be with them.

I decided I needed to see them all right away. I needed to go up a day early—plan with Em how best to tell them, and make sure everything was okay. Suddenly, I was uneasy and wished I had gone up at the beginning of the week, like I had wanted to.

Chapter Nineteen

―

Thursday, July 21, 1988

I was anxious to get an early start for Bainbridge, but first I went over to Toby's to give him the key, so he could feed Oreo.

"Can I do some work while you're gone?" he asked eagerly.

"If you want to, but no power tools, okay?"

"Ah, okay." He frowned and looked away.

"I'll only be gone over the weekend, so if you run out of things to do, you can always scan the surrounding neighborhoods for more ideas. Oh, and just leave the mailbox in the den alone. That's someone else's that I have to work on when I get back."

I trusted that Toby would follow directions, and that the angel would keep out of sight. I knew she'd find her way outside using the doggy door to the backyard, and I also knew that she could do a lot more than I thought she could—just like she'd told me in the beginning.

I packed the truck and made it into Seattle in time to catch the 11:15 a.m. ferry, which would put me on the island a little before noon. Reaching the dock, I pulled up behind the line of cars already waiting to board, killed the engine, rolled down my window, and breathed in the salty sea breeze. Overhead, hungry seagulls soared in erratic circles, their shrieks echoing over the water. The sights and smells of the dock reminded me of the camping trips my dad and I would take on the islands all those years ago, and I relaxed and smiled, thinking about the weekend I'd spend with the kids. Except for sharing the news about Sadie, I looked forward to our time together.

The incoming ferry docked and disgorged its stream of cars, a mix of islanders out for their weekly shopping and people who had jobs in the city. I drove on, parked, and then followed the other passengers up the metal stairs. I grabbed a coffee and headed out onto the deck. As we pushed through Puget Sound, I scanned the view of downtown Seattle, the skyscrapers shimmering with the sun sparkling on hundreds of windows. It reminded me of the glittering angel, and I became lost in the colors of my garden and daydreamed of how things would turn out.

Soon the Bainbridge dock appeared, and the loudspeaker squawked for the passengers to return to their vehicles. I shuffled along with the others down the chipped yellow stairway and waited in my truck. With a soft bump, we arrived at the dock, and then the huge metal mouth opened and poured us out onto the island.

I followed the line of cars into the small downtown area, a section of neatly arranged restaurants and shops, including a small hardware store, a mini-mart, a florist, and a few retail shops along two short blocks. Right before I passed the lone diner, I spotted what looked like Em's minivan parked in front. Slowing down, I stared through the restaurant glass, hoping to catch a glimpse of her. And there she was, sitting at a window table—with Ryan!

Slamming on my brakes, I caused the car behind me to jump on their horn, which got Ryan's attention, and he glanced out at the street. Luckily, I had already passed the diner, and he didn't see me. I sped up, made a quick U-turn, and circled back around.

Ryan and Em?!

Was this why she'd been sticking up for him all this time? In a flash, my old jealousy from high school raged, and gnawing memories flooded back in: Ryan and Em in his silver Trans Am with the giant eagle decal on the hood, two rich kids thinking they owned the school and the future. I thought about their breakup after Ryan's parents died in the car accident, and then the day Em had sidled up to me in the cafeteria, asking me what I was doing that weekend. The chills of excitement from that day now mixed with the chill of jealousy I had never gotten over. Ryan and Em... Dammit, it couldn't be!

The parking spots across from the diner were angled to pull in nose first, and I found a spot a few spaces down and whipped in. I stalked down the sidewalk, fists clenched, and ducked between two cars parked on my side of the street. Heart pounding, I choked down the urge to run across the street and confront them. Instead, I crouched, watched, and waited.

They were seemingly having a wonderful time, two old friends, both of them laughing, with Em throwing her head back, making her hair fall to one side of her face, then tilting it the way she did when she was happy. Ryan was sitting up straight, leaning forward, almost jumping over the table to get closer to her. Em sipped her tea, Ryan drained his coffee, and they both pushed food around their plates.

I fumed and stewed with suspicion as I agonized over what to do. I almost ran across the street several times, but a recurring fear stopped me: had Ryan told her about seeing me and Patty together? My hand shook as I wiped my forehead, and I decided to wait and watch a bit more to see how this little date unfolded. The sun burned on my side of the street, and I squinted through the sweat to keep an eye on them. I stood up after a while and paced back and forth along the sidewalk, so people would stop giving me wary looks. After what seemed like an eternity, the waitress finally picked up their check—which Ryan paid—and they stood to leave.

Ryan held the door for her, and they spilled out onto the sidewalk. He had a toothpick dangling from the left side of his mouth, and Em, still smiling, stood awkwardly as they faced each other. If Ryan had told her about Patty, she didn't look upset; instead, both she and Ryan seemed uncertain as to how to end their rendezvous. They looked around, then back at each other, opened their mouths at the same time, then looked away again. I thought of all the romantic comedies Em loved so much, where the couple tried to decide whether they were going to kiss after the first date. Boiling now, I stood poised on the lip of the sidewalk. If they kissed, I'd jet across the street and knock the daylights out of Ryan.

After a few uncomfortable moments, they hugged briefly, and thankfully stiffly. Ryan went one way, and Em got into her minivan and headed down the street toward her parents' house. I raced back to my truck and followed at a safe distance, then hung back until she pulled into the tree-lined driveway and disappeared around a short cobblestone bend. Shaking with rage, I passed the house, pulled off onto a small side street, and screeched to a stop.

Calm down, calm down, calm down! It took several minutes

for me to just steady my breathing and stop shaking. Unbearable betrayal, laced with a burning fear, colored all my thoughts. What the hell was going on? I couldn't make sense of what I had just seen, couldn't justify it in any way. What did it mean? How long they had been meeting like this? And yes, this had to be the reason she was always defending Ryan! Ugly questions jumbled in: What did this mean for our marriage? Was she leaving me for Ryan? How long had they been carrying on this secret affair here on Bainbridge? Was this the whole reason she hadn't wanted me to come up with her on vacation?

And then there was Patty! What had Ryan told her about seeing us together? I shivered thinking about Patty sitting next to me when Ryan had waltzed in, his smirk and wink, and how he and the waitress enjoyed our little drama at the diner. Was he using this to squirm his way deeper into an affair with Em? I couldn't believe they were having an affair, but what other reason could Ryan have for being on the island at the diner with my wife?

As I gripped the steering wheel, my heartbeat quickened again, and a new thought pounded through my head. He could afford a house here, and Em was accustomed to this lifestyle. Was she sick of struggling to get by in Tacoma, with me being out of work and without prospects? Had she given up on me? On us? Panicking now and sweltering inside the stuffy truck, I could feel sweat soaking through my T-shirt. Even though I knew I should have gotten out to walk it off and cool down some, I couldn't contain my desperation any longer. I cranked the engine and sped back to her parents' house to confront her.

Driving through the perfectly manicured garden that hugged the driveway, I rounded the final bend, and Mitch's mansion dominated the view. The magnificent custom build, fronted with floor-to-ceiling windows and two huge white doors sided by colorful stained glass, still intimidated me, but my anger overrode these feelings, and I charged on. Sneaking to the front door, I could make out Em moving from one room to the next. I punched the doorbell, and moments later, she answered, wearing a white string bikini bottom and a light pink lacy top with red pull strings hanging on each side. She flashed a bright smile, but her smile faded to shock as she stared into my eyes.

"Expecting someone else?" I snapped.

She took a slight step back and stuttered, "Wha— What are you doing here?"

"You're my wife, remember? Remember our kids? I thought I'd surprise you a day early. Happy to see me?" I pushed past her and into the living room, half expecting to catch Ryan there, and I sensed for movement, but it didn't seem like anyone else was in the house.

"Where are Sammy and Dylan?" I asked roughly.

She shut the door and followed me in, closing the strings on her top. Quickly recovering from her shock, she answered, "They're out with my mom, at the stables. Ben, what are you doing here? I thought you were coming up tomorrow?"

"Yeah, well, I thought I'd surprise you. Surprise!" I taunted her, then moved into the spacious white kitchen with its stainless-steel refrigerator big enough to service a restaurant. I glanced up at the all-wood ceiling, pitched and perfect and painted white, the dream home of Big Man Mitch and his wife. I thought of his money and privilege and Em's upbringing, and this stirred my insecurities. My jealousy only grew.

She followed me into the kitchen and found her composure. "Why are you acting so weird? What's going on with you?"

I spewed it all out. "Ryan? Really? You're seeing *Ryan*? What the hell?!"

Em's eyes widened as large as quarters, then she creased her forehead. "You were *spying* on me? What the hell is with you, Ben?!"

"Oh, no. This isn't about *me* doing anything wrong—don't try to play that card. What the hell were you doing with Ryan? How long have you been seeing him? Tell me what's going on right now!"

"Nothing is going on! What are you even talking about? I'm not seeing Ryan! How dare you accuse me of going out on you?!" she seethed, and this took a bite out of my attack. Had I been wrong?

"I saw you two at the diner just now, having lunch, carrying on like young lovers, hugging goodbye. Explain that to me! What the hell are you doing seeing Ryan?! What's he doing here, if not seeing you?"

The more I persisted, the angrier she got. Soon, the indignation became hers, and it came out thick.

"Is that what you really think? Damn you, Ben!" She stormed out of the kitchen and through the sliding glass door, plopping down on a lounge chair on the back patio. I chased after her and sat on a lounge chair facing her. I glared at her, waiting for her to explain herself.

She measured her breathing, slowed down, and calmed herself. She grabbed a large brown-striped beach towel and covered her bare legs, then said in an even and slow tone, "I can't believe you. What was I doing with Ryan? Defending *you*, that's what! I ran into him this morning down at the post office, and I asked him what he was doing here. Turns out, he's opening a boutique nursery shop downtown.

"As soon as he said that, I thought of you—of *your* mailboxes. A boutique shop here on Bainbridge? What better place to sell mailboxes to all the people here on the island? They can afford it, and everyone compliments Dad's mailbox! So, I started in on him. I told him it was wrong of him to steal your idea, and that he should be ashamed of himself. He said he had given up on it anyway because Scott couldn't make them nearly as nice as yours. He said we should talk about it over brunch, and I agreed. That's all!"

Her glare dug like a dagger into my gut. She continued, "I can't believe you'd think it was for anything more—especially what you're thinking! God, Ben, really?! What is wrong with you?" She turned sharply away and stared down the long, sloping green lawn to the shimmering water of the bay beyond.

Well, that took it out of me. I went from indignant to in trouble in an instant. I stumbled and tried to recover. "What do you mean, he's opening a boutique nursery? Here?"

Em turned, now red in the face. "Yeah. Here. And it would be the perfect place for you to have a mailbox display, here on Bainbridge—and one in his main nursery in Tacoma, just like you've always wanted."

I didn't quite know how to process all this, so I said, "He's not making his own? What else did he say?"

"Oh, *now* you're interested? Now I'm not your cheating wife, huh? What about you and Patty, by the way? How long have you been seeing her? Sneaking around Seattle... Are you sneaking into her little apartment, too? Sneaking into *her*?" Her voice shot up, and her indignation turned to full-on rage.

Piece-of-shit Ryan... I bet he couldn't wait to tell her about seeing us at the diner. I tried to explain. "That was totally nothing! And no, I'm not sneaking around with her!"

"Well, what are you doing, then? Ryan told me you were both sitting side by side, pretty cozy when he walked in. What's going on with that?" she fumed.

"Nothing's going on! Toby has been working with me in the shop, and his grandparents are worried because Patty's making noises about him coming to live with her in the fall, and they don't want that. Then she called me out of the blue, and I was in Seattle for supplies anyway, so we had breakfast. Nothing else! And by the way, she's not looking too good. I mean, she's in trouble—"

"Oh, so you're gonna save her, huh?" She did the taunting now.

"No! I told her she needs help. I haven't seen or heard from her since, and I'm not going to." I paused. "That's all there is to it."

It was my turn to look at the water. Moments passed, and I said, "Well, Ryan wants too much control and too big of a percentage. He'd only be interested if he could have it all his own way."

"Ryan's a businessman, and whatever is good for business is good for him. I told him there's no way we would do an unlimited-time agreement; a one-year exclusive is all he gets. He said he'd want the first right to renew at the same terms, and I said I'd talk to you, but yeah, he agreed to a one-year deal."

"What about the split? He wanted some crazy percentage going to him, and I'm not doing that—no way!" I found my anger again.

"How about fifty/fifty? I told him that benefits both of us, and if he wants the exclusive for a year, then he's going to have to play fair. He agreed to that, too," she said smugly.

I stared at her. She stared back at the water. We both sat still, unwilling to give in.

Finally, she said, "I can't believe you thought I would cheat on you—and with Ryan! What are you thinking? Have you no trust, no faith in us?"

"Me? What about you thinking I'm seeing Patty? God! And I *do* have faith in us! Do you?"

"It hasn't been easy this summer, and it's not easy right now. Sneaking up here early like this... What, are you checking up on me?"

"I *missed* you! You and the kids! I thought I'd come up early, and we could talk about what we're going to tell them about Sadie. I thought you'd be happy to see me."

"I would have been. I've been looking forward to seeing you—the kids, too. But God, Ben! Really, I mean..."

We both were facing away from each other, staring at the water and watching two kayakers paddle by, each wearing a bright orange vest and matching orange helmet.

A moment later, a car's tires crunched on the driveway, doors slammed, and the kids yelled, "It's Daddy's car!"

Em moved to the patio table and tucked the beach towel around her waist. I got up and moved to the sliding glass doors, and I saw Sammy running behind Dylan as they rushed out to the patio.

"You're here!" Dylan yelled as he hugged me, and Sammy shrieked, "Daddy! What are you doing here? You're supposed to come tomorrow!"

I sat back down. Sammy crawled into my lap, Dylan stood in front of me, and they both poured out the things they had been doing.

"I caught the biggest fish ever!" Dylan cried.

Sammy pleaded, "I want to get a horse! Grandma said I could if you said it's okay. Oh, please, please, Daddy, can I?"

Em's mom, Dianna, came out with a designer purse over her shoulder and looked surprised to see me. She nodded a quick hello and took a seat at the table across from Em. Fashionable and fit, with short, stylish auburn hair, Dianna was confident and attractive, and she knew it. She said coolly, "Ben, weren't you coming up tomorrow? I mean, it's nice to see you... Is everything all right?"

The kids looked from her to me, like they were watching a tennis match.

"Yeah, everything's ... well, okay, but—"

I suddenly remembered Sadie. Dylan watched my face fall and said softly, "What's wrong, Dad?"

Sammy looked up at me, and her eyes held only innocence and trust. I hated what I was about to say.

"It's Sadie."

Dylan moved closer to me. "What about Sadie?"

Sammy grabbed my hand and darted her head around. "Is Sadie here, Daddy?"

I pulled Dylan onto the lounge chair. "Sadie had to leave us. She's in doggy heaven now. She—"

They both broke into tears, and Sammy fell into me and hugged me tight. "No! No! I wanna see her!"

"Sammy, Sadie told me to tell you she loves you very, very much," I said softly. "You, too, Dylan. She said she'll always be thinking about you in heaven, and that she's so sorry she couldn't say goodbye."

Em moved to a lounge chair and pulled it closer to us, and

Dylan, whimpering now, reached out for her. I said, "I know it's sad, but it was her time, and she had to move on. It doesn't mean she doesn't love you, and I know how hard this is for you. But she'll always be in our hearts. You won't ever forget her, will you?"

They both cried through sniffles and said, "No!" and Sammy added, "But we love her!"

Sammy buried her little face into my side again, her tears soaking through my T-shirt, and Dylan held on tightly to Em. All of us were crying now, and even Dianna wiped away her tears.

The night dragged by, with the kids subdued and visibly shaken by the news. Sammy, especially clingy, made sure she stayed close to either me or her mom throughout the night. Mitch came home and grilled some hotdogs and burgers on the barbecue, and we all ate on the patio, gazing at the lights of downtown Seattle. He had a million-dollar view, and most times, it reminded me of our wedding night. But not tonight. I snuck glances at Em, but she seemed guarded, distant. I couldn't tell if she was sad about Sadie, or still upset over our fight, but everyone could feel the tension between us.

Before the kids went to bed, we made plans for a day of kayaking in the bay, and both Sammy and Dylan were already fighting over who got to be in my kayak. They would both take turns with me and their mother, we said.

Later, Em surprised and disappointed me by pointing me to the spare bedroom.

"Ah, c'mon, Em!" I objected.

"Not tonight. I can't spend the evening fighting with you again."

I grabbed my bag, grumbled down the long hallway, and slammed the door.

It took a long time for me to fall asleep, and I replayed every bit of the day. I felt like a heel for doubting Em, but I was also pissed off at her. I couldn't believe she still thought Ryan was the way—but I was also surprised he was open to the idea again. Something didn't make sense. Em could fool herself and think she'd saved the day, but Ryan was playing her. Why didn't she see that? It made me so mad! That, and her thinking I couldn't do this without his help. Damn them both! Just to show her, maybe I'd take his offer, see how fast he'd change the deal once we got going. "If something can go wrong, it will"—especially where Ryan was concerned. But taking his deal was the quickest way to calm her down, to get her back on my side. I wouldn't give up on finding the right way, though. She might not believe it was possible, but I still did. It wasn't perfect, but maybe it didn't have to be. Maybe this was just another piece of the puzzle. We'd see.

Meanwhile, I'd go out of my way to have a good day with Em and the kids tomorrow. I had to smooth things over, apologize for my jealousy, and make sure the incident with Patty was forgotten. She and the kids were still the most important thing to me, and I had to make sure she knew that. Most of all, I'd get out of this spare bedroom and be back sleeping in my wife's bed tomorrow night.

Chapter Twenty

Friday, July 22, 1988

I awoke alert and on edge. Where was I? Bainbridge. Kayaking with the kids, Em and me... The diner... What kind of mood would Em be in? Me sleeping in the spare bedroom brought back memories of our fighting. Had she put yesterday behind her? I cracked the window, and the sweet smell of roses wafted into the room on the slightly cool morning air. I peeked outside. Wispy clouds brushed the sky, and seagulls skimmed the sea—a perfect day to be out on the water.

Both Dianna and Em were in the kitchen, busy with breakfast, while Mitch sat at the dining table with a French press of delicious-smelling coffee on a silver serving tray. The aroma of buttermilk pancakes filled the open dining area that faced the kitchen, and like the front of the house, it was surrounded by floor-to-ceiling windows with transoms framing the huge back lawn, the shimmering water beyond, and the view of Seattle in the distance.

"Morning, Ben," Mitch greeted me. "Coffee for you?"

I nodded, all the while keeping my eyes on Em, who moved silently in the kitchen, helping her mom with breakfast. She had her back to me and didn't turn around to acknowledge me. Both Sammy and Dylan swarmed around her, each pleading their case for who got to ride in the kayak with me first. She finally turned, glanced at me, looked down at them, and said, "We'll talk about it after breakfast. Now go help set the table." She handed them napkins and silverware, and they tromped over to the table and plopped down, still arguing over who would go first.

I poured the coffee, stood next to my seat, and called out, "Good morning," hoping Em would turn around.

Dianna nodded. "Morning, Ben. How'd you sleep?"

"Fine," I said and glanced again at Em, who made eye contact, but quickly looked away. Her eyes were red and puffy.

"Good morning, Em," I said directly, watching intensely for any hint of her feelings.

"Morning," she finally managed. She approached the table and busied herself with serving the kids first, and they greedily helped themselves to butter and syrup. Before I could ask her how she'd slept, she spun away and headed back for more pancakes.

"So, Em tells me you're going boating today?" Mitch asked me.

"Kayaking," I corrected him.

Em spun around sharply and shot him a disapproving look. Mitch caught it and said, "Oh, okay, good. Well, fine day for it." He quickly poured himself more coffee and got busy drinking it.

What was going on? The mood from the night before was coloring the morning. Em sat quietly, avoiding my eyes. Dianna seemed stiffer than usual, all business, fiddling over the kids, making sure their plates and glasses stayed full, while Mitch squirmed a little—something I'd never seen him do before.

After breakfast, the kids went to their rooms to get ready for the day, while Mitch and Dianna cleared the table and convened in the kitchen. Em and I sat uncomfortably at the dining table, and I searched her face for a clue as to what was happening. She kept her gaze on the table and only occasionally glanced up at me. She looked weary and resigned to something, and when I opened my mouth, she shook her head and motioned for me to join her on the back patio. I anxiously followed her out.

"What's going on?" I asked.

"I didn't sleep much last night. I kept thinking about what happened yesterday," she said.

"It was a misunderstanding, that's all. When I saw you and Ryan together, I thought... I mean, what would you think if you had—"

"If I had seen you and Patty at the diner in Seattle? Well, I wouldn't have jumped to conclusions and accused you of having an affair!"

"Listen..." I reached for her hand, but she jerked it away and took a step back. She crossed her arms.

"I'm sorry, all right?" I sputtered. "I made a mistake. I ... I shouldn't have thought that, okay?"

"But you did. And it really hurt me that you don't trust me. I'm your wife. I've been in your corner from day one! I was talking to Ryan for *you*!" she seethed, stabbing her finger at me.

"I—"

"No," she stopped me. "You should spend time with the kids alone today. You can take the powerboat and do some fishing, or have a picnic—whatever you want to do. I'm not coming along. It would only create tension, and they've been through enough stress with the news about Sadie. They want to spend time with you, not with us fighting," she insisted.

"But Em—"

She raised her hands. "No, it's settled. I'll pack you all some lunch, and you can decide what to do with them today." Before I could continue, she turned and slipped past me back into the house.

The kids were happy to be going out in the motorboat as opposed to having to paddle the kayaks. As we walked down to the boat, carrying coolers, hats, sunscreen, and other gear, I couldn't get my head to settle down. I was shocked and scared and pissed at the same time. Walking down to the dock, I looked back up to the house, and I saw Em and Dianna watching from the patio. Mitch was inside, sipping coffee and looking down on us. Suddenly, it seemed like them against me, and I felt the bond between me and Em slipping away. I could only imagine the conversation she'd had with them about what happened yesterday.

Sammy, still clingy from the night before, held my hand as we walked down to the dock, but Dylan skipped excitedly ahead. He called out, "Can I drive the boat, Dad? Grandpa showed me how, and I can do it out on the open water. I'll show you! Can I? Please?"

"Sure, sure," I said absently.

Sammy joined in, "I wanna drive, too!"

"You're too small," Dylan complained, and this started the inevitable squabble between them.

"That's enough, you two. Sammy, you can sit on my lap when we come back, and I'll let you try." This seemed to quiet them both.

At the boat, I lifted them in and then helped them into the faded yellow life preservers while they jabbered and jostled for a position at the front, near the controls.

"Are we going fishing today?" Dylan asked excitedly.

"No, we're going to have a picnic in one of the coves, and do some hiking," I said.

"Aww, but I wanna—"

"If you still want to steer, then come over here." I diverted his grumbling by telling him we'd cruise for a while so he could practice steering the boat. Sammy quickly begged for her turn, and I promised I'd let her steer on the way back. When they settled down and we had everything loaded, I fired up the motor and chugged away from the dock.

The water gleamed, calm and blue, a sharp contrast with the deep green of the forest on the island. It smelled like the crabs we'd eaten at the docks in Seattle. We cruised slowly, keeping close to the shore, sipping cans of soda through long red-and-white-striped straws. Soon Dylan took over the controls, his face dead serious as he steered thoughtfully and carefully, while I worked the throttle. Sammy stood close by, watching his every move and anxious for her turn. We cruised like this for nearly a half hour before I found the cove.

There were many coves on Bainbridge, but my favorite was on the south end of the island, a horseshoe-shaped opening with a small pit of sandy beach and trails leading into the woods. I took the controls and steered as close as I dared, dropped the small anchor, and helped the kids into the shallow water and then onto the beach. After a couple of trips to gather our picnic gear, I spread out a blanket in the shade, and we devoured our bologna-and-cheese sandwiches and potato salad.

After lunch, we spent the warm afternoon lazily looking for interesting rocks, then skipped the smooth stones across the water. Later, we went for a hike down a well-worn trail leading into the shaded forest of hemlocks and Douglas firs.

"I miss Sadie, Dad," Dylan said with a pout.

Sammy started sniffling, and Dylan put his arm around his sister. Together they ambled along the trail in front of me. I hadn't seen them in over a month, and even in that time, they had grown and matured. Dylan seemed more independent, sure of himself, and I could see that his time with Mitch had given him opportunities to swell in confidence, like steering the boat. And Sammy had changed as well; she seemed more comfortable being vulnerable around Dylan, easily allowing him to comfort her on the trail. Being around the stables with her strong grandmother, riding horses together, and having more freedom on the island had made her more self-assured. I missed not being there to watch them grow and change in this way.

When we got back, Sammy wandered down to the water, searching for stones to skim across it. Dylan stood and looked at me. "I wish Sadie had waited for us to get back, so we could have said goodbye." He teared up.

I searched his serious face, looking for a way to comfort him. "She wanted to, believe me. I was with her, and I told her how much you both missed her. She just couldn't stay any longer." I teared up again as well, but I stayed strong for him. "We'll visit her on our hikes in the backyard, and someday, when you're ready, maybe we'll get another dog we can love and who can love us back."

"It won't be Sadie, though!"

"I know, and right now, none of us are ready. But it's something to keep in the back of your mind."

Dylan began searching the sand for rocks, wandering down to the water to join his sister. They were growing up right in front of me—actually, without me, and I felt left out. We needed time alone as a family, without Em's parents around. I decided I'd take us all into town for dinner when we got back, just the four of us. Em would see how bonded we all were, and we could feel the closeness our family had been missing these last few weeks. Suddenly, I couldn't wait to get back, to get the kids away from their grandparents, even for one night—to laugh and talk and shed the heaviness we'd been feeling.

After our hike, I packed our things and made several trips to the boat to put away the coolers and blankets, while the kids scoured the beach, looking for the last perfect stone to skim across the sea. Watching them do this, I wondered what they would think of the glowing stones the angel had given me, and what they would think of the shinning angel herself. I knew I couldn't tell them, but just thinking of the angel, and of their reaction to her, gave me shivers and created a burst of yellow and blue in my garden.

As we cruised along the coast, Sammy crawled into my lap for her turn to steer the boat. Her wet hair smelled of sunshine and sea spray. She gripped the steering wheel tightly and did a pretty good job of keeping the boat in a straight line. The gentle slap of the water against the hull lulled and relaxed me for the first time that weekend.

After a while, Sammy looked up at me and said, "I miss Sadie, Daddy."

"I know, honey. So do I."

She furrowed her little forehead for a moment, then added, "And I miss you, too."

I hugged her tightly, and my eyes welled up. "I'm here now. And soon, you'll be coming back home, and you can give Oreo a great big hug, because with Sadie gone, he's lonely and can't wait to have you back."

Sammy squinted away a tear. "Now I really want to go home! Can I go home when you do?"

"No, but soon enough. Meantime, you'd better watch where you're going."

She blinked up at me once more, then turned back to the water. I put my hands on top of hers, and together we steered a course back to her grandparents' house. I squinted over at Dylan to see if he had heard our interaction, but he was sitting facing the sea, his chin on his arm, leaning over the port side while water sprayed and splashed over his small, outstretched hand. I filled with determination to be a family again, and as I watched them, I concentrated on our dinner that night and tried to feel the emotions of us all being happy together.

By the time we got back, and the kids had showered and changed, the grandfather clock in the hallway chimed five times. The sun hung at an angle over the western woods, and as the heat of the day released its grip, faint gray clouds gathered over the horizon. After I cleaned up and came out into the living room, I found that Mitch and Dianna had collected the kids and were standing by the open front door. They saw my look of surprise.

"Ah, we're just taking the kids into town for a quick dinner," Mitch offered, "to give you guys some time to talk."

I felt the ambush and reacted immediately. "Wait a minute! I wanted to have a family dinner in town tonight." My voice trembled.

"Ben, it's only dinner," Em cut in. "Besides, you just spent all day with them."

Dianna directed the kids down the driveway, herding them toward the Range Rover. She opened the back door for them to climb in, and Sammy glanced back at me with a puzzled look, seeming unsure of what to do. Dylan climbed in, and Dianna shooed Sammy in after him. Mitch remained in the living room, standing next to Em.

"Come on, let's take a bit of time to talk, okay?" Em's eyes were firm, and when I looked at Mitch, he stood ramrod straight. I looked back at Em, and she took my arm and led me out to the backyard.

We walked down the sloping lawn toward the water, and she took a seat on the grass. I looked down at her, and she patted it, inviting me to sit. The afternoon was one of those perfect times on the island, still warm with a gentle breeze, the water shimmering beneath a burnt-orange sky.

I started in, "Listen, I'm sorry about the whole Ryan thing. I didn't mean, ah... I really don't think you'd cheat on me. It's just that you've been pushing and pushing me toward him. I just can't believe you don't see through him."

She gazed out over the water, her stare far away. When she finally looked back at me, she had tears in her eyes. My heart sank below my stomach, and I braced for what she had on her mind.

"Your reaction really upset me," she said. "I've been thinking of nothing else since—"

"But I—"

"Let me finish." She drew in a deep breath and said, "We can't go on this way. You're going to have to give in at some point and let someone help you. Maybe even let Ryan help you." She paused.

My gut boiled with anger again. I wanted to say something—a lot of somethings—but I bit my tongue and let her continue.

"I know he's been greedy, but it's different now that he's opening a nursery here on the island. He sees the value of your mailboxes, and he's willing to give you what you want. He's not as bad as you make him out to be."

That was enough. "See? This is exactly what I'm talking about! You've never seen my side of it, not really. He's treated me like shit, and you're still thinking he's the only answer. It pisses me off that you still don't see him for what he is, and it pisses me off even more that you don't think I can do this on my own!"

"Dammit, Ben, I approached him *for* you. To help you—to help us. It's everything you wanted. A one-year deal, a fair split on profits, and in a few months, your mailboxes will be in *two* nurseries. This is a good deal! Think about it. Do you have anything else going on?"

Colors swirled in my head, and I longed to tell her about the angel, all about the Source, and about believing in my dream, about imagining better than the best I knew. I wanted to drive her back to our house to show her the shimmering stones and the radiant angel, but I couldn't. She would never believe such a crazy story.

"But there's something better out there for me."

"What, Ben?" she snapped. "What is it?"

"I don't know yet! But I'll find it, I swear I will. I just need more time," I pleaded.

Her eyes had dried, and she turned toward the water again. In the distance, the foghorns of the Bainbridge ferry blared as it slipped up to the island. A line of gulls rushed by overhead, hungry to see what the new crowd might bring. A cool breeze enveloped us, and she wrapped her arms around her bare legs. She had a light sweater on with dark green shorts. She looked so lovely sitting next me. I wanted to hug her, cradle her, and tell her it would all work out.

Instead, she faced me and said, "I can't wait for something that might not come. I can't continue to be this unhappy, and the kids can't suffer through our unhappiness together." She fell silent.

My scalp tightened. "What are you saying? You're not talking about us splitting up? That's not going to happen. I won't let it happen! I love you, and you love me. What are you saying?"

"I... Oh, Ben! I love you, too. I don't want to split up! I just don't know what the solution is here. Something has to change. *You* have to change. You have to make some decisions on your mailboxes. If you took this deal, we could move on. That would be settled, and then, if you got enough orders, you could get some part-time work, and we could go back to how it used to be before all this. I don't know, you just... You should do this."

I'd had enough. "You know what? I'm going to take Ryan's deal; I decided that last night. I'm going to show you how that will turn out. He isn't the end all be all that you keep thinking he is. I'll take his deal, but you let me handle him from this point forward—no more meetings with him without me, got it?" I was shaking now, my voice pitched up a level.

She matched my tone. "Geez! This is what I'm talking about! Why can't we have a civil conversation about this? I just don't see why—"

"Yeah, and that's exactly the problem: you *don't* see why. You just don't get it." I tried to pull her arm toward me, but she yanked it away.

Her cheeks were red, her brow set, and she said in a measured tone, "Fine. You handle this from here on out—but you need to handle it. Go back home, and start making decisions that are based on *us*, not just you. Until this is settled, I'm not doing this."

"Go back home? You want me to leave?" I stammered.

"I'm not doing this with you all weekend. You saw how we were at breakfast; everyone was on edge. I think it would be best if you went home in the morning. My parents have planned to take the kids to a horse show. They're telling them right now that you have to go back home tomorrow for some work stuff."

I jumped up. "What?! You did this without talking to me first? How *could* you?" My heart raced, and anger fueled my reaction. I whipped around and stomped back up to the house, and Em trailed behind me.

When we reached the back patio, I turned on her. "I can't believe you! Your parents can't tell my kids what I'm going to do. I'm not leaving!" I spun around and stormed back into the house, and out of the corner of my eye, I saw Em collapse onto a lounge chair, slamming her hand on the table.

Back in my room, I was so agitated that I immediately changed my mind and started packing. But then, I stopped. I couldn't do that to the kids. But I couldn't stay tomorrow either, because the decision had already been made, and facing Mitch and Dianna—who were both in on it—would make it impossible for me to argue otherwise. I'd leave in the morning before breakfast. The more I thought about Sammy and Dylan, I realized Em was right: this couldn't go on. I had to make something happen, and I would. I wouldn't lose Em and my family, and I sure as hell wouldn't let Ryan, of all people, be the cause of us splitting apart.

He wanted my mailboxes? Fine. He could have them. I was convinced it wouldn't work out, but maybe the Source had another lesson in store for me. Having my mailboxes in both of Ryan's stores in Tacoma and Bainbridge was better than anything I had ever imagined happening with him, so why not? I'd still look for something better, but I'd get Em and the kids back, and that would be a start. I wouldn't give up, but I wouldn't lose my family either. I was boxed in with only one way out: Ryan.

Chapter Twenty-One

Saturday morning, July 23, 1988

At first, I didn't notice the small crowd of neighbors gathered next to the police car parked in front of Toby's house. What the hell? I accelerated, pulled up to my driveway, and jumped out. Toby! As I sprinted to his house, my mind switched to Tom and Laura; maybe something had happened to them. But there was no ambulance, only the police car. I pushed through the neighbors huddled on the sidewalk and searched for a sign, any clue to what had happened, but all I got were blank, worried stares.

I took the front steps two at a time and drilled the doorbell. Tom answered it immediately and swung the door open to reveal two police officers standing at attention, one holding a file on a clipboard. Laura stood beyond them in the hallway, wiping moist eyes that pleaded as they questioned me. I flashed a worried look at Tom, and as I did, Toby came around the doorway leading into their living room. Seeing me, he rushed over and did something he had never done before: he hugged me. His eyes spilled tears on red cheeks as he looked up and mumbled something that sounded like...

It was Patty.

Tom closed the door behind me and pointed to the living room, and we all shuffled out of the hallway. Toby let go of me and followed the officers, and Tom put his hand on my back and whispered, "They found Patty's body late last night in some hotel downtown. She apparently OD'ed."

In the living room, one of the officers, a woman in her late twenties with short black hair framing her sharp face, shot me an accusing stare. Thankfully, Tom said, "It's okay, this is Ben. He's our neighbor from across the street."

She nodded to me and scribbled something on her pad.

"What happened?" I asked.

She explained, "We received a call around one forty a.m. from an anonymous source reporting an unconscious woman in room 904 at the Fairfield Hotel. We dispatched an ambulance, and when the paramedics arrived, they found..." She looked down at her clipboard. "... a young woman, Patty Stack, unresponsive. They pronounced her dead at the scene. The police were called, and after a while, they found her parents' contact information."

The other cop, an older, more senior officer—Berg, by his silver name tag—studied me the whole time his partner related this. Then he asked me, as casually as he could, "What were you doing last night?"

I didn't think anything of his question at first, but then I did.

"I was with my wife and kids on Bainbridge the last few days. I took the ferry back this morning."

He grunted and nodded at me. Tom went over to Laura and put his arm around her. Toby tottered next to the couch, unsure of what to do with himself. He looked scared and lost.

"Where is she now?" Toby asked unexpectedly.

Berg answered, "She's down at the morgue, awaiting identification."

"I don't wanna see her!" Toby cried.

Laura rushed over to him and put her arm around him. "You don't have to, dear. Your grandfather and I will follow the officers down." She looked over to me.

I moved closer to Toby, who broke away from Laura and inched toward me. "Toby can come over with me until you get back," I said.

The cops stayed for another half hour while they arranged to have Tom and Laura identify the body. At each mention of this, Toby's eyes widened, and he began twitching his fingers and scanning the floor. Once the cops left, Tom and Laura got dressed and left for Seattle. Toby and I waded through the dispersing crowd and tried to ignore their inquisitive stares.

I made Toby pancakes and put on some coffee. When I poured myself a cup, he asked for one as well—the first time I'd seen him drink coffee. He coated the steaming pancakes with butter, then upturned the syrup and poured a full quarter of it over the stack. As he stuffed the gooey mess into his mouth, his eyes seemed to clear each time he swallowed. He tried the coffee, but turned his nose up after the first sip.

"It's better with sugar," I said, then put a couple of teaspoons in it for him.

He took another sip, nodded, then took a bigger gulp.

We sat in silence while we ate, his eyes rarely leaving his plate. After I cleared them away and he started in on his second cup of coffee, I asked, "How ya doing?"

His eyes darted up to meet mine. He stared at me as if he had forgotten I was in the room. Finally, he said with force, "Why'd she have to go and do that?" His eyes bubbled with tears, and he cast his gaze back down to the table.

"I don't think she meant to do it. It was an accident."

"It wasn't an accident! She knew what she was doing! She did it because she *hated* me!" He broke out sobbing, and I pulled my chair up next to his. I laid my arm around his shoulders, and he started shuddering while he cried.

"Oh, Toby. Your mom didn't hate you at all. She wanted to get clean so she could be with you, have you live with her in Seattle. It's just that... Well, drugs are no good, and sometimes they take people from you. But it wasn't you, I swear it."

His next words were a jumble, and I couldn't make them out. He needed to cry, and so did I. We sat like that for a while, too distraught to get any work done.

Later that morning, Tom came over, and he and Toby ambled back to their house. As they closed their door, I could only think about the life Toby had in front of him. I didn't know how, but I promised myself I would be a part of it.

Wednesday, July 27, 1988

I spent a busy few days helping Tom and Laura make arrangements for Patty's memorial service and funeral, and I also looked after Toby, keeping him busy in my workshop. I taught him the delicate finish work of installing the tiny windows and doors, and how to carve the miniature grooves in the chimneys, trying to draw him out of the shell he had retreated into. He refused to talk about his mom or his feelings, but the time spent working together seemed to calm him. Both my dad and Em were shocked to hear what had happened, and my dad stopped by a couple of times to see Toby. We spent those warm evenings barbecuing and hanging out in the backyard.

One of those nights, my dad said to Toby, "You know, son, my mom also died when I was young—just a few years older than you are now."

Both Toby and I looked over at him, and I was just as surprised as Toby was.

"What happened?" Toby asked.

"The cancer got her," he said flatly.

We both remained quiet. I had never known much more than that, because my dad never really talked about it. It was just something I knew had happened.

"Yeah, it was awful. Damn near turned her into a skeleton. She was so beautiful before that, so alive…" He broke off and looked away. I felt the tears in my eyes, and Toby's eyes filled as well.

"Damn, she was my everything. I was just … sad. *Dark* sad. Colored everything. Heavy sad… I can't really explain it. After a while, though, I got angry. Angry at life—at God, I guess. I mean, why? Why'd He have to take her from me? What did I ever do to Him? Then after a while, the fights at school started… My dad couldn't understand it. Hell, me either."

"What happened?" Toby asked again.

My dad lit a cigarette, and for the first time, the smell of the smoke appealed to me. He drew it down deep and exhaled long and slow. With a faraway stare, he said, "Time fades things, and after a while, the pain wasn't as sharp, not as deep. It became a hole I covered up with … well, life, I guess. I know this pain is sharp for you right now, and I know you think she didn't love you, or want you. But let me tell you, she was as sick as my mom was, just a different kind of sick."

"But my mom didn't have cancer! She just wanted to do drugs!"

My dad thought about this and slowly crushed his cigarette butt in the ashtray. "Naw. I've known a few guys at the mill who struggled with drugs. Some of them OD'ed as well. They didn't want to; they just didn't have a choice. Once those drugs get into you, they change you. I've seen it."

He looked Toby right in the eyes. "Son, a mother always loves her kids, and nothing changes that, ever. You may not believe that now, but in the end, with time, trust me, you'll see her differently. Until then, we'll be your family—your grandparents and us. Is that okay?"

Eyes filled with tears, Toby just nodded and looked away.

I got chills. I had no idea that my dad had such a depth of feelings. I had a new appreciation for him, a deeper respect and love. I looked up to the trees, looked for the angel, but she wasn't there. Then I felt her inside of me, in the color of my thoughts. She was here with us.

We cleaned up that night, and before Toby went home, he hugged my dad. As he did, my dad looked at me, and we shared a moment.

During some of those nights, I did spot the angel in the distance, and seeing her shining, colorful light bounce from tree to tree comforted me greatly. She kept away while we sorted through all of this, and I looked forward to spending time with her, processing it and making sense of something that seemed so senseless.

Patty's funeral was as short as her life, and after a small gathering at Tom's house, I got home and found both Oreo and the angel waiting for me in the kitchen. The answering machine flashed twice. Not having Sadie around made me miss my family even more. I missed the noise, the life in my kids, and the warmth of Em's smile. I sat at the dining table, and Oreo jumped onto my lap and butted his head against my stomach, purring loudly. The angel sat nestled on a napkin on a saucer, a glittering being who looked up at me with eyes full of love and compassion. Slowly, I let out a deep breath, and the heaviness I'd been carrying lifted somewhat.

"Why? Why did Patty have to die?" I implored the angel. "Why couldn't she get clean? Why couldn't she see the gift that Toby was in her life?"

The angel stared up at me, slowly closed and opened her eyes, and flew over to me. "Let's spend some time together outside."

I set Oreo down and opened the back door to the sun-drenched forest, and the angel zoomed out, painting the air with a dazzling streak of colors. In an instant, I realized how much I'd missed the angel over the last few days—missed the lessons, the magical stones, and the guidance I had sought from the Source.

The Source! I hadn't given it much thought over my weekend with Em, nor during the last few days, which I'd spent in a daze. Fear had returned and clouded out much of what the angel had taught me, and I felt ashamed as I followed her out to the patio table, guilty over how quickly I had abandoned the faith I had worked so hard to develop. But what about Patty? Where had the Source been in her life? I wanted, *needed* to talk with the angel about all this and more.

The air hovered hot and still in the backyard. I could faintly make out the odor of the aroma, but the smell of honeysuckle from my neighbor's yard, pungent and sweet, swept around the table. Oreo drifted over to the wall where Sadie used to sit, and I followed his gaze to the vegetable garden, which had grown even bigger, fuller than when I had last checked on it. Shiny purple eggplants gleamed on their vines, and the stalks of broccoli and cauliflower and small green tomatoes were sprouting to life, so innocent, so hopeful. Some of the flowers were blooming now, and other small, colorful buds filled in, ready to pop open and soak up the summer sun.

I glanced down at the angel, and together we slipped into a garden, but not the garden we'd been in before. Instead, we entered a vast open space, the color of a soft yellow rose, with gentle green hills stretching into the distance. The setting had the soothing ambience of a dream, and together we sat down, as if on clouds. She smiled up at me proudly, and I tingled with excitement. We were in the angel's garden!

Her whole being glistened and sparkled, and the vibrancy of her color glinted off the thin veil of yellow light, which reflected back on us. It filled the space with a dazzling array of radiant hues: azure and sapphire, crimson and pink, violet and lilac and plum, and hundreds more—every color and shade imaginable. It was as if a giant disco ball twirled above our heads, beaming and reflecting the colors. And then all at once, it stopped, and the angel grinned up at me. She was showing off! I grinned back at her, and looking around, I felt not only the warmth of the colors, but the actual life of the colors as well. The slowly pulsating light reminded me of the vibrant energy of the Source, and as I breathed it in, a profound sense of calm washed through me. But another emotion cut into the calm: deep sadness for the tragedy of Patty's loss. I wondered, as I gazed at what seemed to be the life force itself, why Patty couldn't have experienced this. Why hadn't the love and reaffirming life I felt in this space healed Patty, made her whole, as I knew this energy could?

Understanding this, the angel said, "I have been working with you to let this power manifest through your dream. With the lessons, I've tried to teach you that your role in the grand expression of the Source is to embrace your dream, to develop the faith to pursue it, and to let the Source flow into and through you, while you stay focused on nothing but the absolute, pure expression of its purpose for you." She paused, and the colors coalesced into a thicker barrier of sorts, the pulsing light dimming ever so slightly.

She continued, "Patty had this same light flowing through her as well. Everyone does. But at some point, she refused to surrender to its call, and instead, she chose to block herself off from the Source, chose to pursue her own will and self-serving beliefs, a selfish vision twisted and magnified by the illusion and insanity of drugs. As she got further away from the light, the life-giving energy that could have saved her, that could have given her life meaning beyond itself, became dammed up inside her, and its power raged against her. Locked in the prison of self, the energy of the Source, with its power to free her, was instead trapped, and with no outward expression, it turned against itself, destroying Patty and the promise it once held for her salvation. Many people manipulate this power to serve their own ends, and sadly, it becomes their end."

Our bubble of color dimmed, and the light of the Source retreated. Shadows fell across the clouds we sat on, turning them gray. She turned to me, her face glowing amidst the gloom, and all at once, like the sun emerging from behind a dark cloud, the light returned, radiant and warm, and the membrane of color that surrounded us appeared translucent once again.

The angel held her gaze steady and said, "It takes much more energy to block the Source than it does to let it shine, to let it flow through you. But you have to believe. You have to develop the willingness to trust, to sustain your faith. You must continue to have more belief in faith than in fear."

I thought about Ryan and Em and the opportunity. I said, "I now have—"

"I know, Ben,"

She surprised me again. I still didn't understand how she did that. She had once told me that life was a series of tests, each of which contained a lesson. If we didn't learn the lesson, then the test would reappear in a different form. Was that happening here?

She said, "You have learned enough now to follow your own light, to retreat into your secret garden and make decisions based on faith. And this is what you must do now. Soon, I will reveal the last lesson to you, lesson six, and once you have received this truth, you will have all the inspired teachings, and you will be able to make the right choice in this and in any decision, as long as you are true to yourself—true to the Source. But you will know; you will always know the right way."

I wanted to ask her more, but she closed her eyes and breathed in all the light and color from the garden. When she exhaled, we were back at the patio table, and the night sky, dark enough now to reveal its depth and beauty, shone with stars stretching on through eternity.

Later, I checked the answering machine and found that both Ryan and Em had left messages. Ryan and Em… At first, I was shaken by this combination, jealous that those two voices were so close together, even on my answering machine. I ignored Em's call and dialed the nursery. It was well past 8:00 p.m., but if I knew Ryan, not only would he still be there, he would have put in over twelve hours by now.

"I left you a message hours ago! What took you so long to call back?" he shot at me.

"I've been kind of busy with Patty's funeral."

Silence. Then, "What do you mean? Patty died?"

"Yeah, she OD'ed. They found her body in some hotel in downtown Seattle."

He exhaled loudly. "Damn. What a drag."

"So, Em tells me you're opening a nursery on Bainbridge, and you think my mailboxes would be a big hit there, huh?"

"Yeah, well, we'll have to see. I'm willing to give it a shot, on a temporary basis, see how it plays out. Hey, listen, I'm swamped right now with the day's inventory, and tomorrow I'm booked solid. Tell you what: why don't you meet me in Seattle on Friday morning? I'm going over to Bainbridge to see the new store, and we can wrap up the details before I catch the ferry. Say, about nine o'clock? Briggs Diner?"

"Briggs?"

"Yeah. You know the spot. We'll have a cup of coffee in Patty's memory. I'll see you then." Without saying goodbye, he hung up.

A shiver shot through me, and I felt the dark clouds return to my garden. I drifted into my workshop and looked at my mailboxes, my dream. The stones were bouncing with light, and I moved over to them and stared at their lessons. What the hell was I doing? Ryan's deal was colored with fear, but couldn't I also have faith that it would all work out? Couldn't this be part of the Source's overall plan? I closed my eyes and tried to talk myself into it, but my head clouded as the blue of my dream wrestled with the all-too-familiar gray. I opened my eyes, and the colors froze. I picked up the *Fear or Faith?* stone, slid it into my pocket, and turned off the light. I trusted that the Source would guide me tomorrow.

Chapter Twenty-Two

Friday morning, July 29, 1988

I opened the door of the restaurant, and the savory smell of pancakes and fresh coffee calmed me a bit, until I saw Ryan. He was sitting at the counter, chatting up the waitress. As I approached, I glanced at the first booth, where Patty and I had sat just ten days ago. Everything seemed to swirl for a moment, and the déjà vu was thick and sticky. The restaurant simmered with the usual morning crowd, and I watched as the pert waitress poured Ryan's coffee, laughing and flirting. I took a seat next to him, and Ryan swung around and looked at his watch, then up at me, shaking his head.

"Dude, it's almost fifteen minutes after nine! My ferry leaves at nine forty-five. What took you so long?"

"Traffic, that's what. I forgot how bad Friday traffic can be in the morning, sorry."

The playful waitress—the same blonde with the bob haircut, and just out of high school, by the look of her—pointed to my cup. I turned it over, and she poured coffee, smiling at Ryan as she did. I turned back to the first booth and thought of Patty getting off the bus, of her smile and her pain. Why hadn't I seen it then? How much trouble had she been in?

"So, Emily tells me you're moving to Bainbridge, huh?" Ryan said, snapping me back to reality.

"Bainbridge? What do you mean?" *Here we go again...* Ryan always found a way of putting me at a disadvantage, of making me instantly defensive.

"What, she didn't tell you?" He cocked his head, raised his eyebrows, and smirked, like he knew everything—everything I should know, but wouldn't until he rubbed my nose in it.

I tried to recover by lying, "Yeah, we spoke about it last night. But that's not happening any time soon." I couldn't help myself, and I asked, "What did she say about it?"

Now he had me.

"She thinks Bainbridge would be a much better place to raise the kids than Tacoma. She likes it up there. Hell, so do I. I might even get a place on the island myself." His smirk tightened, and he shook his head and chuckled as he reached for his coffee.

Trapped, my back stinging, I fidgeted on my stool. Our meeting wasn't supposed to go this way—but then again, wasn't this always how it went with Ryan? I cursed myself for thinking it would be different this time. I put my hands on my lap to steady them and thought about grabbing my car keys and leaving, but then I felt the stone. I had forgotten I had it, but when I looked down, I saw the glow from my left front pocket. *Fear or Faith?* Suddenly, it hit me: I was in nothing but fear at the moment. Faith hung far, far away. I breathed in slowly and exhaled even slower. The stones, the lessons, and the angel filled my garden.

Ryan continued, "Yeah, it's real nice up there, and I expect my nursery will do well." He checked his watch, then glanced at the big clock over the fryer, where two cooks in stained white aprons flipped bacon, chopped onions, and mixed a pool of scrambled eggs. "Anyway, about the mailboxes. To start with, you're lucky I ran into Emily. Hell, she's a better businessman than you are!" He smirked again.

I wanted to punch him.

"She told me how much her dad likes his, and how everyone who comes over always comments on it. I figured, hell, why not give it a shot? Maybe she's right, and offering those things would help bring in the local crowd." He stopped and waited for me to buy in.

"And the Tacoma store as well, right?" I asked.

Ryan paused, then said, "Well, I've been thinking about that. I'm not convinced the Tacoma homeowners are the right market for this yet. What I want to do is see how it goes on the island first. If they sell well there, then I'll consider bringing them into the main store."

"That's not the deal!"

"Yeah, but that's what makes sense to me."

I tried to reason with him. "But with the Big Box store coming, offering custom mailboxes would give you an edge in Tacoma and on the island. Besides, Em said you already agreed to it."

Ryan swiveled his red-topped stool to face me, his smirk gone, replaced by a scowl. He stared at me and said, "I said I'd see. These are my stores, not yours. I'm willing to do Emily a favor and offer them on Bainbridge, and I'll see how that goes. If they don't sell on the island, they sure as hell won't sell in the Tacoma market. But if they do catch on, then I'll try them in the main nursery, like I said I would."

He held my gaze, challenging me. *"Take it or leave it,"* his look said, and he had me reeling now, off balance. All I could think about was getting Em and my kids back. I slowed my breathing and tried to look calm. Then I turned away and stared again at the booth Patty and I had sat in. I thought of Toby and my dad. Everything seemed to be riding on this moment. I turned back and said, "How long before we'll know how they're selling? How long before you can commit to putting them in the main nursery?"

Ryan drummed his fingers on the counter and gazed up at the stained ceiling. "I'd say in two to four months, we'll know."

"And if they're selling well, then you'll put them in the Tacoma store, right?"

Ryan nodded and looked at the clock again.

I stammered, "So, Bainbridge first, then Tacoma, a fifty/fifty split on profit after costs, and a one-year exclusive, right?"

His scowl vanished, and when he looked at me again, his stare bored into me, a steely poker face, all business. "Here's the deal. My costs on Bainbridge are a lot higher than in Tacoma, but I think we can charge more on the island. So, yeah, it'll be fifty/fifty, like I promised Emily, even though I'm taking all the risk."

I exhaled, relieved.

But then he said, "And I'm willing to do the one-year exclusive, but I want a six-month grace period. We'll try this for six months first, and if it's going well, then we'll start the one-year deal. So, the first six months is a trial period only." He drained his coffee and stared at me with a deadpan look.

Sweat prickled on the back of my neck. It was just like Ryan to get the deal the way he wanted and twist it enough to make it seem like he was keeping his word. But he wasn't—at least, not until he knew it would work out his way. And what would he want then?

"Looks like I'm taking the risk here, not you," I said.

"That's not the way I see it. Without me, you've got nothing, right?" he said.

I stiffened as my fear boiled into frustration. He saw this and said calmly, "Take it or leave it. It doesn't matter to me." He then reached into his pocket to pay for the coffee. The waitress, who had barely taken her eyes off Ryan, caught him looking in her direction and scurried over, beaming at him.

"That'll be it, sugar," he said to her.

I reached into my pocket and pulled out the pulsating stone. I rubbed my thumb over the words *Fear or Faith?*, and they glowed brighter. I closed my eyes and slipped into my garden, and it appeared again: the light of the Source above and behind the membrane of my blue-and-gray bubble, bright, urgent, and pushing to connect through my fear. I flashed on what the angel said: *"You'll know what to do when the time comes."*

And I did. In one great release, I surrendered to the light, and it came crashing through, bathing me in a vibrant explosion of color and warmth and truth. And in that moment, I knew: this wasn't the way. Everything with Ryan was based on fear. This wasn't the fulfillment of my dream, and it certainly wasn't what the Source wanted for me. I still didn't know the right direction, but I knew for sure that this was the wrong one.

Ryan turned back to me and said, "What'll it be, partner?"

"It won't be, *partner*," I hissed.

Ryan lifted his eyebrows in mock surprise and smirked. "What's that?"

"You heard me. This isn't the deal Em made with you, and it makes no sense for me. I'll pass, thanks." I sat up straighter and held onto the faith that competed with the fear I felt. He smirked again, but it didn't faze me; I looked through him, beyond him to some further manifestation of my dream.

Ryan shook his head and smiled. "You're a fool, Ben. This is the best deal you'll get, but once I walk out that door, the deal walks with me."

The old fear tugged at me, but the warmth of the stone in my hand steadied me. I didn't know how this would turn out, but I knew it wouldn't be with Ryan. It wouldn't be here. It wouldn't be like this.

"It's your funeral. Emily's gonna be pissed when she finds out, you know. Pissed!" He grinned and raised his eyebrows while standing and putting a five-dollar bill on the counter. "Coffee's on me," he said, and leaning in, he whispered, "And don't come crawling back to me after you talk to her. I'm through with you."

He turned, nodded and smiled at the waitress, who winked and waved back, then he shook his head at me in disgust and brushed past me as he moved to the door.

I sat on my stool for a moment, and vaguely, the sounds, smells, and energy of the diner floated back to me. Looking down at the glowing stone again, I slipped it back into my pocket. I slowly got up, zipped up my hoodie, and followed some diners out onto the sidewalk. Drizzle misted the streets, and I didn't know what to do or where to go, so I put my head down and wandered along 1st Avenue, then headed toward the waterfront.

The rain, the gray, and the clouds all matched my mood as I crossed Western and reached the little park across the street. The usual crowd of homeless people and those smoking and selling pot looked at me hopefully, but I stared straight ahead and went to the railing, gazing across the water toward Bainbridge.

What *would* Em say when she found out? Would Ryan tell her the moment he got to the island? Surely, she would see how he had changed the deal again. I mean, this wasn't the agreement they had made, not exactly—but that was the point, wasn't it? I searched the dock and stared at a ferry pulling out—the 9:45 a.m. ferry, no doubt, and Ryan would be on it. Should I get on the next one, so I could tell Em myself? And what about the ferries scheduled to come back in August, when Em and the kids were supposed to come home? Would they even be on one? The drizzle fell around me, and my mood darkened.

Lost in my thoughts, I turned and followed the flow of people feeding into Pike Place Market. The market, as always, buzzed with vendors selling homemade crafts, varieties of honey, even a stall selling all things lavender: soaps, lotions, ointments, and creams. Busy flower vendors arranged vibrant bouquets of rich red dahlias, bright yellow sunflowers, orchids, and lilies. Colorful vegetable stalls with neatly arranged rows of radishes, carrots, and red, yellow, and green bell peppers lined each side of the aisle. At the far end of the market, applause erupted as fishmongers finished their show of throwing fish from one black-aproned employee to another.

I found the Starbucks store across from the market and snuck out of the rain for some coffee for the road. I got a large cup of their dark brew, ordered an apple pastry, and found an empty stool at the crowded counter facing the market. As I sipped, I once again thought about all the vendors at the market. They were all taking a risk and living their dream, weren't they? Some of the smaller craft vendors—heck, they showed up every day, pushed their wares, and made their rent somehow. They were doing it; they had faith. And dammit, if they could, I could, too.

A warmth in my pocket nudged me, and I reached in and brought out the smooth, dark stone. It felt soothing in my hand, its round edges comforting. I placed it on the wooden counter, and the woman next to me glanced over at it. The golden words glowed: *Fear or Faith?* The path of fear no longer worked for me. It would be faith from this point on. I would have faith that Em would understand, and also have faith that the Source had something better for me, though I couldn't imagine what it might be.

The woman next to me turned and stared at the stone and said, "That's neat. Where'd you get it?"

Without thinking, I said, "An angel gave it to me."

She raised her eyebrows, smiled, and looked away.

It was the first time I had mentioned the angel to anyone, and it felt good. An angel *did* give it to me. Imagine that.

The drizzle paused for a moment, so I gathered up my stone and coffee, stood and nodded to the woman, and headed back through the crowd to Pine Street, to my truck. I didn't know what would happen next, but I had a strange stirring of faith that the Source did.

Chapter Twenty-Three

Friday afternoon, July 29, 1988

As I drove up Seneca Street toward the I-5 back to Tacoma, brilliant sunlight burst through the rain clouds over the water and lit up my rearview mirror. The gray clouds had parted, and a patch of blue sky allowed the startling rays of the sun to glitter off the shimmering sea. I marveled for a moment at how such a dreary sheet of rain just a half hour earlier could be transformed by the power of the patient light of the sun. Later, the traffic slowed to a bumper-to-bumper crawl, and an orange detour sign signaled the closure of my exit, funneling the traffic to the one before it.

The neighborhoods in this part of Tacoma were even more spread out, with houses on big lots hidden behind thick forest on either side of the road. At the bottom of the exit ramp, I looked to the right and saw a heavy dump truck pulling into what seemed to be the forest itself. A spark of light appeared to follow it as it turned, and I immediately thought of the angel.

Without thinking, I swerved after it. As I turned into the forest opening, the truck went around a bend, and I saw the light flash again, but realized it was simply the sunlight bouncing off the truck's mirror. There was no way to turn around, so I kept going down the dirt road and soon found the cause of the detour: a large housing development, in the beginning stages of its build, lay spread out before me.

The short road led to a large sign announcing the soon-to-be-released homes of The Sherwood Estates Properties. An ornate green-and-beige sign, curved and engraved at the top—very Robin Hood-like—stood at the entrance, presenting three renderings of the types of new homes in progress. They were all large two-story, single-family homes. The base model had gray stone facing covering the front part of the house, which featured a three-paneled front door and a small porch. The next house up in the model line—a slightly bigger home with a small balcony on the second story—also featured a red brick chimney and ornate molding along the roofline. The third house, obviously the top model, had it all: a three-car garage, a larger front porch with two ceiling fans, and high-end, red-veined slate encasing the front and wrapping around both sides. This had to be the new housing development that Toby had told me about.

I pulled over and studied the layout of the development. A new road snaked into the cleared field, and thirty-five fresh driveways pointed to flat, barren plots of land. The overall grid of the development was shaped in a large U, and the road wrapped around and came back to the opening where I'd parked. Deep green woods surrounded it all, adding to its Sherwood Forest feel. A quarter of the lots held homes in various stages of development, some with just a concrete foundation, others with the beginnings of a wooden frame, some with Sheetrock and insulation, while others were further along with gray cedar-mill siding and roofs covered with shiny black shingles. To my immediate right, at the entrance to the development, stood a completed model home draped with colorful banners: the sales office, opening in two weeks' time.

As I took in the layout of the new neighborhood, one thing struck me: each home already under construction had a two-by-four post in front of it, waiting for a mailbox. I looked back at the model home and saw the same post now topped with a standard rounded black mailbox. I glanced over to the sign with the drawings of the three different models, and each of these had the same ordinary mailbox in front of them.

It came to me slowly, gathered momentum, and then burst inside of me—*"Imagine better than the best you know."* The feeling reverberated through my secret garden, and I imagined how much better these homes would look if they each had a matching custom mailbox standing in front of them. Chills gripped me, and I nodded. This was the *how*!

I scurried back to my truck, sat with my door open, grabbed a pen and paper from the glove box, and wrote furiously. This had to be the pro market Mike had referred to—developers who needed local access to the building materials the Big Box store specialized in, and in large quantities. Best of all, this was also the perfect market for my mailboxes. What better way to customize a beautiful new development community?

From a build standpoint, since there were only three models —three variations of a standard design—I could turn them out quickly. Right now, I made every mailbox to order, and that took a lot of time. But if I had thirty-five or even fifty-five orders of a similar design, it would cut production time by well over half, or a lot more, if I had enough help.

Scalable? Absolutely!

I wrote and wrote, and the ideas tumbled over themselves to

get out. In no time, I had three pages of notes. I needed one more thing, so I reached into the glove box, hoping I had it with me, and luckily I did: the Polaroid camera. I took pictures of the three designs on the display board, then stepped across the street to the sales model and took pictures from all angles. Luckily, one of each design had already been completed, no doubt to help sell them, and soon I had captured enough images to make samples of each.

I hurried back to my truck, then surveyed the development one last time. The sky had cleared, and sunlight shone down on the new street, reflecting off the puddles of water on the shiny driveways. With the forest surrounding the grid, the neighborhood appeared enchanted, like a scene from a fairy tale. Excited and anxious now to get home, I couldn't wait to begin making samples of all three models, to call my dad, and to get Toby over to help with the work. I needed to pitch to Mike again; would he take another meeting with me? I'd call and see, but I'd need at least a week to put the samples together first. Plus, I'd need time to sort out all the production details; I wasn't going to pitch this unprepared again.

When I got home, Toby was sitting on his front porch, and I waved him over.

"What happened?" he asked when he saw my smile.

"Only the thing we've been waiting for! I just saw the Sherwood Estates development, and that house with the second-floor balcony you told me about!"

"What about it?"

"Come in and I'll show you."

He followed me into the workshop, and on a side worktable, I laid out the pictures of the housing development.

"This is it!" I pointed at the pictures. "Three designs that we can build out and mass-produce with enough help. This is what Mike has been waiting for. Hell, it's what we've all been waiting for!"

My enthusiasm caught on and lifted his mood, and his questions poured out.

"How long will it take to make these?"

"We can knock these out in a week, for sure."

"Does Mike know about them yet?"

"Not yet. I have to call him and set up an appointment."

"What if he doesn't like them, or want them?"

"You leave that to me. Trust me, he'll like them," I said.

We spent the next few hours mapping things out, and I showed him how I planned to make them based on the pictures I had taken. After we finished, Toby went home and promised to come over by ten o'clock the next morning to begin the work.

I called my dad next.

"I've found it!" I said.

"Found what?"

"I've found the answer for Mike."

A pause. "Well, spill it out, then."

"Nope! This is something you have to see. Can you come by tomorrow to help me prepare?"

"Yeah, yeah, but at least give me a hint."

"Imagine if I told you I finally have a way to scale the mailbox business, and I've found something that Mike can't say no to."

"And?"

"And I'll show you everything tomorrow!"

"But..."

"Tomorrow!" I promised him it would be more impressive if he saw it first. He told me he couldn't wait.

The day had flown by, and by six o'clock, I eagerly searched for the angel and couldn't wait to tell her about the housing development. I went to the backyard and found her perched on the back of a patio chair at the table, beaming at me with the broadest smile she had ever worn.

"You know what happened, don't you?" I asked.

Her little cheeks blushed pink. We blinked at the same time and instantly arrived in my garden, and it had changed dramatically, unlike anything I had seen before. My blue appeared transparent now, backlit by bright white light, alive with energy and movement. The sky above shone an iridescent blue, and in the distance, the gray clouds had dispersed, and only faint traces of them remained, diffused and undefined.

"Do you think it will work?" I asked her.

"What do you think?" she asked me back.

"It has to! This has to be it!"

"And if it isn't?"

It hadn't occurred to me that it might not work out, and I didn't expect the angel to suggest it, but after considering it, my answer came spontaneously. "If it isn't, then I'll keep looking. I'll go directly to the builders themselves if I have to. I'll find a way to make this happen. I will."

"Do you see how the Source works now?"

I did. "It keeps presenting opportunities, just as you said it would. Ideas, situations, different *hows* keep appearing, but I have to have faith and keep taking action, don't I?"

Her necklace pulsed, and her wings closed softly and then burst open, a cascade of colorful sparkles falling from them like tiny jewels. "Now you've got it."

Later, I found that I had a missed message. When I played it back, it was Em, and she didn't sound happy. I immediately called her.

She picked up on the third ring and snapped, "What happened, Ben?"

Ryan, damn him... "What do you mean?"

"Don't play games. I saw Ryan in the village today, and he told me you turned him down. Why didn't you take his offer, like we agreed?"

"I thought I told you to let me handle Ryan! Why do you keep meeting with him?" Pissy now, I wasn't going to let her off easy.

"I happened to be in the village. Don't start all that again. What the hell happened?"

"He changed the deal! Did he mention that to you?"

"No, he just said you turned him down, and that the deal was off. What's going on?" It was more an accusation than a question.

"To start with, he said he wouldn't offer the mailboxes in both stores, only on Bainbridge, and then he would see how it goes. And he wouldn't agree to a one-year deal until six months go by and he sees how they sell. Only then would he consider signing a one-year deal. So, he's already changing everything, not honoring what he agreed to, so I said no deal."

She remained silent for a moment. "I see. But Bainbridge could still be a start, right? It's better than anything you've got now, isn't it?"

"Dammit, Em! Didn't you hear what I just said? He changed the deal and isn't giving me the huge market in Tacoma! And even with the Bainbridge store, there's no guarantee and no one-year deal. And who's to say that if they do sell, he won't change the deal again, and again? Don't you see how he is?"

"I know it's not perfect, and yes, I see how he is. But..." Her voice fell away.

"And by the way, what's all this about us moving to Bainbridge with the kids? I never agreed to that!"

"What the hell are you talking about? I didn't tell him we were moving to Bainbridge!"

"Oh, no? He said you told him the island is a much better place to raise the kids than Tacoma. He said he might even move there as well. What's up with that?"

"Hell, Ben, I simply told him the kids liked the island, that's all!"

"Well, it seemed like there was much more to it than that. I'm telling you, Em, stay away from him, would you? It's really pissing me off!"

She deflected this by asking, "So, now what?"

"What do you mean, now what?"

"If you're not going with Ryan's deal, what *are* you going to do?"

This annoyed me, but I said smugly, "Something better, that's what. I have a much better idea."

"Oh, really?" she said, thick with taunting.

"Yeah, *really*. I saw something on the way home that I think is the answer. It's—"

No, I wasn't letting this out. Not yet. Did I think she would tell Ryan? Probably. Instead, I said, "It's something big. But I'm not going to tell you until I get it wrapped up. But trust me, this is it."

"Yeah, well, we'll see."

"What does *that* mean?"

"Well, what if this new thing you're excited about doesn't work out either? What then?" she asked.

"Why are you always so negative? Why can't you have any faith in me just once?"

She ignored that, and the phone line seemed to go dead.

"Em? You still there?"

"I'm not fighting with you anymore."

"Yeah, well look who's—"

"Hi, Daddy!" Sammy said.

"Ah, oh, hi, sweetheart. Where's your mom?"

"She went out back. Guess what?"

"What?"

"I won a ribbon at the horse show!"

Sammy went on and on about how her grandmother had introduced her to all the judges and other kids competing at the show.

"I wanna get a horse!" she yelped.

"Whoa, there. Horses are a lot of work, and besides, you couldn't take care of it living all the way out here in Tacoma. Let's wait until you're back home, and we'll talk about it. Put your mom back on, okay?"

She begged a bit more, then the phone banged on the floor.

"What?" Em huffed.

"Listen, this new thing is gonna work out, I'm telling you. Just be patient for a little while longer. Can you do that for me? For us?"

She breathed out in resignation. "Yeah, whatever you say."

"Geez, Em!"

"Are we through?"

Apparently, we were.

After we hung up, I was anxious and glanced down the hallway toward the den, but I knew the angel would be tucked in for the night. I grabbed a beer, went to the nearly dark backyard, and found Oreo silhouetted along the top of the vegetable garden's wooden frame. I could see the vegetables glistening in the moonlight. The kids would be so excited to see them. They would come back in a few weeks ... wouldn't they? Of course they would; they had school, and Em had to get back to her job. No, they would come back, but she was right: come back to what? And for how long?

My faith was shaken, but when I looked over to the tall pines, there she was: the angel, radiating golds and reds and yellows from the top of the highest tree. My spirit jumped at the sight of her, and *"better than the best you know"* came into my head. I wanted to believe it. I *did* believe it. But when? It had to come true soon, and as I began thinking about meeting with Mike again, I shifted my thoughts to the Source, as the angel had taught me.

In that moment, I turned it all over: Em, my family, my dream, and the light within. As I did, my faith brightened. One way or another, I *would* make my dream come true.

I just hoped Em had enough faith in us to wait for that to happen.

Chapter Twenty-Four

Wednesday, August 3, 1988

The house had been buzzing with excitement over the last few days. Once my dad arrived and saw the pictures of the housing development and heard my plan to pitch to Mike on the pro market, he was sold. He moved with purpose around the workshop, carefully building and assembling the samples. I hadn't seen him this excited in years.

He looked up one day, and with a gleam in his eye, he said, "I've got an idea."

Both Toby and I stopped what we were doing and bent an ear toward him.

"Since there are only three basic designs, if Mike likes this and orders more, why don't we ask him to precut and deliver the pieces of plywood for the frames of each design? That would be a huge time-saver, and all we'd have to do is the finish work and assembly. Heck, we could move closer to a hundred-plus production in no time!"

Nodding, I jumped right in. "Yeah, yeah, yeah! If we knew the number of mailboxes in advance, we could easily prepare all the detail pieces and have them ready once the wood pieces arrived!"

"I know how to do the chimneys now, and I can also paint the trim and windows. It's totally doable! How many do you think we could handle in a month?" Toby asked me.

I scrunched my eyes and figured the best I could. "I don't know… Certainly a hundred or more. But we'd need more space right away. I don't think we could do more than fifty in the shop as it is. If we get the remodel done, that'd probably give us room for another fifty or more. But—"

"We'll need more room…" my dad completed my thought.

We racked our heads all week trying to solve both the space problem and to find more ways to scale production. The days flew by, and I worked past midnight each night after my dad and Toby left, keeping to a tight schedule dictated by Mike's limited availability. When I called his office on Monday, there were no openings at first, but I convinced his assistant that Mike would want to know about this new product before his next trade show. After a long hold, she fit in a meeting for Friday, 11:30 a.m. It would be tight to complete all the samples by then, but we had all day today and would work right through tomorrow night. Things seemed to be falling into place.

Energized by our activity, the angel soared and sparkled around the house in the mornings, and she and I spent an hour in the backyard after breakfast before Toby and my dad arrived. Our time together had moved beyond words now, and we dwelled exclusively on color and feeling. I was now directing the quality and color of the light by focusing on my emotions only. Faith in the wisdom and flow of the Source, and in the best manifestation of my dream, turned the colors closest to white.

If my mind moved toward doubt, the angel would urge me to shift my thinking back to the Source and focus on its presence alone. She reminded me that it didn't matter if I had to do this multiple times a day, because the power of this technique came from thinking about and surrendering to the Source as often as possible. The more time I spent with the presence of the Source, the faster my manifestation would be. My skeptical mind rejected this as being too simple to work, but each time I surrendered to it, I felt comforted and strengthened. The angel assured me that if Mike wasn't the right channel for this expression, it was because another, better one was waiting for me. "Fear or Faith?" the angel constantly asked me.

I chose faith.

As far as having faith where Em was concerned, well, that proved to be more of a challenge, and she was always at the back of my mind. We hadn't spoken much, and when we did, the conversations were strained and short, mostly summaries of what the kids had been up to. I still hadn't gone into detail about what I was planning with Mike, still didn't trust that she wouldn't tell Ryan and that he'd somehow find a way to sabotage it. She felt this distrust, and it had driven a wedge deeper between us. I kept telling her I'd have an answer for her by Friday, and she begrudgingly agreed to wait until then. She hadn't mentioned how Ryan was doing with the Bainbridge nursery, and I hadn't brought it up. It killed me to think of them being on the island together, of them being in contact, and of him doing all he could to drive us apart. It all added urgency to my meeting with Mike. This had to work!

In the meantime, something totally unexpected happened. On Monday, after Toby had gone home for the day, my dad and I were having a beer in the workshop, puttering around, putting the final touches on house number two and lining up the materials we'd need for the final mailbox. I had opened the garage door to let the smell of primer and paint out, and a slight breeze lifted sawdust off the floor, swirling it into a small cloud that floated away. The fresh air energized the space and heightened the familiar smells of the workshop, bringing back a lifetime of comforting yet mixed memories. I glanced over at my dad as he rummaged through a drawer for something or other, and feelings of comfort, longing, and even loss stirred inside me.

Suddenly, he twirled around, holding the mahogany-handled planer. He grinned and said, "You've still got this?"

I looked up from preparing the final chimney and laughed. "Yeah. I got it from your garage a few weeks ago and figured I'd shine it up a bit. Changed out the blade, and it works as good as new."

My dad cradled it in his left hand, walked over to the open garage door, and patted his pocket for his smokes. He lit one and slowly shook his head as the smoke curled over his shoulder. "Hell, I remember when I picked this up for you. You must have been, what, eight or nine years old?"

"Twelve," I said. "I was twelve. And I remember that day, too."

He gazed into the distance, then put the planer down on a table and absently caressed the smooth mahogany handle. He flicked the cigarette away. "You know, it killed me to let you down like that, all those years ago."

I wanted to play dumb, to ask what he meant. But the look in his eyes, both pleading and hurt—a look I'd never seen from my dad—forced me to put the paintbrush down and turn toward him.

He continued, "I remember picking up this planer, ordering

it from the hardware store. They had a bunch of regular ones, some with plastic handles, but not many mahogany ones. Special order, they said. I was so excited to give it to you." He paused.

I shifted uncomfortably. "And I was so excited to get it. I remember that, too."

"Yeah, well ... I didn't want to do it. I knew how much this meant to you. Hell, it meant a lot to me, too. Your dream to be in business with me, to make mailboxes together, a father-and-son business... I wanted that, too, you know." He searched my eyes and waited.

"It wasn't just my dream; it was *our* dream. It's all I ever knew, all I ever wanted." My eyes blurred, and I looked down.

"Dammit, Ben. I needed work; I needed a solid future. The mill offered that to me, to your mother and me. You still had your whole life to figure things out. I didn't have the time you did; I couldn't take the risk on a boyhood dream. You gotta understand how it was for me." He fell silent and turned his back on me.

After an awkward silence, I said, "Yeah, but I didn't understand. All we ever talked about, all we worked for was making mailboxes. You taught me how to make them. You told me we would do this together. And I believed in you. I believed in us." A tear now fell down my cheek. I couldn't believe we were having this conversation, and the emotions I'd buried for years burned my eyes.

My dad flipped around, his own eyes tearing up now. "God, son, I'm so sorry to have turned my back on you. It's haunted me from the day I told you. I still see your little face, filled with disappointment in me, in your dad. I felt like such a heel." A longer pause now.

He picked up the planer and walked toward me. Then he looked me in the eye and said, "I've thought about that day for over seventeen years now, and each time I do, I've tried to justify it, but I never could. And now, with the mill letting me go, with you still trying to make this work... Well, I don't know. It still bothers me. I keep wondering, 'what if?' You know?" He stood still and held my gaze.

"Yeah, I do know. I've thought it, too—what if? But I don't have an answer for it."

"I know it's probably too late, but can you forgive me for being such an ass? For letting you down like that?" His tears magnified the red in his eyes, and he stared down at the planer, which he held in both hands now.

I walked over and embraced my dad, and he wrapped his big left arm around me and hugged me tightly. He smelled of sawdust and cigarettes.

I let go and stepped back. "I do forgive you. I know now what it's like to put your dream on the backburner and get a job so you can look after your family. I didn't like it then, but I understand it now."

He squeezed my shoulder, then wiped his eyes on the back of his hand. Taking an awkward step back, he patted his pocket for his smokes. He looked up at me and said, "I guess you can still make your dream come true, huh?"

I reached over and took the planer from him, held it up, and said firmly, "No. This is still *our* dream. It's always been our dream. And now we're going to make it happen—together."

My dad raised his eyebrows, surprised by the force in my voice.

I faced him and said, "This dream—*our* dream—is just getting started again. Don't you see? Maybe you got laid off from the mill for a reason. The Big Box store—maybe it's opening for a reason. What if all this is unfolding exactly as it should? What if it's all working out the best way it could? Have you ever thought about that?"

He shook his head and opened his mouth to say something, but I cut him off.

"I think about it. All the time these days."

He frowned. "Yeah, but what if Mike says no? What if this doesn't work?"

"Then we'll find another way. I'll go to the builders directly, one at a time. I'll approach other stores, other lumber wholesalers. I'll market in Seattle and approach stores and builders there. I'll take it to surrounding counties. I'll keep trying, and I won't give up until I find the right way. And there *is* a right way; I know there is."

My dad smiled and shook his head. "I believe you will."

"*We* will," I corrected him. "What we need to think about is how we can scale this bigger than the best we know. Fifty orders, one hundred orders, two hundred orders... What's the best way to scale this even larger? I keep thinking about what you said a few weeks ago, about the other guys from the mill looking for work. We might need some of them after all. With the assembly line we're developing, some of them could handle this work, couldn't they?"

My dad's face lit up. "Hell yeah, they could!" He paused and then said, "I'll tell you what we could do. If Mike says yes, and we need more space, I could rent us some in one of the warehouses in the downtown complex opposite the mill. They've been getting emptier and emptier over the years, and I bet I could get one for a song. Probably even short-term, too—you know, in case this really takes off, and we need even more production space."

He stopped and gazed far away down the street. The light had turned to dusk, and the sounds of crickets filled the summer night. From somewhere down the street, the smell of burgers being grilled wafted over to us. Even in this light, my dad's furled eyebrows told me he was busy thinking, planning, scheming for a way to make this work.

I said, "That's gonna cost money I don't have. Plus, we're going to need even more equipment: heavy-duty table saws, industrial sanders, finishing tools, and materials. It would cost a lot."

"Listen," my dad interrupted me, and full of conviction, he said, "this could really, really work out. If you get this first order, and it goes well, then we could take it one step at a time. We could rent the new space—don't worry, I'll borrow the money on our house, we've got the equity—and we could move a lot of the equipment from this shop, and even my shop, over to the new space. Enough to get us started. If Mike can deliver us precut plywood, we could knock out the initial order within a month. And if I could get the space on a month-to-month basis, I could buy enough supplies to keep it going. From there, we could roll the income over for the second and third set of orders."

"Whoa! I can't let you borrow all that money and take that big of a risk. I mean, you're not even working right now. I can't let you do it. We'll find another way."

My dad, animated now, looked me squarely in the eye and said, "Naw. This is my second chance at a dream I should have made come true years ago. I'm not going to miss it again. Besides, this will work, if..." His voice trailed off.

If.
We both stared at each other and knew what the other was thinking. At that moment, I wished the angel could burst in and paint the shop with her vibrant colors, and as I thought it, I remembered: either Mike was the way, or the Source had something better for us. I smiled at my dad and said, "Let's find us some space. Let's be ready."

My dad nodded slowly. "We will. But let's get Mike on board on Friday first."

Chapter Twenty-Five

Friday, August 5, 1988

The Big Box store had changed even more since we'd last been there. More cars were scattered around the parking lot—employees, no doubt. The nursery on the side now had its own cash register booths just inside the gates, and the last of the summer flowers stood in cheerful rows outside the enclosure. We parked close to the front doors, and before we unloaded the mailboxes, I went in to see where we could set up.

Inside, the store was stocked and ready for business. Every aisle bulged with items, new cash registers stood ready, and the customer service counters by the front entrance buzzed with employees. I moved to the back of the store, and a woman named Cathy came out of the first office and guided me to the same room I had been in before. As she went to get Mike, I asked her to wait until I brought my samples in.

Back in the parking lot, my dad, Toby, and I each took a mailbox. I tucked the new flyers under my arm, and we headed into the store and back into the interview room. We arranged them on the table, and I spread out the flyers in front of each one.

Once again, they looked amazing, and I briefly wondered if Mike would finally see their potential.

"Good luck," my dad said when he turned to leave.

Toby awkwardly put his hand out, shook mine quickly, and mumbled, "Yeah, good luck." Then he followed my dad out.

Unlike the store, the room hadn't changed: same white interrogation table with two folding chairs, same big clock on the far wall, and my samples and flyers crowded the small table. Before I even sat down, the door swung open, and the stocky football player in business dress burst into the room. Mike was wearing a tie this time, and I immediately thought of his promotion and his need to dress up a bit more. He frowned when he saw me and the mailboxes on the table.

"What's all this?" he said with slight irritation.

My spirits fell, and I struggled to regain my confidence.

"Hi, Mike. Ah, thanks for seeing me again." I rushed over and shook his hand.

He relaxed a bit and glanced down at the mailboxes and then back up at me. He raised his eyebrows. "I've seen all this, haven't I?"

I heard the ticking of the large clock on the wall, and I knew I had a brief window to make an impact.

"Actually, no. What you saw before were mailboxes for the residential market, and we both agreed that market wasn't right for this place." I picked up a flyer and handed it to him. "Have you heard of the Sherwood Estates development just north of here?"

At the word "development," his eyes flashed, and he took the flyer and studied it.

"Thirty-five high-end new homes, with three models at price

points sure to go up as the neighborhood fills out. Presales start in a couple of weeks. You're in charge of the pro market, aren't you?"

His eyes flickered again, and he looked up at me and said, "Yeah. So, what's this got to do with it?"

"Mike, the last time we spoke, you said that finding a way to capture the pro market—meaning contractors, developers, and other large-scale builders—is the real future and would make the biggest impact for the Big Box stores, right?" I let him buy in, and he nodded impatiently.

I continued, "Well, what does every builder want?" I didn't wait for him to respond. "They want—no, they *need* an edge over their competition. They need a way to distinguish themselves, and that's why they all have unique housing designs and offer exclusive communities like this, right?"

Mike's bulldog-like face changed as recognition dripped over it. His frown softened, and the barest hint of a smile appeared. He scanned the flyer again and then moved closer to the mailboxes, and in an instant, he got it.

"Ah, I see. So, you think the builders themselves would be the market for these, huh?"

"What better market could there be? Also, don't forget large-scale contractors who are remodeling homes across the city—heck, across the state. But builders—that's the pro market we'd go after with these designs." I paused and waited for the hook to sink in.

"It's interesting," he began, then he stopped and walked around the mailboxes to get a closer look. All three mailboxes were stunning, but the third model stood out the most. It was bigger than the other two, with a larger porch and tiny ceiling fans, and the red-veined siding on the front and sides gave it an impressive, rich feel. I had found plastic molding resembling marble flooring for a dollhouse, and it matched the outside casing of the houses perfectly. Mike ran his finger over it, then opened the front of each sample to test the hinges and the fit.

He nodded and said, "You sure do beautiful work, and your timing couldn't be better. I was at a trade show in Atlanta last week, and every large builder on the East Coast attended it. They all had booths, and I must have made over a hundred and fifty new contacts. And at each of their booths, they all had pictures or renderings of their housing developments and their model homes. Just like this one." He tapped the flyer.

But then he stopped and tapped his chin. "But as I remember, you didn't have a way to scale this. I think we talked about a hundred orders, and that already surpassed your ability to produce. I don't know if this will sell, or how many builders might want these, but a hundred fifty times a hundred is fifteen thousand mailboxes. If you can't even produce a hundred, then surely, fifteen thousand is out of the question."

Fifteen thousand! Oh my God! This was bigger than I had ever imagined, and better than the best I could have dreamed of. I responded quickly, "I'm already gearing up production by taking warehouse space downtown and hiring workers. Because these houses are unique to each developer, but similar in their design, they're highly scalable. In fact, once we have the basic specifications, we can put an order into your store for prefabricated design pieces, which would speed up production for us even more. We can handle any amount you'd have." I didn't quite believe that at the moment, but I did believe we could find a solution, no matter what number of orders we got.

Mike's eyebrows went different ways, and it made me think of a cartoon character with a light bulb appearing above his head. "This has potential. But I'm not the only decision-maker, and I'll have to get a lot of buy-in. First, I'd have to run this by my boss, the senior VP of the pro market, and then we'd have to run this by some builders to see what they say. They can be a strange bunch—highly competitive, you're right, but also highly suspect. Image is everything to those guys, and the last thing they want to risk is their reputation."

Mike bent down to the high-end mailbox, reached into the porch, and twirled the miniature plastic ceiling fans. He continued, "But this could be something they might go for. If they want these, though, we'll have to be able to guarantee both delivery and quality." He paused and said, "There's a lot to think about and a lot of work to do... Can you leave these with me?"

"Absolutely. Do you need anything else?"

"Naw, this should do it. I'll be in Vegas for a trade show this weekend, and I'll see what I can do and get back to you. Fair?"

"Yep, fair," I said. I reached into my pocket, took out some Polaroid photos of the completed mailboxes, and handed them to him. "Here, these might come in handy."

When I got back to the front of the store, my dad and Toby, who were milling around the new table saws and blades, turned and searched my face. I was calm—perhaps too calm—and my dad put his head down and started walking to the back of the store to retrieve the samples.

"No need to get them. He wants to keep them for a while."

My dad whipped around and broke out into a grin, and so did Toby.

"Now, don't get excited yet. He's got to talk to a lot of people before any decision is made. But at least he wants to keep them in-house for a while."

My dad whistled and shook his head, and we headed back to the truck. As we drove, they both drilled me for details, and I gave them a play-by-play description. My dad chain-smoked, and Toby rubbed his fingers together so quickly, they could have started a fire. Dad, all business now, asked question after question.

He started with, "Did he really say fifteen *thousand* orders?"

"Yep."

"There's no way we could produce fifteen thousand orders!"

"We don't have even one order yet," I said.

Toby asked, "What if he says no?"

"Then we'll pitch to the builders directly. Think about all the builders here in Tacoma, and in Seattle, Vancouver—heck, all over. We'll go to each and every one until we get a yes," I said confidently.

By the time we got home, we had more questions than answers, and while we were happy that Mike hadn't said no right then, too many doubts kept us from really celebrating. My dad told me to let him know the moment I heard something, then he left. Toby, also nervous, declined my offer of a sandwich and went home.

In the backyard, the sun soared high above the trees, the sky mostly blue with billowy white clouds, and out of the corner of my eye, a flashing glitter of color landed on the patio table. The angel sat under the shade of the umbrella and gazed at me curiously, expectantly.

I simply said, "It either will or won't be this way; it's up to the Source now. Either way, I'll keep taking the next step."

She beamed up at me and said, "You've learned the secret!"

I puttered around the workshop the rest of the day, trying to come up with the best way to tell Em what had happened with Mike. She still didn't know the whole plan about the housing development, and I was worried how she would take the news that he hadn't yet made a decision. I called her after dinner.

"What?" she said when she answered the phone.

"'What'? That's the hello I get?"

"I'm in the middle of a couple of things, and the kids still need dinner."

"Well, I saw Mike again at the Big Box store and pitched him my big idea…"

Silence.

"Remember I told you I had a big thing lined up?"

"Yeah, I guess."

I tried to ignore her mood and plowed on. "Well, this is a big deal—could mean everything for us. Mike is now in charge of what's called the pro market, which consists of new builders around the city and beyond. There's a new development here called The Sherwood Estates, and I pitched him on the idea of me making new mailboxes for that market. Overall, it's huge, and this could be the start of something that could mean everything for us!"

"And?"

"Well, there are a lot of layers, many people who have to buy in on the idea before he can commit to it, but he kept the samples. He likes it."

Em remained silent. I wanted to keep talking, but I kept my mouth shut.

Finally, deliberately, she said, "So, you've got nothing, and we're essentially at square one, right?"

"We've got a lot more than nothing! He likes the idea, and he's going to pitch to the builders at his next trade show. This could be—"

"And if he doesn't want to do it? What then, Ben?"

"Then I'll reach out to the builders myself. There's got to be a way, Em. You gotta have some faith here."

"I've been having faith! But nothing's changed since we left on vacation. It's almost the end of summer, and you haven't worked since I've been up here. Our bills are piling up. What are we going to do about income?"

Cornered, I said, "I'll get a job before you come home and start school again. I'll do whatever I have to do, but we've got to ride this out right now. This could be big. You've got to trust me on this, okay?"

More silence. Then, "I've *been* trusting you."

"What's that supposed to mean?" My stomach quivered, and her dull tone numbed me.

"This isn't working out. This whole summer has been nothing but stress. My mind keeps going round and round trying to find a solution, but nothing has changed. The only time I'm happy—the only time the kids are happy—is here on the island."

I reacted too quickly, saying sarcastically, "You mean without me, right?"

"See? That's what I mean. I can't even have a conversation with you! I'm just so, so ... *done* with it all."

Panicked, I said, "What do you mean, 'done'?"

"It means I'm done with all this. I'm not doing this anymore."

"Doing what anymore?"

"This! You and me arguing, being unhappy. I can't take it."

"What are you saying?"

"No." Em's voice turned cold and distant, almost as if she wasn't even talking to me anymore. "I'm not saying anything else tonight. I'm not in a good headspace to talk about this right now." She paused and whispered to someone. Her mom? Ryan?

Then she said, "I need to think about what I'm going to do. Let's talk another time."

"What do you mean, 'what *I'm* going to do'?"

"Another time. I'm sorry, I gotta go."

She hung up, and I stood holding the receiver, shaking slightly. My world grew smaller, and the kitchen seemed to close in on me. I'd heard about fight or flight, but without the option of doing either, I felt trapped and doomed. What were my options? Ryan wouldn't take me back, and I didn't want to go back anyway. A job? I hadn't been looking for weeks. I could get one, and work weekends, but what about my mailboxes? And what *if* Mike said no? I wouldn't have the time to pursue this, to chase other builders—not with Em like this.

I slowly set the phone down and shuffled to the dining table. All the excitement of the day, the promise of the pitch, and even the magic of the angel evaporated. My mind raced, trying to think of a solution, trying to make sense of something I couldn't accept. And then fear surged back in as I replayed her words: *"I'm done with all this."* I vaguely thought of the angel and tried to conjure faith, but as I searched my colors, the realization descended like the darkest cloud: without Em and the kids, I'd have nothing.

Chapter Twenty-Six

Monday, August 8, 1988

"Our time together is nearing its end."

The angel's words chilled me. I felt like someone had drained all the air from my lungs. Stunned into silence, I didn't know what to say at first.

Finally, I managed, "But ... what do you mean? How could you go?" My words floated away on a gray cloud.

It was after a productive weekend, where I had spent the days with my dad and Toby in the workshop, reviewing pictures I had taken the day before of two other new developments by different builders around Tacoma. I'd had no idea that there were so many new houses under construction until I started looking for them. The angel always told me that when I was ready, the whole world would be ready, too, and she was right.

But I wasn't ready for her to leave. We were in the backyard when she told me, and she read my colors and tried to calm me.

"Not today, don't worry. But some time in the upcoming week, it will be time for me to answer another call."

I exhaled deeply, and she snapped her wings, sending colors shooting off like fireworks. Then she flew over to the planter where the flowers and vegetables were blooming. I followed her over and knelt down, and she focused on me and then nodded to the garden. It was thriving with life. The carrots' green stalks were splayed out, bushy and bright. The shiny, purple-veined leaves of the beets bulged with energy. The wildflowers grew in a tangled mass of color. It was a breathtaking display, all reaching toward the light of the sun.

She said, "All things planted will bloom and flower in accordance with the grand design within them. Your dream will, too, if you continue to follow the lessons as I have taught them to you, Ben. Do you see how the lessons all fit together now?"

Something inside of me pulsed. "I do, and I feel the presence of the Source in my garden and within me. I see its light and color, and I feel its power." I hesitated, then added, "I'm not sure I fully understand what it is, but I do believe in it."

"That feeling of belief you have is faith. Faith is a knowing that goes beyond explanation, and even beyond reason sometimes. But once you connect with the truth of the Source and follow its vision for you, at that moment, you are on the journey to fulfillment of both your dream and your purpose."

I listened to each word, and they resonated within me. The presence of the Source grew stronger each time I connected with it in my garden. Its light and color, its very presence was there each time I sought it, and it was now as real to me as my own heartbeat.

"It's always been a part of me. I feel that now," I said.

"You have accepted the truth of the first lesson, and from that place, you opened to the next lesson: thoughts are things."

That had been a major "ah-ha" moment for me, and when I looked at things in the world, I often thought of the visions and the thoughts that preceded them.

"Yes, we're all channels for the Source, I see that. Our thoughts direct its energy. But there's often a time delay before thoughts manifest as things, isn't there?"

"That's why it's so important to embrace the next lesson: fear or faith? If you want to shorten the gap between thinking and manifesting, the fastest way is to reduce your fear and doubt, and instead live in and cultivate faith. Faith leads to action, and action turns your thoughts into things."

When she said this, I could see the words on the black *Fear or Faith?* stone glow, and I could feel their warmth. I also flashed on how fast fear colored my thoughts when things went wrong—like when Mitch turned me down, or when I'd met with Ryan for the last time at Briggs.

"I didn't even know how much fear ruled my thoughts, or how quickly I reverted to it when something didn't go the way I planned," I admitted. "Those dark clouds were always there, just waiting to descend, until I pushed them away with the light of faith. That was the lesson I had to keep returning to, and the third stone helped me so much. When I was down and afraid, it reminded me that I had a choice, and that I could choose to return to living in faith."

"Once again, awareness was the key, wasn't it? Knowing you actually had that choice, and then choosing to cultivate faith led to the next revelation: focusing on what you want to see happen."

"And now I get that connection to 'thoughts are things.' By maintaining my focus on what I wanted to see happen, my thoughts did guide my actions and steer me to the resources I needed to bring my dream to life, didn't they?"

The angel nodded slowly while peering up and into me. "And how about lesson five?"

Suddenly, the rainbow glow of earthy-colored light that danced above the light taupe stone flashed in my mind. Its words, *Vision the Why; the How Will Come*, lit up my inner garden. I instantly held the vision of my family and me in our new home in Seattle, and I remembered my flight over the islands with the angel by my side. I was awash with feelings of happiness, of contentment, and most of all, with the completeness I'd feel once my dream came true.

"Lesson five helped keep me in faith, didn't it? Even though the various *hows* might fail, the *why* stayed strong. This lesson, and the vison of my *why*, kept me going, even though I couldn't always see the right way clearly. It encompassed all the lessons; I see that now!" I bubbled with energy, and as I looked around the yard, I saw something new—a glow, a glimpse of the color that was inside everything: the trees, the garden, the blue sky.

"You have begun to see the light of the Source in everything now, and you will soon learn that realizing your dream will serve as a beacon for others to follow, to be inspired by. This is the divine intention of the universe, and it is what I came to give you. You have done more than just learn these lessons; you have become one with them. By you continuing to practice them, your dream will blossom. It's coming alive even now, either with Mike or through another channel. It will manifest whether I am here to see it or not."

She fell silent and looked up at me like an innocent child again, trusting and believing in me.

I felt the burning sting of tears. "But I don't want this to end."

The angel smiled tenderly, buzzed closer to me, and put her small hand underneath mine. Her warmth surged into me. "This isn't the end; it's the beginning of something new and wonderful. All endings are just that, aren't they? New beginnings. And the ending of our time together is the beginning for you and many others who will be inspired by your dream."

And yet I felt as if my world was ending. I must have known she would leave at some point, but I didn't want her to go—not now. I gazed at her and tried to capture her presence, tried to hold onto what I knew would soon become a fading image, like a mirage. I refocused on the bright being sitting before me, her necklace of light glowing softly, her wings fluttering easily, her eyes gentle and knowing.

I whispered, "But what will I do without you?"

Her smile softened. "Don't you see, Ben? My light has combined with your light now, and I will always be a part of you. You won't ever forget me, will you?"

I exhaled sharply, almost a laugh. "How could I? I'll always think of you. You will always guide me."

And with that, I had my answer.

The angel and I sat in the warmth of the midmorning sun, this time on a lounge chair against the back of the house—the same chair Em had sat on when we planted the garden that Sunday afternoon, a day that seemed far away. The angel perched on my shoulder, and I breathed in her sweet fragrance and felt the hum of her vibration against my ear.

"Are you ready for your final lesson?" she whispered.

We entered my garden in our new, magical way: we simply blinked. All at once, we were side by side in the now familiar and comfortable place I recognized as my seat of true power. The intensity of the baby blue surprised me. It had grown more vibrant now, and it pulsated on its own, without the seeming influence of the Source. Wispy gray clouds scattered and floated in the distance. Light peeked behind those clouds now, seeping through and around them, like sunbeams after a storm. We sat in silence while the angel created her own stream of color that rose around her like a bubble: dreamy whites and pastel yellows, luminous and airy. She expanded this aura until it encircled us both.

She began, "Can you imagine what the final lesson might be?"

I didn't have any idea, but I was anxious for direction, for any kind of sign of what might come next. I shook my head.

She continued, "I know you're hoping this current channel is the right one. Regardless of what happens, though, you have all the insights needed to carry on, no matter what happens. All the lessons hold the key to your manifestation."

"But how will I know for sure when the right *how* comes along?"

"You can use lesson six as your guide. And it is:

"Recognize everyone else as points of consciousness for the Source, and support them in letting its energy flow by helping them manifest their dreams."

The angel fell silent and looked up at me with a little frown. My face said it all: confusion.

She said, "Even though this doesn't appear to answer the questions you have now, you'll see, in time, that once you frame all your decisions around this abiding truth, then you'll not only expand your own dream, you'll see how manifesting your destiny will directly help many others achieve theirs, too. This is the ultimate test whenever you are unsure of how to proceed. Always start by asking, 'Will it help others as much as it may seem to help me?'"

In an instant, her bubble expanded and consumed all of my colors, transmuting even the gray of my distant skies into her pure white. Her light was all-powerful, all-knowing, pure truth. It had merged with mine, and together we cast vibrant white halos that reminded me of billowy smoke rings. They extended, one following another, into the upper reaches of my garden, with no limit to how high they could climb. The angel pulsed with this light, each vibration stirring within me, and soon my heart beat with the same rhythm. We sat together, side by side, and I could no longer tell the difference between us. The weight of gratitude I felt was overwhelming, and I wept as I glimpsed the meaning of life and our true purpose in the universe: becoming channels for the light. We were all unique channels through which the light of the Source could express its magnificent design.

The brilliant light pulsed sharply one last time, then descended on and through us. In a snap, we were in my backyard, back on the lounge chair, and I felt Oreo's warmth on my lap. The angel sat next to us for a moment, then exploded in a burst and disappeared into the forest. For the next fifteen minutes, she led all the flying beings in the garden in a final parade of light. Hummingbirds, dragonflies, yellow-and-black bumblebees, and every other kind of flying creature followed her as best they could, all swept up in and floating on her magic trail of shimmering light. As the display grew, and the glimmer of light blurred into continuous color painting the forest, the angel suddenly shot straight up into the sky, and all the wildlife instantly dispersed, darting in every direction. In a flash, everything returned to normal.

Both Oreo and I searched the sky for her, and when the angel reappeared, she landed on the telephone wires at the far end of the yard, sitting amidst a group of crows that had gathered together.

The crows hopped and changed positions, each taking a turn to be near her. After a few minutes, they launched off the wire, and cawing and crowing, flew as a group overhead, disappearing over the roofline. Oreo meowed, leapt off my lap, and jumped to the top of the fence to watch them soar over Toby's house.

Then the angel floated back to the table and smiled playfully. I sat breathless with joy and wonder, and she said, "This magic is always here. It's in you and all around you, and you will always see it if you remember to look for it."

The sun shone overhead, and I took it to be about noon. The wind had kicked up, clearing the air, carrying in the sound of a car in need of a new muffler. From a distance, I heard a familiar whistling—Alan, coming with the mail. What was that dang song he kept whistling...? Ah! It was the theme song of *The Andy Griffith Show*. Black-and-white memories flooded in, reruns of the sheriff, Andy Taylor, and his deputy, Barney Fife. And of course, of Opie and fishing, of walking down a country lane on a sunny summer day. It reminded me of my childhood and the mailbox dreams I'd had with my dad.

The angel stood and puffed her plumage like a bird sunning itself. She buzzed her wings and shot off into the forest.

I met Alan at my mailbox by the curb. He approached me, still whistling, his bag of mail strapped over his shoulder.

"Hey, Alan, how it's going?"

"I couldn't be having a better day, Ben! How about you?"

I stared at his freshly ironed blue postal shirt, his blue shorts, and the broad smile lighting his face. His eyes sparkled with sincerity, and I didn't get what made him so happy being just a mail carrier.

"Alan, you know, with an attitude like yours, you have the

power to be whatever you want in life. You could be much more than a mailman—anything you wanted to, really."

Alan shifted his bulging leather bag and looked at me with a curious expression. "But I'm already doing exactly what I want. I love being a mailman, and I've wanted to do this since I was a little boy."

I scrunched my eyebrows and titled my head.

He continued, "I remember as a kid that the mailman was the most exciting person I knew, because I always filled out coupons and offers to get free samples: coloring books, small toys, comic books, and other stuff. And each day, I'd wait to see what the mailman might bring me. Every day felt like Christmas, and the mailman was like my own personal Santa Claus. He made it all happen. I decided right then that there was nothing else I wanted to do but to bring this same joy to others. What a life that would be! And, well, here I am, doing what I always wanted to do. You see, my dream has already come true. That's how I look at it, anyway. The way I see it, I *am* living the dream."

I scratched my head and slowly smiled. Alan shifted his weight from one foot to the other, almost bouncing, grinning like a child. I understood now what the angel meant with the final lesson. Alan was a living example of lesson six: his light was visible, and his dream spoke through him. Seeing him live it motivated me to reach the same level of contentment, to be that happy. I wanted *my* dream to come true, too!

Alan handed me my mail and nodded, then turned and walked down the street, whistling the same tune, happy as sunshine.

Instantly, the angel appeared. She hovered over the mailbox and smiled. "Did you see his light shine through?"

Before I could answer, she shot back to the house and

through the open front door in a curling arc, leaving her trail of color—something I still marveled at. *Magic*, I thought. *The light looks like real magic.*

"Truth," she corrected me. "Alan showed you the truth that shines through the light of the Source, the essence of the one spirit. The light is already shining through you as well. Don't you think that Toby and your dad have felt it?"

My dad's and Toby's enthusiasm rushed back to me, and I made the connection.

"I have felt it! I see it in their eyes. I see their light of hope, their faith in my dream, come alive when we work together. I do see it!"

"That's why having dreams come true is important. That's why you are destined to make your dream come true: to inspire and help others. That's what's this has been all about," the angel said.

Later, in my workshop, a sixth stone appeared. A stunning white opal, opaque, yet sparkling with the hues of the other stones—salmons, grays, and light browns—sat in the middle of the others, its words burning brightly: *Let Your Light Lead Others*. I caressed it and felt its warmth while watching the golden color of the words glitter and glow. I soaked up the other lessons on the stones before me:

Your Dreams Are Inspired by the Source
Thoughts Are Things
Fear or Faith?
Focus on What You Want
Vision the Why; the How Will Come
Let Your Light Lead Others

I closed the door to the workshop and had a quiet dinner, waiting for a call from Em that never came. I decided to turn in, and as I passed the den on my way to bed, I stood in the doorway, staring at the faint light shining through the little windows and seeping around the edges of the roof on the angel's mailbox. I finally understood: the sixth lesson had been right in front of me all along. The angel had come to shine her light on my mailbox dream, and she had been shining a light from inside it from day one.

Chapter Twenty-Seven

Wednesday, August 10, 1988

The last time I had spoken to Em was Sunday night. She immediately put Dylan and Sammy on the phone, and I listened to their endless adventures. When she finally came back on, we struggled to connect. She had grown more distant and silent. I remembered that when we had decided to get married, she sat me down, took both my hands, and told me that while we might disagree at times, and while we might fight with each other, one thing she would never stand for was what she called "silent scorn."

"You must always promise to talk to me and never withhold," she said.

It had taken some work on my part, but she had always been able to get me to open up. Now she had retreated into that silence herself, and I didn't know how to bring her out of it.

My thoughts constantly went back to Mike and the Big Box store, and then to the builders and the pro market, and to the warehouses my dad and I were searching for. Like a steaming locomotive chugging out of the station, my mind barreled down the tracks of my dream. The next stop might be Mike, it might be the builder community, or it might be a further destination I didn't know about yet. But it would arrive.

I wished I could share all this with Em. Alongside my enthusiasm, though, was a growing unsettledness, a sense of dread around everything that had happened between us. This summer had been hard on us both, and I felt further away from her than I ever had. Would good news with Mike—should that even come—be enough to repair the gulf between us? I couldn't say for sure, and I struggled to stay in faith.

To be prepared for Mike, my dad and I had identified a ten-thousand-square-foot warehouse to rent. While it was bigger than what we currently had the equipment for, it could work for getting started. In addition, I'd already found two other builders to approach if Mike passed on this, and I'd taken pictures of their nearby developments and even begun working on those new samples. Toby, meanwhile, had become convinced that Mike would say yes.

"This has to be it!" he'd say over his shoulder as he cut and sanded frames for the new developments. "There are lots and lots of these—enough to keep us busy for years!"

I wanted to believe him, but the Source had control of this now, and whatever happened, my job was to keep taking action and be prepared for what might come next.

It happened a little after nine that morning.

"Hi, can I speak with Ben, please?"

It was Mike's assistant. My heart fluttered, and every hair on my neck tingled.

"Yes, speaking."

"I'm calling on behalf of Mike Donavon here at the Big Box store. I know this is short notice, but Mike wondered if you had time to drop by today to meet with him?"

"Just name it!" I said.

We set an appointment for ten thirty, and I thought about calling my dad next, but decided I'd see what Mike had in mind first.

I grabbed a few pictures from the two new developments I'd found, then headed off to meet with him. After two days of hot sun, the day had turned cloudy, with no breeze, and the aroma hung thick in the air. As I breathed it in, my thoughts floated to my dad and the mill. What would have happened if he still had his job? What would happen next with Mike? It all seemed connected, and I realized the Source had been behind it all, that everything was unfolding as it was meant to be.

Cathy led me down the familiar white hallway, but instead of turning left into the room I'd been in before, she kept going toward the executive offices. Mike's office was the second to the last, and the setup surprised me. He had a high-end dark wood furniture set, with a matching desk, credenza, and bookcase, and by the far wall, a heavy oak table held all my mailbox samples, with the flyers fanned out in front of them. He saw me through the office window and sprung from his seat to greet me.

"Hey, Ben, thanks for coming in on such short notice! Would you like a cup of coffee or something?" he asked. He was smiling and much more friendly than he'd been before, and when I declined, he dismissed Cathy with a quick nod and asked me to take a seat in front of his desk. He went back to his side, settled in, and began.

"It's been a busy few days. Well, here's the deal: I showed your mailboxes to my boss, Jack Davis, and while he liked them, he wasn't convinced of the overall marketability of them. He suggested I do some market research, so I did.

"The builder in charge of Sherwood Estates is called MJB Builders, out of Portland. They had a booth in Vegas this weekend, and I met one of their reps there. He put me in touch with their supervisor for the Tacoma/Seattle area, and it just so happens he was on site at Sherwood on Monday. I met him at the development, and I took your samples with me..." He paused for dramatic effect.

So, I bit: "And how did he like them?"

"He didn't," Mike said with a frown.

My heart dropped.

Then he smiled broadly. "He loved them!"

My heart took a quick elevator ride from my stomach back to my chest, and I grinned. I wanted to hug and punch him at the same time!

Mike jumped up, came around his desk, and sat on the corner of it. He looked down at me and sped on, "He loved it the minute I showed him the first mailbox. Then, when I showed him the other samples, he asked me how many of these I had made up. I told him just the three, and he thought about it for a moment and then decided on the spot. He asked how many I could get within ninety days, and when I asked him how many he needed, he said thirty-five for this development, and another seventy-five for a development he's working on over in Seattle!" Mike paused to let that sink in.

I quickly added them up. "A hundred and ten?" I asked, sitting up straighter.

"That's for now. For him. To start. Next, I visited a guy I know who works for Milton Home Builders, Gary Stevens, who's based in Seattle proper. They're a huge outfit, an account I've been trying to land for weeks now. I'll tell you a little secret I learned in sales years ago: when you've just made a sale, that's the best time to make another one. Strike while the iron's hot!

"So, I packed up your mailboxes and met Gary for lunch at his office. Now, here's the best part: Because I'd made a sale with Sherwood, guess what Gary wanted? That's right—the same thing! He was blown away by the samples, and these guys don't want to be outdone. If one of them is doing something new in the market, they all jump on the bandwagon. And he did. Here..."

With this, Mike rustled some papers on his desk and brought out a brochure of Milton Homes. He opened it to the second page, a full-color display of a housing project called Hillside Homes, already underway in a neighborhood in northeast Seattle.

He tapped the picture and said, "Forty-five high-end homes that begin construction within two months. He wants forty-five mailboxes to match these four designs, and that's just the start." He grinned at me and said, "This is gonna be big!"

With my adrenaline pumping, I felt my eyelids push my eyebrows up. I opened my mouth, but Mike cut me off. "Now, we've got to talk about production and your ability to deliver on these orders. I've got something in mind, but first I want to hear about your setup. How could you get me a hundred and fifty-five mailboxes within ninety days, with perhaps a lot more to come?"

I told him about the ten-thousand-square-foot warehouse space I had lined up, the equipment I had access to, and the guys I could hire at a moment's notice. He pressed me for production details and quotas, and we talked again about his ability to deliver precut pieces of plywood based on my design needs.

He waved this off and said, "Yeah, that's not a problem, but I have an even better idea. But first, tell me about the detail work

—the windows, doors, roof shingles, all the other stuff. Where do you source those?"

"There's a couple of smaller craft stores in Tacoma I use, but the biggest, with the most selection and capacity for special orders, is in Seattle. It's called Kit Kraft."

He waved me off again. "We'll handle the ordering of all those parts. As a nationwide chain, we buy in bulk—huge bulk—and this gives us a significant price advantage. How soon could you get me a list of what you'd need to produce these initial orders?"

"Ah, I could get you a definite list for The Sherwood Estates by…" I tried to remember the different parts we used for the samples. "… probably this time tomorrow. But I'd need to get more pictures of the other developments before I could tell you what I'd need for those. As soon as I do, I could give you a list of parts for those, too."

"Perfect. I'll set you up with the builders' foremen, and you can arrange to get the pictures you need. Plus, they'll want to meet with you anyway. Now let me ask you, if you had the right production facilities in place by the end of this week, how soon could you get me the first thirty-five for Sherwood?"

I quickly did some calculations. "Within thirty days, I'd say. As for the other samples, we could turn those out in a couple of weeks."

He loved it, and I was elated, obviously. But there was more —way more.

Mike got up and went over to a large, colorful map of the United States. Each state was a different color, a mixture of reds, yellows, greens, and blues. Five black lines separated the map into regions, and bright blue pins highlighted several cities in each state, with larger states having more than others.

"You see these blue pins?"

I nodded.

"These are our current stores. And you see the twenty red pins?" He pointed and moved his hand around the map.

"Yeah, what are those?"

"Those are our new locations, already zoned, and they'll be completed within the next eighteen months. There are builders and housing developments in all of these cities. That's why we're putting stores there."

He turned back and faced me, growing serious. "Now, here's the thing. I'm going to a nationwide trade show next week, and I'm anxious to pitch to the other builders there, but I think it's too soon. My strategy is to first deliver these initial orders, and then, if all goes well and they want more, to fulfill those orders and then spread down the West Coast first." He pointed to the states west of the first region border. "You with me?"

I nodded enthusiastically.

"Now, here's the deal. At some point—again, if this goes well—we could be inundated with orders, and I'll need a guarantee of production and fulfillment." He paused. I was about to speak, but he held his hand up. "My number one responsibility is to ensure timely production and delivery of anything these builders need. They're all on tight schedules, and if you mess them up once, they quickly go elsewhere. You understand me?"

"Yeah, I—"

"I know you've got good intentions and all, but I can't take the risk. So, here's what I propose: You start cranking out these first orders, but you don't do it at an off-site production facility. Rather, you do it here, in our warehouse. We've got everything you need, and I'll show you what I mean in a minute. By keeping it in-house, we'll be able to efficiently scale production and cut costs. Then we'll be able to ramp this up here in Washington and duplicate it elsewhere.

"As soon as we max out production at this facility, I propose we set up a mirror production workshop in one of our other stores—which you can oversee—and this way, we'll be able to roll out design facilities across each region by replicating production and assembly across our other stores. Would you be open to something like that?"

My head buzzed with the scale of his plan, and giving up the independent warehouse idea caused a wave of relief to flow through me. And the idea of rolling this out nationally? Better than I could have ever imagined!

Caught up in Mike's energy, I said, "Absolutely! And after I've organized the best way to produce these, I can easily duplicate the assembly line in each region. And if you've got all the materials in place, I could train a team at each location to turn these out. It's totally doable!"

Mike grinned and said, "I was hoping you'd say that. Okay, now, let's talk about these first hundred and fifty-five orders."

We spent the next hour going over everything I'd need for the first thirty-five homes in Sherwood Estates, and I promised him a complete list of all the parts needed from the craft stores, item numbers included, as well as the types and sizes of wood I'd need him to precut. My next move was to meet with Mike's other contacts and get detailed pictures of the houses in their model lines. Once I had them, I'd get him a new list of parts for those as well. The idea that he'd order, stock, and provide me with all the parts made the job even easier than before, and it allowed us to scale this production to any demand we'd have.

Next, we talked about pricing, costs, and profits, and because I didn't have to come out of pocket for any of the materials, and since Mike had access to wholesale pricing, we worked out an initial split that made him happy and me very happy. The key to profitability was scale—and the scale he was talking about was mind-boggling.

We shook hands, and he walked me back out into the middle of the store, then gave me a tour of the lumber facility. I hadn't seen this portion of the warehouse on the west side of the store, and it was gigantic. He walked me through a large set of doors that opened into another warehouse space filled with lumber and woodworking equipment. I gawked at the size of the warehouse and drooled at the stockpile of fresh lumber lining the walls, stacks and stacks of plywood as high as the ceiling. Forklifts crisscrossed by, while men shouted and scrambled around the bay, unloading even more lumber and supplies. In the center of the space, a serviceable workshop was set up with huge table saws, power planers, and jointing machines, with band saws and every hand tool you'd need. With the right organization and planning, I could turn out hundreds of mailboxes—heck, a thousand or more a month with the right crew.

Mike grinned, turned to me, and asked, "Would something like this do?"

I gaped and asked, "One question: I'm going to need a good foreman—someone who knows my business inside and out—and that's my dad. If I can bring him in here to run this with me, I'm in."

Mike held out his hand, and I shook it. "You've got a deal, partner."

Chapter Twenty-Eight

Wednesday afternoon, August 10, 1988

I raced home excited and overwhelmed with joy, mixed with relief and recurring amazement at what had just happened. *"Imagine better than the best you know;"* the magic of these words held me in their trance. My dream was coming true beyond my wildest imagination, and at a stoplight, I pinched myself to make sure I wasn't dreaming. *National...* The word kept coming back to me, and I kept seeing the colorful map of the United States with the little pins on Mike's wall. Could it be *that* good? It sure seemed like it; Mike already had orders from local builders, and he couldn't wait to go to the next trade show to get more.

I tried to take in what all this meant, what it could mean for me and my dad, for Toby, and for Em and the kids. Mike had asked me if I was willing to travel to other stores nationally, to oversee setting up production facilities, and help this—this, my dream—expand around the country! I became aware of the other cars around me, of the houses I passed, and everything had changed. The whole world seemed lighter, friendlier, and I finally felt as if I'd found my proper place in it. The struggle, the weight of uncertainty I had carried with me for so long had been lifted. Empowered now, I couldn't wait to start planning the next steps with my dad and Toby. We had a lot of work to do.

Pulling up to the house, I found Toby riding his bike up and down his driveway, and when he saw me, he pedaled over. He took one look at the smirk on my face and asked, "What's going on?"

"Come on into the workshop, and I'll show you what's going on!"

Inside, I pulled out The Sherwood Estates pictures and said, "I've got some good news, and I've got some better news! Which do you want first?"

His eyes popped open. "Ah, both!"

"Well, first the good news: Mike got the Sherwood Estates deal—all thirty-five homes—and they want another seventy-five for another development they're working on!" I paused to let him digest that.

"That's great!" He did a little dance of joy, then turned and clapped.

"And now for the better news: he then went to another builder in Seattle, and they want forty-five mailboxes for a new development *they're* working on!"

With this, Toby flew into my arms and gave me a big hug. We jumped up and down and howled like dogs.

Next, I called my dad. "Are you sitting down?" I asked.

"Is it that bad?"

"Nope! You're going to need to sit down so you don't fall over at the good news!"

"Tell me!"

"How would you like to have an initial order of a hundred and forty-five homes from two builders?" I asked.

Silence on the other end. Then, "When does he need them by?"

"If you're worried about workshop details, equipment, and the warehouse space, you can forget all of it! Mike is going to set us up in the lumber warehouse at the Big Box store, and he'll supply us with everything we need!"

"What do you mean?"

"Just come over, and I'll tell you everything."

"On my way!" The phone went dead, and I imagined my dad running to his truck.

Toby followed me into the kitchen, and I handed him the pizza menu. "Time to celebrate! Order two of the largest pizzas they have, and put anything you want on them!"

He licked his lips and dialed the phone.

Outside, a whistle wafted up the sidewalk, and I went out to meet Alan.

"Beautiful day, huh, Ben?"

"More beautiful than you know," I responded.

This stopped him in the middle of handing me my mail, and he searched my face and said, "That's good to hear. Really good to hear!" He then reached down to pick up the newspaper and handed it to me.

The paper! God, I wouldn't be needing the classifieds section anymore! My back tingled at the thought of it. I smiled. "Thanks."

Alan handed me the mail, rummaged through another pocket of his bag, and pulled out the latest music magazine. "Em will be looking for this."

I flashed on our family planting day in the backyard, Em on the lounge chair, sipping her iced tea, smiling at us while turning the cassette over. The music of that day brought back the happiness of that moment, and suddenly there was a hole where my heart used to be.

Alan brought me back by saying, "About time for the family to come home, isn't it?"

"Yeah," I said. "Any day now."

"Well, look at that! You'll be right as rain in no time."

He adjusted his mailbag, turned, and sauntered down the sidewalk, whistling the *Andy Griffith* tune again.

"Right as rain." Until that moment, I didn't know what that expression meant, but now I did. Rain just was. It wasn't good or bad; it was perfect the way it was, like we all were when we followed the dream that burned within us. And now, to complete my dream, I needed to bring the most important part of it—my family—back home.

My dad arrived right after the pizzas did, and we took them and a pitcher of iced tea into the backyard and began our celebration.

"So, what's all this about Mike's warehouse space?"

"Mike says that because of the scale of this thing, they need to guarantee production, and that the best way to do that is to keep it all in-house. They'll buy all the parts for the mailboxes, supply all the lumber, and even customize the workshop for us!"

He thought about this and frowned. "But what about us keeping control of everything? I mean, if we don't have our own space, how are we… I mean, how am I going to…"

Toby frowned and looked over at him. I knew what he was thinking.

"That's the best part! I told him the only way I'd take the deal was if you joined me as the foreman. He agreed, and we shook on it."

"But … really?" He raised a few weak objections, but overall, I could tell he was relieved he didn't have to go into debt and take on the responsibility of rent and employees. We strategized our next moves, and he offered to meet the builders with me. Toby got out a sheet of paper, and we listed all the parts we'd need to make the first thirty-five mailboxes for Sherwood. We worked excitedly, and new ideas came quickly. The list grew, and soon the whole dream took on a definite shape.

After we polished off both pizzas, I raided the freezer and brought out a carton of chocolate chip cookie dough ice cream, and we each helped ourselves to big bowls. As we sat, full and happy, I gazed into the woods and then up at the top of the pines, looking for the sparkle of the angel. What would she think of this when she came back? She *would* come back, wouldn't she?

Suddenly, a chill descended.

Toby saw my expression change. "What's wrong?" he asked.

"Oh, nothing," I said absently.

Toby frowned and cast his eyes down.

"What's going on with you?" I asked.

He kept his head down and pushed at his ice cream. My dad, smoking now, turned and looked over at him. Toby scrunched his forehead and said, "Well, I was wondering... Can I work at the Big Box store, too?"

This stopped me. I hadn't thought about that. Toby was only thirteen years old, and I didn't know what the laws were or what Mike would say. I glanced at my dad, but he averted his eyes and took a deep drag of his cigarette.

I said, "I'll have to ask Mike, but there's a lot of work to do, and you know how to do it. Besides, you're a part of this team, and he'll need your expertise."

Toby looked up hopefully, then stared back into his bowl.

I got up and went into the workshop. When I came back out, I walked up to Toby, holding it behind my back. "I've got something for you."

Toby stood up and raised his eyebrows. I brought out the mahogany-handled planer and presented it to him. "This belongs to you now. You've earned it."

Toby's mouth fell open, and he took it carefully with both hands. "Really? Mine?"

My dad looked over and winked. I smiled and put my hand on his shoulder. "Yep, yours. You'll need it for all the mailboxes we're going to make together."

Toby beamed, shot a smile at me and my dad, and then sat down and put the planer on the table. He picked up his bowl and clinked his spoon, scooping out the final bits of syrupy ice cream and cookie dough. He devoured it all, then ran his hand over the finely polished handle of the planer.

After another cigarette and a few more details, our celebration came to an end, and we each had a list of things to either do or plan for. We cleared the table and carried our bowls into the kitchen, and then I walked my dad and Toby to the door. Then I remembered something else I had been thinking of giving to Toby. I slipped back into my shop and unlocked the drawer where I'd put the pellet gun many weeks before.

When my dad saw me with it, he held up his hands and said, "Don't shoot!" Toby looked at it as if he'd never seen it before.

I handed it to him and said, "Can I count on you to give this to your granddad?"

He took it solemnly and nodded his head. He then turned, and with the planer in one hand and the gun in the other, dashed across the street to his house.

My dad stared at me and asked, "What's that all about?"

"I'll tell you later."

My dad watched him go and then said, "I'm not so sure about Toby working at the Big Box store."

"I know," I said. "Don't worry, I've got a plan."

I walked him back to his truck, and we paused after he unlocked the door. He quickly patted his breast pocket for his smokes, then dropped his hand and held it out for me to shake. "Good job today, son. I'm proud of you."

I moved past his hand, gave him a firm hug, and stood back. "I'm proud of *us*, and of everything we're going to build together." I paused and added, "I told you you'd see it when you believed it. And I think, in the end, we both finally did."

I watched my dad pull away and then took in the fading afternoon sky. The dark clouds from the morning had slowly drifted by, and the high pitch of a leaf blower whined down the street. Birds feverishly pelted out their love songs, and a new breeze had driven the aroma away. "Right as rain," I whispered.

I went into the house and headed straight to my workshop. It was after five by now, and my head buzzed with lists to make, item numbers to track down in catalogues, lists of equipment to give to Mike, and plans for the design of thirty-five mailboxes. My mind flittered around these items and then flew over to the other builders, then to the other cities and states. I soared through the unfolding of my dream and became lost in its vision.

Snap! A burst of light and color shot by the corner of my eye, and the angel landed on top of my list on the counter. No longer startled, I put my pen down and grinned at her. She smiled shyly back and slowly batted her eyes. I had never seen her more resplendent; her necklace now glittered like diamonds, and every tiny feather on her body shone with light, each colorful tip glistening and translucent. Pure joy spilled out of this wondrous being, and we both sat still, sharing this moment together.

"How does it feel to have your dream come true, Ben?" she asked.

Delight surged through me, and I shivered with happiness. "Unlike anything I could have imagined, and beyond anything I could have thought up for myself," I answered.

"There is one thing left to do, you know."

And I did know.

"It's time to bring your family home," she said.

"I wonder if she still wants me?"

"I think she wants you as much as you want and need her. Having your dream come true wouldn't mean much if you couldn't share it with those who mean the world to you."

"Who *are* my world," I said quickly. Hearing myself say it out loud brought back the longing and emptiness that had eaten at me all summer. Instantly, my heart ached for my family. "What should I do?"

"Go tell her you love her," the angel said.

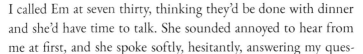

I called Em at seven thirty, thinking they'd be done with dinner and she'd have time to talk. She sounded annoyed to hear from me at first, and she spoke softly, hesitantly, answering my questions with one-word answers.

Finally, she came out with it. "I've been looking at schools here on the island, and there may be a teaching position opening up in the spring." She let this hang in the air.

My heart sped up, and I said angrily, "I don't want to move to the island; you know that. What are you talking about?"

"Well, *I* may," she whispered and fell silent.

"'*I* may'?" That meant without me. My stomach tightened, and I continued, "What are you talking about? We're not separating, and you can't just take a job elsewhere without talking to me. What about the kids? What are you saying here?"

"It's no good for any of us anymore." She hesitated and then said, "We've tried, both of us, this summer, but just when I think it's going to be okay, you... Oh, I don't know... We don't have to make a decision now; we'll see what happens at the end of this school year, and I'll decide then what I'm going to do."

"*You'll* decide? Ah, we're a family, and this is a decision we'll make together. I still love our family, and you do, too ... don't you?"

"Yeah, I do. But sometimes love isn't enough, is it? I mean, I thought being apart this summer would pull us closer together, but it hasn't. It's just made things worse in a way."

"Listen, Em, we're not making a decision on this now. And besides, there have been developments with the Big Box store. Big developments! I've got—"

"That doesn't matter anymore, don't you see? We're broken, Ben, and your mailboxes aren't going to fix us! We don't work together like we used to. I think we should..." Her voice went faint and then stopped.

"Em, we're not broken, and we're not breaking up our family. We need to talk. I need to see you, sit down with you and explain—"

"It's not going to help, Ben. We've been talking, and all we do is end up fighting. I—"

"Listen to me. I'm done fighting. I promise. You've got to let me talk to you, please. I need to tell you what's been going on, what's happened, and what it means for us. Let me come up Friday. Give me that chance, Em. Friday, okay?"

"You know, Ben… Fine, but I'm not going to argue with you anymore."

When I hung up, I had the feeling of the entire house spinning, like in *The Wizard of Oz* when Dorothy's house was torn off the ground by the tornado. I paced the kitchen, too agitated to get any work done. I wanted to talk to the angel, but found her tucked into her little house, radiating her light through the windows. It calmed me as usual and reminded me that the Source held the key to everything now: my dream, my family, my future.

I went into the backyard and waited for the first stars to appear. Then I entered my secret garden, but anxiety gnawed at me, and the fear of losing Em colored my consciousness. But it was there—the bright, glorious light of the Source—and I did what the angel had taught me in lesson four: I focused on the feelings I'd have once my family was back, and my life was once again right as rain.

Chapter Twenty-Nine

Friday, August 12, 1988

The day finally arrived; it was time for the angel to leave. She didn't say so specifically, but over the last few days, our connection had dimmed, and the distance between us had given way to a space—a space in which I had fully become myself. The deep sadness and fear of her leaving had been replaced by new feelings of completeness. I felt independent now and wondrously whole. And yet, I still didn't want her to go.

I found the angel in the den that morning, on the floor next to Oreo, holding onto his right ear as he laid his head between his paws. Her soft white feathers contrasted sharply with Oreo's black fur, and her wings, as vibrant, delicate, and magical as ever, beat slowly, brushing against his shoulder. The angel's eyes were closed, and I stood in the doorway, gazing at them both, my mind peaceful and clear.

I moseyed into the kitchen and prepared the angel's favorite breakfast these days: small crumbs of buttermilk pancakes, brushed with a hint of butter and honey. I fixed a big plate for myself and carried her pistachio shell, filled with this delicious mixture, out into the warmth of the August morning while I waited for her to join me.

Within minutes, she flew over. She took a deep breath, and with an earnest smile, said, "I'll miss your pancakes, you know."

My eyes teared up immediately.

"I may not be here physically, but I will always be a part of you. You will always be able to feel my presence..." She touched her chest. "... inside of you."

I wiped my tears away and gazed at her angelic smile, the softness in her eyes, and the light that hung over her head like a halo.

"But what will I do without you?"

"You'll do what you did *with* me: you'll listen for your truth and let the Source guide you, and you'll help this same light shine forth in others, just as I have done for you."

I thought about this and felt wholly inadequate. "But there's so much I still don't know."

The angel buzzed onto my shoulder, and her presence radiated into me. "Don't worry, Ben," she whispered in my ear, "I will return to you when you are ready to learn more. But now that you've learned to listen to and trust in the Source, you can do a lot more than you think you can. It's time for you to stretch your own wings."

We sat at the table after eating, and she glanced around and breathed in the moist morning air. Lawn mowers, leaf blowers, and kids playing provided the summer playlist in the background. The quick flutter of a hummingbird's wings caught my ear, and the tiny bird landed on the table next to the angel. She looked over at him and smiled, and in a flash, the hummingbird launched back into the air.

The angel peered up at me, crinkled her tiny brow, and said,

"You'll soon be bringing Em and your kids home, and you should get ready for them. I'm going to spend some time saying goodbye out here, and we'll meet again just before you leave."

I nodded down at her, and she disappeared into the forest. I spent the rest of the morning in my workshop, repairing Sirena's mailbox. When I removed the roof, the remnants of the angel's nest still glowed softly, casting a colorful reflection on the paisley scarf. It sent chills through me as I reflected back on our journey together. Seeing Sadie and Oreo sitting so close together in the workshop, gazing up at the mailbox. Lifting the roof off for the first time and seeing the tiny universe of color swirling like a galaxy of light. Discovering the angel, accepting the lessons, and working through the maze of opportunities and false paths. It had all turned out just as she said it would—in a way I never would have imagined.

I worked carefully, so as not to disturb the nest, replacing the rusty hinges and filling a small crack in the roof where the rain had gotten in. I finished by applying a new coat of varnish and then placed it on the counter to dry. In the background stood my mailboxes with five of the bright stones streaming their lessons against the small porches and rooflines. *Real magic*, I thought to myself.

I wandered into the den, plopped down on the couch, and looked over at Oreo, who lay snoozing on his pillow. The den already seemed so empty without the angel's presence, and soon, my sadness and even some fear returned. What would I do without her? And how would my meeting with Em go? Just then, the stone *Fear or Faith?* pulsed in my pocket, and I pulled it out and set it on the coffee table. Watching its words glow with their soft amber light calmed me, and soon I was ready.

I packed an overnight bag—*"Imagine better than the best you know,"* right?—and carried it to the truck. I needed some help with Oreo, so I went over to Toby's. He answered as the doorbell chimes silenced.

"What's up?" he asked.

"I'm going over to the island to meet with Em. Would you mind feeding Oreo while I'm gone?"

"Sure! Can I do some work in the shop this time?"

"Not yet. But when I return, I might have a surprise for you."

His look of disappointment morphed into a smile. "Really? What?"

"You'll have to wait and see. Meantime, take these..." I handed him Polaroids of the new mailboxes we were going to start working on. "... and write out all the steps you can remember to make a completed mailbox. I've made my own list, but I need someone else to make a list so I don't miss anything, okay?"

He snatched them out of my hand, took the key, and quickly disappeared back into his house.

By eleven thirty, it was time to leave. When I looked for the angel, I felt the soft rush of air as she landed on my shoulder, and I breathed in her delicate fragrance. As she held onto my right earlobe, the peace I'd felt from her the first time, I now felt within me. She *had* merged with me, and I knew she would never be far away. With great reverence, I slowly made my way out to the driveway and to my truck.

I opened the door, and she buzzed onto the roof and looked down at me. I stared *into* her for the first time and caught a glimpse of her own magnificent garden. Small fireworks exploded inside of her, and I quickly got lost in their trance. As the fireworks descended, they turned into thousands of lights, like tiny candles flickering and swaying in her endless garden. I imagined them to be other lives, other channels she had helped the light shine forth in, and then it hit me: she would go on to help many others follow and realize their dreams as well. I thought about Toby, and Dylan, and Sammy—might she even visit them one day? The thought sent chills through me. I refocused and gazed into her shining eyes, and a tiny, glistening tear formed and slowly slid down her little cheek. I searched for something to say, but she gently shook her head, became a whirl of light, and shot off into the sky, disappearing over Toby's house and into the woods beyond, her rainbow of light vanishing for the last time.

The eager weekend gardeners were out in full force, prowling through the open tables of colorful annuals and plants, and already I had trouble finding parking at the nursery. Ryan was doing well two weekends before the opening of the Big Box store. He had ratcheted up his coupons by mail and expanded his summer furniture display. *Good for him,* I thought as I made my way into the main store; this could only help.

I glanced through the window of Ryan's office and saw him talking to two of his landscape contractors. I meandered over to the bird feeders and shelves stacked with bird feed, imagining how my mailbox display would look there. Then I waited for them to finish. Shortly, the two guys skulked out of his office, looking at each other and shaking their heads. Ryan still called the shots and seemingly had gotten his way again this morning.

I snuck around the corner and slipped into his office just as he turned to sit down behind his cluttered desk. I caught him off guard, and he did a double take, then his expression turned sour. "What the hell do you want?" He plopped down at his desk and glared up at me.

"Nice to see you, too," I said calmly.

He shifted impatiently, raised his eyebrows, held his hands in the air and blared, "What?"

"I have some news from the Big Box store you're going to want to know about," I said coolly.

His irritation faltered, but he recovered his scowl and said, "About what?"

"I've entered into an agreement with the store to supply new home builders in the area—including Seattle and beyond—with custom mailboxes for all the new housing developments being built. Looks like it's going national," I said with a steady and unemotional voice.

Ryan didn't miss a beat. "So what? Did you come here just to gloat? Because if you did, I don't give a damn." He glanced down and quickly dived into the paperwork on his desk.

"Naw, I'm not here to gloat. Instead, I've got a proposition for you."

He looked back up, scowled again, and said, "I'm not taking on your mailboxes; I told you that at the diner. That deal is dead."

"Good, I don't want that deal, don't worry. I've got a better one for you—and this is one you're going to want to take, now that the local builders are signing on and ordering hundreds of mailboxes." I paused to make sure I had his attention. I did.

"See, here's the thing. People are going to see these new housing developments, and the first thing they're going to notice are my beautiful custom mailboxes, and many of them are going to want to upgrade their own homes with them. Now, here's the deal: I'm willing, right now, to give you a limited, exclusive residential agreement in Tacoma, Seattle, and Bainbridge. You can be the exclusive dealer through your two stores for this residential market."

I paused. I had rarely seen Ryan perplexed and at a loss for an angry argument, but he looked truly confused.

He mumbled, "And why would you do that?"

"I've got my reasons. The deal is fifty/fifty. You advertise to your list, put up prominent displays in both your stores, and I'll give you a six-month exclusive. If you're successful with them, then we can negotiate a yearly deal based on sales and incentives."

"Six months? That doesn't sound like a good deal to me," he huffed.

"Oh, it is. And after you think about it, you'll realize it's a great deal for you and your stores. It'll be the one thing you can offer customers that the Big Box store doesn't. And you're no fool, at least when it comes to business. You'll take the deal.

"But a word of warning: I'm about to get real busy—I mean, like, tomorrow. So, don't think about it too long, as I'm likely to change my mind, and this deal will be gone forever. I'll give you 'til Monday morning to say yes." I stared him down for a moment, then turned to leave.

Ryan called after me, "Why are you even offering me this if you've got it so good with the Big Box store?"

I stopped at the doorway and faced him. "Monday," I said simply, then turned my back on him and walked out of the store.

Back in my truck, I went through the logistics of taking on and fulfilling residential orders again. The whole point of roping Ryan in was to help Toby. I didn't think there would be a place for him at the Big Box store, but Toby could definitely make side orders out of my workshop, with some hands-on guidance from me. Plus, with my new income, I could finish the remodel, and we'd have enough room to handle all the orders we'd get. I still loved designing custom mailboxes, and while the cookie-cutter mailboxes of the new housing developments would earn me a very good living, my heart still beat for the one-offs—the individual custom mailboxes that made homeowners feel so proud and special.

I caught the 1:15 p.m. ferry from Seattle to Bainbridge and made my way up to the deck and into the glorious sunshine of the early afternoon. I adjusted my Seattle Seahawks cap, walked to the front of the boat, and faced Bainbridge. I thought about what Em had said when we last spoke—that she had done a lot of thinking. What had she decided about us?

As we neared the island, the seagulls circled above and followed us to the dock. I got into my truck, and with a heavy heart —a heart with a hole that only my family could fill—I made my way to meet with Em.

Chapter Thirty

Friday afternoon, August 12, 1988

Em was up for a fight.

When I pulled into Mitch's big driveway, both his and Dianna's cars were gone. The house stood quiet and empty, like in a Western when all the townsfolk had cleared out in anticipation of a big shoot-out, and now it was just Em and me facing each other down.

She met me at the door, and my heart melted. She looked stunning in a simple summer-white cotton skirt, with a light blue button-down blouse, open to reveal a hint of her tanned cleavage. She had pulled her hair back in a ponytail, a look I always liked, because it revealed her sharp jaw and long neck. I wanted to grab her and kiss her, but she spun around and retreated into the house.

She turned abruptly, crossed her arms, and said, "You want water or something?"

"Ah, no. Hi to you, too," I said with a scowl.

"Let's go out on the patio." She turned her back on me, and I followed her out.

She plopped down at the table where we'd sat before, then

she reached into a red cooler on the patio, pulled out a beer, and twisted off the cap. She wrapped her long brown legs up onto the chair, took a swig, and sat in silence, staring at the sparkling sea at the end of the lawn. The quiet amplified the distance between us.

I tried, "Well, the mailboxes—"

"Stop right there," she cut me off sharply. "I don't want to hear it anymore. I'm sick of hearing about it. It's all about you, about your mailboxes, and nothing about us—your family."

"But—"

"No, Ben! You need to listen now, and don't interrupt me." She stared at me, her face firm and determined. "I've had a long time to think about everything, and it's not working. Your dream has become an obsession, and it's gotten completely out of control. It's making you do things I don't understand. I don't even know who you are anymore." She paused to catch her breath. "I still can't believe you took money—*our* money!—without telling me, and then you went behind my back and begged my dad for a loan. I go out of my way to help you with Ryan, and you turn that against me. Your mailboxes have torn us apart!"

I couldn't help myself. "Yeah, what about that? Ryan? You went behind *my* back, and you kept just 'running into him' all over the island! I took that so-called deal you made with him just to show you what a sleaze he is! I told you he'd change the deal, and he did! He was more interested in worming his way back into you than he ever was in helping me. The fact that you can't see that—or won't admit it—is the real problem! And now you're talking about getting a job here, and he's opening a store here and is even thinking about moving here? How do you think that makes me feel?"

She stuttered a quick answer. "I... We've been through all that before! There's nothing going on between us, and your jealousy really pisses me off! It tells me just how much faith you have in me—which is none!"

"Faith?!" I yelled breathlessly. "*Faith?!* Are you kidding me? You haven't had faith in me all summer! You've always believed in your dad, and you call Ryan's business 'a little goldmine,' but me? Have you ever had faith that I could make it happen for us? That I could make my business work without their help? Well, have you?!"

"I'm not even going to answer that. Who do you think has stood by you all these years? Who was behind you trying the farmers' market? Who confronted Ryan..." She broke off at that, and I pounced.

"You weren't helping me with Ryan, you were *undermining* me! Every time you pushed me toward him, you just set me up even more! It was like you were saying, 'You can't do it, so let Ryan do it for you!' Well, I've got news for you: I *did* do it! I've been working all summer to make this happen, so that you and the kids would be coming back to something better than when you left!"

"Coming back to what? Have you found a job? Have you even been looking for one? All I hear when I call the bank is money going out and nothing coming in! That isn't something I want to come home to!"

"Oh, you *are* coming home, all right. This is not your home; it's your *parents'* home! And I'm sick and tired of them meddling in our lives, of them feeding your head with all this crap about moving to the island and living a perfect life without me. You're married to *me*, not them! I've been working too hard this summer to make my business work for us—"

"No, Ben, you've been doing this for *yourself*, not for us!"

"Yeah, I had to do it by myself! You never supported me or asked me how things were going! I had faith I could do it, even though you didn't!" I was shaking now, and out it came: "And deep down, I don't think you *ever* had faith in me—or in us." I shook and exploded, "You wanna live on the island with your parents, close to Ryan, you go for it!"

I pushed my chair out and bolted up. She glared at me and slammed her hand on the table.

"See? See?! This is exactly what I knew would happen! There's no talking to you anymore!"

Shaking, blind with rage, fear, and a stark emptiness, I turned and stormed through the house.

Em chased after me, grabbing my arm. "Don't you—"

I whirled and faced her. "Don't what? Pull away, like you pulled away from me? Doesn't feel too good, does it?"

I ripped my arm away, jumped into my truck, and tore down their driveway.

Colors—reds and grays. An explosive display blasted in my mind as I wiped my eyes and barreled down the road toward downtown. Damn her! Damn it all! I had been doing it all for her, for Sammy and Dylan. I screeched to a stop at a red light and pounded on the steering wheel. How could it have all gone wrong like this? This wasn't how my dream was supposed to end! But it seemed like there was no way back. There was nothing but arguing. She was right; we *were* broken.

The light turned green, and the color blurred through my tears. Shaking still, I pulled over and wept freely, all my fear and anger emptying out of me. As my mind cleared, a space formed, and the image of us all back in our house, with Sadie, too, jumping and barking with the kids playing with her, rushed in. I saw Em in her big floppy hat, saying, "That was a nice afternoon—we should have more of those." Then I saw her sly smile, her intimate grin, and I cried even harder, choking on my sobs. I couldn't, I *wouldn't* lose her! Damn it all! This couldn't be the end!

"Go tell her you love her." The angel's words echoed in my head.

I wiped my eyes and nose, pulled a U-turn, and raced back up the road. I tried to calm myself, tried to source the love I had always had for her, for my family, and as I approached the house, the hollowness I felt without her ached and prodded me up the driveway.

I hopped out of the truck and entered the house without knocking. I saw her through the sliding glass door. She whipped around at the sound of it opening, stiffening as I tumbled out onto the patio. I sat opposite her and tried, "Listen..."

She shivered, and her eyes filled with anger, but there were also tears. "No, Ben, no," her voice crackled. "I can't deal with it anymore, and I won't put the kids through it anymore." She paused and collected herself.

Steadily, she said, "This summer has been like a different world for them, and I love seeing them so free and happy, seeing them be kids again. I'd almost forgotten what it was like to hear Sammy sing with the radio, without you yelling at her, without her cringing with fear just for being who she is!" Her tears fell freely now, and she reached into her skirt pocket and pulled out a tissue.

I surrendered completely, and my eyes filled with tears, too. "Em, you're right. You're so right. I've been such a fool." I stopped and took her used tissue from the table, wiping my eyes with it.

She looked at me, and her face softened for the first time. For an instant, I saw an opening in her anger, a brief moment of love.

"I've been blind to you all summer, you're right. I've shut you and the kids out. I've tried so hard to make the mailboxes work out, to prove I could do this, that I neglected the most important thing in my life—and that's you and the kids."

She wiped her eyes and blew her nose.

"I've wanted nothing more than for my dream to work out, thinking that if it did, it would make everything else work out, too. But I realize something now. The only dream that mattered already came true the moment I fell in love with you. It came true again when Dylan and Sammy were born. If having my mailboxes work out means losing you, it means I'd lose everything. And I can't let that happen; I can't lose my family."

We were both crying now, and Em removed a bundle of tissues from her pocket and handed one to me. She left her hand on the table, and I took it and squeezed it tightly.

"I didn't realize it until now, but you were right. I was only thinking about myself when you left, and I forgot how much I already had." I stared into her tear-filled eyes and said, "I love you. I've always loved you, Em, right from the beginning, from the first time I saw you. I've been selfish and scared and couldn't see how you've always been on my side, always wanted the best for me, for us. And for the way I treated you, doubted you, I am truly sorry. I love you. You're everything to me..." My voice fell away, and I reached for a clean tissue.

Em's face softened at my confession. She hesitated a moment, her eyes darting around the table.

"You can't possibly move here and break up our family! Think of Sammy, of Dylan. You have a life in Tacoma with your family ... with me. *We* are our family." I swallowed hard, my tears warm on my cheeks.

Em was crying harder now. She pulled out another tissue and handed it to me. Then she pushed her chair out from the table and came over to me, motioning for me to pull mine out, too. She sat down on my lap and wrapped her arms around me, giving me a wet hug.

She leaned back and said, "You have no idea how hard this has been on me and the kids. Almost every night, they ask when you're coming up, where you are, and why you're not here yet. Each time they did, it broke my heart. What could I tell them? You kept getting further and further away. I tried to help you..." Her voice choked up, and she looked down.

"I'm so sorry, Em. I will never let this happen again, I promise."

She stood up, took my hand, and led me over to the couch against the house, sitting down next to me. She interlaced my hand in hers, draped a leg over mine, and looked up at me.

"I love you. I love the kindness I feel from you right now, the kindness I fell in love with. It went missing this summer, and I was afraid I couldn't get it back. I was scared I was losing you, and I ... I just shut down, I guess. I'm sorry, but I didn't know what else to do. Things just seemed to be getting worse and worse, and I didn't see a way out. I know I haven't had the kind of faith in you that I should have, but I was just scared—scared of losing everything, including you."

She hesitated, then said, "And you're right about Ryan and my parents. I just ... I just lost faith in you—in us. I'm so sorry. I love you, and I want *this* Ben back; I want what we had. But we can't keep fighting…"

I leaned in and kissed her. She began to press her lips against mine, but then withdrew. She creased her forehead.

"But what are you going to do now? About work? Are you okay with getting a job—I mean, can you be all right with putting the mailboxes aside for a while? Can we go on like that?" she asked.

"I took Ryan's deal."

She stared at me and raised her eyebrows. "You did?! When? What did he say?"

"I went by the nursery before I came here. He'll take it, even if he hasn't said yes yet. Trust me, he'll take it."

"What about the one-year deal, and six months, and all that?"

"Yeah, ah, it's interesting. Now that I've got a better offer, he has to take the deal the way I want it. I'm giving him a six-month exclusive, and if it works out, then we'll negotiate on my terms." I smirked.

"And he said yes to that?"

"Not yet, but trust me, he will. Especially after my deal with Mike."

"Mike? You mean at the Big Box store? I thought he turned it down?"

"Well, he didn't want the mailboxes for the residential market, but like I said, he got promoted into what's called the pro market, and now he's in charge of all the new builders around Tacoma and Seattle. You've seen the new developments, haven't you?"

"Yeah, of course. They're hard to miss. My dad has been selling land right and left."

"Yeah, well, I pitched him on making mailboxes for all those new builds, and he loved the idea. He met with a couple of local builders, and they put in an order for over a hundred and fifty mailboxes!"

She covered her mouth. "What?! But how in the world can you make so many mailboxes?"

"That's the best part. Mike wants to scale this, and he's going to set up a complete workshop in his store, and he wants me and my dad to start working there next week!" I beamed.

"Oh my God!"

I then told her about Mike's map, about going national, and about setting up and supervising stores throughout the country. Her eyes dried, then shined, then sparkled and got bigger and bigger with each part of the story.

"Ben, I had no idea!" She teared up again and frowned. She looked up at me, and I glimpsed Sammy in her eyes and expression. "I can't believe I missed all this. All I saw were the failures, and I never knew how hard you were trying! Why didn't I...? I just didn't know." She looked down at her hands, then slowly said, "You were right: I didn't think you could do this on your own. I kept thinking that Ryan was the answer. Oh, Ben, I'm so sorry I doubted you. I feel... I don't know what to say. I feel so ashamed. Can you ever forgive me?"

"I do, I do. I wish I could have told you what I was doing. But there was so much other stuff going on, too—stuff no one would have believed. And toward the end, I didn't know how to reach you. I just felt so far away from you." My eyes burned again.

She hugged me tight, and when she pulled back, her face shined with relief—and joy. "I won't doubt you—won't doubt *us* again."

"And it's going to get better and better! You know the home in Queen Anne you've always wanted? Well, by this time next year, we can begin shopping for it. It'll be time for your dream to come true, too."

She hugged and kissed me, and I kissed her back. She climbed on top of me, and our kisses turned deep and passionate. We hugged and pulled ourselves into each other.

"What time are your parents due back?" I panted.

"Come," she said. She pulled me up and led me back into the house and into her bedroom.

Chapter Thirty-One

―

Saturday morning, August 13, 1988

I awoke out of a deep, blue dream. The bedroom, with its high white ceiling fan, was unfamiliar to me, and for a moment, I was disoriented—but just for a moment. I turned and found Em lying on her side, gazing at me, her face animated by a mischievous smile.

"Good morning," she said.

I reached over and pulled her into me, and she fit the contours of my body like a missing puzzle piece.

"Good morning back." I smiled while caressing her.

"Ah, I don't think we have time for that, but I've got a good idea," she said.

"I like your good ideas."

"How about the kids and I come home with you today?" she asked.

"But I thought you weren't coming home 'til next week?"

"Naw. We've been away from home long enough."

We decided to leave right after breakfast. I'd take the 9:35 a.m. ferry, and Em—because Sammy had promised to help Dianna feed the horses that morning—would follow on the next ferry with the kids. Em scrambled out of bed and went to tell them all about the change of plans.

When I got to the dining table, I found both Mitch and Dianna subdued while going through the motions of preparing breakfast. But the kids rambled on excitedly about coming home.

"I'll bet my tomatoes are as big as baseballs!" Sammy raved.

"And my broccoli, too! Mom, can you make us a broccoli casserole with lots of cheese when we get back?" Dylan asked.

"I will," she said, "but first we have to say hello to Oreo. I'm sure he'll be very happy to see you both."

"I wanna!" they both cried in unison.

Em nodded and cleared their dishes, then convened one last time in the kitchen with Dianna, and they carried on a quiet conversation. The kids bounded to their rooms and emerged after a while, lugging their little bags. Once they reached the minivan, they raced around it, arguing and begging for the front seat during the ride home, but Em corralled them.

"You'll both be sitting in the back seat, just like on the drive over," she told them.

The kids, too excited to be discouraged, shrugged free of Em and skipped back to the house, jumping up and down and jabbering the whole way.

Mitch ambled onto the cobblestone driveway and kissed Em on the cheek, then came over and shook my hand, his viselike grip less firm than before. His hair glistened with Brylcreem, and he wore a crisp orange polo shirt with white shorts. He looked ready for an all-day sail.

We stood awkwardly for a moment while he glanced around his meticulous garden, and then he faced me, raised his eyebrows quickly a couple of times, and said, "So, Em told us about your deal with the Big Box store. National, huh?"

I was happy Em had told them, and I wasn't going to miss the opportunity.

"First things first, of course: we have to fulfill the hundred-plus orders we have. But yeah, if it goes well with the builders on the West Coast, then we'll roll this out nationally." I paused, gauging his reaction, but he was well practiced at keeping his emotions in check.

He raised his eyebrows a couple of times again—it didn't bother me as much this time, for some reason—and said, "I always thought if you could find the right market, then you could scale this thing." He sighed and added, "I'm glad this worked out for you. Good job."

He extended his hand again, and I grabbed it firmly and said, "Me, too."

I walked past him and over to the doorway, where the kids now fidgeted next to Dianna. I hugged them goodbye, and Sammy cried up at me, "Tell Oreo I'll be home soon!"

I faced Dianna, and she shrugged and smiled.

"Thanks for looking after the kids this summer," I said. "I'm sure we'll be back up again soon."

Dianna nodded and simply said, "Sure, anytime," then swept the kids up and ushered them back into the house.

I smirked and shook my head at Em.

"Give her time," she said. "She was looking forward to spending more time with the kids if we moved here."

"Well, when we move to Seattle, we'll be just a ferry ride away. She can come visit us any time she likes."

I took Em's hand and nodded to Mitch, and we strolled back to my truck.

I took in the grounds one last time, listening to the chorus of birds and watching the busy bees flitter from flower to flower. Somehow, the whole scene had changed overnight, and not only did I not feel less than—a first for me, being surrounded by Mitch's immaculate property—but I began thinking about what our own garden in Seattle might look like.

"What's in the house?" Em snapped me out of my daydream.

I flashed on the angel and immediately felt guilty about the secret I'd been hiding. Of course she didn't know about the angel, nor about the magical summer we'd spent together. I gazed at her with a puzzled look on my face.

"Food?" she asked.

"Oh yeah, food. Not much," I conceded.

"How about we make a run to the farmers' market after we get back? I'll make a list before we leave," she suggested.

I nodded and squeezed her hand, and she leaned up and kissed me. My pulse quickened. I couldn't wait for her and the kids to come home. When Mitch walked back into the house, I took her by the shoulders and kissed her slow, and she kissed me back.

I held her and said, "I love you, Em."

She moved into me, put her hand on the back of my neck, and pulled me into her.

We untangled ourselves, and I drove down their winding driveway and back through downtown on my way to the dock. When I passed the diner, it looked like any other diner to me, and I felt relieved that we had moved past the misunderstanding from before. And then farther down, I spotted it: RYAN'S NURSERY, with a team of carpenters hustling in and out of a good-sized corner store. I studied my rearview mirror as I passed and saw Ryan coming out of it, leading one of the workers and carrying on an animated conversation. *Go get 'em, Ryan.* He would do well with my mailboxes. I smiled to myself as I joined the line of cars for the morning ferry.

As the ferry cut through the water, the sun bounced off the waves, and the sea spray cooled my cheeks. I stood at the front of the boat and closed my eyes, and for the first time, I felt as if I had the answer to the riddle of life. *"Trust the Source," "Have faith," "Imagine what you want," "Keep taking action,"* and more —the lessons of the angel reverberated within my garden, and I realized I had now made them my own. These were the truths I would live my life by, and the truths I would pass on to others. I opened my eyes and saw the dock approaching, and I knew there was one last thing to do before I got home.

The interstate toward Tacoma moved quickly on a Saturday morning, but my exit remained closed, so I took the detour. Waiting at the stop sign, I glanced down the road toward The Sherwood Estates development and saw a truck lurch out of the hidden street and onto the road. As I was lost in thought, thinking about the angel and all that had happened this summer, someone honked impatiently behind me. I turned the other way toward home. As I approached a Thrifty Drug store, I hoped they had the one thing I needed for our homecoming to be complete.

An hour later, the doors of the minivan opened and closed in the driveway, and then the voices of my family approached the front door.

"We're home!" the kids yelled as they stampeded into the house. They dumped their bags on the couch, and Dylan ran out to the backyard while Sammy snuck into the den.

Em greeted me with a hug. I took the bags from her, and together we piled them onto the floor in the bedrooms. Passing by the den, I saw Sammy petting and cooing at Oreo, who rubbed back and forth against her, his tail sticking straight up.

"I missed you!" Sammy said as he purred deeply and fell into her.

I joined Dylan in the backyard, and then Sammy and Em followed us out. Sammy pointed at the hummingbird feeder, which had two glistening hummingbirds bouncing around it.

"They're back, Daddy!" she said.

"They've been here all summer, just waiting for you to come home," I said.

We gathered around the vegetable garden, and the kids wooed and wowed at how large the eggplants and cucumbers had gotten. All the vegetables were bursting with life, and butterflies and dragonflies hovered over the brick-red heads of the wildflowers. The tomatoes, plump red jewels gleaming with the fading morning moisture, attracted Sammy the most, and she began picking one after another until her little hands were full. She called to Dylan, "Help!"

Dylan bounded over and started picking them as well. Em was busy gathering the colorful wildflowers, so I went back into the kitchen for a vase and a bowl for the tomatoes.

On my way back, a glint of light in the forest caught my eye, and I turned quickly, hopefully, but saw only dappled sunlight reflecting off the leaves. Searching for any sign of the angel, I saw only birds as they darted between the branches. I looked over at the kids scurrying around the garden, chattering away. I closed my eyes, and the colors in my garden pulsed a soft baby blue. Just as the angel had said, I felt her presence, her warmth and peace. Opening my eyes, I sensed a part of her with us here in the garden.

Sammy, her bowl of tomatoes overflowing, looked up at me and made a little frown. I knelt down, and she said, "I wish Sadie was here."

At the mention of Sadie, Dylan stopped picking tomatoes, and Em came over and put her arm around Sammy.

"Sadie is here with us in our memories, and she's always waiting for us to visit her in the forest." I pointed to the familiar trail, and Em brought some wildflowers over and handed a bunch to both Dylan and Sammy.

"Can we go say hello to her?" Em asked.

The kids looked up hopefully, wiping away their tears, and I nodded. I led them down the trail, and Oreo followed behind us. When we reached Sadie's grave, Em helped the kids place their flowers over the slightly raised mound, and together we all held hands.

I said, "Sadie, we've come to visit you, Sammy and Dylan and Em. We all miss you so much, and you'll always be a part of our family."

Sammy broke down and blurted out, "And we'll never forget you!"

Dylan added, "And we love you!" and then burst into tears and fell into Em's legs.

After a while, I picked Sammy up, and she cried on my shoulder as I carried her back. I held her tightly and inhaled her little life, my tears falling onto her tangled hair.

The Lonely Pines parking lot sparkled with a sea of cars when we arrived at the farmers' market. The kids, excited to ride the ponies again, unlocked their doors and jumped out, but Em intercepted them and grabbed their hands, and they dragged her toward the market. As I got our bags and cart out, the warm August wind blew by, cleansing the air. I looked over to the road and saw the tops of the trees swaying and the early fall leaves dancing in the streets. I turned back to the truck bed and removed Sirena's mailbox.

I caught up with Em, who was waiting in line for the ponies with the kids. Giving her the cart, I tucked Sirena's mailbox under my arm. I smiled and winked, making my way through the crowd and into the market. I caught a glimpse of a flashy red-and-yellow Hawaiian shirt and saw Bud dashing between the booths with his clipboard. He didn't see me, and I didn't bother to say hello.

I strolled down the aisles, and on the left, I saw the colorful scarves and blouses of Sirena's booth waving high in the breeze. It reminded me of the festooned booths at the Renaissance fair we had taken the kids to the summer before. Her stall was a wonderland, a little bit of magic in the busy market. A line of people, baskets in hand, waited for their weekly eggs, and I took my place behind them. I bobbed between the heads in front of me and caught Sirena's eye. She flashed a knowing smile, then turned to the back of her booth to fetch more eggs.

When I got to the counter, a large rooster and a couple of hens pecked their way out of the back curtain and hopped up onto the bales of hay at the sides of the booth. All three of them sat down, settled in, and looked obediently at Sirena. She grinned at me as I put her mailbox on the counter, and with her eyes sparkling, she said playfully, "Were you able to fix it?"

"Oh, yeah, it's all good now," I replied with a nod.

In a whoosh of energy, Em and the kids ran up behind me.

"It's good to see you all together again!" Sirena said.

Sammy rushed up to the table and asked, "Do you have baby chicks today?"

"For you? Absolutely!" Sirena reached under the counter and pulled out a large basket filled with ten fuzzy yellow chicks.

"Wow!" both the kids yelled as they cupped their hands and dove into the chirping chicks. Em locked eyes with Sirena, smiled, and reached her hand into the basket as well. Sirena, along with the rooster and the two hens, watched while the chicks climbed over their hands.

Sirena said, "I hear the Big Box store is going to feature your mailboxes?"

I did a double take, wondering how on earth she would know that. But then, of course, she knew a lot more than I thought she did.

"Yeah. It looks like it's going to work out better than I could have imagined."

Sirena smiled and said, "It's amazing what happens when you follow your dream, isn't it?"

Em, hearing all this, looked up, bemused. I nodded at Sirena and moved aside to let her help the people in back of us. The kids finally put the chicks down, and we gathered our eggs, thanked her, and walked out of the booth. I turned back and saw Sirena beaming at me, the sun glinting off her bracelets.

We waded back into the bustle of the market and stopped at the ice cream stand on the way out. Each of us got a double scoop of fresh blackberry ice cream for the ride home.

Back at the house, we unloaded the food, and the kids

crammed into the kitchen to help put things away and examine the treats we had picked up. They grabbed the salted caramels, but Em snatched them away and promised them one each after lunch. The little kitchen buzzed with their energy again, and my heart throbbed. God, I had missed them! Drawers opened and closed, the pantry stood open, and Oreo climbed in to have a look. Sammy and Em continued with the groceries while Dylan wandered back into the house.

Just as we finished putting things away, Dylan came back in, holding a glowing stone: *Fear or Faith?* "What's this, Daddy?" he asked curiously.

Suddenly, all eyes were on me.

I moved over to him, scooped it out of his hand, and said, "It's a reminder that dreams come true, if you can learn to have faith in them."

Em raised her eyebrows, and Dylan was about to ask another question, but in that moment, Sammy raced into the living room and turned the boom box up. Cyndi Lauper's "Time After Time" blared from the living room, and Sammy started singing along. I turned and rushed into the living room after her. Em soon followed and glanced at Sammy, who now held her hairbrush, singing into it. I disappeared into the hallway. Em's eyes darted over to me when I came back out, and at first she didn't see the bag I had from Thrifty.

I knelt next to Sammy. "I've got a present for you."

I pulled out a battery-operated toy microphone. Sammy's eyes grew large as I switched it on and handed it to her. She yelped and did a little dance. I smiled over at Em, and she smiled back with relief. Then we both listened to Sammy sing—in pretty good key, I might add—the final lines of the song.

When it ended, the Bangles' "Walk Like an Egyptian" came on, and Dylan ran out of the kitchen to join his sister in the ritual. Together, they bobbed their heads and jutted out their hands. Em took my arm and pulled me in line behind them, and we all pranced around the living room. As the chorus filled the room, I looked at my family and wiped away a tear as I realized all my dreams had come true.

Acknowledgments

―――

The fulfillment of this dream has been years in the making. From the first inspiration I had, over thirty years ago, to the writing, rewriting, editing, and now publishing, I have received the generous and insightful help of many people.

    I would first like to thank the presence of the Source in my life —a vibrant, enduring, and ever-present knowing—who planted the seed of this idea, and who wouldn't let me forget it for even a moment during all that time. It constantly urged me to keep notes and jot down ideas, characters, and plots, and I have many boxes of outlines, chapter starts, and more. In fact, even today, when I read through some of my favorite spiritual books, I find notes in the margins with a big "A," meaning "angel." I was destined to write this book, to bring this little angel to life, and to bring her lessons into the lives of all who read this tale. I rely on the Source for so much more in my life, and I know it is not finished speaking through me yet.

    As far as the people who contributed throughout the writing process, I'd like to first acknowledge the persistent early help I received from my sister-in-law, Laurei Brooks, who read through many of my early drafts and made the most helpful, loving, and practical suggestions that made this book better. Laurei, you know how much of your soul is within these pages, and your enthusiastic and unwavering support of this story, the spiritual lessons within it, and your deep spiritual presence is found throughout this story. I can't thank you enough.

I'd also like to thank other early readers of the manuscript who helped me make this a much better book by reining me in and helping me paint the characters with the brush that made them both more relatable and more likeable. These include my dear writer friend, Kathleen Woods, who gave me needed feedback on how to handle several female characters in the book, and also reminded me of how much we love our pets, and what we would do to be with them in the end. Thank you, Kathleen, for not only that feedback, but also for your ongoing support. My dear friend, Lizzie Houck, who read my early manuscript with a down-to-earth and practical view, and helped me ferret out those sections that might have detracted from the overall spiritual message. Also, Lizzie, your knowledge of Seattle and the surrounding areas helped me tremendously. Your friendship, as well as the time we've spent together in Los Angeles and Seattle and hiking Mount Rainier, remain the fondest memories of my life. I value you more than you know. I'd also like to thank Doug Davison, writer, producer, and dear friend, who read several drafts of the book and gave me straight feedback that helped make this book better and better. Thank you, Doug. I can't wait to read your first mystery! Kathee Kelly, a dear working associate and client, also offered her time freely, and enthusiastically read, proofread, offered helpful suggestions, and gave me continuing support throughout the later versions of this book. Kathee, thank you for your constant support and encouragement on both this book and my previous book. Your kindness means the world to me.

I'd also like to acknowledge the immense support I received from some very talented and dedicated editors. First was Nicola Perry, who works out of London. Nicola, thank you for your wonderful structure of breaking down this story into manageable parts, and for your insightful view into both the characters and overall structure. Your seasoned eye and delicate approach helped me rearrange the plot perfectly, and thanks to you, the book began to take the shape I had always intended it to. Next, someone to whom I owe the greatest debt is Nela Trninic of Gold Feather Editing. Nela, how can I ever begin to thank you? You provided so much loving guidance, you gave so much of yourself to this book, and I relied (and still do!) on your skill, your intuition, and on your expert storytelling and editorial skills. Rewriting this book chapter by chapter with you and knowing that you were always just an email away was such a comfort to me. You helped me immeasurably. And of course, your expert help with social media marketing and your ongoing and enthusiastic support for this book mean the world to me. You are a special woman, and I can't thank you enough. I'd also like to acknowledge the copy editing and proofing skills of Robin Fuller. Robin, you turned this manuscript into a real book, and I'm grateful for the time, careful eye, and patience you invested in it.

There were many other talented people involved in the publication of this book, and they include the most amazing cover designer, Tatiana Villa, of Villa Design. Wow, is all I can say. Tatiana, you are a star, and you captured the essence of the dream I've held in my heart for so many years. I'm so lucky to have found you. I'd also like to thank Jesse Gordon, who formatted this manuscript and was always prompt, professional, and kind through my many questions and requests. Thank you, Jesse! Also, I couldn't have self-published this without the steady and experienced hand of Kerrie Flanagan. Kerrie, thank you for your consistent patience throughout my endless emails and questions, and for your calming and professional presence throughout this dizzying process. This book is now available because of you.

Lastly, I want to thank the real angel in my life, my amazing wife, Qi Han. Darling, you know how much you mean to me and how grateful I am, every day, that our lives came together. Thank you for fueling, encouraging, and always believing in me and my dreams. You are the light and the love of my life.

Author Bio

Michael Zajaczkowski earned his master's degree in marriage and family counseling from Antioch University, Los Angeles. Using the insights and understanding gained as a trained therapist, Michael pivoted into the business community where, as an international business coach, he uses the tools of goal setting, visualization, self-talk, and more to help clients imagine better than the best they know and take consistent action to make their dreams come true. His previous titles include *The Owner's Manual to Life: Simple Strategies to Worry Less and Enjoy Life More*. Each week, he sends out three inspirational and thoughtful quotes to help you get more centered and see your life from a new vantage point. Remember, "We don't see things as they are, we see them as we are." —Anais Nin.

To sign up for quotes like these, read more about Michael, or download a sample of *The Owner's Manual to Life* or his other titles, please visit: www.MichaelZBooks.com

Jacket design by Tatiana Villa
Author photo @ Carina Gonzalez
Follow Michael on social media:
https://linktr.ee/michaelzbooks

The Color of Dreams

Michael Zajaczkowski

Reader's Guide

THE COLOR OF DREAMS

(Warning: contains spoilers!)

1) *The Color of Dreams* is a book that brings the Law of Attraction to life through the inspiring story of Ben, who has a dream of making custom mailboxes with his father. Through years of frustration that bring him to the brink of ruin, losing his job as well as almost losing his marriage, Ben receives a very special visitor, an angel, who teaches him six spiritual lessons for manifesting his dream. What is your opinion of the Law of Attraction? Have you had any practical experience with using it to manifest things in your own life?

2) The book opens with change in the air. First, Ben and Emily's relationship is reaching a breaking point. Then Ben loses his job at the nursery. Next, we learn that Ben's dad's work at the mill might change if the mill doesn't win the contract with the Big Box store. Given this uncertain beginning, which character or situation did you most fear for and why?

3) When the angel appears, she speaks to Ben of the first lesson and introduces him to the mysterious concept of the Source. What does the Source represent for you?

4) Ben's secret garden is a key concept throughout the book. This is where the angel directs him to make the essential changes in his consciousness, which then result in the changes in his life (thoughts are things). Do you have a secret garden? If so, how do you interact with it?

5) There are six lessons:

Your Dreams Are Inspired by the Source
Thoughts Are Things
Fear or Faith?
Focus on What You Want
Vision the Why; the How Will Come
Let Your Light Lead Others

Which of these spoke to you the most and why? Which one do you think is the most important overall and why?

6) Early in the book, we learn that Ben's father disappointed him deeply when he chose to take a job and turn his back on their shared dream. Do you have someone in your life who has turned their back on your dreams as well? Who might that be, and how did you react?

7) We all know someone like Toby. Toby is a neglected and seemingly unwanted kid who turns to trouble because of lack of guidance and direction. Has this ever happened to you or someone you know? Is there someone in your life right now who could use your love and support?

8) Patty is a lost soul who has turned to drugs and alcohol to deal with her problems. Unfortunately, alcoholism and other kinds of addiction are common forms of escape, and they can cause terrible consequences not only for the addict, but for those in relationship with them. How could Patty have implemented the angel's six lessons to get clean? Which one should she have started with?

9) Both Sadie and Oreo are adorable pets who might remind you of pets you have had or currently have. All pets provide us with unconditional love, and it is always heartbreaking when one of them gets sick or passes away. How did Sadie's death affect you?

10) While both Dylan and Sammy are just young kids, they do have a character arc in the book. Did you recognize it? If so, describe it and how that made you feel about your own kids.

11) The theme of the book is spiritual, referencing the Source, spiritual lessons of manifestation, visualization, colors that interact with our thoughts, and more. How do you differentiate "spiritual" from "religious"? Or do you see them as the same thing? What do the spiritual elements in this book mean to you in your life today?

12) If you could spend one day with the angel, a being full of wisdom, understanding, and peace, what would you ask her? What do you think she would tell you?

13) What inspires you to follow your own dreams? Is there any special mantra or belief that you've used in your life to help you make your dreams come true?

14) In the book, the angel tells Ben that she will return once he's ready to learn more. What other lessons do you think the angel might teach Ben, and us, one day?

Printed in Great Britain
by Amazon